The Light of the World

Leonard E. Rook

The Light of the World
by Leonard E. Rook

Printed in the United States of America

ISBN 978-1-60647-671-0

www.xulonpress.com

Enjoy Dave!

Lew Cook.

DEDICATION & ACKNOWLEDGEMENTS

First and foremost it is with my deepest love, heartfelt thanks, and gratitude that I dedicate the writing of this Book to, God the Father, His Son Jesus Christ, and to the Holy Spirit, who is my teacher and guide. I feel very deeply that God has only used me as the pen in His hand, to get His message to you the reader of this book. You will without a doubt, find Gods message, within its pages that He wants you to hear and understand. When you receive His message, thank Him for it with all of your heart.

Also, I would like to acknowledge Gods richest blessings to me, which is my family. To my loving wife Lorriena, who has stood by me and has encouraged me throughout all of our married life; and helping me to raise our four wonderful children, Deborah, Leonard Jr., Randall, and Patricia, I love you all from the bottom of my heart. You have all been, and always will be, a great source of inspiration to me in whatever I choose to do. Someday God willing, they will all be jewels in my crown when I reach Gods great and beautiful Heaven. Then I can present them all to the Lord with unspeakable joy in my heart. In (Ps.127: 3) the scripture say, "Behold, children are a heritage from the Lord; the fruit of the womb is a reward."

I also owe a great deal of thanks and gratitude to my wife Lorriena, my Granddaughters Dana Marcellus, and Shanda Keenan; for their great work in helping me to design the cover of this book. I am also very thankful and grateful to my daughter, Deborah Keenan for her expertise in helping me with her insights on many things along the way. Likewise I am very thankful to my Grandson Derek Keenan for his expertise in keeping my computer in good working order. Words alone, cannot express a persons' thanks and gratitude enough to someone you love so much. I know God will bless each and every one of them in His own perfect way, for great will be their reward in Heaven.

PREFACE

There are so many ways in today's world for a person to lose their soul, and before they realize it, they will be lost forever. Once you die, there is positively no second chance for you to gain eternal life. You will spend your eternity in one of two places, Heaven or Hell. These are the only two choices God has given mankind. In the Bible God makes it very clear, in (Rom. 6: 23) that the wages of sin is death. But God in His great love, wisdom, and mercy toward mankind when He created us, gave us the ability to choose what we want to do with our life. We can serve Him or Satan. It's your choice. Because of the way the world is today, it is very easy to become so confused over which religion or faith, or belief speaks the truth and which one is just another man made religion that serves themselves and Satan. There is only one true faith or religion in the world today, and that is the Christian Religion and its faith that is taught from **Gods Holy Book, THE BIBLE.** If you trust any other man-made religion or faith to try to help you to gain eternal life, then you are headed in the wrong direction. You will reap nothing but certain destruction in your second spiritual death that, will occur in the life to come after your death here on earth. **Jesus made it very clear in the Bible when He said in (Jn.14: 6), "I am the way and the truth and the life. No one comes to the Father except through me."**

Also in (Jn.10: 30) Jesus says, **"I and the Father are one".** Jesus could not have made this warning any clearer then it is. This is absolute proof that Jesus is the Son of God and also that He is God in human form. It is my fervent hope and prayer that, as you read this book that, you will receive the messages that God has in it for you. One of the most important facts in life that you will ever learn is that; **"Gods Promises, His Everlasting Love, and His Forgiveness are carved In Stone and they cannot be erased."**

Throughout these great stories, you will come to know God in a very special way, and realize the great love that He has for you and all of mankind (Mt. 28-18-20) **"All authority in Heaven and on Earth has been given to me**. Therefore go and make disciples of all nations baptizing them in the name of the Father and of the Son and of the Holy Spirit, and teaching them to obey everything I have commanded you. And surely I am with you always, to the very end of the age." This scripture is more absolute proof of the deity and majesty of Jesus Christ our Lord and Savior. In (Col.2-9-10) Paul said. "For in Christ all the fullness of the Deity lives in bodily form and you have been given fullness in Christ who is the "Head over every power and authority."

"JESUS IS THE LIGHT OF THE WORLD."

CONTENTS

INTRODUCTION

In this book there is not just one story to read, but is a collection of five different unique stories. They are all taken from different sources of Gods Holy Book the Bible. Each of these stories, show the reader Gods awesome and magnificent power, His great and unchanging Love for mankind, and His forgiveness and patience with those He loves and cares for. The main focal point of each story points to God; and the way that He worked out His plan in the lives of the people who were involved in accomplishing His will throughout the stories. It was God who engineered and controlled each situation and not the people who were involved.

Through Gods guidance and the work of the Holy Spirit, who deserves all the credit, I have been able to explain the scriptures that are in the stories so that people from 9 to 90 years of age can read and understand them. There are no confusing words in my book so that you will need a dictionary to understand them... In my book I have included such things as, times, dates, customs and locations of many of the events that have taken place throughout the stories. As you read these wonderful true and exciting stories, let the great imagination that God has given you, take you back in time that you will enjoy beyond your wildest dreams. Stop and pause once in awhile in this journey, as you read these stories, and reflect back on what you have just read, and then you will enjoy and learn much more than you ever thought possible. It is my greatest hope and prayer that you the reader will tell these stories to your children, grandchildren, and your friends. You will receive a special blessing from the Lord when you tell these stories to anyone young or old alike. Throughout my life, one of my greatest blessings from God is that, He has always helped me to meet people and to enjoy them as I, listened to their stories of life. Who knows! Perhaps someday, a complete stranger may walk into your life and become a good friend to you just because, you have told these beautiful stories to someone who was willing to listen. Then you will know for certain that it had to be under Gods direction and guidance that, you two have met and have become good friends. God Bless.

Yours in Christ,

Leonard E. Rook

Part One

THE STORY OF CREATION

-1-

THE BEGINNING OF ALL THINGS IN THE UNIVERSE

In the beginning God Created the Heavens and the Earth. This is the very first sentence in Gods Book the Bible. No one, or anything else created the Universe and all that is in it. God did it by His almighty spoken word. If you open your Bible to (Gen; 1-1) (if you have one) and begin reading, you will be able to read just how God performed His magnificent work. He didn't create it by some big bang theory or by some magic trick. All He had to do was to speak the word and it was done. In (Ps. 33; 6-9) the scriptures say:" By the word of the Lord were the heavens made, their starry host by the breath of His mouth.

He gathers the waters of the sea into jars. He puts the deep into storehouses. Let all the earth fear the Lord. Let all the people of the world revere Him. For He spoke, and it came to be, He commanded and it stood firm." As you read on in verse 3, God said," Let there be Light," and there was light. Then God separated the light from the darkness. God called the light "Day" and the darkness He called "Night." By separating the light and the darkness God also created the evening and morning of the first day.

Light is necessary for making Gods creative works visible and life possible on the earth. Without the light and the heat of the Sun that He has placed in the Universe we could not exist. In the Old Testament the word "Light" is also symbolic of life and a blessing from God. For example the following scriptures in (Job 3:20; 30; 26, 33; 30, Ps; 49; 19,

All of them refer to the light of the soul. Paul uses this word to illustrate Gods recreating work in sin-darkened hearts (2Co.4; 6).

In the New Testament Jesus refers to Himself as the "Light of the World." (SeeJn.12; 46), (Jn.1; 1-10),"In the beginning," these verses stress the work of Christ in Creation. The verses open with the same phrase. GOD CREATED. The Hebrew noun Elohim is plural but the verb is singular, a normal usage in the Old Testament when reference is to the one true God. In the Old Testament the Hebrew verb for "Create" is used only of divine intent, never of human activity.

The creation as fashioned and ordered by God had no lingering traces of disorder and no dark threatening forces arrayed against God or man. Even darkness and the deep seas were given benevolent functions in a world fashioned by God to bless and sustain life. The world was "formed out of water" (Ps; 24-2) (2Pe; 3-5) and founded upon the seas. The waters will not cross the boundaries set for them (Ps; 104 7-9; Jer; 5; 22.). Because God sets these boundaries and it is His laws, nothing can change them. In the scriptures (Ps.33; 7) it says, He gathers the waters of the sea into jars. He puts the deep into storehouses. The seas cannot overflow these boundaries and flood the world again like it did in Noah's time.

On the second day God said;" Let there be an expanse between the waters to separate the water from the water." So God made the expanse and separated the water under the expanse from the water above it. And it was so. There is only one possible outcome, whether it is stated (vv. 9,

11, 15, 24, 30) or implied, to Gods words: For example, "Let There Be." It is that, whatever He spoke, it turned out absolutely perfect. So God called the expanse "Sky". This is the atmosphere as we see it from the earth today." Hard as a mirror," (Job 37; 18), and "like a canopy" (Isa. 40; 22) these are among the many pictorial phrases used to describe the Sky. When this was completed; there was evening and there was morning, of the second day.

Then God said," Let the water under the sky be gathered unto one place, and let the dry ground appear." And it was so. This was also Gods very special way of referring to the "Seas" in (Ge.1: 10) that surrounded the dry ground on all sides and into which the waters of the Lakes and Rivers flow. God called the dry ground "Land "and the gathered waters, He called "Seas."

Also on the 3rd day, God said; "Let the land produce Vegetation: seed-bearing plants and trees on the land that bear fruit with seed in it, according to their various kinds, The land produced vegetation, plants bearing seed according to their kinds, and trees bearing fruit with seed in it according to their kinds. Here you can see how God stressed orderliness, and symmetry, of His creative work. Now there was evening and there was morning of the third day and God saw that His creation was good.

After God had created something He would look at it, (as He states in the Bible) so He could see that it was good. It had to be good because God created it. Everything He made was perfect. Everything has its own order with no exceptions. Both creation and the reproduction of all things are specifically kept in a perfect order. God cannot create anything that is bad because, it would go against His own nature, His will, and His great love for what He creates. We as humans do much the same thing when we create something with our own hands. We stand back and take a look at it to see if we need to do anything else with it to improve it or not. We as humans, usually have to improve on things that we make, but it is not so with God.

On the fourth day of Creation, God said; "Let there be lights in the expanse of the sky to separate the day from the night, and let them serve as signs to mark seasons, and days, and years, and let them be lights in the expanse of the sky to give light on the earth. It is here that God is referring to the uncountable stars in the sky that we see at night. Then God made two greater lights. The greater light would rule the day, and the lesser light would rule the night. The greater light is the Sun, and the lesser light is the Moon. Then God saw that it was good, and there was evening and there was morning of the fourth day.

On the fifth day, God said;" Let the waters bring forth swarms of living creatures and let the birds fly above the earth across the expanse of the sky. This also included all insects that fly, (Dt.14; 19-20). After God created the swarms of living creatures, He then created great creatures of the sea, and every living and moving thing with which the waters swarm, according to their kinds and every winged bird, according to its kind.

Then God blessed them saying;" Be fruitful and multiply, (or increase in number) and fill the waters in the seas, and let the birds increase on the earth." This was Gods benediction on all living things that inhabited the water and that flew in the air. By His blessing, they flourished and filled both realms with life. All of the people on the earth, who have lived, or will ever live, are under this same benediction that God has given to the rest of His creation. So it was that, the evening and the morning of the fifth day were completed.

Gods rule over His creation promotes and blesses life, each and every day we live on this earth. Therefore we should give Him thanks and praise for everything we have, or ever hope to have each day of our lives. It gives God the greatest of pleasure, to give to His people that believe and trust in Him, the many new blessings that they receive each day of their lives. He does this out of the goodness and the love in His heart that radiates from His very being. His great storehouse of blessings is beyond our greatest imaginations.

On the sixth and final day of Creation God said, "Let the land produce living creatures according to their kinds, livestock, creatures that move along the ground, and wild animals, each according to its kind." Now God speaks as the Creator-King, announcing His crowning work of creation to His Heavenly Court. Then God said; "Let us make man. Let them have dominion over the fish of the sea, over the birds of the air, over the cattle, over all the earth, and over every creeping thing that creeps upon the earth."

So God created Man in His own image, in the image of God He created him, Male and Female He created them. In (Gn.3; 27) God said to them, "Be fruitful and increase in number, fill the earth and subdue it." In this scripture, God has given man dominion over everything on the earth with no exceptions. The vegetation, seed-bearing plants for food, the trees, the fish of the sea, the creatures that crawl upon the ground, the beasts of the earth, all the birds of the air, and the creatures that move on the ground, everything that has the breath of life in it. God made it so, and He saw that it was good.

Since God created man in His own image, every human being is worthy of honor and respect. The scriptures state in (Gn.9; 6) (Jas.3; 9). That he is neither to be murdered nor cursed. The word "Image" also includes such characteristics as "righteousness, holiness," (Eph.4; 24) and "knowledge." (Col. 3:10). Believers are to be "conformed to the likeness of Christ, (Rom. 8; 29) and we will someday be like Him" (1:Jn.3 2). Man is the climax of Gods creative activity, and God has "crowned him with glory and honor" He has made him ruler over the rest of His creations. It says in (Ps.8; 5-8), that man was made a little lower than the heavenly beings. (Angels). God saw all that He had made and it was very good. And there was evening, and there was morning of the sixth day.

So it was that, the heavens and the earth were completed in their vast array in six days. By the seventh day God had finished His work, so He rested from all His labor and God blessed the seventh day and made it Holy. Now, God didn't rest because He was tired of working so hard. It was because there was nothing that was formless or empty remaining. His creative work was completed and it did not have to be repeated, repaired, or revised in any way. It was totally effective, and absolutely perfect. As God says in (Gn.1; 31) "and it was very good."

The seventh day, which is also called the "Sabbath", has special meaning for God because He made it a day of rest and worship to keep it Holy. God did this so man would have one day in seven to rest from his labor, and also to worship and honor Him their Creator and God. In (Eze. 20; 12) the Lord said: "I gave them my Sabbaths as a sign between us, so they would know that I the Lord made them Holy." It is only through Jesus Christ our Lord and Savior, who gave His life on the cross and "Shed His Blood" for all of mankind for the remission of sin that, we are made holy and righteous before God once again.

The origin of the noun, "Sabbath," is translated from the Hebrew word "Rested," so the two words have the same meaning; there is no distinction between them. The first record of obligatory Sabbath observance occurred when the Israelites left Egypt and were in the Sinai Desert. (Ex. 16; 23) According to (Ne. 9; 13 -14), the Sabbath was not an official covenant obligation or (agreement) between God and the Israelites until God gave the law to Moses at Mount Sinai. Then it became Gods law.

Although God has set aside one day in seven for man to rest, we as humans, who are the crowning glory of His creation, do not keep this day holy any more. The god of money has taken over our lives. We should worship Him every day of our lives, and we should do this without having to stop and think about it. God loves to hear and to see us worship Him, any time of the day or night. He has no set time for you to call on Him. He knows what you are thinking, and what is in your heart. The darkness of the night, and the darkness that you hold within your heart, is like daylight to Him. You cannot hide anything from Him. The scripture in (Job.28; 11) says; "He searches the sources of the rivers and brings hidden things to light."

Also in (Mt.10; 26) Jesus said; "There is nothing concealed that will not be disclosed, or hidden that will not be made known." This is Gods guarantee that all things are visible and known to Him, no matter what you may try to hide, say, or do. You cannot see God, but He is always near you, wherever you go. In (Ps. 139; 7-10) it says this very clearly. "Where can I go from your spirit? Where can I flee from your presence? If I go to the heavens, you are there. If I make my bed in the depths, you are there. If I rise on the wings of the dawn, if I settle on the far side of the sea, even there your hand will guide me; your right hand will hold me fast." These scriptures make a very clear and comforting statement for all believers in Christ. They should help the unbelievers as well to realize that, God is always present and near to all who will call upon the name of the Lord.

When you believe in God, although you cannot see Him, you can feel His divine presence. You will have a joy in your heart that you cannot contain, because God will make you a new person inside. God says in (Dt.16; - 15) "For the Lord your God will bless you in all your harvest and in all the work of your hands, and your joy will be complete." These words will prove to you to be absolutely true beyond a shadow of a doubt as you continue to read and enjoy this book.

-2-

SATAN

In the beginning, after God had created the earth and everything in it, He knew that Satan or the Devil would come along and spoil everything He had so perfectly created. As you can see in the world today, every time there is something good created by God through mankind, there is something bad or evil that will soon follow it. There is no getting away from it. God and His word is the only thing left in this world that is perfect, holy, and just. Through the Devil, sin came into the world, and the whole human race has become corrupt and evil with no exceptions because of it.

For example: Look at some of the governments and rulers of the different countries of the world today. They look after themselves and make themselves very rich, while the people of their country go hungry and homeless and have little or no clothes to wear. Human life has no value in many countries today. These rulers will pay for their greed and cruelty when they stand before the Lord to be judged. Theirs' will be the greater damnation, when the Lord Jesus Christ comes back to earth the second time. At this point I believe I am getting a little bit ahead of myself in the story, so please permit me to go back and explain who Satan is, and where he came from, and just how sin came onto the world.

Although there is no record of time, like we have today after God had created the Earth, that Satan who was a Cherub in Gods great realm of angles, decided that he wanted to be better than God. He was very beautifully adorned and he had great wisdom, power, and a great deal of responsibility. So one day Satan decided to rebel against God and His authority. In (Isa. 14; 13- 14) Satan said in his heart, "I will ascend to heaven; I will raise my throne above the stars of God; I will sit enthroned on the mount of assembly, on the utmost heights of the sacred mountain. I will ascend above the tops of the clouds; I will make myself like the Most High."

He also persuaded a great number of other angels to rebel against God, and to follow him in his quest for more power and honor. In (Rev. 12; 3-4 NKJV) the scriptures say; "And another sign appeared in heaven; behold, a great, fiery red dragon having seven heads and ten horns, and seven diadems (crowns) on his heads. His tail drew a third of the stars from heaven and threw them to the earth." The dragon spoken of here is the Devil or Satan. Dragons abounded in the mythology of the ancient peoples, and they are still being used or symbolized, in the same manner today in many countries. They are normally used symbolically to depict the enemies of God and of Israel. In reference to the one-third of the stars that were swept from heaven, many understand this reference to speak of the rebellion, of a third of the angelic host that followed Satan. The seven heads, ten horns, and seven diadems or (crowns) refer to Satan's brilliance, power, and glory as a god of this age.

The scripture states in (Rev.12; 7-9), that there was a war in heaven. Michael and his angels fought against the dragon, (who is Satan) and the dragon and his angels fought back. But he was not strong enough, and they lost their place in heaven. The great dragon was hurled down, that ancient serpent called the Devil, or Satan, who leads the whole world astray. He was hurled to the earth, and his angels with him.

Not all of the angels that rebelled against God that were cast to the earth were permitted to roam free. The most wicked and vile ones are still being held in dungeons in Hell bound in chains. They will remain there until the great White Throne Judgment on Judgment Day. On that day, they will be judged by God and cast into the Lake of Fire (or Abyss) (Lk.8; 31) along with all unbelievers. Also in (Jude 1; 6) it says this; "And the angels who did not keep their positions of authority, but abandoned their own home, these (He God) has kept in darkness, bound with everlasting chains, for judgment on the great day. This will be their just reward for rebelling against God and His authority.

As you may or may not know, the Devil has many names. In (Isa.14; 12) he is referred to as the morning star, and the son of the dawn, the Prince of darkness, Lucifer, or Satan. The Devil or Satan is the most common names used today in our language. He was the opposite in power but not equal to Michel the Archangel. He is very crafty and sly. Sometimes he is also referred to as the great deceiver, because he uses deception and deceitfulness as one of his prime weapons against the human race. When you are deceitful in the things you do, you are creating a lie and you are committing a great sin in Gods eyes. The truth is not in you. In (Rev. 12; 9; - 20; 2), the Devil is referred to as "that ancient serpent." He instituted lies and rebellion as innocent cleverness, when he deceived Adam and Eve in the Garden of Eden.

When you cheat, lie, steal, kill, degrade, or covet, other people's things, or goods, you are playing right into the Devils hands. You are going the way of the world, and going against Gods' will. When you sin and go against Gods' will, Satan is the one who will win your soul, not God. You will become the only loser in the end. Then you will spend eternity in hell with the Devil in eternal pain and torment. There, you will be in complete and eternal darkness. Not only, will you be in total darkness but also you will be completely separated from God forever. This complete separation from God will be totally unbearable to say the least.

Jesus felt this total separation from God when He hung on the cross, and cried with a loud voice saying; "My God, My God Why Have You Forsaken Me?" Also, you will never be able to fellowship with any of your relatives and friends again that were believers in Christ, who have died and gone on to heaven before you. There will be no second chance for you to be redeemed by the Lord Jesus Christ, our Lord and Savior. You will be as we say, TOAST.

Let me try to describe to you in some very small way what it would be like in hell. I believe it is impossible for the human minds to even imagine, or to understand what it will be like in hell. Try to think of the worst pain and agony, that you have ever experienced. Then think of how you suffered, and how long the suffering and pain lasted. Now, multiply that pain and suffering by one hundred million times, and you might have some small idea what it is like in hell. Hell is so bad that, not even the demons that were Satan's evil spirits that, Jesus had cast out of the possessed man, wanted to be sent back to hell. They knew how bad it was in hell. You can read about this in (Mk.5; 1-17)

This event that I am referring too, took place in a Gentile community where Jesus was going about teaching. A man with an evil spirit came from the tombs to meet Him. No one could bind him any more, not even with chains. When he saw Jesus he ran and fell on his knees in front of Him. Then the evil spirit that was in the man shouted at the top of his voice, "What do you want with me, Jesus, Son of the Most High God?" then Jesus said to him, "come out of this man, you evil spirit!"Then the evil spirit said to Jesus, swear to God that you won't torture me.

Then Jesus asked him, "What is your name?" "My name is Legion, he replied, for we are many." He begged Jesus again and again not to send him out of the area.

Some farmers in that area raised pigs for a living. As it happened, there was a large herd of about two thousand pigs feeding on the hillside nearby. The evil spirits begged Jesus to allow them to go into that herd of pigs. They knew that Jesus was the Son of God, and they also knew, that He had the power to send them back to hell permanently if He chose to do it. So Jesus gave them permission to go into the herd of pigs. As a result, the whole herd ran down the hill and was drowned in the lake.

There is one more example of what hell could be like, that I would like to convey to you at this time. If you have a Bible handy, you can read about it in (Lk.16; 19-31). But in case you don't have a Bible handy, I feel that I should relate the story to you. It is the story of The Rich Man and Lazarus.

This rich man possibly could have come from a very rich family and had inherited his wealth through the family, or he could have accumulated it through many shrewd business deals that he was able to pull off at some other person's expense. But in any case Jesus did not say how he had become rich.

His possessions could have included such things as, large herds of sheep, cattle, and all kinds of livestock. There was no limit to the things he might have possessed. He could have had hundreds of men servants and maidservants at his beck and call. It is also possible he could have been of Royal Blood. I say this because of the description that Jesus gave of the clothing that he wore. The fact that he wore clothes of purple shows he could have been of Royal Blood. People of Royalty; usually wear some part of their official dress cloths with the color purple, in it. It is still worn by Kings and Queens of today, as a sign of Royalty. If we compared him to the rich and famous people of today, it would probably sound something like this.

He would probably have a four-car garage, with the most expensive vehicles on the market parked in it. His house would be a four level split; somewhere in the neighborhood of three to four thousand square feet, with marble floors, and the finest of Prussian rugs, to walk on. He would have a large swimming pool in the back yard with men and women servants doing all of the work that had to be done around the house. He would not have to lift a finger to do anything. This man had the whole ball of wax. He was on top of the world.

Jesus does not condemn people because they have a lot of money and are well off. He is only concerned as to the way they use their gifts from Him. What you give back to Him for His use, and how you help others who are in need, this is what is important to Him. When you use your riches wisely and keep His commands, then He will bless you with more riches and other gifts. You will receive more then what you can contain. No doubt you have heard the old saying,"what goes around comes around". So it is the same thing with God. Whatever seed you sow that is what you shell reap. When you do His will and you trust Him to do what He says He will do, it is then that you show your faith and love for Him.

I hope that you understand that this is my description of how it could have been, and it is not Gods description. "Please," do not take my meaning wrong here as I am only trying to make a point. If you receive many good or great rewards here on earth, but you do not give, or share your good fortune and gifts with someone who is less fortunate when God presents you with the opportunity, then you will miss the whole meaning of what Jesus was trying to teach here, and my point as well?

One day while Jesus was teaching a group of people around Him, He told them this parable. Jesus said; "There was a rich man who was dressed in purple and fine linen and had lived in luxury every day. At his gate was laid a beggar named Lazarus, covered sores and longing to eat what fell from the rich man's' table. Even the dogs came and licked his sores. The time came when the beggar died and the angels carried him to Abraham's side. The rich man also died and was buried.

In hell, where he was in torment, he looked up and saw Abraham far away, with Lazarus by his side. So he called to him, ' Father Abraham, have pity on me and send Lazarus to dip the tip of his finger in water, and cool my tongue, because I am in agony in this fire.' But Abraham replied, 'Son, remember that in your lifetime, you received your good things, while Lazarus received bad things, but now he is comforted here and you are in agony. And besides all this, between us and you a great chasm has been fixed, so that those who want to go from here to you cannot, nor can anyone cross over from there to us.'

He answered, 'Then I beg you father, send Lazarus to my fathers' house, for I have five brothers. Let him warn them, so that they will not also come to this place of torment.' Abraham replied, 'they have Moses and the prophets; let them listen to them. "'No, Father Abraham, he said, 'but if someone from the dead goes to them, they will repent. ' He said to him, 'If they do not listen to Moses and the Prophets, they will not be convinced even if someone rises from the dead.' "

By the way that the scripture is written I would say that the rich man did not care for the beggar and his plight in anyway shape or form. He ignored the beggar completely. He may have even said to himself at some point in time something like this. "Why should I care for this man who has nothing? He means nothing to me. He is only a beggar; let him solve his own problems". Unfortunately a big percentage of the people of the world today think in this same way. This kind of attitude cannot please the Lord.

It was so hot there, that even a drop of water on the tip of his tongue, would have felt like a world of relief. He was begging for just one moment of relief from his agony. This story should tell you what you have to look forward to if you choose to follow the Devil and turn away from the Lord Jesus Christ and God our Father.

The chasm that is spoken of in the story has been fixed by God Himself, and not by anything, or anyone else. These are only two, of the stories in the Bible that relate to what it is like in hell. There are many more. Thanks, be to God the Father that He gave the human race a chance to choose between good and evil, between God and Satan.

Each and everyone, who ever lived, or will ever live on this earth, have to make their own choice. No one else can make it for you. I pray to the Lord in Heaven, that you will make the right choice today because; you might not have tomorrow to make that choice. You only have this choice while you are a live on this earth. After you die, it is too late.

But God will Judge you in any case. You will stand before Him and give an accounting of what you have done in this lifetime. Then you can tell Him face to face, why you have rejected His Son, the Lord Jesus Christ, if that is your choice. If you reject Christ, then, you have rejected the Father who sent Him. It will be too late for you too even wish you had another chance. There will be weeping and gnashing of teeth. (Mt.8: 12). Jesus made this statement I did not. The second you die, you either wake up in Heaven, with the Lord, or you wake up staring at the Devil. Take your pick. "You alone, have to make the choice."

-3-

THE CREATION OF MANKIND

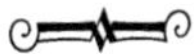

Now that you know how the Devil came into existence, and how sin was first committed, let me explain how sin entered the human race and its consequences. I would like you to think back to the sixth day of creation. After God had created all of the plants, trees, vegetation, and all of the creatures that creep upon the ground, and all of the animals that have the breath of life in them. God said; "Let us make Man!" I would think right about now, a question might come into your mind. Who is "God talking to?" It says in my study Bible that God speaks as the Creator-King, announcing His crowning work, to the members of His heavenly court, which would consist of God the Father, God the Son, and God the Holy Spirit.

So now God is ready to add to His work of creation, and to make a man. The man could worship and honor Him, and he would also be a companion for God. The man would be someone else He could talk with, and the man could care for the beautiful garden that God had created. God said in (Ge.1; 26) "Let us make man in our image, in our likeness, and let them rule over the fish of the sea, and the birds of the air, over the livestock, over all the earth, and all the creatures that move along the ground." This passage of scripture tells you that God delegated sovereignty, or (kingship) on man, because he was created in Gods' image. He was righteous, he was holy, and he had no sin.

I would suspect that possibly another question might have entered into your mind right about now? How did God, our Sovereign Lord, create man? In (Ge.2; 7) it tells you how God created man. We did not evolve from Apes or Monkeys, as some people would have you believe. The scripture says; "The Lord God formed the man from the dust of the ground and breathed into his nostrils the breath of life, and the man became a living being." God called the man Adam. This means "Man." There is the answer to your question, pure and simple?" The man had an excellent body and he was healthy, strong, intelligent and perfectly sinless. (Holy) He was perfect in every respect.

Now the Lord God had planted a garden, in the east, in Eden, and there, He put the man He had formed. Although the exact location of this garden is not known for sure, the Bible says that it was probably located where the Tigris and the Euphrates rivers come together. These two rivers come together in what is known today as Southern Iraq. The name Eden is synonymous with the word "Paradise" and is related to either a Hebrew word meaning "bliss" or "delight" or a Mesopotamian word meaning "A plain." Jesus used the word "Paradise" when He hung on the cross between the two thieves, when He said; to one of them; "Today you will be with me in "Paradise!" But I believe, when He said it at that time, He was probably referring to Heaven, which would be like Paradise. The garden had to be a very beautiful place, because God had made it, and it was perfect in every respect.

Sometimes God would walk in the garden in the cool of the day, to see what the man Adam was doing and to talk with him. There were all kinds of trees and shrubs planted there. Also fruit trees with blossoms on them, and some with fruit on them, and all kinds of flowers that grew out of the ground. All of these trees were very pleasing to the eye, and their fruits were good for food and very pleasing to the taste.

In the middle of the Garden, God had planted two special trees. They were the tree of "Life" and the tree of "Knowledge of good and evil." The Tree of Life signified the giving of life without death, to those who eat its fruit. The tree of "Knowledge of Good and Evil" signified the giving of knowledge of good and evil leading ultimately to death, to those who eat its fruit. It also refers to moral knowledge or ethical discernment.

Adam possessed both life and moral discernment because he came from the hand of God. The access to the fruit of the Tree of Life showed that it was Gods will and intention, for Adam to have an abundant life. A river that flowed from Eden watered the garden. From this same river, four other rivers were formed. The four rivers were called the Pishon, Gihon, Tigris, and the Euphrates. These rivers flowed throughout the land.

Then the Lord God took the man, and put him in this beautiful Garden of Eden that He had planted, so he could work it and care for it. This was the first responsibility that God had placed on man. Then the Lord God commanded the man saying; "You are free to eat from any tree in the garden; but you must not eat from the tree of, Knowledge of Good and Evil, for when you eat of it you will surely die." (Ge.15-17). When God spoke of mans' death here; He was referring to mans spiritual death which is the second death that man can experience. It is not his physical death that he would have to experience a second time.

After some time had passed, God could see that Adam was not completely contented and happy. So God brought all of the beasts of the field, and the birds of the air, that He had formed from the dust of the earth, so Adam could give them names. This was his first act of having dominion over all the creatures around him. So now, God has given Adam a second big responsibility. After Adam had named all of the beasts of the field, and all of the birds of the air, God knew in His heart, that the man was not completely happy. Even with all of the added responsibility that God had given Adam, no suitable companion or helper was found for him.

Then God said; to his heavenly court "It is not good for the man to be alone. I will make a helper suitable for him." Then the Lord God caused the man to fall into a deep sleep. While he was sleeping, God took one of the man's ribs, and closed up the place with flesh. God then took the rib, and from it He made a woman. When God had finished, He brought the woman to Adam for a companion and a helper. This pleased Adam, and he said; "this is now bone of my bones, and flesh of my flesh. She shall be called woman, for she was taken out of man. For this reason, a man will leave his father and mother, and be united to his wife, and they will become one flesh." Together, they would form an inseparable union, of which the words, "one flesh" is both a sign and an expression of togetherness.

Without female companionship and a partner in reproduction, man could not fully realize his humanity. The start of the human race is completed, and man would be able to reproduce, like the rest of Gods creations. Adam named his wife Eve, because she had become the mother of all the living people. The man and his wife were both naked and they felt no shame, because they were still morally innocent, and because there was no sin in the world at this time.

-4-

THE FALL OF MANKIND

It is not known just how long it was before Adam and Eve fell into sin, after God had created them. However, as you know, the end results and the consequences are still the same, and mankind has been paying for his sin ever since. Because of the sin of our first parents Adam and Eve, we as their descendants inherited their sin as well. The blight of sin and rebellion brought a threefold curse that darkens the story of Adam and Eve in Gods good and beautiful garden. This event, the fall of man, takes place in (Ge.2; 4 to Ge. 3; 24).

It appears from the scriptures that, the serpent was one of the most beautiful and attractive creatures that God had created. They had legs and they walk upright on the ground. It was not mentioned in the Bible, that the serpent had to crawl on the ground until after God had cursed it sometime later in the Garden of Eden.

I also suspect that, the serpent was one of Gods' most beautifully colored animals, and very pleasing to the eye to look at. The Bible says that it was the most "crafty" of all the other wild animals that God had created. One other point I would like to make here to clarify my statement is that, Satan would not have picked just any animal to disguise himself as, so he could deceive Adam and Eve. It would have had to be an animal that was crafty and beautiful enough at the same time, to attract Adam and Eve, to come near it. At this point in time, they had no reason to fear anything in Gods' creation.

So when the time was right the Devil or Satan or, "That Ancient Serpent" as he is referred to later on in (Rev.12; 9 -20; 2) discussed himself as a serpent to tempt Eve. Now watch how Satan uses his craftiness to twists Gods words of warning around, so that he could achieve his evil purpose of deceiving Eve.

As I stated before, deception is the number-one tool that Satan uses to deceive people and it actually causes people to sin against God. So now he uses deception on Eve, and he causes her to commit the first sin of mankind against God. One other tool of the Devil is to, make a person doubt and question God and His motives. Doubt also causes people to think that they can get away with things with God without suffering any consequences. This is the wrong way to think because it is the way of Satan. As you may recall, God had told Adam that they were forbidden to eat from the tree of Knowledge of Good and Evil, because if they did they would surely die. This was a specific and a direct command from God.

So Satan said to the woman; "Did God really say you must not eat from any tree in the garden?" This question, and the woman's response, would change the course of human history forever. By causing the woman to doubt Gods word, Satan brought evil and sin into the world. It was here that the great deceiver Satan under took to alienate man from God. Now watch how Eve replies to the Devil. "We may eat fruit from the trees in the garden, but God did say, "You must not eat fruit from the tree that is in the middle of the garden, and you must not touch it, or you will die!" It is here that the woman adds to Gods words of warning. In the last part of the sentence," and you must not touch it." She was distorting Gods prime directive, and it was demonstrating that the serpent's clever challenge was working its poison. "You will not surely die," This was one of the biggest lies the Devil ever told anyone. It was a blatant denial of a specific divine command of God. The Devil continued to say to the woman: "For God knows that when you eat of it your eyes will be opened, and you will be like God, knowing good and evil!" In the two words "God knows", Satan accuses God of having unworthy motives.

As it is written in the scriptures in (Job; 1; 9-11), (2; 4-5) Satan accuses God and the righteous man Job of the same thing. When Satan told Adam and Eve that their eyes would be opened, he was only telling them half of the truth. Their eyes would be opened to be sure but, not in the way that they had anticipated. The results would be catastrophic and quit different from what the serpent had said it would be, of knowing good and evil.

When the woman saw that the fruit was good for food and that it looked so delicious, the damage was already done. Satan had already put the desire in her heart to eat the forbidden fruit. She thought she would have wisdom like God and she would know all things. After all, the Devil had just said she would be like God. So she took one of the apples and she began to eat it. She also gave some to her husband and he ate it too, and immediately their eyes were opened, and they realized that they were naked. They had a new awareness of themselves and of each other in their nakedness and shame, which only God could cover.

As you know sometimes, little children will run around the house naked and think nothing of it. Adam and Eve were that innocent before they sinned. After they had sinned, they could see their nakedness, so they sewed some fig leaves together to try and cover themselves and their nakedness. Now they were feeling their first sense of shame and guilt.

Now that they could see their nakedness and shame, they were probably experiencing other kinds of feelings as well. For example, Fear. This would be one of the greatest fears that they would feel right away, because they would realize that they had broken Gods commandment and they had sinned, by disobeying God. Also, fear is another tool that the devil uses against mankind. Another feeling that they would experience would be guilt. Their holiness and rightness was gone. Stripped away by the sins they had committed. The feeling of guilt would be there every time they looked at each other. Their peace of mind and the joy that they had in their hearts was gone. No longer were they happy and care free like they once were. Anger, would be another feeling that they would be experiencing right away because of the great loss of their rightness and holiness. They knew that they had lost something very precious, and that they did not know what to do about it. Adam and Eve knew that they had committed a terrible sin, and they did not know what God would do to them, or how God would react when He come to the garden to talk to them.

In (Ge.3; 8-24) the event continues. It is not recorded just how long it was before God came to see Adam and Eve in the garden. (Ge.3:8) says; Then the man and his wife heard the sound of the Lord God walking in the garden in the cool of the day, and they hid themselves from the Lord God among the trees of the garden. But the Lord God called to the man, "Where are you?" The man answered, "I heard you in the garden, and I was afraid because I was naked, and so I hid." Then the Lord God said: "Who told you that you were naked?" Have you eaten from the tree that I commanded you not to eat from?" Right now, at this point in the story, in the very next words to follow, is where for the first time in human history, that the practice of blaming someone else for all of your troubles, heartaches, and problems comes from. Adam answered the Lord and said: "The woman you put here with me, she gave me some fruit from the tree, and I ate it." Adam is blaming God and the woman now and not himself for his sin. Now God turns to the woman and it is her turn to answer to God.

The Lord God said to the woman: "What is this you have done?" Now it is Eve's turn to blame someone else for her troubles. She said: "The serpent deceived me and I ate." By this time I would suspect that the Devil would have left the serpent to suffer his own fate. He certainly would not have hung around until the Lord God showed up. Satan knew the damage had been done. There was no turning back. The Devil had accomplished what he had set out to do. He had alienated the whole human race from God, because of sin. He had destroyed the perfect holy relationship, between God and mankind. Now all of mankind would have to suffer and die because of the sin that had been brought into the world by Satan.

Then the Lord God said to the serpent, "Because you have done this, Cursed are you above all the livestock and all the wild animals. You will crawl on your belly and you will eat dust all the days of your life. And I will put enmity between you and the woman, and between your offspring and hers; he will crush your head, and you will strike his heel." When God used the words "cursed are you," He was only cursing the serpent and not the man and the woman. The ground was cursed because of Adams sin. The word dust, is the symbol of death it's self. (v.19) it would now be the serpent's food. In (v 15), when God said, "He will crush your head and you will strike his heel." Here God shows us His grace for the first time. The antagonism, or the open hostility, between people and good and evil is used to symbolize the outcome of the titanic struggle between God and the Devil.

But one day this struggle will end when Christ judges the Devil for the last time and throws him into the lake of fire forever. The offspring of the woman would eventually crush the serpent's head. This promise was fulfilled when Jesus Christ died on the cross and rose again from the dead. The Lord Jesus Christ has completely defeated all sin, the power of Hell Death and the Grave, and the power of Satan. It is a total and complete victory that Christ has won for all believers in Christ when, He was raised from the grave early on that first Easter Morning, over two thousand years ago. It is Gods free gift to all who will accept Him. It also shows Gods grace toward His prize possession, the human race.

After God had finished cursing the serpent, He turned to the woman and said, "I will greatly increase your pains in childbearing; with pain you will give birth to children. Your desire will be for your husband, and he will rule over you." Having great pain in childbearing was her judgment. Her judgment fell on what was most uniquely hers as a woman, and as a suitable helper for her husband, and that was the bearing of children.

In (Ge.3: 17) to Adam God said; "Because you listened to your wife and ate from the tree about which I commanded you, to not eat of it!" Cursed is the ground because of you. Through painful toil you will eat of it all the days of your life. It will produce thorns and thistles for you and you will eat the plants of the field. By the sweat of your brow you will eat your food until you return to the ground, since from it you were taken, for dust you are and to dust you will return."

This is Gods judgment on the whole human race. God will never reverse His judgments on anything, because He never changes. God is the same today as He was yesterday. In the Hebrew language the words "painful toil" mean burdensome labor. But He has provided a way for you to be released from His judgments. That is by His grace, which is through Jesus Christ our Lord. He paid our sin dept in full by the shedding of His blood, and His death on the cross.

Then the Lord God displayed His further concern and love for Adam and Eve by killing some animals and then making garments out of skins for Adam and his wife Eve to wear... The Lord God banished Adam and Eve from the Garden of Eden, to work the ground, from which he had been taken. After God drove them out, He placed a cherubim angel and a flaming sword flashing back and forth to guard the way to the tree of life, on the east side of the Garden of Eden.

It is hard to even imagine in your mind, just what Adam and Eve must have been feeling, when they were told, that they had to leave Gods beautiful and peaceful garden. All of the scriptures in (Rev.2; 7; 22; 2 14 (19) refer to the "Tree of Life. Only through Gods redemption in Christ, will mankind have access once again to the tree of life in Heaven.

Because they had once experienced such a close and unique relationship with the Lord God, their remorse must have been just about too much to bear. Just like you and I today, they would be crying, and worrying about what they would do from now on. Just think about the situation that they had just placed themselves in. In Gods beautiful garden they had all of their needs met. Everything was there. Now, without even a hope of the things that were past, they had nothing. All that they had were the animal skins that they wore when they left the garden. They would have no home or shelter, no food to eat, that they would know of at that time, and they would be utterly devastated and totally lost. Adam and his wife Eve were now more than ever, becoming totally dependent on God for everything in their life. It was a complete reversal of the life that they were so used to having.

When they lived in the Garden of Eden and had a strong personal fellowship with the Lord God, He supplied all of their daily needs. They had none of the worries and sorrows that they would have now that they were completely on their own. Now they would have to forage for themselves. Their own human nature, would have to take over and somewhat replace, what God used to do for them. They would have to think for themselves more than they wanted to admit.

It does not state in the Bible just exactly what happened at this precise time, but we know that God is a very loving and caring God. He would not have left Adam and his wife Eve all alone without any thing, to protect them, or food to sustain their life. Because we know that God will never forsake us or leave us on our own, we can always take all of our troubles and problems to Him, anytime and anywhere, with no restrictions, and no strings attached.

Now that you have had a brief history lesson on how the world was created, and how sin came into the world by Satan. I will now continue with some of the most fantastic stories, of the great men of the Bible. These stories will show you, Gods great and magnificent power as well as how He helped and delivered His people from the many predicaments that they would get themselves into. These stories will also illustrate to you Gods great love, and His caring for and the protection of His people. These stories will also advise you of His wrath, His patience, and His forgiveness.

When you read these stories, use your imagination, and put yourself back in Biblical times, when these stories and facts took place. One of the greatest things that God has given all human beings is the ability to escape from reality by the use of our imaginations. You must also remember however, that the people of that time in history, did not have the tools, and the modern convinces that we enjoy today. They did not have any cars or fast moving planes that would fly at twice the speed of sound to go somewhere. All the people had at that time was manpower, foot power, or horsepower. Also, only the very rich could afford to have slaves, to do their work. The families were quite large at that time in history, and it was quite prestigious to have many sons to carry on the family name. It was also not uncommon at that time for a man to have more than one wife. But this is not an accepted practice in our culture today in many countries.

-5-

CAIN AND ABLE

This is the story of Cain and his brother Abel. It is not known just how long after Adam and his wife Eve were expelled from Gods beautiful garden, that she became pregnant for the first time. The Bible only states that, Adam lay with his wife Eve, and she became pregnant and she gave birth to Cane her first Son. She said: "with the help of the Lord, I have brought forth a man." When Eve used the words "with the help of the Lord," she acknowledged that God is the ultimate source of life. In the scripture it says in (Ac 17; 25- 27) that He (God), is not served by human hands, because He Himself gives all men life and breath, and everything else they need. From one man, He made every nation of men, that they should inhabit the whole earth. He determined the times set for them, (mans' life span) and the exact places where they should live. God did this so men would seek Him, and perhaps reach out for Him and find Him. Although He is not far from each of us, at any time in our lives, He still wants us to call upon Him at all times and in every situation that we find ourselves in.

So now we have the first human baby, born to human parents, and it was a boy! I can well imagine how they must of felt. They must have felt a great deal of joy along with a little bit of fear thrown in. Caring for the baby would be a big chore for them because, they would not have any of the modern convinces that we enjoy today. But by the same token, now they would have someone else to love and to care for, and to take up their spare time. For the first time in their lives, they would have sore aching muscles, from having to work hard just to live from day to day.

They would have to build a home for the family, gather food and store it, as well as make some extra cloths to wear. The everyday routines, would take its toll on their bodies as well as their minds as it does for us today. There is no doubt that many times throughout their lives, they would look back and remember that their Garden Paradise was gone forever and that they could never get it back. Their pain of remorse and their utter disgust must have been over whelming to say the least. To go from total joy and complete happiness to a state of total despair is a road that no human being should have to travel.

Sometime later, Eve gave birth to her second son, and they named him Abel. His name means "Breath" or" Temporary" or" Meaningless" which hints at his short life. I would imagine that the boys grew up much like the boys of today do. Playing games, working together, fishing, hunting, and just enjoying each other's company. In my imagination, I can see the two boys as quite different in body build, and in height. I would think that Cain would be the stronger of the two boys, because he was the oldest, and he would be the big brother type, plus he was a worker of the soil. I imagine him as a much rougher looking, tough, strong, and ready to take on the world.

Abel on the other hand, was the keeper of the flocks, a Shepherd. He would be lighter in body build, than and not as strong as Cain, and he would be kinder and gentler of soul and spirit. He would be the more handsome of the two boys.

I also see him as the quieter and softer-spoken of the two boys. I believe he must have enjoyed being alone, because tending and looking after flocks of sheep, and goats, would be a lonely occupation. Because, he was the younger of the two, and the smaller and gentler type, he could have well become the favorite boy of the family. This would possibly cause a great deal of trouble and strife between the two boys and their parents.

In the course of time, Cain brought some of the fruits of the soil as an offering to the Lord. But Abel brought fat portions from some of the first-born of the flocks. The Lord looked with favor on Abel and his offering, but He did not look with favor on the offering that Cain brought to Him. This made Cain feel very downcast, and very angry. Cain could not understand why God was not pleased with his offering, because he brought what he thought was good enough but it was not the first fruits of the season. It was not good in Gods eyes. This was the reason why God looked with favor on Abel's offering instead of Cain's. God had apparently instructed His first human family, what they were to sacrifice, and how they were to do it, and at what time of the year it was to be done. You will see later on, just how important it was to make an offering or a sacrifice to God. It was a very big part of the people's lives in the Old Testament times.

The contrast or the problem was not between an offering of plant life, and of animal life. But it was between a careless, thoughtless offering, and a choice, generous, offering. Motivation and heart attitude are all-important, to God. In (Lev.3; 16), it says: "The priest shall burn them on the altar as food, an offering made by fire, a pleasing aroma." All the fat from the animals that were sacrificed belonged to the Lord, at that time in history. But in today's world, God is more interested in how you offer your heart, and soul, to Him, rather then what you can offer Him materially. He is not interested in material thing, because He already owns all of these things. It is Gods great pleasure, to give us the material thing that we need and desire.

Also, in (Heb. 11; 4) it says: By faith, Abel offered God a better sacrifice offering than Cain did. By faith, he was commended as a righteous man, when God spoke well of his offering. It was Abel's faith in his heart, and his humble attitude towards God, that pleased God more than anything else. The fact that Abel wanted to please God in everything that he did; this was what was important to God. So God counted it as rightness to Abel. What Abel wanted was not important. Also, the fact that Abel offered a burnt offering of fat, which be-longs to God, and that he kept Gods command, this pleased God much more than the way Cain had presented his offering to God.

Abel offered the first-born, of the flock, which is a form of recognition that all of the productivity of the flocks is from the Lord, and all of it belongs to Him. But, if you want to offer something to God today that will please Him the most, offer Him your love, your heart, and your soul, and obedience to His word. When you do that, you will be heaven bound. There is nothing greater, that you can offer the Lord, than these four things. God will pour out His richest blessings on you. You will not be able to contain the blessings that God will give you. This is His promise to you and all of mankind. Try Him, and see what happens.

The biggest problem with Cain's offering was that, he did not do what God wanted him to do. He had not obeyed the Lords command. His motivation and his attitude were bad from the beginning. He reacted predictably, because of his anger with God. He was blaming God for his not doing things right, and not himself. God told him what was wrong in (Ge.4; 6-7). The Lord said to Cain, "Why are you angry? Why is your face downcast? If you do what is right, will you not be accepted? But if you do not do what is right, sin is crouching at your door, it desires to have you but you must master it."

Here God shows us, that we can master the Devil and his demons, if we ask Him for His help and we really want to do it. God has given mankind the power over Satan, through Jesus Christ His Son. Jesus has broken Satan's power. You no longer have to remain in Satan's power without any chance of escape. (Ge.4; 6-7), is a very important piece of scripture for everyone to remember. It pertains to all of the cultures of today, as well as the cultures that have died out and disappeared long ago.

The Hebrew word for crouching is the same as an ancient Babylonian word referring to an evil demon crouching at the door of a building, to threaten the people inside. Sin may be pictured here as just such a demon, waiting to pounce on Cain. That is the way the Devil and sin work together. They are waiting for any opportunity to devour you and to lead you astray, away from the loving and caring God that loves you. You need God to help you fight Satan and his evil demons; you cannot do it by yourself. The fact that the words," It desires to have you," it would appear that Cain was already plotting Abels murder, and that he had murder in his heart, and God knew it. He could not hide his thoughts from God, and neither can you or anyone else, so it is advisable to watch, even what you think.

Sometime after the Lord had spoken to Cain, and he had fully realized that God was not pleased with his offering, he decided to take out his frustration and his anger on his brother Abel. It seems that he had to have someone else to blame beside himself for the trouble that had occurred between God and himself. So, who would be better for him to blame than his innocent brother Abel? So without a second thought, Cain sought his first opportunity to kill him. As far as he was concerned his anger with God had to be appeased. Satan was working his terrible poison of hate and jealousy within the heart of Cain without him even knowing anything about it. The Devil knew that he would have his own way with Cain because of the terrible attitude and anger that he was packing around. The Devil had him right where he wanted him because his mind was set on murder.

One day Cain said to his brother Abel, "Let us go out to the field." He probably used the excuse that he wanted Abel to go hunting with him, or some other kind of lame duck excuse to get Abel to go with him. While they were in the field, Cain attacked his brother Abel and killed him. It was the first murder ever committed by anyone, of the human race. This murder was especially monstrous, because it was committed with a deliberate deceitful act. ("Let us go out to the field"). The murder was committed against a righteous good man, as well as a brother. This is a striking illustration of the awful consequences of the fall of man away from God and His grace.

Sometime after the murderous deed was committed, God said to Cain; "Where is your brother Abel?" This was a rhetorical question because God already knew what had happened to Abel. Cain replied to the Lord and said; "I don't know." This of course, was an outright lie. "Am I my brothers' keeper," he replied. He was very callous and indifferent to God. This kind of attitude is all too common throughout the whole course of human history. People just do not care how they address God, or what they say about Him, or how much they take His name in vain. Some day God will judge these kinds of people by casting them into the eternal Lake of Fire unless they repent of their sins before God and before they die.

Then God said," What have you done?" Listen! Your brother's blood cries out to me from the ground. "Just as Abels' innocent blood cried out to God against Cain at that time, so does the innocent blood of murdered victims of today. Their blood too cries out to God for Justice.

Now Cain will see the awful consequences of his action of murder, and the terrible judgment that God places on him because of it. God said to him; "Now you are under a curse and driven from the ground, which opened its mouth to receive your brothers' blood from your hand. When you work the ground, it will no longer yield its crops for you. You will be a restless wanderer on the earth." Now no longer would the ground produce food for him as it once did because, Gods curse was on him. He would have to find other ways to support himself. God had now passed His judgment on Cain and it was irreversible because, God does not change His mind after He has spoken.

Then Cain said to God, "My punishment is more than I can bear. Today you are driving me from the land, and I will be hidden from your presence." Just being hid from Gods presence would be totally unbearable in itself. "I will be a restless wanderer on the earth, and whoever finds me will kill me." But the Lord said to Cain: "Not so. If anyone kills Cain, he will suffer vengeance seven times over." Then the Lord put a mark on Cain, so that anyone who found him would not kill him. God has spared the life of the world's first murderer. So it was that, the first murder and punishment for the deed that had been committed, was dealt with in the history of mankind. Then Cain went out from the presence of the Lord, and dwelt in the land of Nod, east of Eden. The word "Nod" means Wandering.

When Cain said to the Lord; "my punishment is more than I can bear," he was not repenting to God for his sins, or for what he had done. But, it was because he was feeling all kinds of self-pity for himself, and the situation that he had gotten himself into. Anger, jealousy, deception, lying, self-seeking, and murder, are all sins that he could claim for himself. But now he was cast out from the presence of the Living God and he could do nothing about it. That was the price he had to pay for disobedience to God, and for his sin of murder.

Although there is no recorded number of the population at that time as such, the following words in (Ge.4; 14-15) (whoever, anyone, and no one) seem to imply, that there was a substantial number of people already on the earth, outside of Cain's immediate family. When He marked Cain; God could have been referring to the people who were not yet born, so no one would kill him.

Sometime after Cain went and dwelt in the land of Nod, he took a wife from some of the local inhabitants. In the Bible, it says that Cain lay with his wife, and she became pregnant, and she gave birth to a Son, and she named him Enoch. At that particular time Cain was building a city, and he named it after his Son Enoch. Possibly part of the reason why Cain would build a city is because he was trying to stop his wandering ways, and God had forbidden him from ever working the land as he had before. By using his hands in this manner he could keep busy, and not have to wander around the country like a lost sheep so much. Also, he could hide in the city as well, when he had to.

As time passed, and Adam had turned 130 years old, God gave Adam and Eve another Son, and they called him Seth. God in His great love and mercy had given Adam and Eve another Son, to replace Abel their murdered Son, so he could carry on the family line of Adam and Eve.

As the years passed by, Seth grew into manhood and he too took a wife, and he lay with her, and she bore him a Son and they named him Enosh, which also means "Man." When he had grown up, he began to call on the name of the Lord. Now once again, God has reestablished a righteous line of people for His Son Jesus Christ to descend from. As you can see that there is a very sharp contrast between the two descendent lines of Seth and that of Cain.

There are ten generations from Adam to Noah. These generations alone could have accounted for millions of people. The reason why I make this statement is because of the longevity of the people in those biblical times. Some people lived almost a thousand years. This longevity that the people had, also demonstrates Gods awesome power that He has over all of His creation. He can do whatever He wants to do, no matter what the circumstances are. The following, is a list of the years that some of the people lived. You can read this list in (Ge.5; 1-32).

Name	years lived
Adam	930
Jared	962
Seth	912
Enoch	365
Enosh	905
Methuselah	969
Kenan	910
Lamech	777
Mahalalel	895
Noah	950

As you can see from the chart, that at one time in the history of the world, longevity played a very important part in Gods' plan in populating the earth. But, that is not the case any longer. In (Ge.6; 3) God said, "My Spirit will not contend with man forever, for he is mortal, his days will be one hundred twenty years. So, now God has set the human life span, to be no longer than one hundred twenty years maximum. As you know, the human race does not live that long today.

In (Ge.6: 5) the Bible says: The Lord saw how great mans wickedness on the earth had become, and that every inclination of the thoughts of his heart was only evil all the time. The Lord was grieved, that He had made man on the earth, and His heart was filled with pain. Mans sin is Gods greatest sorrow. God cannot bear to look at sin. But in this day and age, He covers our sins, with the blood of the Lord Jesus Christ, and He no longer sees our sin. This shows us how wonderful, Gods Grace is, and how much He loves us.

So the Lord said, "I will wipe mankind, whom I have created, from the face of the earth; men and animals, and creatures that move along the ground, and birds of the air, for I am grieved that I have made them. We as His people are not to grieve the Holy Spirit either. In (Eph. 4; 30), it says, "Do not grieve the Holy Spirit of God, with whom you were sealed, for the day of redemption."

The Lords wrath was truly justified; because of the way the people of the earth had turned against Him, and rejected Him. They chose to follow the way of the Devil, instead of following the way of the Lord God, who had created them. But God, once again will show the human race, His Mercy and Grace. He did not kill the whole human race in the flood, but spared Noah and his family, as you will see in my next story.

Part Two

THE STORY OF NOAH

-1-

NOAH AND THE ARK

The story of Noah is recorded in the first book of the Bible. (Ge.Ch.5-9; - 28.) (NIV). The story of Noah spans 950 years in the history of the world, as we know it today. Although it will be a short story, it is nonetheless very important in the history of mankind. Noah was a righteous man, blameless among the people of his time, and he walked with God. That is; he kept Gods commands and did what God told him to do without question. The godly life that Noah and his family led was a powerful contrast to the wicked lives of the people who lived around him. God loved Noah and his family with a deep and abiding love, just as any father on earth loves his children.

Noah had three sons. Their names were, Shem, Ham and Japheth. The Bible does not tell us how old Noah's family was, but the Bible does state that Noah was six hundred years old when the floodwaters came upon the earth. His three sons were married, but they did not have any children of their own at the time of the flood. The story of Noah's salvation from the flood illustrates Gods redemption of His children.

In the scriptures (Heb.11; 7) it says that, by faith Noah, when warned about thing not yet seen, in holy fear built an ark to save his family. By his faith he condemned the world and became heir of the righteousness that comes by faith. When the flood came, Gods word was proven to be true. Noah's faith was vindicated, or proven to God when he expressed complete trust in God and His word, even when it related to "things not yet seen," (namely the coming flood). So it was that Noah, also fit the description of Gods righteous ones who live by faith. His faith in Gods' word moved him to build the ark in a dry, landlocked region where it was inconceivable that there would ever be enough water to float the vessel. Without faith it is impossible to please God, because anyone who comes to Him must believe that He exists, and that He rewards those who earnestly seek Him.

There are many people in the Bible who lived by righteous faith throughout the Bible. A few examples would be: Abel because of his better sacrifice and obedience to God. Abraham and Sarah; they were both very old, and Sarah herself was barren. God gave them a son named Isaac in their old age. By faith Enoch, was taken from this life, so that he did not experience death. He could not be found, because God had taken him away. Before he was taken, he was commended as one who pleased God. Elijah was taken to heaven in a fiery chariot and he did not experience death.

So, God said to Noah, "I am going to put an end to all people, for the earth is filled with violence because of them. I am surely going to destroy both them and the earth, and all life under the heavens, every creature that has the breath of life in it. Everything on earth will perish. I am going to bring floodwaters on the earth. So make yourself an ark of cypress wood. Make rooms in it and coat it with pitch, inside and out." The Hebrew word for "Ark" is used elsewhere only in reference to the basket that saved the baby Moses. The mother of Moses made his basket watertight in the same way, by coating it with pitch.

As the Lord continued to speak to Noah He said; "This is how you are to build it. The Ark is to be four hundred and fifty-feet long, seventy-five feet wide, and forty-five feet high. Make a roof for it, and finish the Ark to within eighteen inches of the top. Put a door in the side of the Ark and make a lower, middle, and upper deck." An overhanging roof was put on it to keep the rain out, 18 inches from the top. Noah's faith in the Lord was so strong that he didn't even question the Lord when He was told what He was going to do.

You can well imagine that all of the people who knew Noah and his family at that time, probably thought Noah had lost his mind. After all, no sane man would build a boat out in the middle of nowhere, with no water, or lake around to put it in. He would be the laughing stock of the century. I would suspect, that Noah told the people who came around to see what he was doing, just exactly what God was intending to do? But they would not believe him. The people had become so corrupt and evil, that they would just laugh, and sneer, and make fun of him and his God. Satan had become the God of the people and the world is no better off today in many places. The Lord God of Heaven and Earth had given up on the whole human race, and now He had passed His judgment on them. There was no hope for them in any way shape or form. They were doomed to total extinction.

As God continued to speak to Noah He said, "You are to bring into the Ark, two of all living creatures, male and female, to keep them alive with you. Two of every kind of bird, every kind of animal, and of every kind of creature that moves along the ground, will come to you to be kept alive. You are to take every kind of food that is to be eaten, and store it away as food for you and for them." Also in (Ge.7; 2) it says, "Take with you seven of every kind of clean animal, a male and its mate, and two of every kind of unclean animal, a male and its mate, and also seven of every kind of bird, male and female, to keep their various kinds alive throughout the earth. The number seven symbolizes completeness. Also multiples of the number seven is used many times in the Bible, in the religious cycle.

In reference to the words "clean animal and unclean animal," a clean animal that is used for food, has a split hoof. For example, cattle, sheep, deer, moose etc. are all considered clean animals. The unclean animals would be animals like horses, donkeys, or any kind of animal or bird that eats blood or carrion. Insects that do not have hind legs for jumping, and water creatures that do not have scales or fins. Only two of the unclean animals were taken because, the ceremonially unclean animals would only have to reproduce themselves after the flood. But the ceremonially clean animals would be needed for the burnt offerings that Noah would sacrifice to God in (Ge.8; 20) and later on for food for all of mankind. God did this because He had given everything to man, to have control over it (Ge.9; 3).

After the appointed length of time had passed that, God had set for the building of the Ark, God spoke once again to Noah and said, "seven days from now I will send rain on the earth for forty days and forty nights, and I will wipe from the face of the earth every living creature that I have made."

It was God the great creator, who chose the exact animals, birds, and all of the creeping things that live on and in the ground that, He wanted to save and keep alive for His new world. Everything that God had told Noah, that He would have to save and keep alive on the Ark, came to the Ark by Gods command. God knew that the task of choosing the right species that He wanted would be too great a task for Noah to complete because he was only human. As it says in (Ge.7; 9), male and female, came to Noah and entered the ark, as God had commanded Noah. All of the sea creatures and fish that God wanted to preserve would remain alive outside of the Ark in the water. God didn't leave anything to chance.

The use of the number forty, often characterizes a critical period in Gods redemptive history. Here are some examples. (1) When the earth was flooded, it rained for forty days and forty nights. (2) Moses was on the mountain forty days and forty nights, when God gave him the Ten Commandments. (3) God caused the children of Israel, to wander in the desert for forty years, because of their disobedience to Him. (4) Jesus was in the desert for forty days and forty nights, when He was tempted by the Devil. (5) It took the twelve Israelite spies forty days to complete their journey into Canaan and to report back to Moses. These are only a few instances, where the number forty is used. So you can see that God used certain specific periods of time, and numbers to represent the events that have occurred in human history.

Noah did all that the Lord commanded him. This statement proves that Noah was completely obedient to God and therefore God considered Noah to be righteous before Him. It was his faith in God that saved him, and his whole family from certain death in the flood to come. When the seven days that the Lord had spoken of were past, the rain began to fall just like God had said it would. This shows you that Gods word is true, and that He does not change His mind at any time, because He is true to His word. Then God said to Noah in (Ge.7; 1) "Go into the ark, you and your whole family, because I have found you righteous in this generation." So it was that, in true obedience to the Lord that, Noah and his family entered the life saving Ark that he had built with instructions from the Lord.

Then the Lord shut them in the Ark and He closed the door behind Noah and his family. This would be the last time that God would speak to Noah, in the old world as they knew it. The next time that they would converse with each other, it would be in the new world after the flood. God has displayed

His redeeming love to mankind once more, by saving Noah and his family. They alone would be a new start for mankind, and a new generation of people for God to love, and care for on the new earth that was to come. Up to this point in time, the story of the flood is a story of Gods judgment on mankind. But from this point on, it will be a story of Gods unfailing love and the redemption of mankind. In (Ge.7; 11) the scriptures gives us a hint as to the date when the flood occurred, but not a specific year. The scriptures state it this way. "In the six hundredth year of Noah's life, on the seventh day of the second month, on that day all the springs of the great deep burst forth, and the flood gates of the heavens were opened, and rain fell on the earth for forty days and forty nights." The full fury of the flood was unleashed on sinful mankind. As the waters increased, they lifted the ark high above the earth. It lifted it up above the highest mountains under the entire heavens. It covered the mountains to a depth of twenty feet. Every living thing that moved on the earth perished. The old wicked world as Noah and his family had known it was gone forever.

The water covered the surface of the earth for one hundred and fifty days or approximately five months. To Noah and his family, it must have seemed like an eternity of time when you consider the problems that they may have had to put up with for that length of time. They may have felt that God must have forgotten about them. Noah tried several times to see if the water had receded or not.

But God remembered Noah and his family. When the word remembered is used here in the Bible, it is not merely to recall to mind, it is to express concern for someone, or to act with loving care to them. When God remembers His people, He does so with "favor." In (Ne.5; 19) the scriptures says, "Remember me with favor, O my God, for all that I have done for these people." Then God sent a wind over the earth, and the waters receded steadily from the earth.

After forty days, Noah opened one of the windows that he had made in the ark and sent out a raven. It kept flying back and forth until the water had dried up from the earth. Then Noah sent out a dove, to see if the water had receded enough from the ground. But the dove could not find any place to put its feet because there was water over the surface of the earth. So the dove returned to Noah and he took it back into the ark. Then Noah waited seven more days, and then he sent the dove out again.

When the dove returned to him in the evening, there, in its beak was a freshly plucked olive leaf. So Noah waited seven more days, and sent the dove out again, and this time it did not return to him. Then he knew that the earth was dried up. It was on the first day, of the first month, of Noah's six hundred and first years that the water had dried up from the earth. On the twenty-seventh day of the second month, the earth was completely dried up. The date mentioned here signifies the beginning of the new world after the flood. Now mankind had a new start in the history of the world.

Then God said to Noah. "Come out of the ark, you and your wife and your sons wives. Bring out every kind of creature that is with you, so they can multiply on the earth and be fruitful, and increase in number." After Noah and his family had left the ark, everything that remained on the ark, came out in an orderly fashion. There was no big stamped, or animals and birds, running or flying in a disorderly manner. They came out as the scripture says: "one kind after the other."

It had been a little more than a year after the flood began, that Noah and his family came out of the ark. Also, it was the first time that God had spoken with Noah and his family, in the new world. It would probably be about this point in time that the full impact of the flood, and what God had done, would impact upon Noah and his family. They would now fully realize what a great and glorious blessing God had bestowed on them because; now they would realize that they were the only human beings on the whole earth.

One of the first things that Noah did, after he and his family came out of the ark, was to give thanks to the Lord God of Heaven and Earth. Then he built an altar, so he could offer up a bunt offering to the Lord, which was his custom. He took some of the clean animals and clean birds and killed them, and sacrificed them on the altar to God. The Lord smelled the pleasing aroma and said in His heart; "Never again will I curse the ground because of man, even though every inclination of his heart is evil from childhood. And never again will I destroy all living creatures, as I have done. As long as the earth endures, seedtime and harvest, cold and heat, summer and winter, day and night will never cease." When God makes a promise, He will not change it or His mind, no matter what anyone thinks, because God is unchangeable. As the saying goes, you can say that His words are the only words in this world that are carved in stone.

When the four words "smelled the pleasing aroma" was used here, it is a figurative way of saying that the Lord takes delight in His children's worship to Him. In (Eph.5; 2) it says: Be imitators of God, therefore, as dearly loved children and live a life of love, just as Christ loved us and gave Himself up for us as a fragrant offering and a sacrifice to God. Your worship to God should be a very personal matter, because it comes from your heart and soul. God sees what's in your heart as well as everything else that happens in your life. Everything in the world is like an open book to Him.

Now at this particular point in time God renews an old covenant with Noah and his sons. He blessed them and said: "Be fruitful and increase in number, and fill the earth. The fear, and dread of you, will fall upon all of the beasts of the earth, and all of the birds of the air, and every creature that moves along the ground, and upon all the fish of the sea, they are given into your hands. Everything that lives and moves will be food for you. But you must not eat meat that has its lifeblood still in it. Also, for your lifeblood, I will demand an accounting. I will demand an accounting from every animal. And from each man, too, I will demand an accounting for the life of his fellow man." Once again God has given man dominion over His creation. This was not a new covenant with man, but a renewing of the old covenant that was established with Adam and Eve in the Garden of Eden when God created the earth. Meat would now supplement mankind's diet again.

"For your lifeblood I will demand an accounting!" These words pack a very powerful meaning. They mean exactly what they say. If an animal kills a man, then that animal will have to give an accounting for it. Likewise, if a man takes another man's life, by premeditated murder, by man shall his blood is shed. The blood in its self is what contains life, not the body. The body is only the container or the holder of that lifeblood. Without the blood there is no life.

Life is a precious and mysterious gift of God, and man is not to seek to preserve it, or to increase the life-force within himself, by eating the "life" that is in the blood." The scriptures clearly states in (Lev.17; 11) why God forbids this practice. It says: "For the life of the creature is in the blood, and I have given it to you, to make atonement for yourselves on the altar." This is why people of the Old Testament were required to sacrifice animals to God. It was so the animals blood would be shed on the altar as a substitute for mans sin and not his own. The animal's blood was also a representation, of the blood of Christ that makes the full atonement for a person's life and their sins. This is why, our Lord and Savior, Jesus Christ, had to shed His precious blood for all of mankind, on the cross at Calvary. Jesus was the full atoning sacrifice for all of mankind that God the Father required. His blood makes us Holy, sinless, and acceptable in the sight of God.

When we confess our sins before God the Father, and we are sorry for committing them, God looks down on us and sees the blood of the Lord Jesus Christ. Then God covers our sins with His blood and they are forgiven. Jesus is our mediator between the Father and us. There is no other substitute whereby we can be saved. This is Gods decree and the absolute truth.

Now the God of Mercy and Grace makes a New Covenant with Noah and his descendants after him. God said in (Ge. 9; 8-17) "I now establish my covenant with you and your descendants after you. With you and all the living creatures on the earth. Never again shall all flesh be cut off by the waters of a flood; never again shall there be a flood to destroy the whole earth. This is the sign of the covenant I am making between me and you and every living creature with you, a covenant for all generations to come. I have set my rainbow in the clouds, and it will be the sign of the covenant between the earth and me. Whenever the rainbow appears in the clouds, I will see it, and remember the everlasting covenant between God and all living creatures of every kind on the earth."

This covenant was a different kind of covenant between God and man, because this time, God used the visible sign of the rainbow in the sky. This covenant and all other covenants that God has ever made with man will remain unchanged until Gods Judgment Day. Then He will make all things new again. After the flood Noah lived three hundred and fifty years. Altogether, Noah lived nine hundred and fifty years. Then he died. Noah was the tenth and last member of the genealogy of Seth, the third son of Adam and Eve.

So it was that now mankind would reproduce and fill the earth. He had received Gods full blessing. Man still retained his long life cycle, for a little while longer to repopulate the earth. God had not yet shortened mans' life to a maximum of one hundred and twenty years, as He said He would do in (Ge.6; 3). This was not a sign that God would not keep His word or change His mind. As you know, people of today very seldom live past one hundred years old. So you can see how God has shortened mans' life span even more than one hundred and twenty years. You can also see how God repopulated the whole earth, by using only eight people. It was through Gods richest blessing, and His great love for mankind, that man has been able to multiply and to prosper so well on the earth. Through His awesome power, and His mighty word, God had given man a long life at one time in history. But now man has lost this privilege because of his sin and a rebellious heart.

The three Sons of Noah, Shem, Ham and Japheth, represent seventy different nations of people that are spread throughout the earth today. The number seventy is multiples of the numbers, ten and seven. Both of these numbers signify completeness. It is with the word "Completeness" that I will end the story of Noah and the flood, and his part in the history of mankind.

Part Three

THE STORY OF ABRAHAM

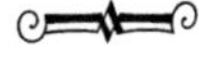

-1-

ABRAHAM THE PATRIARC

The story of Abram or Abraham, as God later renames him, is a story of a man who demonstrated his great faith and love for his God. The strict obedience that he felt towards his God was one of the compelling forces that drove him to do what he did throughout his life. He is sometimes referred to as the father of many nations. Abram, (this is the name I will call him until later on in the story.) was a descendant of Shem, one of the sons of Noah.

There were ten generations from Shem to Abram. Terah, who was the ninth in line from Shem, had three Sons. Their names were Abram, Nahor, and Haran, but this is not necessarily the order in which they were born. Haran became the father of Lot, and Haran died in the land of Ur in the land of the Chaldeans where he was born. The name of Abrams wife was Sarai, and she was unable to have any children because the Lord had made her barren. God had made her barren for a very specific reason. This reason will be revealed much later in the story.

It was very demeaning, for a woman in those days not to be able to bear children. It was very important to have a big family, and in this way, to be able to produce a lot of descendents. The name of Nahor's wife was Milcah. She was the daughter of Haran. He had the same name as the city that he would later settle in. In the Hebrew language, the two names are spelled differently.

Terah the father of Abram and Nahor took his whole family, and they set out from Ur, to go to the land of Canaan. But when they came to a place called Haran, they settled there for a while. It is not known why they settled at this place. I would suspect one of the reasons for settling there could have been the fact that Terah was an idolater, and he worshiped idols. The moon-god was worshiped in both Ur and in Haran. For this reason alone, he would feel more at home, and would be inclined to settle in such a place as Haran. Also, Haran was a flourishing caravan city at that time and this could have influenced him as well to stay there. It is not known how long the family of Terah lived in Haran, or if in fact, that they ever left that city and later returned, but Terah died there when he was two hundred and five years old.

Abram was a great deal different than his brothers both in character and spiritually. He was a devout and faithful servant of the Lord. He obeyed God without doubting or questioning Gods commands or motives, and the Lord credited Abrams faith to his righteousness.

Now the Lord had spoken to Abram previously while he was still in Mesopotamia, before he lived in Haran. The Lord had said to Abram: "Leave your country, your people and your fathers' household and go to the land I will show you." The fact that Abram left his home, not knowing what lay ahead of him showed that his faith in God was deeply rooted within him, and that he trusted God to lead him, and protect him no matter what came his way.

At this same time, God had made a promise to Abram. The promise that God had made to Abram was a seven-fold promise. (1) I will make you into a great nation, and (2) I will bless you, (3) I will make your name great, and (4) you will be a blessing. (5) I will bless those who bless you and (6) whoever curses you I will curse, and (7) all peoples on earth will be blessed through you."

As you can see Gods promise to Abram contained seven gigantic blessings. God was restoring His original blessing on mankind once again, as He did in (Ge.1; 28). But this time He is going to fulfill His blessing to mankind through Abram and his offspring. I do not believe that Abram could have realized at this time, the full impact of what God had told him, or what God was going to do through him. It would not be until sometime later when God spoke to him for the second time, that Abram may have had some idea of the magnitude of the covenant that God was making with him.

Abram was seventy-five years old when he left Haran and departed for Canaan. Although he was well advanced in years, as we say we are in today's world at seventy-five, Abram would live another full century before God would take him home to heaven. The Bible says that when he departed from his home country, he took all of his possessions with him. This included all of his people, his livestock, his gold and silver, everything that wasn't nailed down. He left nothing behind him to tie him to his old country or to his old way of life. He was to be totally separated from his homeland. This would be a huge leap of faith for any one regardless of who they are. We as Christians today, may have to do much the same thing if, we are to serve the Living God as He wants us to. We have to step out of our comfort zone with boldness and confidence to proclaim Christ and His saving grace, and His kingdom to all people.

God had made Abram a very rich man at this stage in his life. The people, mentioned here, are the men and women servants that Abram had acquired in his lifetime, before God asked him to move. They would be responsible for looking after flocks of sheep, goats, cattle, and camels, or any other animals that Abram might posses. As you can see, it would be a huge undertaking, to move everything that Abram had acquired in the seventy-five years to another country. There were no airplanes, trains, or trucks to move Abrams possessions with. Not like we have today at our fingertips. You can well understand that he must have had many problems even getting started, and then continuing on his journey to the land of Canaan.

Although, Abram might have been accustomed to moving around with his flocks, he did not complain or grip to God about his problems. He just did what God told him to do. This expressed his great love and trust for his God. He knew that God was with him, and that God would give him the solutions to whatever problems that might come his way. To top it all off! He took his nephew Lot with him and all of his possessions as well. By doing this, it would cause Abram more problems later on. Lot was also very rich and he had many possessions and many people to care for as well. But there was a vast difference between Lot and Abram. Lot was a self-seeker and his desire was to serve himself any way he could, even if it was at someone else's expense. Abram on the other hand, depended on God completely for everything.

As the Bible relates in the scripture in (Ge.12; 5), it says: "and they arrived there in the land of Canaan." They had no doubt selected a dwelling place where they had a good supply of grass and water for their flocks and herds. After Abram had settled down for a while, he started to travel throughout the land. He wanted to see the land that the Lord had brought him to.

As he traveled about in the central part of Canaan, he came to the great tree of Moreh at Shechem. There was also a famous holy sanctuary located there as well. A large tree was often a conspicuous feature at such holy places. Because it was a holy place of worship, he paused and rested, and gathered his thoughts. It was there that, he too worshiped his God. But he wouldn't worship or bow down to the statues that the local people worshiped in that part of the country. The land at that time was controlled and ruled by the Canaanite people.

From there he went toward the hills east of Bethel and pitched his tent, with Bethel on the west and Ai on the east. Bethel was located just twelve miles north of the present day Jerusalem. While he was at this location, he built an altar to the Lord, and he called on the name of the Lord. It was customary, for Abram to build an altar to the Lord, in places where he had a memorable spiritual experience, with the Lord.

The altars Abram built were made in a very special way. The altars that animals were to be burnt and sacrificed on were made from materials from the earth. But the altars where God caused His name to be honored, and where He would come to bless the people, were made from natural uncut stone. That is, no hand tools or anything else that was made by man was to be used, to reshape the stones in any way. If any hand tools were used they would defile the altar. Also, there were to be no steps leading up to the altar. This was because; they might expose a person's nakedness, as they stepped up to the altar.

When the Lord appeared to Abram at this place He said to him: "To your offspring I will give this land." The Lord frequently appeared visibly to Abram and other people in those ancient times, but He does not do this in today's world. Sometimes He appeared in the form of an angel. He would speak to them, but He did not appear to them in all of His glory. So now, Abram knew why the Lord had brought him to the land of Canaan. He acknowledged that the land of Canaan belonged to the Lord in a special way. After God had spoken to Abram at Bethel, Abram set out and went to Negev. This was a dry wasteland stretching southward from Beersheba, and south of Hebron. This is the place that he would return to later on to live. After he had seen all of the country that God had wanted him to see, he returned home to his family and his people.

Some time had passed after Abram had returned home, and there arose a great famine in the land of Canaan where he lived. He had no doubt, heard from God, or someone else, that Egypt was the land of plenty. Once again, Abram was faced with the monumental task of moving all of his possessions to a different country. But he trusted in the Lord and just went ahead and moved to Egypt. The Lord had made Egypt a land of wealth and power at that time. Egypt was a land of plenty, because of the Nile River that flowed through it. The Nile was normally dependable, and it supplied the country with all of the water it needed to sustain a good life that was closely tied to agriculture.

Just before Abram entered Egypt, he said to his wife Sarai: "I know you are a beautiful woman, and when the Egyptians see you they will say: "this is his wife", and they will kill me and let you go! Tell them that you are my sister, and they will treat me well because of you, and my life will be spared. At this time, Sarai was sixty-five years old, and still a beautiful woman. Abram must have understood the costumes and the laws of Egypt because of what he told Sarai to say to Pharaoh the King and to his officials.

After Abram had settled down and He was going about his business, some of the Egyptians seen how beautiful Sarai was, and they reported it to the Pharaoh. So the Pharaoh took her into his Palace to be one of his wives. After all, the Pharaoh knew a beautiful woman when he saw one. He took her as a wife only for his own selfish reasons. It was not necessarily to have sex with her.

For example: some of the reasons may have been (1) because she was so beautiful and pleasing to the eye. (2) Anything that was within his power to possess, he would have to have control over it. (3) She would give him a little more prestige, and she would boost his ego a great deal when she was presented to his officials in his court. (4) He knew that if he controlled the women of Abram, he also could control the power and the wealth of her husband.

Because of Sarai, the Pharaoh made Abram even wealthier, than he was before. He gave Abram even more livestock, sheep, cattle, donkeys, camels, silver and gold, as well as menservants, and maidservants to care for all that he had. It would have taken most men a lifetime to accumulate what Abram had accumulated while he was in Egypt.

In Abrams time, the possession of large herds of live-stock and servants was a measure of a person's wealth. There is an interesting point here that I would like to bring to your attention and that is to say that; Abrams experience in this episode foreshadows Israel's later experience in Egypt, when the Egyptians held the Israelites captive for 430 years as slaves. The Israelites would then be led out of Egypt by Moses to the Promised Land. The Exodus is another story in its self. This also proves that Abram was truly the "Father" of Israel.

There is no mention of the length of time that Sarai stayed in the Palace of the Pharaoh, or how long Abram stayed in Egypt. In (Ge.12; 17- 20) it says; "But the Lord inflicted serious diseases on Pharaoh and his household because of Abrams wife Sarai." Somehow, probably through the grape vine, Pharaoh learned that Sarai was Abrams wife. This made the Pharaoh very angry. Pharaoh than sent for Abram and asked him saying; "What have you done to me?" Why didn't you tell me she was your wife?" Why did you say; "She is my Sister, so that I took her for my wife?"

It appears at this point, that the Pharaoh will catch Abram in a big lie. Egyptian ethics emphasized the importance of absolute truthfulness. Then Pharaoh said to Abram; "Now than, here is your wife. Take her and go." At the same time, the Pharaoh gave orders about Abram to his men, and they would watch over him and send him on his way out of the country with his wife and all of his possessions when he was ready to go.

So as time passed, and the famine was over in the land of Canaan, and the land had returned to normal, Abram departed from Egypt, and went back to Negev with much greater wealth, than what he had, when he came to Egypt. Lot, Abrams nephew, also left Egypt at the same time. From there, they wandered from place to place until they finely came back to the same place at Bethel and Ai, where they had originally came from. You may recall that it was here that Abram had first built an altar to the Lord. He had come full circle back to where God wanted him to be.

The scriptures in (Ge.13; 1-18) do not state how long Lot stayed with Abram after their return from Egypt. But as time went on, there was trouble brewing between Abrams herdsmen, and Lots herdsmen. They were arguing over pasture and the water they needed to feed their livestock. This was one of their main problems. The herdsmen probably had a number of other things that they were squabbling about, but it is not mentioned in the Bible. But at any rate, there was a great deal of dissention in both camps.

To compound the problems, there were Canaanites and Perizzites living nearby in the land at the same time. I believe this is the reason why Abram called on the Lord when he did and now, the problems were getting to be too much for Abram and Lot to handle. So Abram took his problems to the Lord. (This is what all people can do, and let God solve the problems for them). If all people would do this simple thing, we would be living in a much better world today.

After Abram had called on the name of the Lord, he took the solution to his nephew Lot. Abram said to Lot, "Let's not have any quarreling between, you and me, or between your herdsmen and mine, as we are brothers." As you will notice, Abram who was always generous gave his young nephew Lot, first choice. He said; "Let us part company. If you go to the left, I will go to the right. If you go to the right, I will go to the left." The choice was up to Lot. In that way Lot could not accuse Abram of any wrongdoing. Abram knew that the Lord would bless him no matter which way he went. Also, Abram did not want to obtain any wealth except only by the Lords hand and through His blessings.

So Lot looked up, and saw that the whole plain of the Jordan was well watered, and like the garden of the Lord. The words like the garden of the Lord. Refers to the garden of the Eden and its perfect conditions. It would also be like it was in the land of Egypt. So Lot chose for himself, the whole plain of the Jordan. It was the best land in the area. Then he moved all of his possessions toward the east, away from Abram. He went and settled in the cities of the plains, near Sodom and Gomorrah.

As I have stated before, you will probably notice that there is quite a contrast between Abram and his nephew Lot. When Lot looked up, he looked up with a selfish desire in his heart. He wanted to have the very best land, and the very best of everything under his control. It was very evident that he didn't care too much about how Abram would make out. Lot cared more about material thing, and what he could get out of other people to further his own cause, than he cared about what God would have wanted for him. The Bible says that God truly blessed Lot because of Abram. God had made him very rich at the same time as Abram. Also in (Heb.7; 7) it says; "the lesser person is blessed by the greater." Abram on the other hand, when God told him to look up, he looked up because God had commanded him to look up. He had love and obedience in his heart, and God blessed him for it.

After Abram and Lot had parted company, in (Ge.13; 14-18) God said to Abram, "Lift up your eyes from where you are, and look north and south, east and west. All the land that you see I will give to you and your offspring forever. I will make your offspring like the dust of the earth, so that if anyone could count the dust, then your offspring could be counted. Go, and walk through the length and breathe of the land, for I am giving it to you." Similar phrases are used in (Ge. 22; 17). For example "as numerous as the stars in the sky" and "as the sand on the seashore." God was once again renewing His covenant with Abram that He had made a long time ago. Also, when God told Abram to walk through the land, it was either to inspect it or to exercise his authority over it, thus demonstrating the promised ownership of the land to his descendants.

So Abram did what God had commanded him to do. He moved his tent and all of his belongings near the great tree of Mamre at Hebron. There he built an altar to the Lord. The building of an altar was probably a great honor and a privilege to Abram, because of his great love for his God. He would not need God to tell him to do so.

Sometime after Abram and Lot had parted company, a war broke out between the Kings of the land, near the cities of Sodom and Gomorrah. As luck would have it, Lot had moved into the city of Sodom, and he was living among the wicked people in that city. Now Lot was righteous, in respect to all of the other people who lived there. But; by moving into such a city as Sodom, he had put himself and his family in danger of imitating the filthy lives of the lawless men and women who lived there. It would have been very easy for Lot and his whole family to slip into the same form of Idolatry because of the environment that they lived in. This very same thing applies to us today as well. We also can be drawn away from the Lord and into the ways of the world if we are not careful.

The Kings of Sodom and Gomorrah were defeated and driven off into the Valley of Siddim. After the battle was over, the victors of the war went into the cities of Sodom and Gomorrah and ram sacked them. They took everything that was not nailed down, and carried it off to their cities. Lot was no exception. He and his family and all that he possessed, were taken captive and taken to one of the victors cities.

However, one of Lots servants who had been captured escaped, and he went and reported to Abram what had happened to Lot and his family. When Abram heard this news, he knew that he must do all that was within his power to rescue his nephew Lot. At that time, Abram was still living by the great trees of Mamre, near an Amorite, a brother of Eshcol and Aner, who were very close allies of Abram. They and their armies were willing to go and fight alongside of Abram and his men. But Abram refused their help. Then he took 318 trained men who had been born of his household, and went in pursuit of the King that had taken Lot and his family captive.

It is here at this point in the story, that Abram is called the "Father of the Hebrew people in the Bible." He is the "First Biblical" character to be called a Hebrew. The fact that Abram took only 318 men from his household is a clear indication of his great wealth and power. It also displayed the fact that he had great faith in God to support and to protect him.

When Abram had located the place where Lot and his family were being held captive, he divided his men and attacked the opposing army. The Bible says that he completely routed them, and caused them to flee pursuing them as far as Hobah, north of Damascus. After the battle was over, Abram recovered all of Lots family and his possessions, and returned them to their home. Then he departed from Lot and his family and returned to his home at Mamre.

There is no mention of any loss of life in Abrams army. This clearly indicates that God had gone before Abram and his army to protect them. It is also possible that God had put great fear into the hearts of the Kings army and it caused them to flee in terror. It also, demonstrates Gods awesome power over all things and in any kind of situation. The Lords arm is never to short when it comes to helping His people.

Shortly after Abram and his army had returned home, the King of Sodom came out to meet him in the Valley of Shaveh. (That is the Kings valley east of Jerusalem.) Then Melchizedek who was the Priest of God Most High, and King of Salem, (a shortened form of "Jerusalem") brought out bread and wine, and blessed Abram and said in: (Ge.14; 19-20), "Blessed be Abram by God Most High, Creator of heaven and earth. And blessed be God Most High, who delivered your enemies into your hand." Then Abram gave Melchizedek a tenth of everything he had taken from his enemy as a tithe offering. This was the first time that Abram had ever gone to war against anyone, and God had shown His great love for him by protecting Abram and his army.

Just a word or two here about the "High Priest Melchizedek. The meaning of the name Melchizedek is "My King is Righteousness" or "King of righteousness." (Heb. 7; 2-3). Melchizedek is later spoken of in scripture as a type or prefiguration of Jesus our "Great High Priest." (Heb. 4; 14) whose priesthood is therefore in the order of Melchizedek, not in the order of Aaron?

Abram would not accept a single thing from the King of Sodom not even a thread or a thong of a sandal, because he had taken an oath to the "God Most High." (This was a standard practice in ancient times.) Also, he didn't want to be obligated to anyone but the Lord. He knew that God was the only one that had made him rich. It was his great desire to make sure that it was known to all the people that it was God who deserved all of the credit. Likewise if; Abram had accepted anything from the King of Sodom, the King might have tried to exercise lordship or kingship over Abram at some future date.

It is not stated in scripture, just how long it was after Abrams encounter with Melchizedek and the King of Sodom that the Lord appeared to Abram in a vision. This vision is the next great happening, and excitement to occur in Abrams life. Let's pause here for a second or two in our story, and just think of what is happening to Abram. He is actually seeing his Creator in a vision. Can you imagine just what an experience it would be, to have God our Father, appear to us in a vision or in the form of an angel?

To me it would be an experience of a lifetime, and also somewhat frightening. But God in His great wisdom handled the whole situation with loving care. Listen closely to what the Lord says to Abram in (Ge.15; 1). He said; "Do not be afraid, Abram. I am your shield, your very great reward." Where the word Shield or "Sovereign" is used here and elsewhere, the reference is to the Lord as Abrams King. The first thing that God did was to silence Abrams fear, of what was happening to him. Although Abram was very rich, God Himself was shown as Abrams greatest treasure, as He should be too all of mankind. But that is not the way it is. Mankind has gone its own way and it has had to suffer the consequences of its actions since the beginning of time.

Because Abram and his wife were very old at this time, and they had no children, Abram showed some concern as to why God hadn't fulfilled His promise to him up to this point in time. So Abram said to the Lord; (Ge.15; 2) "O Sovereign Lord, what can you give me since I remain childless, and the one who will inherit my estate is Eliezer of Damascus." Eliezer was one Abrams chief servants that he had acquired on his journey southward from Haran.

In ancient times, a person who had no children or heirs to their estate could adopt one of his own male servants to be heir and guardian of their estate. They did not have to be a relative. It appears; that this is what Abram had done or had, contemplated doing before he received this vision from the Lord. Now once again God shows His great love to Abram by renewing His covenant with him, and telling him what He is going to do for him.

Then the word of the Lord came to him and said; "This man will not be your heir, but a Son coming from your own body will be your heir." Then God took him outside his tent and told Abram to look up and count the stars, "if indeed you can count them. So shall your offspring's be." Abram believed the Lord, and the Lord credited it to him as righteousness. This promise was initially fulfilled in Egypt, as you can read in (Dt.1: 10; Heb.11: 12). In the Bible it says in (Gal. 3:29) that ultimately, all people who believe in Christ are Abrams seed and heirs according to the promise. God also renewed His promise to Abram, that He had given the land of Canaan as his possession and that his descendants would also inherit it. But Abram questioned the Lord saying: "O Sovereign Lord, how can I know that I will gain possession of it?" Abram believed Gods promise of a son, but he asked God for a guarantee of the promise of the land.

So once again God told Abram what would come to pass in the future in (Ge. 15: 9-21). That same day after Abram had spoken to the Lord, Abram prepared the bird and animal sacrifices that the Lord had commanded him to do. As the sun was setting, Abram fell into a deep sleep. Than a thick and dreadful darkness came over him and the Lord said to him: "Know for certain that your descendants will be strangers in a country not their own, and they will be enslaved and mistreated four hundred years. But I will punish the nation they serve as slaves, and afterward, they will come out with great possessions. You, however, will go to your fathers in peace, and be buried at a good old age. In the fourth generation, your descendants will come back here, for the sins of the Amorites have not yet reached its full measure."

It is here in this scripture that, God, foretold to Abram, about the children of Israel, who would be his descendants. God also told him of their slavery, and of their return to this Promised Land. God even set out the boundaries of the Promised Land. From the river of Egypt to the great river the Euphrates, and the land of the Kenites, Kenizzites, Kadmonites, Hittites, Perizzites, Rephaites, Amorites, Canaanites, Girgashites and Jebusites. The Lord through Joshua would initially fulfill the scriptures here when he led the children of Israel into the Promise Land. These scriptures are further proof that God knows all things past, present, and future. You cannot hide anything from Him, not even your most secret thoughts.

As you can see God fulfills His promises in His own time but, not necessarily, as we require things to be fulfilled. In (Isa. 55:8-9) hear what the Lord says to all of mankind." For my thoughts are not your thoughts, neither are your ways my ways," declares the Lord. "As the heavens are higher than the earth, so are my ways higher than your ways, and my thoughts than your thoughts."

The Bible does not state how long it was after Abram had spoken to the Lord, that the next big event took place in his life. Now Sarai Abrams wife was barren and she had not given Abram any children. Sarai had become very impatient waiting for the Lord to fulfill His promise to Abram about a son. So she decided to take matters into her own hands and not wait for the Lord to fulfill His promise. In her human way of thinking, she devised a plan of her own to solve her problem. But her impatience would later cause her a great deal of stress and frustration in the years to come. She had an Egyptian maidservant by the name of Hagar. Abram had probably acquired her while Abram and Sarai were in Egypt.

She said to Abram:" The Lord has kept me from having children, go and sleep with my maidservant; perhaps I can build a family through her. This was an accepted practice in ancient times. So Abram agreed to Sarai's wishes. When Hagar became pregnant she began to despise Sarai, because she mistreated her. After a while, Hagar ran away from their home to get some peace of mind.

After she had traveled some distance, she stopped and rested by a spring on the road to Shur, east of Egypt. It was there, that the angel of the Lord found her and he said, "Hagar Servant of Sarai, where have you come from, and where are you going?" "I am running away from my mistress Sarai, "she answered. But she could only answer the first part of the angels question because she did not know at that time, exactly where she was going.

What, the angel told her the next time that he spoke to her; it must have really made her very happy, and somewhat fearful. It was probably even harder for her to believe her own ears. But, because of the message that the angel spoke to her, she must have realized that it was an angel speaking to her. The angel of the Lord said to her: "You are now with child and you will have a son. You shall name him Ishmael, for the Lord has heard of your misery."

The angel also told her what her son and his descendants would be like. He explained to her that he would be like "a wild donkey of a man'. He would live in the desert like a wild donkey, roaming from place to place, and staying away from human settlements. Wherever he would go, there would be open hostility between him and other people. Than the angel told her to go back to her mistress, and submit to her. So the hostility that existed between Sarai and Hagar would be passed on to their descendants. As time passed, Hagar bore Abram a son, and he called him Ishmael. Abram was eighty-six years old when Hagar bore him a son.

THE COVENANT OF CIRCUMCISION

Abram was ninety-nine years old, before the Lord appeared to him again. This time the Lord would make another covenant with him, called the "Covenant of Circumcision." What God was going to doing now, was to confirm His covenant once again with Abram, and to give him further instructions as to what He wanted Abram to do. In (Ge.17; 1) God said to Abram, "I am the God Almighty, walk before me and be blameless."

It is here, that God requests a special commitment from Abram. He was to walk before God and be "Perfect, or Blameless," or his faith must be accompanied by the "obedience" that only comes from faith. In this passage, God refers to Himself as "God Almighty" for the first time. The Hebrew word Ei-Shaddai, is similar to a word for mountain or "God, the Mountain One." With either meaning, it highlights the invincible power of God, or referring to the mountains as Gods symbolic home. It was the special name by which God revealed Himself to the Patriarchs.

This is the fourth time that God has appeared to Abram since he had come into the land of Canaan. God also made it very clear that this was His covenant, and not anyone else's. In (Ge. 17: 1-27) the Lord said: "As for me, this is my covenant with you: You will be the father of many nations. I will make you very fruitful. I will make nations of you, and Kings will come from you. I will establish my covenant as an everlasting covenant between me and you and your descendants after you for the generations to come, to be your God and the God of your descendants after you. The whole Land of Canaan where you are now an alien, I will give as an everlasting possession to you and your descendants after you; and I will be their God."

As well as this covenant, God had another surprise for Abram. He was about to change Abrams name, from Abram to Abraham. This name change is significant because the two names, although similar in pronunciation, they have two different meanings. The first name Abram, means "Exalted Father" which is probably in reference to God, because God is the Exalted Father. Also the second name Abraham, means "Father of Many." By giving Abram a new name, God marked him in a special way as His servant. Also, it reinforced the fact, that he would now become the father of many nations. From this point on, I will also call him Abraham.

Being this was the fourth time that God had appeared to Abraham, I believe that by this time, Abraham was becoming quite accustomed to having the Lord appear, and talk with him. This time Abraham lay face down on the ground. It was either out of fear of the Lord, or out pure reverence for the Lord. Now the Lord makes another covenant with Abraham. But now God has special conditions attached to it. The Bible states in (Ge.17; 9-27) just what the Lord expected from Abraham and his descendants. The conditions are as follows:

(A) Abraham had to keep Gods covenant.
(B) He had to walk before God and be perfect.
(C) His descendants would have to keep Gods covenant for generations to come.

(D) All male adults and children were to be circumcised in the flesh, by the cutting off or removing the foreskin from the male organ.
(E) This included all of the males living under Abraham's control at that time.
(F) All male babies born into Abraham's own household were to be circumcised.
(G) All children were to be circumcised when they were 8 days old; this included all males bought with money from foreigners who were not Abraham's offspring.

In (Ge.17: 13) God said: "My covenant in your flesh is to be an everlasting covenant. Anyone who was not circumcised would be cut off from His people, because he has broken my Covenant." Circumcision was Gods sign of the special covenant. But it also marked Abraham as the one to whom God had made the special covenant commitment. Also, it was done in response to Abraham's faith, which God credited it to him as "righteousness."

We know that God is not a God who will do things halfheartily. Everything has to be complete and perfect. Because He had blessed Abraham, He would also bless Sarai as well. Since God has a wonderful master plan for each and every one of us, He had one more important statement to make to Abraham. He said to Abraham in (Ge. 17:15-16) "As for Sarai your wife, you are no longer to call her Sarai; her name will be "Sarah. I will bless her and will surely give you a son by her. I will bless her so that she will be the mother of nations; Kings of people will come from her." The name Sarah means "Princess." So now, Sarai has a new name as well as Abraham. God has now decreed that Sarah would to be a Princess, and she would become the Mother of Many Nations; Kings of peoples will come from her."

Once again God has told Abraham that He was going to give him a son. But then Abraham laughed and said to himself, "Will a son be born to a man a hundred years old? Will Sarah bear a child at the age of ninety?" Because both him and Sarah were very old at this time, and were well past their bearing years, he must have had some doubts as to what God was promising him. From a humans way of thinking it would have been impossible. But with Gods Almighty Power, nothing is impossible.

Abraham then said to God, "If only Ishmael might live under your blessing?" Then the Lord said to Abraham, "Yes, but your wife Sarah will bear you a son, and you will call him Isaac. I will establish my covenant with him as an everlasting covenant for his descendants after him. (The name Isaac means "Laughter.") Abraham's laugh was quite understandable from a human standpoint, because twenty-four years had elapsed since he had been told the first time that he would have a son, and still he had no son. This is absolute proof that God will always keep His promise to all people. God cannot lie because He is Holy and God does things within His own time frame.

Then God said to Abraham; "As for Ishmael, I have heard you; I will surely bless him; I will make him fruitful and will greatly increase his numbers. He will be the father of twelve rulers, and I will make him into a great nation. But my covenant I will establish with Isaac, whom Sarah will bear to you by this time next year."

So it was that, Abraham came to know for certain that he would have a son for an heir to his vast fortune. Now both Abraham and Sarah have the time line for a son that they so desperately wanted. Then God went up from Abraham. On the very same day that the Lord had spoken with Abraham, he was circumcised along with all males in his household, as well as all males that were under his control. At that time, Abraham was ninety-nine years old, and Ishmael was thirteen years old.

-2-

SODOM AND GOMORRH

The story of Sodom and Gomorrah is a story within a story. I say this because, it still involves Abraham, and it was one of Abraham's greatest tests in his life. This time, Abraham would again, came in very close contact with the Lord. This time, even the Lord was hesitant to show Abraham what He was going to do, and the reason for His sudden appearance.

Our story begins in (Ge. 18; 1 and ends in Ge. 19; 29). Abraham is sitting in the doorway of his tent in the shade, in the heat of the day. This was a common practice for anyone living in the Sinai Desert. The temperature could reach up to 110 degrees Fahrenheit by midday, during the summer months. He was still living by the "Terebinth Trees" at Mamre. This region later became known as Hebron. The people usually did most of the hard physical work early in the morning and late in the afternoon. By working this way, they hoped to avoid the extreme heat of the day. When it was too hot to work they could rest in any shade that was available to them.

As Abraham was sitting in front of his tent, he was probably thinking about the many events that had taken place in his life and the continuing problems of the day. Suddenly, three men appeared out of nowhere to speak to him. When Abraham looked up, they were standing some distance from him. Can you imagine his surprise! We know that one of the men was the Lord, because of what the scriptures say, and that one man, was greater in stature. But this time, the Lord had brought two angels with Him to fulfill the task that He had to do. The Bible says: they were part of Gods heavenly council. This is the fifth time that the Lord has appeared to Abraham since he came into the land of Canaan.

When Abraham saw them he ran to meet them, and he bowed down before them. Bowing down before your guests, was an acceptable custom at this point in time. It was a form of greeting, and it also showed respect, to anyone in authority as well. I believe that Abraham must have suspected that one of the men was the Lord, because of his greeting to the three men. He said: "My Lord, if I have now found favor in your sight, do not pass on by your servant." He desperately wanted to show his hospitality, and to express his deep gratitude to his guests for their visit. He said: "Please let a little water be brought, and wash your feet, and rest yourselves under the tree, and I will bring a morsel of bread that you may refresh your hearts, and then go on your way now that you have come to your servant. "Very well" they answered, "do as you say."

The practice of providing water so your guests could wash their feet was a very common practice in the desert. It was also a pleasure that you afforded your guests, and it gave them a real sense of happiness, as well as a great deal of comfort for their hot tired feet. As you can see, Abraham had now taken on the roll as a devout servant.

So Abraham hurried into the tent and told Sarah to quickly make some fresh bread. In the mean time, Abraham went to a herd of cattle and got a young calf and had it killed and prepared, as well as some butter and milk, and brought it to the three men. Then they proceeded to eat it under the tree in the shade. I believe that, the custom of providing good food and comfort, for your guests when they come to visit you, should be practiced on a much wider scale throughout the world today. If people practiced this small jester of kindness, I believe there would be more love and less hostility in the world.

After the three men had finished their meal, the Lord said to Abraham, "Where is Sarah your wife?" it was a question for Sarah this time, and not for Abraham. Abraham said;" she is in the tent." Then the Lord said to Abraham; "I will certainly return to you according to the time of life, (about the same time next year) and behold, Sarah your wife shall have a son." Once again God has renewed His promise of a son, to Abraham and his wife Sarah. As you can see, the Lord always remains true to His word, with no exceptions. This is also absolute proof, that the man who was talking to Abraham was God Himself because, He used the words, "I will certainly return to you according to the time of life."

As I stated once before that, as you read through the Bible, you will see that God would appear too many different people in many different forms. For example: He appeared to Abraham in the form of a man. He appeared to the children of Israel in the form of a cloud on a mountain. To Moses He appeared in the form of a burning bush, and to Jacob and to Joseph He appeared to them in their dreams.

While Sarah, who was inside the tent at the time the Lord was speaking to Abraham about her, she overheard the men's conversation, and she laughed within herself, and said; "after I have grown old, shall I have pleasure, my lord being old also. (Satan had caused her to doubt the power of God.) When Sarah referred to her lord, she was referring to Abraham. Sometimes the wives referred to their husbands as "Master or their lord." Then the Lord said to Abraham: "Why did Sarah laugh saying, "Shall I surely bear a child since I am old?" Is anything to hard for the Lord? As soon as Sarah realized that the Lord had heard her laugh, she quickly denied it saying, "I did not laugh," because she was afraid of the consequences, and she had compounded the denial with a lie. But the Lord said, "No, but you did laugh!"

Nothing within Gods will is impossible for Him to do. Not even today, or at that particular time for Sarah who was well past her childbearing years. Another example would be Mary, who was the mother of Jesus Christ our Savior. She was a virgin and she became pregnant supernaturally through the power of the Holy Spirit. But the Lord knew that she had laughed within herself, because He knew her thoughts. When Sarah laughed, she had reacted in the same manner that Abraham had reacted earlier when the Lord told him about having a son. However, God in His great mercy did not punish Sarah and Abraham when they laughed, but He forgave them.

After the three men had finished their meal and were about to leave, they turned toward Sodom, and Abraham walked with them for a little ways, as it was customary to do in those days. It was then that the Lord said to Himself; "Shall I hide from Abraham what I am about to do? Abraham will surely become a great and powerful nation, and all nations on earth will be blessed through him. For I have chosen him, so that he will direct his children and his household after him, to keep the way of the Lord by doing what is right and just." In this passage, the Lord allows His thoughts to be heard, as if He were a man. He was reflecting on the fact that Abraham had a vested interest in the city of Sodom because of his nephew Lot who lived there. I would also suspect that by this point in time that, Abraham may have made many friends with the people that he had dealings with in the city of Sodom.

By now, Abraham had become Gods covenant friend, and this time God had convened His heavenly council at

Abraham's tent. He also had permitted Abraham to stand up, and to question Him, almost to the point of an argument. The following conversation also illustrates the mutual accessibility that existed between God and His servant Abraham. In this manner He gave Abraham the opportunity to speak in His court, and to intercede for the righteous in Sodom and Gomorrah. Christians today, can also intercede for other people in Gods heavenly court, through their prayers.

Then the Lord said; "The outcry against Sodom and Gomorrah is so great, and their sin so grievous, that I will go down and see if what they have done is as bad as the outcry, that has reached me, and if not I will know?" When God used the words, "I will go down," He was showing that He does not act in hast or out of ignorance, or on the basis of mere complaints. But when He went down this time, the results would be the Judgment on Sodom and Gomorrah. Centuries later in history, God in the person of Jesus Christ would also have to come down to the earth to die on the cross at Calvary to redeem the world from sin.

Then two of the men turned away and went toward Sodom, but Abraham remained standing before the Lord. When God had told Abraham what He was about to do, Abraham questioned the Lord and said; "Will you sweep away the righteous with the wicked? What if there are fifty righteous people in the city? Will you really sweep it away, and not spare the place for the sake of the fifty righteous people in it? Far be it from you to do such a thing, to kill the righteous with the wicked, treating the righteous and the wicked alike. Far be it from you! Will not the Judge of all the earth do right?" Abraham based his plea on the justice and authority of God, confident that God would do what was right.

Then the Lord replied; "If I find fifty righteous people in the city of Sodom, I will spare the whole place for their sake." Once again, Abraham spoke up and said; "Now that

I have been so bold as to speak to the Lord, though I am nothing but dust and ashes, what if the number of the righteous is five less than fifty? Will you destroy the whole city because of five people?" As you can see here that, Abraham described himself as insignificant, when he used the term "dust and ashes" when he appealed to God the "Judge" of all the earth. "If I find forty-five there," He said, "I will not destroy it."

So Abraham continued to press the Lord and said, "What if only forty are found there?" The Lord said; "For the sake of forty I will not do it." Then Abraham said again, "May the Lord not be angry, but let me speak. What if only thirty can be found there?" The Lord answered and said; "I will not do it if I find thirty there?" Once again Abraham asked the Lord, "Now that I have been so bold as to speak to the Lord, what if only twenty can be found there?" The Lord said," For the sake of twenty, I will not destroy it." So now Abraham asks the Lord once again and said, "May the Lord not be angry, but let me speak just once more. What if only ten can be found there?" The Lord replied, "For the sake of ten I will not destroy it." After this Abraham did not question the Lord any further on the matter. The matter was closed. Perhaps, Abraham had been counting on the members of Lots family to save the cities that could have numbered ten righteous people at that time. But as it was, only four people were saved, Lot, his wife, and his two youngest daughters.

Abraham's questioning of the Lord did not come from a spirit of haggling, but it came out of concern for his relatives and him wanting to know Gods ways. So now the two cities that were so corrupted with homosexuality and all manner of evil had their fate sealed. Soon, Sodom and Gomorrah would be no more. After the Lord had finished speaking to Abraham, He left, and Abraham went home.

Lot, Abraham's nephew, was sitting in the city gate of Sodom in the evening, when the two men appeared to him.

When he saw them, he greeted them, as was the custom. In those days the city gates were used to discuss all of the important matters concerning the city, and its people. It was used much like we use a room as a council chamber today. The Bible doesn't say why Lot was at the city gates, at that particular time of day but it does say that it was there that he met the two men who were Gods angels. There was no way that Lot would have been able to know the real identity of the two men. But he knew that they were two strangers to the city because, he had not seen them around the city before.

After Lot had greeted the two angels he invited them to have a meal, and to wash their feet. He also invited them to stay the night with him. But they refused, and said that they would stay the night in the square. Although Lot didn't know who these men were at this precise time, he wouldn't take no for an answer. After insisting very strongly, Lot finely persuaded the two men to go to his house and to spend the night there. So the Angels accepted Lots invitation and they went to Lots home.

Just before they were ready to retire for the night, a large group of men from the city came and surrounded Lots' house. They said to Lot, "Where are the men who came to you tonight? Bring them out to us so that we can have sex with them. Homosexuality was very commonplace for the men of Sodom in that day. Sodom's wickedness had made it ripe for destruction. Lot went outside and closed the door behind him. He said to the people, "No my friends. Don't do this wicked thing! Look I have two daughters who have never slept with a man. Let me bring them out to you and you can do what you like with them. But don't do anything to these men, for they have come under the protection of my roof."

Ancient hospitality obligated a host to protect his guests in every situation no matter what the cost. Lot even went so far as to offer to sacrifice his two virgin daughters to the mob of people, rather than break an obligation he felt that he had to keep. Because his two daughters were already pledged to two son-in-laws in the future, he would have suffered a great deal of disgrace in the eyes of the city population.

Also, it would have been contrary to the law he was sworn to up hold. He was caught between a rock and a hard place, as we say. But, he was willing to make that terrible kind of sacrifice, to protect his two guests. At this point, I believe that Lot probably wished that he had never set foot in the city of Sodom. As it was, he could barely tolerate the wickedness that existed in that city. (2Pet.2; 7-8). But he was the only one in his family that felt that way.

The people in the mob said; "This fellow came here as an alien, and now he wants to play the judge. We'll treat you worse than them. Get out of the way. Then they pressed Lot as if they were going to break down the door of his house. But the two men inside the house reached out and pulled Lot back into the house and shut the door. Centuries later in (Ex.2; 14, Ac.7; 27) Moses would also be considered an outsider and accused of setting himself up as a judge over the people. Then the two angels inside the house struck all of the men outside of the house with blindness, so that they could not find the door.

The angels then said to Lot; "Do you have anyone else here, son-in-laws, sons, or daughters, or anyone else in the city who belongs to you? Get them out of here because we are going to destroy this place. The outcry to the Lord against its people is so great that He has sent us to destroy it." At this point it must have become very clear to Lot just who the two men were.

After the angels had told Lot what was about to take place, he hurried to his prospective sons-in-laws homes, and told them that the Lord was going to destroy the city. But his son-in-laws thought he was joking. It appears that Lot had even lost his power of moral persuasion among his family members. When Lot came back to his house, dawn was approaching, and the angels urged Lot to hurry, because the time for the destruction of the city was drawing near. The word "time" here, suggests that God has a specific time and place for everything that happens in the world and in His universe.

But Lot, just like the rest of his family was reluctant to leave his home and all of his material possessions. When Lot displayed a great deal of hesitation, the angels forcefully had to take Lot and his wife and two daughters safely out of the city. Then the angels told Lot, to "flee to the mountains and don't look back, or stop anywhere in the plain." If they did, they would be swept away in the destruction of the two cities. "Don't look back." This was a very clear and direct command from the angels.

But Lot complained and said; "No my lords please! Your servant has found favor in your eyes, and you have shown great kindness to me in sparing my life. But I can't flee to the mountains; this disaster will overtake me and I will die. The town of Zoar was not too far away and Lot said; "Look, here is a small town I can run to, and my life will be spared." Then the angel said to Lot, "very well, I will grant this request too. I will not overthrow the town you speak of. But flee their quickly, because I cannot do anything until you reach it."

By the time Lot had reached Zoar, the sun had risen over the land. While they were fleeing for their lives, Lots wife, who really didn't want to leave the city at all, looked back for one last look at the city she loved. But because, she disobeyed the angels' stern command, she was turned into a pillar of salt. Her destruction was very sudden and complete. Nothing was left of her but a mineral heap.

In (Lk.17; 32) Jesus referred to her, in His teaching on the sudden destruction that will come in the last days. "Remember Lots wife," He said. She had disobeyed the angel's instructions. Then the Lord rained down brimstone and fire out of heaven on the two cities of Sodom and Gomorrah. He totally destroyed them, including all of the inhabitants of the cities, and all of the surrounding plain, which, included all of the vegetation that grew on the land. They were no more; the two cities were now history.

The people of the two wicked cities had paid the ultimate price for their sins. The Lord had sent them all to hell, where I am sure the Devil welcomed them with open arms. Lot and his two daughters were the only people to survive the horrific destruction of the two cities. The only reason Lot and his two daughters were saved, was because the Lord in His great mercy, remembered His great love for Abraham. The Lord knew how deeply it would have hurt Abraham to see Lot and his family destroyed along with the two cities.

When Abraham got up early the next morning, he went once more, to the place where he had stood before the Lord. He looked down toward Sodom and Gomorrah and seen the black smoke rising from the destroyed cities like it was coming from a furnace. He must have felt some remorse for the people of the two cities, because he knew that Lot lived there, and he no doubt must have had some kind of business dealing with some of the people at one time or another. So Abraham had a firsthand look, or a front row seat, to see the last of the two great cites. He was also the one and only witness to Gods great and awesome power.

Lot and his two daughters didn't stay in the small town very long because he feared for their lives. They decided to move to the mountains and live in a cave. A short time after Lot had moved to the mountains, his two daughters became concerned about preserving their family line or lineage. This should have been of no concern to them, because it was the Lords concern and not theirs. They too just like Sarah decided to take matters into their own hands. So the two daughters conspired together to get their father drunk. The oldest daughter said to her younger sister: "Our father is old and there is no man around here to lie with us, as is the custom all over the earth. Let's get our father to drink wine, then lie with him and preserve our family line, through our father.

That night the girls got their father very drunk with wine, and the oldest daughter went in and lay with him. But he was not aware of it when she lay down, or when she got up. So the next night, they got their father drunk with wine again, and the younger daughter went in and lay with her father. Likewise, he was not aware of it, when she lay down or when she got up. As a result, both daughters became pregnant, and in the due course of time, both of them had a son. Though Lots role was somewhat passive, he was the one that bore the basic responsibility for the drunkenness and the incest that caused his daughters to become pregnant by him.

The oldest daughter named her son Moab. He became the father of the Moabites. When the youngest daughter had her son, she named him BenAmmi. He became the father of the Amorites. This shameful act of incest that had resulted in the birth of the two sons was indeed a sinful act in the eyes of the Lord. But these two sons would eventually become two great nations in the future. Their descendants would have far reaching consequences for the children of Israel. They would become bitter enemies of Abraham's descendants.

After Abraham had witnessed the terrible destruction of Sodom and Gomorrah, and the awesome power of the Lord, Abraham moved from there into region of Negev, between Kadesh and Shur. But for a while he lived near the city of Gerar. Gerar was located very close to Philistine territory and it was about halfway between Gaza on the Mediterranean coast and Beersheba, in the northern Negev. Abraham and Sarah stayed in that area for quite some time. Abraham knew that he had moved into hostile territory, and that Abimelech the King was a pagan King. He also knew that the people of that region worshiped Idols. Therefore, he had a good reason to fear for his life, and for his possessions. He knew that the King had absolute power within his land. His word was the law with no questions asked.

It was at this particular time that, the Lord prolonged Abraham and Sarah's stay in the area longer, so that He could fulfill His promise to them concerning their Son Isaac. However, before they were discovered, in the land, Abraham had reminded Sarah of what she was to say to the King, if he came to take her away from him. It was the same mistake that Abraham had made in the past, when he was in Egypt. Sarah was to say to the King; "that she was Abraham's sister." This was not a lie, but only half of the truth. It was the only way that Abraham thought, that he could protect his life, his family, and all of his great possessions. After all, this same plot had worked for him in Egypt, so why not try it again. Abraham's son Isaac, who will be born in the future, will also commit this same kind of deception.

As time went on, someone did report to the King that there was a wealthy man living in the land, by the name of Abraham, and that he had a wife who was quite beautiful. I would also suspect that she would still have been mentally and physically strong at her age so he sent for Sarah. When she came before the King, she told him her story. She said that she was Abraham's sister. So then the king put her in his harem, but he didn't go near her. This was because the Lord was protecting her from all harm and danger. The scripture in (Ge. 20; 18), which says; "For the Lord had closed up every womb in the Abimelech household because of Abraham's wife Sarah."

It would have taken a considerable length of time, before the women in Abimelech's household, to realize that they were not getting pregnant and bearing children like they should be. This would have been a great and worrisome concern to the woman. The main reason the King took Sarah for his wife to begin with was, so that he would be able to control Abraham and his wealth through Sarah. The act of taking Sarah was for material gain only, and nothing else. Now that Abraham's plan was in effect, he had to only wonder and to contemplate, how he was going to get her back, which would be no small task for him.

One night God appeared to Abimelech the King in a dream. He said to him: "Indeed you are a dead man, because the woman whom you have taken she is a man's' wife. "These two words "mans' wife," in the Hebrew language clearly indicate that God has put Sarah on a basis of equality and dignity, the same as Abraham. Both are literally spoken of as lords or nobles. "A noble wife of a noble man."

The warning here to this pagan King about committing a great wrong, showed how much God cares for His people. Even though this King didn't know, or worship this God, who spoke to him in his dream, he must have feared for his life, and for the lives of his people. He said: "Lord will you destroy an innocent nation? Did he not say to me, 'she is my sister,' and didn't she also say, 'he is my brother'? I have done this with a clear conscience and clean hands'" He had not known about Abraham's deception, but he put the blame squarely on Abraham's shoulders where it belonged. He didn't want to die for something that he didn't do.

Now the truth of the whole situation is reviled to the King in his dream, and Gods response to him was one of absolution and grace. God said to the King; "Yes I know that you did this with a clear conscience, and so I have kept you from sinning against me. That is why I did not let you tough her." Once again, God intervened to spare the mother of Isaac, the promised offspring of Abraham. He protected Sarah from all harm with His Almighty Power.

God used the King, to demonstrate His will and His power to help His people. There was no denying the fact that God existed, and who He was. Now as God continues His conversation with the King He said, "Now return the man's' wife for he is a Prophet, and he will pray for you, and you will live. But if you do not return her, you may be sure that you and all yours will die." This was not an idle threat from God; because God does not make idle threats He will carry out His plan, no matter what happens or who may be involved.

In the proceeding passage, God has now bestowed another title on Abraham by calling him a "Prophet." Up to this point in the history of mankind, God in the Bible had, never used the word Prophet. The term indicates more of a relationship to God than an ability to speak for Him. Abraham's relationship to God was the basis for Gods command that Sarah be restored to her husband.

The gravity of the situation must have touched the King so strongly, that his fear quickly spread to his family and servants. The next morning when he related the whole dream to them, they were filed with great fear. So the King sent for Abraham and asked him two questions. These questions were the reverse of each other. He said to him: "What have you done to us?" How have I offended you that you have brought on me and on my kingdom a great sin?" You have done things to me that should not be done. What was your reason for doing this?" These questions were very touching but to the point. Now it was Abraham's turn to answer for the deception of his own making.

After the King had put the questions to Abraham, he answered them, without hesitation or fear. He said to the King; "I have two reasons for my actions. (1) "Because I thought surely, that the fear of God is not in this place; and they will kill me on account of my wife. But indeed she is truly my sister. She is the daughter of my father, but not the daughter of my mother. (2) As to the second question, "Indeed Sarah is truly my sister and she became my wife." The marriages of the family of Terah were very close. In this Patrician society the marriages of close relatives was regarded as a sign of rank. Later a law would prohibit the marriage of people so closely related.

As Abraham continued to explain the reason for his deception he said, "It came to pass, that when God caused me to wander from my fathers' house that I said to her: "This is your kindness that you should do for me, in every place, wherever we go. Say to me, he is my brother." Abraham's half-truth was a sinful deception, but not a legitimate explanation. After Abraham had finished his explanation to the King, he was quite happy to let Abraham do what he wanted to do. He also told Abraham that he could live anywhere in the Kings land that he wanted too. Abraham's explanation of the whole situation had pleased the King so much that he made Abraham even richer than he was before.

When the King returned Sarah to Abraham, he gave sheep, cattle, and male and female servants to Abraham as gifts for the wrong that he had committed against Abraham. To Sarah he said: "I am giving your brother a thousand shekels of silver. This is to cover the offence against you before all who are with you. You are completely vindicated." The King realized that he had caused Sarah a great deal of embarrassment and that she may be looked down on by some of her people. Abimelech's generosity was a strong contrast to Abraham's fearfulness and deception. After Abraham had been released of all blame by the King he prayed to God and God healed Abimelech, his wives and his slave girls so they could have children again.

-3-

THE BIRTH OF ISAAC

The Bible doesn't indicate just how long it was after Abraham's encounter with the King, that Sarah became pregnant and gave birth to her son Isaac. But the Bible says that it happened at the exact time the Lord had said it would. The scriptures say in (Ge.21; 1) "And the Lord visited Sarah as He had said, and the Lord did for Sarah as He had spoken. "The verb (Visit) is an extraordinary choice here, because it means that the Lord entered directly into the affairs of His people. The Bible stresses the fact that it is the Lord who causes conception, and children are a gift of the Lord.

The God of heaven and earth had now fulfilled His promise to both Abraham and to Sarah. God had used Abraham's one-hundred-year-old body and Sarah's ninety-year-old body to perform a great and wonderful miracle. It was living proof of Gods Almighty Power, His truth, and His Majesty. It proved beyond a shadow of doubt, that nothing is impossible with God. The people of Abimelech's kingdom must have also witnessed this great miracle that God had performed, and they also celebrated with Abraham and his people.

Can you imagine the joy, and the excitement that was present in the Abraham household, when the baby was born? If you are married and have experienced the birth and the presence of children in your home, you will understand just how Abraham and Sarah must have felt. Sarah's old breasts that had long passed their ability to produce milk were now full of milk. So, now she could nurse the beautiful baby boy that she so proudly held in her ageing arms. God had blessed her beyond her wildest dreams. This was another miracle, performed by God in His grace towards Sarah "His Chosen Princess." The joy in the hearts of the new parents must have been indescribable. It gives God the greatest pleasure to give His children the desirers of their hearts, if it is in His will to do so.

Soon after the baby was born, Abraham named his son Isaac, as God had instructed him to do. The name Isaac means: He (God) is Laughing. It was Gods turn to laugh now because of Abraham and Sarah's doubts long ago. As you might recall that they had laughed within themselves, about having a son in their old age. Now their laughter had turned into unspeakable joy and happiness. From now on they would celebrate every major step in the life of Isaac their Son. Abraham circumcised his son Isaac when he was eight days old, as the Lord had commanded him.

When Isaac was weaned at the age of two or three, Abraham held a big banquet to celebrate this joyous occasion. It was a great opportunity for Abraham and Sarah to show off the beautiful son that God had given them, through His grace and love for them. Whenever Abraham looked at Isaac, it would be a constant reminder of the covenant that God had made with him a quarter of a century ago. Isaac was living proof that God does not forget His promises or go back on them. He is always faithful and true to His word because He is holy and just.

As time went on, all was not well in the household of Abraham. There had been trouble brewing for quite some time, between Sarah and Hagar, the Egyptian slave woman who was the mother of Ishmael. At the time of this banquet, Ishmael was mocking and making fun of Isaac, as boys will do from time to time. Ishmaels mocking of her favorite son was just too much for Sarah to handle. As far as she was concerned Ishmael was mocking the joy that Sarah and Abraham were having in their young son Isaac.

The Bible says that Ishmael was in his late teens, perhaps about seventeen when the lid finely blew off of the two women's relationship. You can understand this because of the boy's difference in age. But the real underlying problem was that Sarah and Hagar just couldn't get along with each other, no matter how hard they tried. The quarreling between the two women must have hurt Abraham very deeply. He was a man that was caught between a rock and hard place because, he had two wives that he had to try and keep happy. But that's double the trouble in any mans castle, no matter how you want to look at it.

To solve her problem, Sarah who was very bitter at the time, went to Abraham and told him that he had to get rid of Hagar and Ishmael. It is also possible now that, Sarah may have realized that she had committed a grave error in judgment when, she took matters into her own hands to try, to acquire a son through Hagar her slave. But far be it from her to take the blame for any of her problems. Many people do the same thing in today's world. They have to blame something or someone else for their problems. In today's world we call it passing the buck. So that's exactly what Sarah was doing to Abraham. She was passing the buck. What was once her problem would now become a problem for Abraham to solve?

This problem would really hurt Abraham now because, he was enjoying the celebration of Isaacs weaning, and he was probably enjoying both of the boys playing around him at the same time. The biggest problem that Abraham had was the fact that, he also loved Ishmael very much. If you recall, Abraham had asked God on one occasion, when he talked with Him, if He would give Ishmael a blessing, and God said that He would. Now both love, and legal custom, would tear at Abraham's old heart and add to his anguish. But Sarah had other concerns and fears as well. Sarah saw Ishmael as a potential threat to Isaacs's inheritance. She thought that if she could drive them away and out of their lives, it would have the same effect as disinheriting Ishmael.

So what was Abraham to do? His love for Ishmael was so deep that he probably felt that his old heart would break. In his mind he had no solution to the problem that he was facing now. In that culture it was a shameful and very distasteful thing to send Ishmael and his mother away. When a surrogate mother bares a son to another woman's husband, that mother and child could not be dismissed even if the first wife subsequently gave birth to a son. This also, partly explains Abraham's demise and reluctance to do what Sarah demanded. There is no doubt that Abraham must have prayed many nights to God for an answer to his problem. There is no way of telling for sure just how long it was before God answered Abraham's prayers about this terrible dilemma he was facing. But God did answer Abraham's prayer in His own time, and not in Abraham's time.

God already knew the trouble that Abraham was having. Abraham desperately needed to hear from God. He wanted God to give him permission to send Hagar and Ishmael away. How was he supposed to solve this problem and ease the aching pain in his heart because of the law? So God came to Abraham and said: "Do not be so distressed about the boy and your maidservant. Listen to whatever Sarah tells you, because it is through Isaac that your offspring will be reckoned. I will make the son of the maidservant into a nation also, because he is your offspring." It is here that God states His preference of Isaac over Ishmael.

This is the sixth time that God has appeared to Abraham since he came into the land of Canaan. When God told Abraham to listen to Sarah and to what she had to say, it was the second time that God has overruled Abraham and the laws of the land. You may recall in (Ge.15; 4) was the first time that God overruled Abraham. God did this because Abraham was going to make one of his servants the heir to his estate. Once again, God spoke of the covenant that He had made with Abraham years before.

Although Abraham was going to lose his oldest son Ishmael, he promptly obeyed God without question. Early the next morning, Abraham took a skin full of water (a bag made out of an animal hide to hold water) and some food and gave them to Hagar his maidservant and her son, and then he sent them on their way into the desert of Beersheba. Although he only gave Hagar and her son meager supplies, Abraham knew that God would look after them, because of His promise to Abraham. This was a hard test for Abraham because of his love for Ishmael. But little did he know that he would have to endure a far greater test later on that would involve his other son Isaac.

After Hagar and her son had wandered in the desert for some time, their water supply and food had run out and they were becoming very desperate. So in total desperation, Hagar put her crying son under a bush and went away for a little distance, and sat down and began to cry her heart out. She must have thought that her life was worthless and over. She said within her own heart; "I cannot watch the boy die." She had completely forgotten about the promise that God had made to her eighteen years earlier when she was pregnant with her son. It was the promise to make her son Ishmael the father of a great nation. In the following scripture in (Ge.21; 17-21) it states that the Lord heard the boy crying.

The words "God heard," are indeed two wonderful words that anyone in trouble would be overjoyed to hear. There is no pain or suffering that God does not see or hear about. He knows your every thought and your every need and you can talk to Him at any time. Unknown to Hagar, God was always near to deliver the child from harm. He would not let him die. God does not forget or cast out people the way mankind does.

Then the angel of the Lord called to her out of heaven and said to her: "What is the matter Hagar? Do not be afraid; God has heard the boy crying as He lies there. Lift the boy up and take him by the hand, for I will make him into a great nation." Then God opened her eyes and she saw a well that was full of water. So she went and filled the skin with water and gave the boy a drink. Hagar was so overcome with grief that she was unaware of the provision of water that was right there before her eyes. How fitting, and wonderful it was, that the promise of God would be renewed to her right there beside a provision of life giving water.

Oftentimes, throughout the pages of the Old Testament, a spring or a well of water is a symbol of spiritual salvation as well as physical deliverance. (Is. 12; 3) says "With joy you will draw water from the wells of salvation." As you may have experienced at some point in your life, when you are thirsty for a physical drink of water on a hot day; an extra cold drink of water is indeed a God given gift to you. When you receive that drink of water, it lifts up your spirit as well as your physical body. The gift of water is indeed life saving in many ways. Without water you can't live very long in the desert or, otherwise for that matter. But Gods spiritual water is as equally important to your mind, soul, and body, and to the pursuit of your eternal life.

It was not long before Gods promise was realized in Ishmael's life, and he became a great archer and hunter. As he lived in the Desert of Paran, he became like a wild donkey as God had said he would. But, God was with the boy as he grew up. This is further proof of Gods' Love and Grace for His people.

As Ishmael grew into manhood, Hagar his mother wanted to make sure that Ishmael got married. So she went to Egypt and brought an Egyptian woman to him to take as his wife. She wanted to make sure that he married an Egyptian woman, because she wanted him to marry into his own race of people. You might recall that it was customary in those days for the parents to arrange their children's marriages when they became a certain age. Later on Abraham would do the same for his son Isaac. Arranged marriages are still being practiced in some cultures in the world today as well.

One day while Abraham was still living near the city of Gerar, Abimelech the King and Phicol, the commander of the King's forces, came to Abraham to make a treaty with him. It appears that, the King was still bothered about the last time they had met, and God had spoken to him in a dream. The King did not want to be deceived by Abraham, or to be threatened by Abraham's God any more. Once was enough for him. The fear of God was in him, and he knew that Abraham would intercede for him if this God appeared to him again. This same commander, Phicol, will be involved with Abraham's son Isaac later on as the years pass by.

King Abimelech said to Abraham: "God is with you in everything you do. Now swear to me here before God, that you will not deal falsely with me or my children or my descendants. Show to me and the country where you are living as an alien, the same kindness I have shown to you." The King was making sure that his family and all of his descendants after him would, never again come under the same situation as he did, with Abraham and his God.

With these words "God is with you," Abimelech and Phicol introduced their desire to form a treaty with Abraham. When the King asked Abraham to swear to him before God, he was calling on Abraham's God to be a witness to the treaty, and a witness against anyone who might break it. This kind of treaty, or covenant was a complete binding obligation to anyone who was involved in its making. As you know however that, whenever you take an oath, it is a very serious matter, and it carries with it a commitment that must be kept. The taking of an oath is still required in the courts of many countries around the world today.

The reason for the uneasy feelings between the two parties was that, there had been some very heated disputes between the two about a well of water. When Abraham complained to Abimelech about the well of water that Abimelech's servants had seized. The king replied in all innocence. (As if he could be innocent at all) "I do not know who has done this thing; you did not tell me, nor have I heard of it until today." This was a boldfaced lie and he knew it.

The water rights to this well, or to any other well for that matter, were very important to the owner or owners in the desert. In many cases it was the only means of a water supply for their herds of livestock, and for themselves in the areas that they lived in. Also, the owners could demand some kind of payment from anyone, who wanted to use the well if they so desired. So the ownership of the well was a very important part of any agreement.

Then Abraham said: "I swear it." Now the treaty was a done deal, and both parties were absolutely bound by it. At that time, there were many treaties made between people just by their spoken word. It was not necessary to have the agreement written down in some form or other. But as you will see, the King had an ulterior motive for making the treaty with Abraham. There was a very strong possibility that he was trying to deceive Abraham just, as Abraham had deceived him earlier. He may have entertained the thought that it was payback time for him, and he would have the last laugh on Abraham.

After the dispute had been settled over the well, Abraham gave Abimelech some sheep and cattle, as was the custom for the celebration that was to follow. There was always a celebration or party after any treaty was made. It proved the good intensions of the parties involved in the treaty. To make the occasion all the more memorable, Abraham set aside seven ewe lambs from the flock. When Abimelech saw the seven ewe lambs his curiosity got the better of him, so he asked Abraham why he did this. So Abraham replied, "Accept these seven lambs from my hand as a witness that I have dug this well." So now Abraham was getting a little more insurance, as to the ownership of the well.

The gift of the seven lambs would make the treaty completely binding and there was nothing the King could do but smile and accept the offer. So once again, Abraham had out foxed the King. When the celebrations were over, the King and his commander returned home with the seven lambs, but they were minus the ownership of the well.

The Hebrew number seven is similar in sound to the verb meaning "to swear." From that time on, the place where the treaty and the oaths were made became known as Beersheba. The town of Beersheba became an important town in the northern Negev Desert. It also marked the southernmost boundary of the Israelite monarchy in later times. An ancient well there, is still pointed out as "Abraham's well." It was there that Abraham also planted a tamarisk tree, in the hope that it would last a long time, and mark the spot where the treaty was made.

-4-

ABRAHAM'S ULTIMATE TEST (Ge.22; 1-19)

This part of Abraham's life is without question, one of the most shocking and memorable texts in the whole Bible; and yet its outcome is one of the finest texts describing the loyalty of the Lord to both His covenant, and to His servant Abraham. It also reveals the remarkable faith on the part of Abraham, Sarah, and their son Isaac. It also points to the future sacrifice of Gods only Son, Jesus Christ. This test would be the greatest test that Abraham would ever have to face in his lifetime.

Now it came to pass, sometime after Abraham's dealings with King Abimelech over the water well problem that, God decided to test Abraham one more time. God in His infinite wisdom decided, to test Abraham's faith, and to give him the opportunity to prove his true character to God. Isaac by this time had grown into a young teenager. I would suspect by this time in his life that Isaac had already been taught a great deal about God and how He works by both of his parents.

In the scripture, the Bible uses the word "tested" and not the word "temped." God does not tempt people. He only tests them. However, God will test everyone somewhere, or sometime, as we journey down the road of life. The Devil is the only one who will tempt you to do something wrong and cause you to fall away from God. God only tests us in order to confirm our faith and our commitment to Him. The term "God" here includes the definite article. (That is to say who is making the demands?) This is a way of indicating that the "Genuine Deity" or the "True God" is making these demands, and not a false god or a Demon.

When God spoke to Abraham on this one particular occasion, He called his name not once, but twice. He said; "Abraham, Abraham." Then Abraham answered God with the response of a true servant, as did Moses and Samuel when God called them by name. "Here I am," he replied. Then God said to him: "Take your son, your only son Isaac, whom you love, and go to the region of Moriah. Sacrifice him there as a burnt offering on one of the mountains I will tell you about."

In Genesis chapters 16 and 25 the scriptures states that Abraham had six other sons by his other wife Katonah but they were not born until after Sarah's death except for Ishmael. But only Isaac was uniquely born, and was the Son of Gods promise to Abraham. The words "your son, your only son, whom you love," is in direct contrast to the sacrifice that God would make with His only begotten Son Jesus Christ centuries later, to save the human race from certain and eternal death. Through His sacrifice on the cross those who are believers in Christ now have the Gift of Eternal, Life and the forgiveness of their sins through His shed blood on the cross. To this I say, Thank You Father.

It is hard to imagine in my own mind as a father, what might have been going through Abraham's mind, after God had asked him to do what appears to be a terrible deed? However, nothing is said in the Bible about what Abraham or Sarah's thoughts were on the whole matter. To kill the son of promise that God had given him, it would take a faith that was unshakeable. But Abraham must have reasoned within himself that if God had the power to give life, He also had the power to take life. Therefore Abraham must have concluded, that if God had to destroy his only son, then God would bring him back from the dead also, if that was what was necessary to fulfill His purpose.

Because God had promised him descendants as numerous as the stars, and the sands on the seashore, this promise alone, would enable him to carry out this demand of the Lord. You may recall that, there was one other time in the past, when God had appeared to Abraham, and he had committed himself to be in complete obedience to God. He was to trust and to follow the will of God no matter what came his way. This commitment also applied to Isaac his son through circumcision and to all of Abraham's descendants.

So with prompt obedience to God and His command, he would obey without question. Although he probably didn't fully understand at the time why God wanted him to do this terrible deed, he had absolute trust in God. It would take a great deal of faith on Sarah's part as well, because Abraham would have told her what God had instructed him to do. It must have taken an enormous toll on Abraham and Sarah's emotions at the time. But by the same token, it is a predetermined heartbreaking picture of what God did too His Son Jesus Christ for us on the cross at Calvary.

Early the next morning, Abraham gathered wood for the sacrificial fire. Then he saddled his donkey, and taking two of his trusted servants and Isaac with him, he departed on what would be about a three-day journey. This journey would take them to Mount Moriah where God told him to go. The name Moriah means, "Where the Lord Provides." or Where the Lord Appears." Right here, is a little bit of a clue as to what the Lord will do for Abraham later on. The author of Chronicles identifies the area as the Temple Mount that is located in Jerusalem (2chr. 3:1). Today the Dome of the

Rock occupies "Mount Moriah". It is an impressive Muslim structure erected in A.D.691. A large out-cropping of rock inside of the building is still pointed to as the traditional site of the intended sacrifice of Isaac.

On the third day Abraham looked up and he saw the place where he had to go. When he arrived near the location that God had spoken to him about, Abraham said to his servants; "Stay here with the donkey, and I and the boy will go over there and worship, and then we will come back to you."

The likely reason that Abraham ordered the servants to stay behind was because, if they would have went with him, they might have tried to stop him from doing what God had commanded him to do. When the Lord told Abraham that he was to "sacrifice his son as a burnt offering," he was to do just that. He was to follow each important step of sacrificing an animal. He was to actually kill Isaac, and to burn his body just like as if he was a real animal. He was not to just wound him and then nurse him back to health.

So Abraham gave the wood for the fire to the boy to carry, and Abraham carried the knife and the fire in a container, and they set off for the mountain. As the two of them went on together, Isaac asked his father saying: "Abraham, Father?" 'Yes my son' Abraham replied. "The fire and the wood are here but where is the lamb for the burnt offering?" Abraham answered and said to Isaac; "God Himself will provide the lamb for the burnt offering, my son."

When Abraham had come to the mountain that God had told him about, there he builds an altar, and he arranged the wood on it. He bound Isaac hand and foot, and laid him on the altar on top of the wood. Isaac at this point is a type of (prefiguration) of Christ when He was laid on the cross at His crucifixion. By this time Isaac must have known that he was the one who would be the sacrificial victim because, there was no other kind of animal or lamb around that he could see. Yet like our Savior, on an even darker day in history;

Isaac was willing to do his father's will. This also required a great deal of love and trust on the part of Isaac. He was willing to give up his life to satisfy and obey his father no matter what the cost.

Then Abraham reached out his hand and took the knife to slay his son. But the angle of the Lord called to him from heaven at the last possible moment. "Abraham! Abraham!" It was God Himself calling out to Abraham. Not once but twice. When God called his name twice with some urgency, this kind of command would demand Abraham's immediate attention with no hesitation on his part. God was about to show Abraham another miracle as well as His awesome power of provision.

"Here I am," he replied. Then God said to Abraham "Do not lay a hand on the boy. "Do not do anything to him. Now I know that you fear God, because you have not with-held from me your son, your only son." Then Abraham looked up and there in a thicket he saw a ram caught by its horns. God had provided the perfect sacrifice that would be needed. Abraham's old heart must have pounded with unspeakable joy, when he saw what God had done for him. He went over and took the ram and killed it and then sacrificed it as a burnt offering on the altar instead of his son Isaac.

As the ram died in Isaacs place, so also Jesus Christ died and gave His life as a ransom for many on the cross as stated by the scriptures in (Mk. 10: 45). Then God called to Abraham a second time from heaven and said: "I swear by Myself, declares the Lord that because you have done this, and have not withheld your son, your only son, I will surely bless you and make your descendants as numerous as the stars in the sky and as the sand on the seashore. Your descendants will take possession of the cities of their enemies, and through your offspring all nations on earth will be blessed, because you have obeyed me."

Abraham's faith was made complete by what he did for God, and not by what he didn't do for God. This part of Gods promise was partly fulfilled in King Solomon's reign. God is still blessing all of the nations of the world today because of Abraham and what he did, but they will not accept it or believe it because the Devil has blinded them to the truth.

"I swear by myself." When God swore this oath He had to swear by His own name, because there is no greater name by which He could take an oath. Abraham's devotion is paralleled by Gods love to us in Christ as reflected in (Jn.3: 16 Ro. 8:32). Before Abraham departed for home, he named the place "The Lord Will Provide." After all things were accomplished by the Lord, Abraham and his son Isaac went back to where the servants were waiting for them and they all returned home to Beersheba.

It came to pass, as time went on, that Sarah, Abraham's faithful and loving wife died in the region of Hebron. She was one hundred and twenty-seven years old when the Lord called her home. It was a sad time for Abraham, but it would have been a joyful time for Sarah. The Lord let her live long enough, so she could see her son Isaac, grow into adulthood. (He would have been about 37 years old at the time she died). Try too imagining what it will be like to live in eternity, and to have perfect fellowship with the Lord forever just as Sarah is now doing.

Now Abraham had a problem because he had no place to bury Sarah his wife. It is true that Abraham was a very rich man in many ways, but he was not a landowner. So Abraham went to some of the Hittites that owned land in the area where he lived. He told them of his situation, and that he wanted to purchase some land so he could bury his dead. He didn't want to have Sarah buried in just any old graveyard. He wanted to be the one in control of her burial plot, and a plot for himself as well. It would also be available for some of his descendants who would come after him if it were needed. However, he didn't want to be obligated in any way to the Hittites.

As Abraham was looking around for some land, he approached a group of Hittites near the city gates. He said: "I am a foreigner and a visitor among you. Give me property for a burial place among you that I may bury my dead out of my sight" Then he offered to pay a sum of money, or in this case, it was a weight of silver, to purchase some land. Money had not yet been invented or used at this point in time so a weight of silver was used as payment for whatever was bought.

He made an offer to a landowner whose name was Ephron. The land that Abraham had looked at and was interested in had a cave on it as well. In those days people would bury their dead in caves if it were possible. In this way they could seal the caves up with stone to protect the dead remains from thieves and robbers. When Abraham asked Ephron about this certain piece of land he answered him in the presence of the other Hittites and said: "Hear us, my lord. You are a mighty prince among us, (he might have said this to honor Abraham because of his wealth, or so he could gain favor with the other people) bury your dead in the choicest of our burial places."

This indeed was a very generous offer but it was not what Abraham was looking for. Then Ephron, offered to give the land to Abraham. But Abraham refused to accept it as a gift, because he reasoned, that if Ephron could so readily give the land away, then he could just as readily take it back if he so desired. But, if there were an exchange of money or any other kind of payment, the land would have to be deeded to Abraham. Then there would be no question of ownership in the future. So Abraham negotiated a price of four hundred shekels of silver. A shekel is about two fifths of an ounce or 11.5 grams. Now at last Abraham had finely become a land-owner. He was not only responsible for the land and the cave, but he was also responsible for the trees that surrounded the property. Trees were of great value in those times, as they are today. Although Abraham was a wealthy man, the only land that he ever possessed was a burial plot for himself and for Sarah his wife. He preferred to love, and honor his God and to do what God wanted him to do, rather than become a great Land Baron, which would mean nothing to him when he died. His wealth was a secondary thing to him.

I believe Abraham would have spent a great deal of his time, telling the people of the land about the loving and faithful God that he served and worshiped. So it was that, Abraham buried Sarah in the cave at Machpelah, near Hebron. By purchasing a burial place in Canaan, Abraham indicated his unswerving commitment to the Lords promise. Canaan was to be his new homeland as promised by the Lord his God.

-5-

THE MARRIAGE AND DEATH OF ISAAC (Ge.24; 1-67)

Some years had slipped by since the death of Sarah, and Abraham took another wife by the name of Keturah. She bore him six more sons. She was also a concubine just like Hagar. That means that she was not legally married to Abraham. The Bible states that Abraham was about one hundred and forty years old when he made Keturah his third wife. Her son's names were, Zimran, Jokshan, Medan, Midian, Ishbak, and Shuah. So the grand total of all of Abraham's children now stands at eight.

However, his greatest concern was for his son Isaac the "Son of Promise." By this time Isaac was forty years old, and he was probably thinking about marriage. No doubt he had probably discussed this desire with Abraham more than once. So now Abraham decided to do something about the marriage of his son Isaac. As was the custom, it was Abraham's responsibility to arrange his Sons marriage. He certainly didn't want his son to marry any woman outside of his own clan of people because, the people of the land worshiped Idols as well as other faults gods. It is possible however that, some of the people may have turned to the

God of Abraham after they had seen what his God had done for him.

It would take a great deal of effort on the part of Abraham to arrange his son's marriage. One of the many requirements that Abraham would have had to fulfill would have been to take a long journey. But he was just too advanced in years to do so. So he called the chief servant of his household, whose name was Eliezer, and he gave him some very strict instructions as to what he had to do.

Abraham said to him; "I want you to swear by the Lord, the God of heaven and the God of the earth, that you will not get a wife for my son from the daughters of the Canaanites, among whom I am living. But go to my own country (Mesopotamia) and my own relatives and get a wife for my son Isaac. By making Eliezer take an oath before God, Abraham was assured that he would follow Abraham's instructions to the letter. Also by the swearing of an oath it also showed Eliezer how important the matter was to Abraham. When anyone swore an oath, there was no way anything could be changed.

Now Eliezer's problems would be starting to grow one after the other. I can well imagine the line of thinking that he may have been developing as he prepared to depart. To start with, he couldn't take Isaac back with him so he could choose his own wife. Then Eliezer would have to choose a wife for Isaac without exception. What if he made the wrong choice? What was he to do if the woman did not want to leave her family and come with him to a foreign land? Added to this, she would be required to marry a man that she had never met, and didn't love. Also, if the woman that he chose decided not to come back with him, he would have to come back to Canaan empty handed. He was trying to cover all of his bases so that more problems wouldn't come up later on.

There is no doubt that if these were the kind of thoughts that may have been plaguing his mind at that time; they would have been very upsetting to him to say the least. But Abraham soon put his fears to rest so that he need not be concerned.

Abraham said to him; "The Lord, the God of heaven, who brought me out of my father's household and my native land, and spoke to me and promised me on an oath, saying: ' to your offspring I will give this land. He will send His angel before you so you can get a wife for my son from there. If the woman is unwilling to come back with you, then you will be released from this oath of mine.'" This statement displayed how great and wonderful Abraham's faith was in the God of heaven and earth. Abraham was not putting his trust into the hands of men who could fail, but he was putting his trust in the hands of the "Almighty God," whose hands are the most trust worthy of all.

Abraham's faith in God would have been quite reassuring to Eliezer also because he too understood that God has a plan for everything in this life. Now he too would also oversee the marriage of Isaac. God would not leave anything to chance. That's why, God sent an angel to guide Eliezer in his quest for a wife for Isaac. God would do the choosing and identify the right woman that He had chosen for Isaac, not Eliezer. There are no half measures with God. Even in today's world He will not do something part way with you and then leave you hung out to dry. God is always faithful and just in all that He does.

So early the next morning, Abraham's chief servant chose ten of his masters choicest camels and departed for the town of Nahor, in Abraham's old country of Mesopotamia. He took extra camels, because, he would have to have transportation for Isaacs bride and her maids, as well as all of their belongings. He also took some other servants to help him on his journey. The town was probably named after Abraham's brother Nahor, but it is also called Haran. The name Mesopotamia means, "Aram of Two Rivers." It is located in the northern part of Syria beyond the Euphrates River.

When Eliezer arrived at the town of Nahor, he was no doubt tired, dusty and glad that this part of the journey was over. It was late in the evening, which was the coolest part of the day. He made his camels to kneel down by a well that was just outside of the town. As was their custom, the woman of the town, would be coming to the well to draw water for the evening and for the next day. It was probably at this point that, the heart of Eliezer began to pound with some excitement that was also mixed with some fear as well. He was starting to become very anxious about what to do. This would have been the part of the journey that would have concerned him the most because, now it had become decision time for him. But he did just what all people should do in their time of decision and need. That is to pray, and give our problems to God. Although you cannot see Him, you can feel His presence. He is always right beside you and He will never leave you because this is one of His greatest promises to you.

When Eliezer seen the women of the town coming out for water he began to pray. He said; "O Lord, God of my master Abraham, give me success today, and show kindness to my master Abraham. Behold, here I stand by the well of water, and the daughters of the men of the city are coming out to draw water. Now let it be that the young woman to whom I say; ' Please let down your pitcher that I may drink,' and she says, 'Drink', and I will also give your camels a drink.' Let her be the one you have appointed for your servant Isaac. And by this I will know that you have shown kindness to my master." Before he had finished his prayer request, to God, God had already begun to answer his request. This is proof that God knows your innermost thoughts, even before you think them, or say them.

I will take a minute here and explain the prayer that Eliezer requested of God, before he met the woman that he was looking for. You will notice that in Eliezer's prayer request to God, that he named each specific requirement. He left nothing to chance or to a possibility for God. He was very explicit in his prayer. We should do much the same thing when we ask God for our needs and desires. God will grant you the desires of your heart if they are in your best interest, and it is what His will is for you. But sometimes you must be patient and wait for Gods answer. He will not lead you astray.

1. The first thing that Eliezer did was to address God with reverence and humility. He said; "O Lord." This would indicate that he held God in very high esteem, and that he knew that God would calm his anxious heart and his fears that seemed to plague him at the moment.
2. Then he said; "God of my master Abraham." Here, he was expressing his faith and that he was addressing the one and only true God of Abraham, a living and powerful God. Not some idol that could not answer his requests.
3. Then he asked for "Success Today." He wanted to find the right woman that day, so he wouldn't have to keep looking and wondering who she was, or when she would show up. He probably didn't want to have any more anxious moments then was necessary. As he prayed, he probably became more anxious for Gods answer than he cared to admit. He likely wanted to settle the matter that he had came for, as soon as possible and return to his home.
4. The next request was for the Lord to show "Kindness or Love to his master Abraham." At this point he was asking God to remember the kindness that He had shown Abraham in the past, when He had made

a covenant with Abraham concerning Isaac and his descendants.

5. Being that he didn't have any Idea who the woman was or what she looked like, he asked God for a sign to validate his errand. Then he expressed to God just how and what he would look for as the sign from God.

The Bible says that; "Before he had finished praying." In this instance, God had already answered Eliezer prayer. The beautiful young and vibrant girl, who was still a virgin, and the one that was chosen by God, came to the well for water. The young woman did exactly, as Eliezer had requested of God in his prayer. This was because God would have put in her heart, what He wanted her to do to fulfill His purpose. You must remember that it is God who is doing what "He requires here," not what any man wants or requires. Man, was only the means by which God would accomplish His will. If she did exactly as he had requested in his prayer, Eliezer would know for certain, that she was the woman that he was seeking. He had placed everything into Gods hands and God had delivered his request.

There are several facts here to show you that God was in control of the whole situation. (1) She was of the lineage of Abraham, Gods chosen people. (2) She was a virgin. (3) She was the chosen one of God Himself. (4) She had to be young, innocent, and righteous in Gods eyes. She was also a prefiguration, of the Virgin Mary, the mother of Christ who was to come in the future.

The young woman's name was Rebekah, which means, "Ensnaring Beauty." She was the daughter of Bethuel, and one of the eight children born to Milcah, the wife of Nahor, who was the brother of Abraham. So she was born into the circle of Abraham's relatives. She would be Abraham's grandniece.

As he was watching the women of the village coming to the well for water, Rebekah, the beautiful young girl went down to the well to fill her pitcher with water. When she came past him on her way to her house, he asked her for a drink of water. After she had let down the pitcher of water from her shoulder, and had given him a drink, she said to him: "I'll draw water for your camels too, until they have finished drinking." This was a domestic chore that she was not required to do for a stranger.

So Eliezer said to her, "Whose daughter are you?" She replied and said, "I am the daughter of Bethuel, the son that Milcah bore to Nahor. Then Eliezer said to her: "Please tell me? Is there room in your father's house for us to spend the night?" She said to him: "there is enough feed for the animals, and there is room for you to spend the night."

When the camels had finished drinking, Eliezer took a golden nose ring, and put it in her nose. It weighed a beka, which is about half a shekel. Then he put two bracelets of gold for her wrists that weighed ten shekels of gold. After she had received the gifts from Eliezer, she ran back to her mother's household. She was probably out of breath when she got there but she expressed with a great deal of excitement, what had happened to her at the well. She also explained to her mother, that they would have guests for the evening meal, and that they would have to provide lodging for them as well.

After Rebekah had departed for home, Eliezer bowed down his head and worshiped the Lord and said: "Blessed is the Lord God of my master Abraham, who has not forsaken His kindness to my master. As for me, the Lord has led me on the journey to the house of my master's relatives."

Now Rebekah had a brother whose name was Laban. The moment that he saw the nose ring and the bracelets on his sister's arms that she was wearing, he knew what they meant. The jewelry meant that she had been spoken for, or engaged. After he had listened to her story, and he had done the things that he was required to do, he ran to the well and seen Eliezer standing there by his camels.

He said to him: "Come, you who are blessed by the Lord. (This statement shows that Rebekah and her family were of the same faith as Abraham.) Why are you standing out here? I have prepared the house and the place for the camels, with straw and fodder for feed. As well, there is water for you and your men to wash your feet."

So the men went to the house where a meal was prepared for them, but Eliezer said that he would not eat until after he had explained his mission to the family. This group of Abraham's relatives, probably had not heard from Abraham, or about what he was doing, or where he might be living, for the past fifty years or so. To add to their curiosity, they certainly did not know who this stranger was.

So they decided to forego the evening meal for a while, so that they could hear what this stranger had to say, and why he had come. At this time, Eliezer would have taken on the appearance of a storyteller. To be able to listen to someone tell a story at the end of a long hard day would be a welcomed treat in that time period as it is today. I know from my own experiences in life that, I enjoy nothing better than to listen to someone who has a good story to tell. It can push a persons' imagination to the limit, and give them peace, joy, and sometimes a great deal of happiness.

The first thing that Eliezer had to explain was who he was, and where he had come from. He said to his inquisitive and wide eyed on lookers; "I am Abraham's servant." I can just imagine the hush and the look of amazement that might have crossed the faces of the family. Then he commenced to tell them how the Lord had so abundantly blessed Abraham his master. He explained how God had blessed Abraham with great wealth, in gold and silver, as well as many male and female servants, and with great herds of livestock. His story probably kept them spell bound, as he continued to relate the experiences of Abraham to them.

When he came to the part of the story, about God giving Abraham and Sarah a son in their old age, it must have totally amazed everyone. The family was probably even more amazed when they were told that God had changed their names. Then he related to them how Abraham had made him swear an oath not to get his son Isaac a wife, from among the Canaanites where he lives. But, he was to go back to his father's family and his own clan to get a wife for his son.

He then told them again what happened at the well. He explained, how he had prayed to the Lord, and how the Lord had started to answer his prayer even before he had finished praying. As he continued his story, he told them of how he had given thanks to the Lord for leading him on his journey, and how God had helped him to find the granddaughter of his master for his son's wife. It was a story that any man would be proud to tell anyone. As an added bonus for Eliezer the storyteller, he would be able to capture the imaginations of young and old alike; it would have brought a great deal joy to his old heart without question.

Now that his story had come to a conclusion, he needed conformation as to what the family intended to do. Would they let Rebekah go with him so she could fulfill her destiny as required by the Lord, or would they say no? He needed to have their reply so he would know what he had to do. It was then that both Laban and Bethuel said to Eliezer, "This is from the Lord. We can say nothing to you one way or the other. Here is Rebekah, take her and go, and let her become the wife of your master's son as the Lord has directed. As you can see, they recognized and respected the authority of the Lord. When Eliezer heard their reply, he bowed himself to the ground and worshiped the Lord, giving thanks, for enabling him to complete his task.

Then he brought out gifts of silver and gold, jewelry, and articles of clothing, and gave them to Rebekah. He also gave costly gifts to her brother and to her mother. The rich gifts that were bestowed on Rebekah and her family indicated the wealth of the household, into which she was being asked to marry into, and that she would be well cared for throughout her life. The downside to this whole affair as far as Rebekah was concerned, was that she would be leaving her friends and loved ones far behind, and going to a strange new land. Little did she know at this point in time, the important role that she would be playing in God's plan, and in the history of mankind?

Early the next morning when Eliezer went to the family to ask for their blessing, Rebekah's brother and mother said: "Let the girl remain with us ten days or so, and then you may go." It was very apparent that the family was having second thoughts, and they didn't want to let her go just yet. This was probably because they loved her so very much and they didn't know if they would ever see her again.

Then Eliezer said to them: "Do not detain me, now that the Lord has granted success to my journey." Here he was reminding the family that it was the will of the Lord that she leaves right away, and not Eliezer's will. So to resolve the whole matter, they said: "Let's call the girl and ask her about it" So they called Rebekah and asked her if she would go with this man. "I will go," she said. So now the matter was clarified and settled.

No further discussion was needed. So then Laban, her brother blessed her and said: "Our sister! May you increase to thousands of ten thousands, may your offspring's possess the gates of their enemies." These two poetic lines reflect the promise of God to Abraham and Sarah. The term ten thousands translated here as meaning, "Myriads" or "uncountable numbers" as it was in Gods promise to Abraham in (Ge.22:

17). The term "possession of the "gates" of one's enemies meant power over them.

After they had pronounced their blessing on her, they gave her some maids and a nurse as well, and sent them on their way. The whole company of people must have made quite an entourage as they departed that day from Haran. Now, Eliezer's mind could finely be at ease. At last, they were on their way back to Canaan. His task was almost completed.

Meanwhile, Isaac had been on the move also. He had moved from the Beer Lahai Roi. This name means, "The Well of the One who lives and who sees me." This area, is the same area that Hagar, Abraham's Egyptian slave had been expelled too years before when Abraham had sent her away the second time. Now he had moved into the some area where Abraham's tent was in the region of Gerar.

One evening Isaac was out walking in his field. It is possible that, he was meditating on the past events of his life, and he was probably also wondering when his soon to be wife would show up? As he was walking he looked up, and saw the caravan that was bringing Rebekah and her maids to him. When Rebekah saw Isaac, she asked Eliezer: "who is the man that is walking in the field, and coming to meet us?" He said: "It is my master." So she covered her face with her veil, as was the custom, for young unmarried girls to do. She then, got down from her camel and waited for Isaac to come to them.

With great enthusiasm and excitement, Eliezer the servant, related to Isaac all of the things that had happened on his journey. He was undoubtedly glad to have completed the task that he had been given and to be back home again. Then Isaac took Rebekah into his mother's tent, where she had lived before her passing. It was here that Rebekah would reside until her and Isaac was married. This was also a public act, to show that she was to become his wife. Quite often, a mother's tent was used for a bridal chamber before the wedding. "And he loved her."

Her presents there in his mother's tent would also help him to get over his mother's death. Isaacs's sense of grief at the death of his mother was now replaced by the joy in the newness of someone else to love and care for. Only rarely, in the Bible do we read of romantic love, spoken of with such emotion. The story of Isaac and Rebekah's love is a beautiful story as it is. It gives a dramatic portrayal of Gods kind providence toward His people. Because Isaac was a special son, by whom God would fulfill His promise to Abraham, so also Rebekah would have had to be a very special woman.

After some time of courtship the two were married, but Rebekah was baron for a while just like Sarah had been. It is not known why God had closed up her womb for a length of time, but as you know, God fulfills His plans at His own timing. So Isaac prayed to God passionately, to open her womb. God heard his prayer and opened her womb and Rebekah became pregnant.

While she was carrying the two boys in her womb, they seemed to be struggling or fighting within her, as if they were competing in her womb for the best position. She was having a great deal of trouble with the pregnancy, so she prayed to the Lord to explain to her just what was happening. The Lord heard her prayer and He spoke directly to her and said: "Two nations are in your womb. Two people will be separated from your body; one people will be stronger than the other, and the older shall serve the younger."

So now she knew what God had planned for her and that everything would be all right. Now she could carry on with her life and not have to worry about her pregnancy. It must have been quite an experience in its self, to have the God of Heaven and Earth speak directly to her. She was to have twin boys. This is the first time that twins are mentioned in the

Bible. To be able to produce twins, it was considered to be a special blessing from God.

In the fullness of time, right from birth, strange thing began to happen. When the boys were born, the first one came out and he was red and "hairy." So they named him Esau. The name sounds like "hairy" in the Hebrew language. Esau would become the Patriarch of the Arab nations or Edomites. When the second boy came out, his hand took hold of Esau's heel. His name was called Jacob. His name sounds similar to, "He grasps the heel," or the word "heel."

Many times the children in those days were named after some thing, or a person, or something that happened to them or the parents at the child's berth. In the ancient Middle East, the firstborn son would have preeminence over the rest of the family and they would receive the birthright of the family. But this time God chose the younger Jacob for His purpose. Through His action here, God shows you that He has the sovereign right to do whatever pleases Him, according to His own perfect will and purpose.

The difference between the two boys was similar to two other brothers in history, Cane and Abel. Esau was a hunter, big and strong, and an outdoorsman. Jacob was like Abel, quiet and preferred to tend to livestock rather than to go out and hunt wild game Because Isaac was the first born and the only legal son that Abraham had, he would inherit everything that Abraham owned. God the Father had also predestined it. Beyond this, he would only receive God's blessings.

Keturah's sons had the same status as that of Hagar's son Ishmael, but they would have been without the particular blessing from God that Ishmael had received. Midian was the father of the Midianites, some of whom, later on in history bought Joseph from his brothers on their way to Egypt. Because there is no other mention of Abraham taking any other wife, it would be safe to say that Keturah was with Abraham until his death. To protect his son Isaac and his inheritance, after his death, Abraham gave all of his other lesser son's appropriate gifts, and sent them far away from Isaac. Then he continued to live near Isaac his Son of Promise until his death.

Abraham was, one hundred and seventy-five years old, and then he died. "At A Good Old Age, an Old Man full of Years," just as the Lord had promised him over one hundred and twenty years before. This phrase was used whenever the Patriarchs were mentioned to have died. It was also used when Job died. Then Abraham was buried and gathered to his people. His two sons Isaac, and Ishmael buried him in the cave at Machpelah beside Sarah his wife. Abraham lived a full century after he had set out from Haran. These words prove that there is an "Afterlife. It also means that his spirit went to be with his ancestors or his other deceased relatives in death.

This is the way it will be for you and for me, and all of mankind until Christ comes in the future. Your spirit and your soul will go to one of two places. It will either go to Heaven or to Hell when you die. It is your choice and you must make that choice alone. No one can make it for you.

So, ends the wonderful story of the great Patriarch Abraham. He was a man, who was loved by God beyond question. Our God has kept His promises to mankind throughout the ages. He still loves us without reservation. All God asks of you, is to believe in Him and in His Son Jesus Christ, and to repent of your sins to Him and ask for His forgiveness. If you believe in Him, you cannot help but love Him?

If you do this one small thing that God asks of you then, you will be guaranteed eternal life through Jesus Christ our Lord. This is His promise to us. So give Him your heart and soul, and live forever in heaven when you leave this old sinful world far behind. This is one more promise that the Lord has made to mankind and it will not change no matter what comes or goes. Some day you will leave this old world when you die and that is a certainty. "What then"?

Just a Foot Note here to say: When Isaac, Gods Son of Promise to Abraham and Sarah died; he was buried in the same cave as Abraham and Sarah at Machpelah. He was one hundred and eighty years old when he was gathered to his people.

Part Four

THE STORY OF JOSEPH

-1-

HIS BACKGROUND

Perhaps some time during your lifetime, you may have heard or read the wonderful story about Joseph and his coat of many colors? In any case, I feel that Gods Holy Spirit compels me, to relate this beautiful story to you, the reader of this book. After you have read this story and you understand it more fully, then you too can become a great and awesome storyteller. Then you may wish to tell it to your children or to other people as well. Throughout this story, you will see just how much "God Loves, Protects, Provides, and Cares for all His children who Love and Honor Him."

Since the beginning of time as we know it, God who is the Great Creator of all things in the Universe has a specific plan for all of mankind that has ever lived, or will live on the face of this earth. He has given mankind the privilege of choice. But there are only two choices that you can make. You can choose to worship God and His Son Jesus Christ and gain eternal life, or you may follow the way of the world and the Devil and spend eternity in Hell in eternal torment and pain. But you will without a doubt, spend eternity in one of the two places after you are judged on Judgment Day. This is written and it's very clear in Gods book the Bible.

To start this wonderful story, I will give you a little back ground on Jacob, who was Josephs father and how this story all came about. Jacob was the man, or the ancestral line into which God had planned to carry on the descendant line of Abraham right up to Jesus Christ His Son. There were a number of events that happened to Jacob throughout his lifetime, but I will only mention just a few and elaborate on them.

The following are some facts that Jacob was noted for.

> God changed his name from Jacob to "Israel, which means He struggles with God." You can read about this in the Bible in, (Gen.35: 9 -12).

> Jacob in his generation, more than any other one of the Patriarchs, represented Israel. He, as well as his people struggled with God and with men, but they overcame their difficulties and they became a blessing to other nations. It is through the life of Joseph, that the covenant family in Canaan became an emerging nation in Egypt. God was setting the stage for Moses and the Exodus of the Hebrew people from Egypt some 430 years into the future.

> It was at this time that God would renew His everlasting covenant with Jacob. This was the same covenant that He had made with Abraham years before.

> Jacob wrestled with God.

> He stole Esau's Birthright for a bowel of stew. The birthright was very important because it meant that the oldest son would receive the greatest portion of their father's estate when he died.

> He was notoriously deceptive, and a liar, when he was dealing with people, as you will see in some of the following paragraphs.

> Jacob was the Father of twelve sons that became the Fathers of Israel's twelve tribes.

He is well known for the dream that he had one night on his journey to Haran when he was running away from Esau his bother. In his dream, he saw a stairway resting on the earth, with its top reaching to heaven, and the angels of God were ascending and descending on it. There above it stood the Lord. This was a sign that the Lord offered to be Jacobs God. Jesus told Nathaniel, one of His disciples in (Jn. 1:51) that he would "see heaven open, and the angels of God ascending and descending on the Son of Man."

When Jesus made this statement He was proclaiming that He is the bridge between heaven and earth. He is the only "mediator between God and mankind." In (Jn.14: 6) Jesus said: "I am the way and the truth and the life. "No one" comes to the Father except through me." (Jn.5: 39) says, "Search the scriptures, for in them ye think ye have eternal life, and they are they which testify of me." Likewise in (Lk. 11:28) it says, "Blessed are they that hear the word of God and keep it."

It was at this time also, that the Lord reaffirmed with Jacob, the covenant that He had made with Abraham and Isaac. Even though he was running away from the consequences of his lies, God said that He would always be with him and keep him wherever he went, and that all of the people of the earth will be blessed through him. When God made this covenant with Abraham, it was an everlasting covenant. All believers and nations that exist today are still being blessed through Abraham and the Jewish nation whither they realize it or not.

When he awoke from his dream the next morning, he took the rock that he had used as a pillow, and made a pillar. Then he poured oil on it, and named the place Bethel, although the city used to be called Luz. This covenant illustrates Gods undying love and faithfulness to His people because, it is Gods promise and nothing or no one can change it.

Jacob, the father of Joseph, had two legal wives. Their names were Leah and Rachel, who were sisters. He also had sons by two other maidservants or surrogate mothers, whose names were Bilhah and Zilpah. Leah conceived and bore Jacob a total of six sons and a daughter named Dinah. Their names were Reuben, Simeon, Levi, Judah, Issachar and Zebulum.

Then Rachel conceived and bore Jacob two sons. Their names were Joseph and Benjamin, but there would be many years between the two boys. Rachel died giving birth to her second son Benjamin and was buried on the way to Ephrath, which would later become known as Bethlehem. The sons of Zilpah were Gad and Asher. The sons of Bilhah were called Dan, and Naphtali. All of these sons were considered to be the sons of Jacob, even though they were born of surrogate mothers. But because the women were not married to Jacob, they would not be entitled to any share of Jacobs's estate, like the rest of his sons would have been. So, if you count them all up, you can see that Jacob had a total of twelve sons and one daughter.

It was a sign of prestige and wealth to have a large family in those days, and also to be in the possession of many sons. But it was also equally bad, to be a woman that could not bear children. This caused a great deal of strife between the husbands and wives in that time period, as it did between Sarah and Hagar, earlier in Abraham's era.

One of the biggest problems that existed between Leah and Rachel was the fact that Jacob truly loved Rachel. The second reason why Jacob hated Leah was because her father Laban had tricked Jacob into marring her. Laban had promised Jacob that he could marry Rachel his youngest daughter, whom he loved. Plus, after being tricked by Laban into marring Leah, who was the wrong woman, Jacob had to work for Laban seven more years, if he wanted Rachel for his wife. Seven years of work was the wages that Jacob and

Laban had first agreed upon, when they had made the agreement for Rachel years before. So you can see how Laban had deceived Jacob. Now someone else had deceived the deceiver Jacob.

Through this deception of Jacob by Laban, you can see the work of Satan, because he is the great deceiver of the ages. Deception is one of his greatest weapons that, he uses against mankind. He is also the father of all lies. You may have heard of the old saying, "what goes around comes around." That's exactly what happened to Jacob. Jacob talked Esau his older brother, into selling his birthright for a bowl of stew. Esau despised his birthright, and in this manner he showed that he despised the Lord who had created it. Esau was not a God fearing man. He did as he pleased. When he become of age, he married a Canaanite woman and so he undoubtedly followed their ways and customs.

When Jacob conspired with his mother Rachel, to steal Esau's blessing from Isaac their father, it was only possible because of Rachel. It was her desire to have Jacob blessed by Isaac instead Esau. So she helped to disguise Jacob, so Isaac couldn't tell which one of his sons that he was blessing. Isaac was old and blind at the time when he performed the act of blessing on his sons. Blindness in old people was quite common in those ancient times, because people could not shield their eyes properly against the desert sun, as they do in this day and age.

Although Leah was unloved by Jacob, she was truly loved by God. He heard her cries for love each time she gave birth to a child, and he turned her sorrow into joy. Her sons become great people, tribes, and nations. Leah had become the mother of Jacobs's first four sons. This included Levi, the ancestor of the"Aaronic Priestly Line," and Judah, who was the ancestor of David and his royal line, and ultimately of Jesus our Lord. What more could a person ask than to have Jesus as one of your descendants? Now that you have some background on the father of Joseph, it is time to get on with the story of Joseph.

As you may recall back in the story of Abraham, that God had made a covenant with Abraham, and He had promised him that He would multiply his descendants, and they would be as numerous as the "Stares in the Sky, and as the Sands on the Seashore!" that is exactly what God was doing. The genealogy of Joseph is as follows.

> Abraham was the father of Isaac.
> Isaac was the father of Jacob.
> Jacob was the father of Joseph.

So as you can see, that Joseph was the third generation after Abraham, so he would be one of the great grandsons of Abraham. As our story begins, Joseph was seventeen years old and deeply loved by his father Jacob. One of the reasons that Jacob loved Joseph so much was because God had given him another son in his old age. Just like his great grandfather Abraham had received in his old age from God.

One day, Jacob made Joseph a beautifully ornamented robe, and gave it to him in the presences of his other brothers. This was a great show of favoritism on the part of Jacob. Also, this act of love that was displayed so boldly to Joseph by his father caused a great deal of anger and hatred between Joseph and his brothers. To make matters even worse and to compound their hatred for Joseph, he had become the bearer of bad news to their father. A tattletale or squealer was something that the brothers would not tolerate and put up with for very long.

Joseph had been out where his brothers had been tending their father's herds of livestock. When he returned home he brought back a bad report, to his father about the poor work that his brothers were doing with the herds of livestock. This act of telling tails on his brothers would do nothing but fuel the hatred that Joseph's brothers felt for him. Bitterness, anger, hatred, lying, murder, steeling, cheating, and deception are just some of the many tools of the Devil, and he uses them to his full advantage on the people of the world every day of their lives. But things were about to start getting a little bit spicier for the brothers, and then their hatred for Joseph would be totally out of control. The bitterness and the anger that they harbored would cause them a lifetime of pain and sorrow, as you will see.

JOSEPH'S DREAMS AND HIS BETRAYAL

One night God caused Joseph to have a dream that would change his life forever. He was quite excited about it and in his youthful enthusiasm; he related his dream to his brothers when the opportunity had presented itself to him. He said to them: "Listen to this dream I had: We were binding sheaves of grain out in the field when suddenly my sheaf arose and stood upright, while your sheaves gathered around mine and bowed down to it." Then his brothers said to him: "Do you intend to reign over us?" When they heard it, they hated him all the more because of his dream, and what he had said to them. Also, it is quite clear from their question that they understood immediately the full meaning of Josephs dream.

Then Joseph had a second dream. As he told it to his brothers this time he said: "Listen I had another dream, and this time the sun and the moon and eleven stares were bowing down to me." While he was telling his brothers about the second dream that he had, he was probably more excited than he was the first time. When he went and told his father about his second dream, his father rebuked him and said: "What is this dream you had? Will your mother and I and your brothers actually come and bow down to the ground before you?" Although his father was insulted and hurt to some degree, he kept the matter in the back of his mind because; he knew that the dreams had to be coming from God.

The dreams were indeed a revelation from God. But the greatest revelation of all was the fact that all of the people, who were involved in the dreams, understood the meaning of the dreams. Although the people did not like the dreams and what they implied, it was only through Gods grace that He revealed the dreams to them at all. How many times have you heard of people having dreams, or having reoccurring dreams, and they have never understood them, or have tried very hard to remember them in great detail, but they could not do it.

By now his brothers were so angry with Joseph that they plotted ways to kill him. Satan himself was orchestrating the anger that was being demonstrated by Joseph's brothers at this point in time. Later on, in the years to come, God would turn this anger into a great blessing. Many times in your life, God will turn Satan's evil work into a rich blessing for you, and you may not recognize it at that particular point in time. But I can assure you that this is exactly what will happen.

As you might recall, I stated once before that, God often revealed the future to His people in dreams. Little did the brothers know at that time, that Joseph's dreams would come true in the years to come and that he would become the "Prince" among his brothers? This would be a prime example of how God used Satan's evil work to being Gods love and kindness to His people. One other example would be the story of Job.

One-day Joseph's brothers took their flocks and journeyed north from the Valley of Hebron to Shechem, in search of better pastures for the flocks. Shechem was the place where Abraham had built his first altar to God. Sometime had passed since they had departed from the Valley of Hebron, and Jacob their father had not heard any word from his sons as to how they were faring, or how the flocks were being cared for. He was becoming quite worried and concerned about this troubling matter.

So he called Joseph to him and said: "As you know, your brothers are grazing the flocks near Shechem. Come, I am going to send you to them. Go and see if all is well with them and with the flocks and bring word back to me." Even though Jacob knew of the open hostility between Joseph and his brothers, he still had to know what was happening with his sons and their flocks. It had never entered his mind for an instant that, something evil could happen to Joseph on his journey to Shechem, or that his brother might try to kill him.

So it came to pass, that God put another part of the plan that He had for Joseph's life into action. There is no mention of how long it took Joseph to reach Shechem, but when he got there his brothers and their flocks were nowhere to be seen. As he was wondered around the fields looking for them, a man saw him and asked him: "what are you looking for?" Then Joseph said: "I am looking for my brothers and their flocks. Can you tell me where they are grazing their flocks?" "They have moved on from here, the man answered. I heard them say, let's go to Dothan. "Dothan was an ancient city, located about thirteen miles north of Shechem near Mount Gilboa.

After Joseph had finished speaking to this man, he set out toward Dothan to locate his brothers and their flocks. Although no time of day is specified in the Bible, I would suspect that it may have been somewhere around mid day when Joseph finely caught up to his brothers and their flocks. From scripture it appears that the brothers were all together and they could have been having their noon meal.

It was probably a bright sunny day as well and a person could see someone coming in any direction for miles. I say this because the brothers had seen him coming at a great distance even before Joseph had seen them. Joseph was wearing his beautiful ornamented robe, and that is how the brothers recognized him at such a great distance. Also, because he was so far away, they may have had ample time to discuss and to make a final decision as to what they were going to do with him when he got to them.

Then Satan entered the brother's hearts once again, but this time with much more persuasive power than before and they plotted to kill him. They said: "Here comes the dreamer. Let us kill him and throw him into one of these cisterns, (an old dry well) and say that a ferocious animal devoured him. Then we will see what becomes of his dreams." They reasoned among themselves, that if Joseph was dead his dreams could not come true and they would not have to bow down to him.

However Reuben, Joseph's oldest brother, didn't hate Joseph as much as his other brothers did. He intervened to try and save his brother's life. Because he was Joseph's oldest brother, he felt that he, more than anyone else, was responsible for Joseph and his safety. Reuben said to his brothers: "Shed no blood!" But cast him into this pit which is in the wilderness, and do not lay a hand on him." He said this, because he planned to rescue Joseph later, and take him back to his father. After he had convinced his brothers not kill Joseph, Reuben left them and went out to the flocks that he was tending out of their sight.

As Joseph approached his brothers and he had greeted them in his usual way, he probably told them why he had come. When he told them that he was there to check up on them because their father was concerned about their welfare they didn't believe him, and they became very angry. So they stripped him of his beautiful robe and threw him into a dry cistern that was located nearby. They knew that he would die within a few days without water. But little did the brothers know or realize at the time, that it was all part of Gods plan to use their anger and bitterness to fulfill His plan for Joseph.

As they set down to eat their evening meal, they looked up and saw a caravan of Ishmaelites or Midianites, coming from Gilead with their camels loaded down with spices, balm and myrrh. The caravan was on its way to Egypt. As you know, only the rich people and traders could afford camels in those days, and Josephs brothers must have realized this when they seen the caravan coming toward them.

The brothers had probably been discussing among themselves at some point in time, how they might turn their crime of hatred into some kind of profit. Judah said to his brothers: "What profit is there if we kill our brother and conceal his blood? Come, let us sell him to the Ishmaelites, and let not our hand be upon him, for he is our brother and our flesh." So Judah's brothers listened to him, and they pulled Joseph out of the cistern and sold him to the Ishmaelites, as a slave for twenty shekels of silver. That was only about two-thirds the price for a young slave of seventeen if, all was well and nothing was physically wrong with him.

Thirty shekels of silver was the standard price that was paid for a slave in those days. This was also the price that was paid for Jesus, to Judas, one of His own disciples, by the High Priests just before His crucifixion. But the traders must have known that there was something wrong, but they didn't care. Joseph was young and in excellent condition and he would bring a high price for them in the Egyptian slave market. Joseph begged his brothers not to sell him but to no avail. The troublemaker would now be gone out of their lives forever. They thought that once Joseph was in Egypt, they would never see him again and his blood would not be on their hands. So it was that, Joseph would now become a slave and be sold into slavery in Egypt.

When Reuben returned from his flock to where his brothers were camped, he went to the cistern to see how Joseph was doing. He probably wanted to tell Joseph what he was planning to do, and that he would rescue him some time soon. But when he got there, Joseph and the caravan were gone. So he tore his clothes, which was a common expression of profound dismay and grief. Coupled with his grief, over losing his younger brother, he also feared that he would be blamed for everything that had happened to Joseph because; he was the oldest one of the brothers.

Now Joseph's brothers had to come up with a story to tell their father. They certainly could not take the chance and tell their father that, they had sold Joseph to a caravan of traders for twenty pieces of silver. If they did that then they would have all been in a lot of trouble with their father, and there is no telling just what he would do to them. There is a possibility that Jacob would have disowned them as his sons and disinherited them.

So they had to make it appear as if Joseph was dead. So they killed a goat and dipped Josephs coat in the blood. When the brothers returned home with their flocks, they took Josephs beautiful coat to their father and asked him if it belonged to his son Joseph, as if they didn't know that already. They said that some wild animal had killed Joseph, and his blood stained coat was all that they found of him. Then Jacob tore his clothes in utter grief and disbelief, in the same manner that Reuben had done, and he wept for Joseph for many days. Now he had lost his first son of his beloved Rachel. As far as he knew his favorite son whom he loved so deeply, was gone forever.

-2-

JOSEPH STARTS A NEW LIFE

Now God was with Joseph. This phrase is used quite often throughout the Bible and it is used many times in the story of Joseph. This means that wherever Joseph went, or whatever Joseph did, God would bless his work, and the people around him. Their households would prosper beyond the people's wildest dreams. Now Joseph was very strong, well built, and a very handsome boy. That is to say that he was pleasing to the eye. Just his appearance alone, would bring a handsome price for his slave traders.

But there was also one other huge difference between Joseph and everyone else that was going to be sold at the slave market that day. That was that, he loved and trusted God, and because of his faith, he knew that God would protect him and bless him no matter what came his way. God had placed Joseph exactly where He wanted him to be.

As our story continues to unfold, you will see just how the Lord has a hand in everything that happens to Joseph. The end result is a show of Joseph's faith and trust in God. As well, you will see and hopefully understand, the great love, protection, and the care that the God has for all of the people who believe in Him and His Son Jesus Christ.

Shortly after Joseph had arrived in Egypt, the Midianites took him to the slave market to be sold as a slave. There is no doubt that the traders, would have kept Joseph in good health while he was in their possession so that, when he appeared on the auction block he would be looking like he worth a great deal of money. However, God had already chosen the person who was to now enter the life of Joseph, so He could continue to carry out His plan for Joseph.

The man, who bought Joseph, was not just any old run of the mill buyer of slaves. This man had a very high position in the court of the Pharaoh, the ruler of Egypt. The Bible says that he was one of Pharaohs officials, the captain of the guard. The officials name was "Potiphar." To be the captain of Pharaohs guards, he would have had to have been held in very high esteem, and above all else, trusted, to carry out the Pharaohs orders to the letter.

Because Joseph was Potiphar's slave, he was allowed to live in his Egyptian master's house. You can see here how God cared for Joseph, by putting him in the captain's house. In this manner, Joseph would be in line for a better position in his life. Also, God would be able to show Potiphar that, his household was being blessed through Josephs presents there. As time passed, Potiphar saw how God was with Joseph, and how God had given him success in everything he did.

So now through Gods grace, Joseph gained the respect and trust of Potiphar. Then he made Joseph his attendant, and put Joseph in charge of everything that he owned in his household and in his fields. So the only thing that Potiphar had to be concerned about was the bread that he would eat. It was indeed a very high position to be put in, and it carried with it a great deal of responsibility. But Joseph did not fear the new responsibilities that had come his way. He knew that God was with him, and that God would give him the wisdom and strength that he needed to complete his tasks and to rule Potiphar's household with truth and understanding. The language bearer and customs would be a stumbling block for both Potiphar and for Joseph alike but that would be overcome with time.

As time went on, Potiphar's wife began to flirt with Joseph and to make bold advances toward him. Many times, she begged him each day to come to her bed. But the Lord was with Joseph, and He kept Joseph from committing such a great sin. At one point, Joseph become very upset with her advances toward him and he said to her; "With me in charge, my master does not concern himself with anything in the house. Everything he owns he has entrusted to my care. No one is greater in this house than I am. My master has withheld nothing from me except you, because you are his wife. How then, could I do such a wicked thing and sin against God." He didn't want to be guilty of such a terrible sin against his God, and suffer the consequences. He was so tired of her begging him to go to bed with her every time she spoke to him that, he even refused to be around her.

When Joseph refused to yield to Potiphar's wife's temptations, he was doing several things that you would expect from a person who was in his kind of position. For example;

- He acknowledged the great responsibility that his master had given him.
- He realized that he was the greatest one in his master's house.
- He understood that his master had held nothing back from him except his wife.
- He had his master's complete trust, which a person in his position would have to earn.
- Last but not least, he stood up for his ethical beliefs, his faith and he refused to commit such a great sin against God, whom he loved and trusted above everything else.

So Joseph did what was in his heart, and he found it very easy to resist the temptation that Satan had put before him in the form of Potiphar's wife. It was the empowering presence of God in his life that helped Joseph to resist the temptations of the woman. Even though he knew that the woman served and worshiped other gods; Joseph had probably told her many times about, the righteousness of the one and only true God that he worshiped with his whole heart and soul. It is also possible that he had explained to her in great detail how it was that this very same God; had delivered him from certain death in the well in the desert.

Likewise, there is little doubt that at the sometime, Joseph would have also tried to explain to her that it was this same God who was blessing everything that he was doing. He gave God the full credit for everything in his life. This in its self would have made Potiphar's wife very angry and resentful. The same problem holds true in today's world as well. When you mention God and His goodness, His love, and His grace, many people become angry and resentful and they try to shrug it off as a joke and say that they did everything themselves.

In the following part of the story you will see how Joseph who was completely innocent of all wrongdoing, and how he was punished for his faith in the God he worshiped, and the principles that he chose to up hold because of his God.

One day while Potiphar was away and there were no men around the house, Joseph went into the house to do his daily duties. He was not expecting any trouble, but trouble found him. As he entered the house, Potiphar's wife grabbed hold of him and she tried to get him into bed with her. In the ensuing struggle, she tore off some of his clothing and she was left holding it in her hands as he fled the house. When she saw that he had left his garment and fled from the house, she became very angry and upset.

In her fiery rage she screamed for her servants and commenced to fill them full of lies. “Look,” she said to them, “this Hebrew has been brought to us to make sport of us. He came in here to sleep with me, but I screamed. When he heard me scream for help, he left his garment beside me and ran out of the house. The servants had no choice but to believe her lies, because they hadn’t seen or heard anything to disprove them.

So she kept the garment with her until her husband came home, and then she showed it to him. After she had retold her pack of lies to him, just like his servants, he had no choice but to believe her. At that time, Potiphar became very angry and upset. But, because Joseph had always been so truthful and honest in all of his dealings with Potiphar, he had his doubts as to the total truth of his wife’s story.

The attempted rape of a master’s wife, by a foreign slave would have been a cause for exceptional outrage. It would have given the master the right to kill the slave and throw his body to the crows. But; because he had some doubts about his wife’s story, Potiphar put Joseph into the prison in the house of the Captain of the Guard. It certainly was not the worst prison that was available, but nonetheless it was a prison. This prison was more like being under house arrest, rather than a prison with cells and straw or the hard ground for a bed.

Potiphar may have put Joseph there, so he could watch over him and protect him, as he was the only one in charge of that particular type of prison. Besides this, he probably didn’t want to kill the golden goose, as they say. He knew that God was blessing him and his entire household because of Joseph. He also knew a good thing when he was it. It is very sad to think, that the unbelieving world of today, doesn’t realize just how much God loves them too, and that He blesses them because they have Christians living around them. The unbelievers are truly blessed by Gods Christian children, just as Lot was blessed because of Abraham.

This would be Joseph's first experience in any kind of a prison, or close confinement, so he must have been a little frightened and apprehensive as to what could happen to him while he was in prison. He probably wondered from time to time why God had permitted him to be placed into this prison type environment. He had certainly done nothing wrong to deserve this kind of treatment, and he knew in his heart that he was totally innocent of any charges against him.

But the Lord was with Joseph even in prison and He showed him great mercy. As time passed God gave Joseph favor in the sight of the prison warden. The warden liked Joseph so much, that he put him in charge of all of the prisoners that were held in the prison. He was also responsible for all that was done there concerning the prisoners. The warden paid no attention to anything that was under Josephs care. The main reason why the warden had no reason to worry was because, Joseph's reputation had preceded him and it showed that he was very trustworthy. There is no doubt that, he had heard how Joseph's God was with him, and that He gave him success in whatever he did. The warden also realized that because of Joseph, his life would be a lot easier and he wouldn't have such a huge responsibility on his shoulders. He could now pass many of his problems on to Joseph and let him have the responsibilities that went along with the job.

As time passed while Joseph was in prison, the Lord was beginning to prepare the way for Josephs rise to power in Egypt. You can read this account in (Gen.40: 1-23-41:1-40). One day, Pharaoh, the King of Egypt, became upset and angry with two of his key officials. They were his chief cupbearer (or butler) and his chief baker. These were two highly prized positions in the Kings court, and these positions carried with them a great deal of responsibility as well.

The Bible does not specify why the King was so angry with them, but he put them under house arrest in the same prison that Joseph was in. After they had been in custody for some time, the two of them each had a dream, on the same night. In the following morning, they were both down cast and a little bit worried and mystified as to what their dreams meant.

As they were discussing their dreams between themselves, they were not aware that the Almighty Hand of God was working in their lives. The chief cupbearer would be the divinely appointed agent for introducing Joseph to Pharaoh. As I mentioned before, dreams, and their proper interpretations, played a very important part in the people's lives in ancient biblical times. It was Gods way of revealing the future to some people, but not everyone could interpret the dreams.

The next morning when Joseph went to see the two men, he asked them saying: "Why are your faces so sad today?" "We both had dreams," they answered, "but there is no one to interpret them." Then Joseph said to them,"Do not interpretations belong to God? Tell me your dreams." You may recall now how in Joseph's life that God had caused him to dream two different dreams as well. Remember the sheaves of grain, and the sun, the moon and eleven stars.

But right from the beginning, Joseph gave God all of the credit for causing the two men to dream. When he said; "Do not all dream interpretations belong to God?" He was expressing and showing his deep faith in God. Also he was saying that God was the only one who could interpret the dreams properly and accurately because He was the one who had sent them. When he said; "Tell me your dreams," he was presenting himself as Gods agent through whom God would make known the revelation contained in their dreams.

It was the chief cupbearer who spoke up first and said to Joseph, "In my dream I saw a vine in front of me, and on the vine were three branches. As soon as it budded, it blossomed, and its clusters ripened into grapes. Pharaohs cup was in my hand, and I took the grapes, and squeezed them into Pharaohs cup and put the cup in his hand." After the cupbearer had explained his dream to Joseph, he waited with great anticipation and excitement, for Joseph's interpretation of his dream.

Instantly, the Lord revealed the dreams to Joseph, and without hesitation Joseph answered and said to the chief cupbearer: "This is the meaning of the dream. The three branches are three days. Within three days Pharaoh will lift up your head and restore you to your former position and you will put Pharaohs cup in his hand, just as you used to do when you were his cupbearer." I can just imagine the joy and the relief that that he must have felt when he heard such good news. The word "Instantly," that is used in the text here is positive proof that God was right there with Joseph as, He is with all of His children who love and worship Him. Joseph didn't have to pray to God first to receive the answers to the dreams God reviled them to him instantly.

After the cupbearer had heard the explanation of his dream, Joseph said to him, "Remember me when all goes well with you. Show me kindness and mention me to Pharaoh and get me out of this prison." Then Joseph told him his story. He told him of how he had been forcibly carried off from the land of his father, and how Potiphar's wife had falsely accused him, and now he was being held in this same dungeon as they were.

The word "Dungeon," here could possibly refer to the dungeons in Hell. It was a slap in the face to the Devil and his home, which is Hell. It also reflects Joseph's despair at being confined in such a place. In the Hebrew language the word is translated as cistern. In this way the author of Genesis has also established a link with Joseph's earlier experience at the hands of his brothers. There is no doubt, that the cupbearer had all of the best intentions in the world to remember Joseph and his plight. But when he did return to his position as chief butler to Pharaoh, he forgot all about Joseph in prison.

Then the chief baker, who had been waiting on the side-lines with great anticipation and a little fear in his heart, said to Joseph, "I too had a dream," Perhaps it was his sense of guilt that held him back. But now he felt that the time was right to tell Joseph his dream. He said; "On my head were three baskets of bread. In the top basket were all kinds of baked goods for Pharaoh, but the birds were eating them out of the basket on my head."

Then Joseph said to him: "This is the meaning of the dream. The three baskets are three days. Within three days, Pharaoh will lift off your head and hang you on a tree, and the birds will eat away your flesh." He would not even receive a proper burial. As you will notice, both dreams contained the number three. This indicates that both dreams would be fulfill on the same day.

When the baker heard the bad news of his impending death in three days, he probably went crazy with grief and fear, for he knew that he was going to pay with his life for whatever his crime happened to be. There is no mention in the Bible of the type of crime that the baker committed. But I would suspect that it was that, there was a plot against the Pharaohs life with poisoned baking of some sort. When the Pharaoh got wind of it, and had an investigation, he found that the baker was responsible for the plot. Otherwise the Pharaoh would have had no reason to behead him and impale him on a tree.

Now on the third day it was the Pharaohs birthday, and he threw a big party for all of his servants and officials of his court, so they could celebrate with him. As the day started out, things happened just as Joseph had said that they would. The two prisoners were brought before Pharaoh so he could put them on trial, and they could answer to the charges against them. The cupbearer was restored to his former position of serving the Pharaoh, and the baker was beheaded and hung on a tree for the entire world too sees.

The baker's execution would also serve as a stern warning and a discouragement, to the rest of his servants and officials or, to anyone else for that matter, who might try to attempt to take the Pharaohs life. It was a clear and precise statement to the people from the Pharaoh. The Pharaoh could be both gracious, and merciful as his will dictated. But he could also rule with a fist of iron at the same time, if he had to. The baker's death, and the way that he died, was a just reward for the deed that was committed. Centuries later, a similar event would take place and John the Baptist would be beheaded by Herod the Tetrarch in Jerusalem. But his fate defiantly did not fit any kind of crime.

-3-

THE PHARAOH'S DREAM

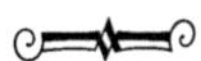

Now the time was right with God, and Joseph's life is about to take a turn for the better. He would rise from a dungeon in prison to the Egyptian Throne Room. Once again God was engineering the circumstances so that through Joseph, He could meet the needs of the nation of Egypt and His people during the coming famine. He would also reunite Jacobs's family for the final time. God will always work out His plan for you if you will let Him, but as you can see, it is all done in Gods timing and not in mankind's timing.

It was not until a full two years had passed that the butler remembered Joseph, and what had happened to him in prison. This shows you how quickly man can forget his fellow mans problems, and that he almost never keeps his promises. But God is always ready, willing, and able to keep His promises to His people. "You can always say that Gods promises and His word are carved in stone, they will not change or fade away.

One night when the Pharaoh had barely fallen asleep, God caused him to have a dream. In his dream, he was standing by the Nile River. This river was one of the most important rivers in Egypt. It was so important, that the Egyptians held it in reverence as a god and worshiped the river as such. At that time and for centuries to come they worshiped many different kinds of idols and gods.

As he was standing there, he saw seven cows come up out of the river. They were all very nice, sleek and fat as they grazed among the reeds. Cattle often submerged themselves up to their necks in the Nile to escape the sun and the insects. After them, there came up out of the Nile, seven ugly and gaunt cows, and they stood beside those on the riverbank. The cows that were ugly and gaunt ate up the seven sleek fat cows. Then the Pharaoh woke up. I can well imagine how utterly confused his mind must have been over this kind of dream.

After some time had passed the Pharaoh fell asleep again that same night, and then he had a second dream. The second dream was similar to the first dream, but yet it was different in some respects. In the second dream, God used heads of grain and the wind to reveal the future. When Pharaoh had his second dream it too was very puzzling to him and it also left him without any answers to his dreams. These two dreams completely unnerved him, and they caused him to become anxious and very ill at ease the rest of the night. Perhaps he even walked the floor for a while, trying calming his shattered nerves. His second dream however, must have really spooked him because the scripture says that, "His spirit was troubled."

In his second dream, suddenly, up out of the ground, there came up seven heads of grain, and they were all on one stalk, plump and good. Then seven thin heads, blighted by the east wind, sprang up after them, and the seven thin heads devoured the seven plump full heads. When the Pharaoh woke up out of his fretful sleep the following morning, he realized that the dreams that he had dreamed were very real. Pharaoh, like everyone else in Egypt, believed very strongly in dreams and he put a lot of faith in their importance. But he did not know the meaning of them, or who would be able to interpret them for him.

So early the next morning, he called for all of the wise men, and all of the magicians that were in Egypt. After he had related his two dreams to them, he soon found out that there was no one who could interpret the dreams for him. At this point, he probably became very upset with all of these so-called wise men and magicians. The wise men possessed great knowledge of the laws, and the rules of the land, that were associated with the courts of the ancient Middle East. They were either functionary of pagan religions, as they are here, or merely observers and interpreters of life it's self.

The magicians on the other hand were priests who claimed to possess occult knowledge and to use the power of Satan. But who else was he to turn to? He certainly did not believe in the God of Heaven and Earth. But he was soon to realize the power of God through Joseph. It is not mentioned how long after the Pharaoh had his dreams, before the chief cupbearer realized that he had forgotten about Joseph in prison, and what Joseph had done for him. But the Bible does say that it was a full two years before he remembered Joseph. When he did remember, he went to Pharaoh and said: "Today I am reminded of my shortcomings." By this statement that was made by the cupbearer, it shows us how God uses ordinary people to do His work, and to accomplish His purpose. Although he didn't realize it, it was God who helped him to remember his promise to Joseph.

Then the chief cupbearer reminded Pharaoh of how he had been put in prison by the Pharaoh two years before. He said to the Pharaoh; "While I and the chief baker were both in prison, we each had a dream. Now there was a young Hebrew there who was a servant of the captain of the guard. When we told him of our dreams, he interpreted them for us, giving each man the interpretation of his dream." Then he said: "Things turned out exactly as he interpreted them to us. I was restored to my position and the other man was hanged." I can just imagine the relief and the surprise on the Pharaohs face when; he had finished hearing what his servant had to say.

So the Pharaoh sent for Joseph and they brought him out of prison. This would in effect be Joseph's permanent release from prison He would never again have to experience any type of imprisonment. It is reasonable to assume that, at the same time that Joseph was to appear in the presence of the Pharaoh; that he may have also called all of the wise men, the magicians, and all of his officials together before Joseph's arrival at the Palace. In this manner, the Pharaoh would have had a great contingent of witness to support his actions against Joseph if, the interruption of his dreams turned out to be a hoax.

When he had bathed himself, and his whole body had been clean-shaven, and he had changed into new clothing, he was brought before Pharaoh in his throne room in the palace. You can well imagine of how Joseph may have felt, when he was ushered into the presence of the great Pharaoh of Egypt. Just coming into the Pharaohs beautiful palace he would have been awestruck and flabbergasted too say the least.

Shortly after a few words of formal introduction, the Pharaoh said to Joseph. "I had a dream, and no one can interpret it. But I have heard it said of you, that when you hear a dream you can interpret it." "I cannot do it, but God will give Pharaoh the answer he desires." Here Joseph was expressing his faith in God and giving God all of the credit once again. Joseph was not trying to plead his innocence so he could be released from prison. He didn't even try to strike a bargain with the Pharaoh in any way, shape or form. But, he was revealing to the Pharaoh, that it was God, the Ruler of the Universe, "and The Creator of all things, including dreams." who would reveal his dream for him. He made it very clear to the Pharaoh that the interpretation would come from the "One True Living God," and not the gods who filled the courts and homes of Egypt. This also included the Pharaoh, who was considered to be a god himself.

After the Pharaoh had repeated his dreams to Joseph, he sat back and waited with great anticipation for the interpretation of the dreams. Then Joseph who was led by the Spirit of God, said to Pharaoh again without hesitation: "The dreams of Pharaoh are one and the same. God has revealed to Pharaoh what He is about to do." Joseph has for the first time testified of the living God in a pagan court. God has enabled Joseph to understand the dreams, so that He could ultimately show that it is He who controls, and will control all things in the Universe.

God had put Joseph in Egypt during this critical time, so that He could bless Egypt through a Hebrew. In this manner, the blessing of Egypt would become known throughout the ancient world, as a blessing from God, and not from the Idol gods of Egypt. It was also a way that God could show, that He was keeping His promise to bless all nations through His people who would someday become the nation of Israel. This is one lesson that the world of today would be well advised to learn. God loves the "Apple of His eye' which is the nation of Israel, and God will not break His promises to them no matter what comes their way. He will keep them to the letter because He cannot lie.

As Joseph continued to explain the Pharaohs dream to him he said: "The seven good cows are seven years, and the seven good heads of grain are seven years. It is one and the same dream. The seven lean, ugly cows that came up afterward are seven years, and so are the seven worthless heads of grain scorched by the east wind. They are seven years of famine. As for the wind, that was mentioned in the dream, it referred to the hot east wind that blows in from the desert in the late spring and early fall. It often withers the vegetation in the whole country.

So now Pharaoh understood part of his dream but what was he to do. He probably had a thousand unanswered questions in his mind and so he asked Joseph to further explain his dream.

Then Joseph continued to speak and to elaborate on the Pharaohs dreams he repeated to him what he had said before. "Repetition, of a divine revelation," was often used for emphasis on such matters as dreams, and any thing that came from God. Joseph wanted to make sure that the Pharaoh fully understood the dreams, so he would know exactly what God was going to do. Joseph was not about to leave any doubt in the Pharaohs mind as to what God meant or what He intended to do.

"It is just as I said to Pharaoh: God has shown Pharaoh what He is about to do. Seven years of great abundance are coming throughout the land of Egypt, but seven years of famine will follow them. Then all of the abundance in Egypt will be forgotten, and the famine will ravage the land. The abundance in the land will not be remembered, because the famine that follows it will be so severe. The reason the dream was given to Pharaoh in two forms is that the matter has been firmly decided by God, and God will do it soon."

Long famines were rare in Egypt because of the regularity of the annual overflow of the Nile. But famines were quit common in other parts of the world at that time, and are still common in the world today. There was another great famine that is recorded in the Bible in Elijah's time. (2 Ki. 8:1) That famine was supposed to last for seven years also. But because of Elijah's intercession with God, and the fact that he prayed earnestly to God, the famine only lasted three and half years. This shows you the power of prayer, and that one believer in God can intercede for many.

The fact that Joseph told Pharaoh that, God would start to fulfill the dreams soon, probably prompted the Pharaoh to ask Joseph what he as King, was required to do. So Joseph said to Pharaoh, "Now let Pharaoh look for a discerning and wise man and put him in charge of the land of Egypt, and appoint commissioners over the land, to take a fifth of the harvest of Egypt during the seven years of abundance. They should collect all of the food of these good years that are coming and store up the grain under the authority of Pharaoh, to be kept in the cities for food. This food should be held in reserve for the country, to be used during the seven years of famine that will come upon Egypt, so that the country will not be ruined by the famine."

JOSEPH'S RISE TO POWER

Everything that Joseph had said seemed like a very good plan to the Pharaoh and to his officials as well. So he asked his officials, "Can we find anyone like this man, one in who is the spirit of God? It was at this point that, the Pharaoh realized that Joseph was the only one who fit the description perfectly. He would be the man he need at his right hand to fulfill such a great and awesome task. The Pharaoh has now just testified in public and before his officials, to the reality of Gods Spirit, and to His Almighty Power that was working in Joseph's life.

As the Pharaoh continued to speak to Joseph, and to show his authority before the people in his presence, he said to Joseph: "Since God has made all of this known to you, there is no one so discerning and wise as you. You shall be in charge of my Palace; and all of my people are to submit to your orders. Only with respect to the throne, will I be greater than you."

Now the Pharaoh was giving Joseph his complete trust, and he showed this trust in Joseph by making him the second most powerful man in Egypt. No other Pharaoh before in the history of Egypt had, ever created the position that Joseph was now to enjoy and to be honored by. God had taken Joseph, a common slave, from a prison dungeon and placed him into one of the highest positions in the Egypt. It was a blessing beyond blessings for Joseph.

This part of the story of Joseph is similar to the book "From a Popper to a Prince." But that's as far as it goes. The big difference in this story is that, in the Bible it is God, and God alone who, has engineered and made all things happen, and Joseph is only the vessel in which God has worked to perform His declaration. You may have noticed that throughout the Bible and throughout the history of the world for that matter, God has used just ordinary people to do His bidding. You don't necessarily have to be someone great or have a high position in life, so God can use you. God is no respecter of persons. He will use whom He pleases, when He pleases.

As he continued to speak, the Pharaoh said to Joseph: "I hereby put you in charge of the whole land of Egypt." It was a statement and a command that only the Pharaoh himself could break. Then the Pharaoh took off his signet ring from his finger and put it on Joseph's finger. This ring would be used by Joseph to sign any documents and laws that he would make. Then the Pharaoh dressed Joseph in robes of fine linen, and put a gold chain around his neck, and presented him to his court.

By presenting Joseph to his court for the second time in one day, after all thing were settled and done with, it show the people who were present there that, the Pharaoh had complete confidence and trust in Joseph. Joseph was the only man who was to hold this high position, and it was he alone, who was to possess the great power that went along with the position. This was the first time in the history of Egypt that this kind of position had ever been created. It is from this time on in the life of Joseph that, God will bestow great wealth and power on His servant Joseph. The young man, who had once been nothing but a mere Sheppard Boy, has now become the second most powerful man in Egypt.

Now he would wear nothing but the finest clothes and have the best place in the land to live. The ring, the robe, and the gold chain, were three visible signs to the people of Pharaohs court and to the people of the country that expressed the transfer and the sharing of royal authority to Joseph.

Then the Pharaoh had Joseph to ride around Egypt in a chariot as his second in command. Men shouted before him "make way, make way." This command would signify the importance of Joseph to the people of the land. The people of Egypt bowed before him, as a sign of respect, and homage to his position, but not as a sign of worship. No one in the land was permitted to lift a hand or a foot, without Josephs consent. This meant that Joseph had enormous power and total control over the running of the whole country of Egypt.

As time passed and Joseph had become accustom to his new position and the country; the Pharaoh decided to bestow more honor on Joseph. He thought that if Joseph were going to have such enormous power in Egypt, he should have an Egyptian name. So he gave him the name of Zaphenath-Paneah, which the Bible says means, "The God Speaks and Lives." These words refer to the true God of Joseph, and not to Joseph himself.

By the time Joseph had risen to power in Egypt, thirteen years had elapsed, since his brothers had sold him to become a slave in Egypt. For thirteen years God had been refining and molding Joseph's character, and getting him ready to become the second-in-command in Egypt. Now he was thirty years old and ripe for marriage. So the Pharaoh who was by now enjoying peace of mind, and was no doubt enjoying the blessings of God as well, decided to help Joseph get married. So he gave Joseph, Asenath, to be his wife. She was the beautiful daughter of Potiphera who was at that time the Priest of On.

After the wedding was over and the partying was all done, the Pharaoh made Joseph to ride around Egypt in his chariot once again to, show the people that he was truly his second-in command. This display of open handedness by the Pharaoh no doubt gave his heart and his ego a huge boost. It was also an open statement to the peoples of Egypt how, gracious and kind the Pharaoh could be when he wanted to be.

In the course of time, Asenath bore Joseph two sons. The name of his firstborn son was Manasseh. Joseph named him this because he said: "God has made me to forget all of my trouble and my entire father's household." His second son was named Ephraim and he said: "It is because God has made me fruitful in the land of my suffering." Joseph's two sons were born in the seven years of plenty, long before the famine would occur.

As Joseph went throughout the land of Egypt, he was very busy seeing to all of his duties in the various cities. The people listened to Joseph and they did exactly what he told them to do. They did not whine and complain to him because they loved and respected him a great deal. They also knew that he carried with him the authority of Pharaoh. When he spoke, he spoke as the Pharaoh and no one questioned him on what he said or demanded.

He had the people to build huge storage sheds for the produce, and large bins for the grain that surrounded each city. The grain was so abundant that it was like the sand of the sea. There was so much grain and produce that Joseph gave up trying to keep a record of it, because it was beyond measure. The abundance of the crops and produce was another miracle from God that displayed His awesome power and His good will for the people.

After the seven years of abundance had come to an end, the seven years of famine began just as Joseph had said it would. There was famine in all of the other countries, but in the whole land of Egypt there was plenty food. Egypt had become Gods earthly storehouse for the rest of the known world at that time. When the famine had spread throughout the whole land of Egypt, the people cried to Pharaoh for food. Then Pharaoh told the people of Egypt, “Go to Joseph and do what he tells you.” With this statement the Pharaoh once again shows that he had complete trust in Joseph and his ability to handle any situation that would arise.

When the Egyptians and the other people went to Joseph, he opened the storehouses and sold them the grain. Now notice here that Joseph sold the grain, he didn’t just give it away. Although he may have given grain away to some of the poorer people of Egypt who had no money, the Bible does not state this as fact.

By selling the grain to the people, he made the Pharaoh and his country very wealthy. All of the surrounding countries came to Egypt to buy grain from Joseph, because the famine was so severe. By selling grain to other countries, and meeting the many different people’s needs, Joseph was able to testify to them concerning the reality of the true God that he worshiped honored. Joseph, more than anyone else in Egypt, would have had the greatest opportunity to explain what God had done for him, and for the land of Egypt.

-4-

JOSEPH'S BROTHERS GO TO EGYPT

Jacob and his family were still living in Canaan at the time of the famine. Even though they were godly people and they worshiped the Lord, they to as well as everyone else were feeling the effects of the terrible famine that was griping their country. No one in the family seemed to know what to do to relieve their distress over the famine. But that would soon change for the better. God was starting to work in their lives just as He had worked in Joseph's life.

As time passed and the famine in the land grew more severe, the family's supply of grain was running very low. Jacob knew that the family could not hold out much longer without grain for food, and for livestock feed. There is no doubt that the severity of the problem was weighing heavily on the mind of Jacob. One day he said to his sons. "I have heard that there is grain in Egypt. Go down there and buy some for us so that we may live and not die."

So it came to pass that, Jacob sent Josephs ten brothers down to Egypt to buy grain, but he did not send Josephs younger brother Benjamin with them. Jacob feared for Benjamin's life more than he did for his own, and with good reason. He could not bear the thought of having something terrible happen to, his youngest son Benjamin. He did not want a repeat of what had happened to Joseph his other beloved son. As far as Jacob knew, Joseph was dead, and Benjamin was the only remaining son of his beloved Rachel, who had died giving birth to Benjamin. It is now at this point in the story that the dreams of Joseph will start to come true.

When Joseph's brothers arrived in Egypt, it was probably early in the day and they went directly to where they could purchase the grain that they so badly needed. It was then that they were told that, they would have to go before the overseer of the country before they could buy any grain. This was because; he was the only one who had total control over everything that the country sold to anyone. No other person was allowed to sell anything in Egypt. Not even a stick of wood.

As the brothers came before the overseer to buy their grain, they bowed down low to him with their faces to the ground. This was done out of respect because of Josephs high position. When the brothers bowed down before Joseph, it was then that he remembered the dreams that God had given him twenty years earlier. But the brothers would not be reminded of the dreams because they didn't recognize who he was until much later. God was starting to fulfill Joseph's dreams to the letter.

When Joseph saw his brothers for the first time, his heart must have just about jumped out of his chest with over whelming joy and excitement. There is no doubt that, he would have loved to put his arms around each one of them and tell them who he really was but, he dared not to do it because of his high position. He would have to reveal himself to them in a private meeting some other time. So he pretended not to know them.

In the twenty years that had passed between them, their appearances had not changed too much. This was because they had been near their middle age when they had sold Joseph to the caravan of traders, and by that time in their life their features were more or less set.

However, his brothers on the other hand would not recognize Joseph for several reasons. (1) He was only seventeen when they last seen him. Now he was twenty years older, and possibly much taller. His body would now be more physically developed than it would have been at seventeen, (2) His whole body was now clean shaven, and he would possibly be wearing a wig or a hair piece, that hung down from the top of his head to the side of his face, and on to his shoulder. This was the custom of all Egyptian males. Egyptians considered hair on the face and on the body as unclean. (3) He was wearing Egyptian clothing, which would cause him to appear to be an Egyptian. (4) He spoke the Egyptian language fluently. (5) When he spoke to his brothers, it was through an interpreter, although he understood them perfectly. He wanted to appear to be a stranger to his brothers because; he wanted to question them about his younger brother Benjamin and his father Jacob whom he loved very deeply.

When Joseph spoke to his brothers, he spoke to them in a very harsh tone of voice, so he could keep his identity hidden from them. He said to them: "Where do you come from?" "From the land of Canaan to buy food;" they replied. As Joseph was remembering his dreams and how his brothers had reacted to them, he let go of all of his pent-up feelings and he said to them; "You are spies! You have come to see where our land is unprotected. He called them spies to put fear into their hearts and to calm his own anger and frustrations.

Joseph was also testing them at this time to see if they had changed their ways for the better. He was curious to see if they still held the bitter hatred in their hearts as they had done so long ago. But his brothers answered and said: "No my lord, your servants have come to buy food." Unwittingly, Joseph's brothers had once again fulfilled his dreams, coupled with their own scornful fears. He wanted to see in the worst way, if they would start to blame each other for their present situation when, they were under the extreme pressure of his authority.

Then one of his brothers said to Joseph: "We are all the sons of one man. Your servants are honest men and not spies." Then Joseph repeated his threat and he called them spies again. He wanted to see if his brothers would volunteer any further information about their family. Joseph was trying so desperately to find out about his younger brother Benjamin who he loved very much. But his brothers replied; "Your servants were twelve brothers the sons of one man, who lives in the land of Canaan. The youngest is now with our father, and one is no more."

When Joseph's younger brother Benjamin was mentioned, Joseph had a great deal of difficulty in hiding his feelings. The compelling desire to ask more questions about the well being of his younger brother was indeed, an over-whelming and a tremendous strain on Joseph's nerves. He feared that if he continued to question his brothers further, his deep heart-felt emotions might give away his identity. That was the one thing that he did not want to do at this particular time.

The words that probably hurt his heart the most at that time were when, they said; "One was no more." But little did the brothers realize that the one who was supposed to be "no more," was standing right in front of them. There is no doubt however; that by now there was an overwhelming sense of fear and dread, that had overcome the brothers and it more than likely showed on their faces as well. They were like an open book to Joseph.

There were two main reasons for their tremendous fear. The first reason was because of the accusation that they were spies. The second reason was just as devastating, but it was more frustrating than anything. It was the fact that they were seemly unable to convince this governor of their good intentions. It seemed to them that this governor would not change his mind no matter what they said. They did not know how they were ever going to convince this man that they were only there to buy food for their families. They must have also realized by now that if they were found out to be spies, this man had the power to execute them on the spot.

But then Joseph said to them: "It is as I spoke to you, saying 'you are spies!" They must have thought that they were walking dead men. They had tried everything in their power to convince this Egyptian of who they were, and why they had come. So now they waited to hear their death sentence that they were so sure was coming. In their minds they were already dead and with no hope of life because, this angry Egyptian overseer still appeared to be so angry with them.

Joseph said to them: "this is how you will be tested. As surely as Pharaoh Lives, you will not leave this place unless your youngest brother comes here. Send one of you to get your brother. The rest of you will be kept in prison, so that your words may be tested, to see if you are telling the truth. If you are not, then as surely as Pharaoh Lives, you are spies!" The most solemn oaths at that time were pronounced in the name of the reigning monarch or of the Lord Himself.

Then he put them all in custody for three days. Joseph probably did this to show his brothers what could happen to them, or possibly to demonstrate his authority and power over them. However it was indeed an opportune time for Joseph to pay them back for the treatment that he had received from them if, that was what he desired. But it is more likely that, he just wanted to be near them so he could observe their actions for a while without them knowing it. By putting them in prison, the brothers would get a taste of what it was like to be treated as a criminal, or to have the fear of what it was like to be thrown into a cistern as they had done to him. They would also have time to reflect and ponder over their past mistakes.

While they were in prison, one of the brothers said to the others: "Surely we are being punished because of our brother. Now we must give an accounting for his blood." Now the brothers started to realize that they were going to reap what they had sown. When Joseph heard this, he went into his house so that his brothers would not see him weep. He was unable to control his emotions any longer because; his heart was so heavy with pain for the brothers that he loved so much.

After the three days had passed, Joseph went to the prison to speak to his brothers. He was going to release them after he had given them further instructions, as to what they were supposed to do. Through an interrupter, he still spoke to them in a rough and authoritative manner, so he could maintain his disguise. He said to them: "Do this and you will live, for I fear God. If you are honest men, let one of your brothers stay here in prison, while the rest of you go and take grain back for your starving households. But you must bring your youngest brother to me, so that your words may be verified and that you may not die."

When Joseph told his brothers that he feared God, he gave them a little bit of a clue, as to who he really was. But his brothers did not recognize the clue because of their great fear of him. They did not realize that the Egyptians at that time did not worship the true God of Heaven and Earth.

Then Joseph took Simeon the second oldest brother hostage, and bound him right there before their eyes. This was to show his authority and that he meant what he said. The reason that he didn't take Reuben, his oldest brother and put him in prison is because it was Reuben who had tried to save Josephs life when his other brothers tried to kill him. So it wouldn't have been fair to Reuben to have to suffer in prison for the acts or the sins of the other brothers.

After Simeon was led away to prison, Joseph gave orders to his men to fill his brother's sacks with grain. But he also secretly, told his men to put each mans silver back in his sack without them knowing about it. By returning the silver to their sacks, Joseph was reassuring himself, that his brothers would make another return trip back, and they would be able to buy more grain to feed their families. He didn't know how rich or how poor his brothers were. Plus, he didn't know how small, or how large their families were. He wanted to make sure that they would return. He wanted desperately to see his youngest brother Benjamin. After they had filled their sacks with grain, they loaded the sacks on their donkeys and departed for their home back in Canaan.

It was about a three-day journey, from Egypt to their home in Canaan. After they had made a long day's journey, they stopped for the night to rest and to feed their donkeys. When one of them opened his sack to get feed for his donkey, he saw his silver pouch in the mouth of his sack. He ran to his brothers and showed them that all of his silver was still in the pouch. So then each one of the brothers looked in their sacks and found their silver also. Then they began to tremble with fear. They said to one another: "What is this that God has done to us?" They had no one else to blame, so they had to blame God for all of their troubles and misfortunes.

But if you stop and think about it for a second or two, these brothers were no different than the people of today! When the people of this day and age have a lot of problems and sorrows, the first one they blame is God. Not themselves. They think that God has caused all of their troubles, and they had nothing to do with it. But the human race could not be further from the truth of the matter. Everything that you do in life has its own set of consequences that tags along with it, be it good or bad.

God only permits problems to come into our lives, so that we will come to Him for the solutions. When we ask Him for His help, He will always hear us with no exceptions. So take your troubles and heartaches to the Lord. He will relieve you of all your stress, your problems, and all of your aches and pains. But you must lay your problems down before the Lord in true repentance; read His word, believe it and obey it, and let Him work out the solutions for you. When God presents you with a problem, He will always give you a way out of it. So take Him at His word because He is only trying to mold and refine your character and make you into the person that He wants you to be. Sometimes He may take something from you, or put you somewhere else where you don't want to be but it, is only because He has something better for you in the future.

Jesus said in (Mt.11-28) "Come to me, all you who are weary and burdened, and I will give you rest." This is Gods promise to you, it is not mans promise to you that can and will be broken most of the time. So try Him out and see what He does. You can talk to God just like you are talking to anyone. You will not be disappointed no matter what comes your way.

Now the brothers had something else to worry about and to stew over because: if, only one of them had gotten their silver back, then it could have been classed as an oversight, or a mistake. But as it was, they all were in possession of their own silver that they had taken to Egypt. Now, if the Egyptians caught them, it would look like the silver was stolen and that they had gotten away with it. They could all be charged with stealing and be executed on the spot. They must have been absolutely terrified and looking over their shoulders, and listening for the sound of Egyptian chariots behind them all of the way home.

When the brothers arrived back at their home, they related everything to their father Jacob, and they told him all that had happened to them while they were in Egypt. Without leaving out any details, they said to Jacob: "The man who is lord over the land, spoke harshly to us, and treated us as though we were spying on the land. But we said to him: 'we are honest men we are not spies. We told him that we were twelve brothers, sons of one father. One is no more, and the youngest is now with our father in Canaan. Then the man who is lord over the land said to us. "This is how I will know whether you are honest men: Leave one of your brothers here with me, and take food for your starving households and go. But bring your youngest brother to me, so I will know that you are not spies but honest men. Then I will give your brother back to you, and you can trade in the land."

After they had finished explaining to their father about their harrowing trip to Egypt, the brothers proceeded to empty their sacks of grain. There in each mans sack was his pouch of silver, which they showed to their father. Then they became more afraid than ever. They did not know what would happen to them when they returned to Egypt a second time. They would certainly have to go back to Egypt again to get more food, and to get their other brother Simeon who, was being held hostage in prison.

When Jacob saw the pouches of silver, he became very depressed and angry. He blamed his remaining sons, for the great lose of his other two sons. He said to them "You have deprived me of my children, Joseph is no more, and Simeon is no more, and now you want to take Benjamin." His whole world seemed to be wrapped up in his two youngest sons, Joseph and Benjamin, and now his world was crumbling right before his eyes.

It was almost unbearable to even think of giving up his last remaining son of his beloved Rachel. His old heart was breaking inside of him. In his anger he said: "My son will not go down there with you; his brother is dead, and he is the only one left. If harm comes to him on the journey you are taking, you will bring my gray head down to the grave in sorrow." Jacob felt that he would die of a broken heart. These were indeed the words of a man who simple could not stand the thought of loosing another son.

So what were the other brothers to do? They knew that they had to return to Egypt. Now, the one thing that they needed the most seemed impossible to get also. Their father didn't want to let them take Benjamin with them because, he feared for Benjamin's life. The brothers felt that it would probably take days or even weeks to convince their father that this is the way it had to be. They were given no other choice in the matter. Once again Reuben who was the oldest son stepped forward to save another brother. This time it was Simeon, he was trying to save from certain death, just as he had done with Joseph.

Then Reuben came up with a plan so that they could possibly get their father to change his mind. He said to his father: "Entrust him to my care and I will bring him back. If I do not bring him back, then you may put my two sons to death." Can you imagine just what he was saying; he was volunteering to sacrifice his own two son's lives to save his Brother Simeon's life? Reuben must have loved his brother Simeon very much, or that he was positive that he could accomplish what he said he would do. He would protect Benjamin at the cost of his own life if need be.

But Jacob still remained stubborn and would not change his mind at that point in time. It seemed that his mind was made up forever, and he was not going to change it no matter what his sons said or did. But time, was not a luxury that Jacob had on his side to be able to ponder the problem that he was facing for very long. He knew in his heart that, he would have to make a decision sooner or later.

As time went on, the family's food supply was getting very low once again and they could no longer afford to sit around and let Jacob ponder his problem any longer. Finely, Jacob said to his sons: "Go back to Egypt and buy us a little more food." Now, the test of the two wills could no longer be permitted to continue their struggle against each other. The will of Jacob the father and the will of the sons of Jacob who, had to do what they were required to do. Just as the people in the ancient world had to make hard choices, so it is the same for people in today's world. There is no difference. You have a choice to make. You can do God the Fathers Will who can give you eternal Life, or you can follow your own will and the will of the world and go to "Hell with Satan." The choice is all yours and no one can make it for you.

It appears at this point from scripture that, Judah was becoming the spokesman for the rest of the brothers. Judah said to his father Jacob. "The man warned us solemnly, 'you will not see my face again unless your brother is with you." If you will send our brother along with us, we will go down and buy food for you. But if you will not send him, we will not go down, because of what the man said to us."

So now Jacob, or "Israel" as the Bible now calls him, because God had changed his name earlier in life, had to make the choice. But he still complained bitterly and said: "Why did you bring this trouble on me by telling the man you had another brother?" Judah replied and said: "The man asked us pointedly, about ourselves and our family saying: 'is your father still alive? Have you another brother'?" The brothers had no choice but to tell the truth at that time. Then they said: "How could we have possibly known that he would say: 'Bring your brother down?" Jacob was still blaming his sons for all of his troubles and he was still very angry with them, because he had been put in such a terrible position. But the choice had to be made. Jacob did not realize at the time, that God was working out His wonderful plan to reunite his family once again, and turn his deep sorrow into unbelievable joy.

As the days passed by quickly, still they argued back and forth with the same old argument with the same old result. Finely, Judah said to his father: "Send the lad with me because if you do not, then we and you and our little ones will die. I myself will be responsible for him. If I do not bring him back to you, then let me bear the blame forever. For if we had not lingered, (argued for days) by now we would have returned the second time." Israel knew in his heart, that he had only one choice to make, and that was to let his sons take Benjamin back to Egypt with them. Now Israel could argue no longer with his sons.

So he said to them, "If it must be so, then do this. As a present for the man, take the best fruit, some balm, spices, honey, myrrh, pistachio nuts, and almonds. Take double the money (silver) plus the money that was returned in your sacks. Perhaps it was an oversight. Also, you can take your brother Benjamin with you. May God Almighty give you mercy before the man, and release your other brother and Benjamin." After some preparation, all of the brothers departed on their second journey back to Egypt. There is no doubt that when the brothers departed this time, they left their homes and their families with, a great deal of fear and doubt in their hearts and minds. The fact that the bags of silver that they had found in their sacks when they had returned home the first time, was probably still weighing heavily on their minds They had no way of knowing what to expect now, from the man that they would soon come face to face with once more. The brothers were truly caught between a rock and a hard place.

They had every right in the world, to worry and to fret over, what they thought might happen to them in the near future. But all they could do for the present time was to sweat it out, and no doubt they prayed a lot too. It probably never crossed the brother's minds for a moment that God was controlling the whole situation, and that God would work things out in His own time, and in His own way. God and His plan, was the furthest thing from their minds.

It was early in the morning, when the brothers arrived in Egypt for the second time. This time they wasted no time with idle chitchat with the people of the land. They knew for certain where they had to go, and whom they had to see. So without any other thoughts what so ever, they went directly to the man that they feared the most; it was Joseph the overseer whom they did not recognize.

As far as they were concerned, he was the one and only man who held life and death in his hands. By his command they could all be killed or sold as slaves and all of their possessions confiscated. As they approached Joseph this time, and they told him who they were, he could hardly hold back the tears of joy that he felt as he recognized his younger brother Benjamin. So he excused himself from their presence, and he went to the steward of his house and said to him,

"Take these men to my home, and slaughter an animal and make ready, for these men will dine with me at noon." When the brothers heard this they could not understand what was happening to them. It appeared that this man, who held their life in his hands, had a complete change of heart. They could scarcely believe what they were hearing. On their first trip to Egypt, this man treated them as spies and criminals. Now on this second trip, they were being invited into this man's home to dine with him. It was just too much for their minds to comprehend.

So without the slightest hesitation, the steward did as he was instructed to do by Joseph. As the brothers came near Josephs home around noon, they became frightened and upset again. They thought that they were going to be punished for the crime of stealing the silver that they had found in their sacks of grain. So they confessed to the steward the whole story, about what had happened to them on the previous trip. They swore up and down, that they were totally innocent of any criminal act.

To make matters even more confusing, they were amazed at the reply that they received from the steward when he spoke to them in reply to their fears. He said to them: "Peace be with you! Do not be afraid! You're God and the God of your father has given you treasures in your sacks." The steward had replied to them with a blessing of peace, instead of accusations of stealing. The steward also was expressing his faith in the same God that they and Jacob worshiped. This must have given the brothers some relief as well, but it also left them utterly confused and dismayed.

After they had entered the house, the steward gave them water to wash their feet and feed for their donkeys. When all this was accomplished, the steward brought Simeon their brother who had been held captive, out to meet them. After many greetings and salutations to each other, the brothers prepared the presents that they had brought for Joseph from the land of Canaan. They were still wondering why this man, who had so much power in Egypt, would invite them to dine with him in his home at noon. It was still a big mystery to them.

When Joseph arrived home at noon, everything was ready and waiting for him and his guests to dine. The brothers came and bowed down before him to pay him honor. This was the second time that the brothers had bowed down to Joseph. It was a further fulfillment of Joseph's dreams, and of Gods almighty power. The first question that Joseph asked them was about their health. Then he said: "Is your father well, the old man of whom you spoke? Is he still alive?" They answered and said: "Your servant, our father, is in good health and is still alive." These words alone would have brought a great deal of comfort to the aching and troubled heart of Joseph.

Joseph then looked around and saw his brother Benjamin with them. He said to them: "Is this your younger brother of whom you spoke to me?" Then Joseph said to Benjamin: "God be gracious to you my son." Joseph said this because of the special relationship that had existed, between him and Benjamin when they were together as a family. At this point, Joseph could hardly control his emotions. He was almost overwhelmed with the joy and the happiness that was being contained within his heart. So then Joseph excused himself and hurried out of the room, and he went into his private chambers where he could weep for joy. He had to vent out his emotions without being heard by his household or his brothers. After all, it had been twenty years since he had last seen his brother Benjamin.

After he had settled himself down, and he had regained his composure Joseph washed his face, and came out again, this time in full control of his emotions. It would not look good for him to show such deep emotions in front of his brothers or his servants. It would be a sign of weakness, and it just was not a suitable thing for such a great leader to do. Then he instructed his servants to serve the food.

Joseph still wanted to keep his identity hidden from his brothers, so he continued to use Egyptian customs, such as their eating habits. As you recall, it was an abomination to the point of almost becoming sick to their stomachs, for an Egyptian to eat in the same room with a Hebrew. The Egyptians even shaved the hair from their bodies, where the Hebrews had beards, and did not shave their bodies.

When it came time to eat, they all sat down for the noon meal at different tables. Because of his status, Joseph sat at a table all by himself. Then, all of the Egyptians sat at another table and the Hebrews at a table by themselves. It was during the seating of the Hebrew brothers that a very curious thing happened to them. Joseph made them to sit in a particular order. They were seated according to their age, from the youngest to the oldest. The brothers looked at each other in astonishment. They could not understand, how this man who had invited them to dine with him, could know so much about them. For this man to know their ages, it seemed to be an impossible feat.

When the food was served, Benjamin was given five times more food to eat then the others. It was not customary to receive extra portions of food, unless you were a very special person, or you were held in very high esteem by the host. The special treatment that Benjamin received also reflects the special relationship between Joseph and Benjamin. This kind of special treatment was something else that, the brothers had to marvel at and to wonder about.

Even though they were curious, about the way things were happening, they kept it to themselves and dared not ask any questions of this man. It was better for them to remain silent for the present than, too open their mouths and be convicted of some wrong statement that they might make. The scriptures in (Pr.17: 28) states that, even a fool is thought wise and discerning if he keeps silent and holds his tongue. So they remained silent and enjoyed their meal to the delight and pleasure of their host.

After everyone had finished the meal and the brothers were well rested, Joseph gave orders to his steward to fill their sacks with as much food and grain as they could carry, and to send them on their way back home with his blessing. But Joseph still wanted to test the character of his brothers. He gave further instructions to his steward and said; "Put each mans silver in the mouth of his sack. Also put my cup, the silver cup, in the mouth of the sack of the youngest, and his grain money." So the steward did as he was instructed to do by Joseph.

At dawn the next morning, the brothers set off for their home in Canaan. Shortly after the brothers had left the city, Joseph said to his steward: "Get up, follow the men, and when you overtake them, say to them why, have you repaid evil for good?" Then the steward was to explain to them what he was looking for. It was Josephs silver cup that he practiced divination with. Then the steward was to accuse them of stealing it and then say to them: "This is a wicked thing you have done?" So the steward went after the brothers and he caught up to them within a short period of time. He told them just exactly what Joseph had instructed him to say word for word.

The brothers were completely dismayed and dumb founded by what was happening to them. This was the second time that they were being falsely accused of a very serious crime. They said to the steward: "Why does my lord say such a thing? Far be it from your servants to do anything like that. We even brought back to you, the silver that we had found in our sacks the first time when we returned to Canaan. So why would we steal silver or gold from your masters house?"

To further prove their innocence, they made a very bold statement and said: "If any of your servants is found to have it, he will die: and the rest of us will become my lord's slaves. It was then that the steward softened the penalty contained in the brother's proposal. He said to them; "Very well, then, let it be as you say." Whoever is found to have it, will become my slave; the rest of you will be free from blame."

Then each of them unloaded their donkeys and placed their sacks of grain on the ground for inspection by the steward. As the steward started to search the sacks, he began with the oldest and worked his way to the youngest. It was there that he found the cup, in Benjamin's sack as well as the silver. When they saw this they tore their clothes, in an expression, of distress and grief because, now they would have to keep the bargain that they had just struck with the steward. So with hearts and minds that were heavy with fear, and frustration, they loaded up their donkeys once more and went back to the city with the steward. Josephs plan had worked to perfection.

Joseph was still in the house when his steward and his brothers returned, and the steward reported to Joseph what had happened. The brothers threw themselves to the ground before him. This was a further fulfillment of Joseph's dreams. Then Joseph removed any thoughts that they might have been entertaining concerning a plot against them by saying; "What is this you have done? Don't you know that a man like me can find things out by divination?" (Divination is the art or practice, that seeks to foresee or foretell future events or, by the aid of supernatural powers such as the will of the gods.)

Then Judah took it upon himself once again to be the spokesman for his brothers and he said to Joseph: "What can we say to my lord? What can we say? How can we prove our innocence? God has uncovered your servant's guilt, and we as well as the one who had the cup, are now your slaves. It was at this point that Judah realized that God must have been in control of everything that was happening to them and he offered no excuses. It was not just by chance, that all of this trouble had come upon them, and they were at their wits end. There was no way, or no place for them to turn to except to God Himself.

Then Joseph said: "Far be it from me to do such a thing! Only the man who was found to have the cup will become my slave. The rest of you, go back to your father in peace." This was a further test, put to the brothers by Joseph. He wanted to see if they would leave their youngest brother Benjamin as a slave in Egypt, as they had done to him twenty years before. As for the brothers, Joseph's words must have been especially bitter. They knew that they dared not return home without their younger brother Benjamin. There would never be any peace in their father's household, if they left Benjamin as a slave in Egypt.

Then Judah came near to Joseph and tried to explain the deep despair that his father would experience if he lost Benjamin. He said to him: "Please my lord, let your servant speak a word to you and do not be angry with your servant even though you are equal to Pharaoh." These words were intended to be more flattering then true. But by acknowledging Josephs power and by telling him how great he was Judah, might have been trying to use flattery to enhance his position along with his plea for mercy.

Although it was very difficult for Judah, he tried to explain everything back to Joseph that had happened to him and his brothers, up to the present time.

As he was searching for words of clarity, the thought must have crossed his mind that, by repeating the questions that Joseph had asked him and his brothers, it would somehow explain the predicament that they now found themselves in. He said to Joseph: "My lord asked his servants, do you have a father or a brother? We answered: We have an aged father, and there is a young son born to him in his old age. But his brother is dead, and he is the only one of his mother's sons left, and his father loves him."

Then you said: Bring him down to me so I can see him for myself." After much arguing and quarreling, we were able to convince our father that our younger brother had to come with us this time to Egypt. It was because of your orders, and the fact that you had kept our other brother hostage to insure our return here, that he agreed to send Benjamin with us. He did this even though it might kill him if anything should happen to Benjamin. I your servant have guaranteed the boys safety to my father. If I do not bring him back to my father, then I will bear the blame all of my life. So please, let me remain here as your slave instead of the boy, and send him home with his brothers. How can I go back to my father if the boy is not with me? Do not let me see the misery that would come upon my father."

No doubt, Judah was remembering how his father had reacted, when the brothers had told him that his beloved son Joseph was dead. This pleading and begging by Judah was very sincere and to the point. Judah was expressing his great love that he felt for his aged father and for his younger brother Benjamin. He was willing to sacrifice his own life so his brother could go free and return home to his father.

The kind of sacrifice that Judah was willing to make here is, a reflection of the sacrifice that our Lord and Savior Jesus Christ, would be making for the sins of the world centuries into the future. Jesus willingly gave His life on the cross at Calvary, for you and for me so that we can go to Our Father in heaven when we pass from this earth into eternity.

After Judah had finished speaking to Joseph, and expressing such great concern for his father; Joseph could no longer control his emotions. He ordered all of his Egyptian attendants out of his presence, so that there would be no Egyptians with him when he made himself known to his brothers. He wept so loudly that the whole Egyptian Palace heard him. He could not stand the strain of hiding his identity any longer.

After he had controlled his weeping, and he had settled his emotions down to a point of respectability, he went back into the room where his brothers were seated. Then Joseph called his brothers to him, and he announced the best news to them that their ears could have ever heard in years. With a show of great emotion, he told them who he really was. He said to them: "I am Joseph! Is my father still living?"

But his brothers could not answer him immediately because, they were utterly terrified at his presence. Now, what were they to expect next. Was this man lying with some hidden motive behind what he said, or was he telling the truth. They were at a complete loss for words. Joseph must have realized that the reason why they didn't really recognize him was because he was still dressed like an Egyptian.

Also at this time just as before, he spoke to them through an interpreter. Now it was Joseph who would have to prove his identity. The second time that Joseph spoke to them, he spoke to them in Hebrew.

He said: "Come close to me. I am your brother Joseph, the one you sold into Egypt. Do not be distressed or angry with yourselves for selling me here. Because it was to save lives that God sent me ahead of you. For two years there has been a famine in the land. There will be no reaping or plowing for another five years. But God sent me ahead of you to preserve for you a remnant on earth, and to save your lives by a great deliverance. So then, it was not you who sent me here, but God. He made me father to Pharaoh, lord of his entire household and ruler of all Egypt."

Joseph gave all of the credit to God and not to himself, or for anything that he might have done. When Joseph called his brothers a remnant of people, he was in the confidence that they would live to produce a great people. Jacobs's descendants did become a great nation centuries later. They would become the future slaves of the Egyptians.

The over whelming joy that Joseph must have experienced, would have been hard to express in words. After all of the apologies and greetings were over with, Joseph said to his brothers: "Now hurry back to my father and say to him. This is what your son Joseph says: God has made me lord of all Egypt. Come down to me; don't delay! You shall live in the region of Goshen, and are near me. You and all of your children, your grandchildren, and all that you have. I will provide for you there, because five years of famine are still to come. Otherwise you and your entire household will become destitute. You can see for yourselves, and so can my brother Benjamin, that it is really I who am speaking to you."

He was using his brother Benjamin as a witness to prove who he was. It appears that Joseph and Benjamin may have had a long conversation together at some time without the other brothers present. The two, may have spoken to each other of thing in their past that, only they knew about. Then Joseph had a long intimate conversation, with his brothers. It is very possible also that, at this particular time Joseph showed his brothers that he had been circumcised just as they had been when they were eight days old. To further identify who he really was this time, he only spoke to them in their Hebrew language. Now there was no more hostility or fear between them for the first time in over twenty years. There was no reason for the brothers to hang on to any kind of resentment or bitterness any longer.

Then Joseph said: "Tell my father about the entire honor accorded me in Egypt, and about everything you have seen." With a show of great urgency in his voice he said to his brothers, "Bring my father down here quickly." Now it was Josephs turn to wait with anticipation in his heart, and with many questions in his mind that, only his father could answer.

After he had hugged and kissed all of his brothers and he had stopped weeping over them, he talked with them awhile longer. No doubt, they were discussing the events of the past twenty years, when the Pharaoh received the news about Joseph's brothers arriving in Egypt. This news made the Pharaoh and all of his officials very pleased. So now the Pharaoh had an excellent opportunity to express his appreciation and gratitude to Joseph one more time. He sent a messenger from the palace to summons Joseph to his presence. When Joseph arrived at the palace, he went directly into the presence of the Pharaoh in his throne room. After Pharaoh had expressed his joy to Joseph at the news of the arrival of his brothers, he then instructed Joseph as to what he was to tell his brothers to do.

He said to Joseph: "Tell your brothers, do this; Load your animals and take some carts from Egypt, for your children and your wives, and return to the land of Canaan. Never mind about your belongings. Bring your father and your families back to me. I will give you the best of the land of Egypt, and you can enjoy the fat of the land." So Joseph did exactly as the Pharaoh commanded him and He gave his brothers provisions for their journey home.

To each of them, he gave new clothing. But to Benjamin, he gave five sets of clothing, and three hundred shekels of silver. To his beloved father, he sent ten donkeys, loaded with the best thing of Egypt. Also, he sent another ten female donkeys loaded with grain and bread and other provisions for his journey back to Egypt.

After all of the preparations were completed, Joseph sent his brothers on their way back to Canaan. The last command that he gave his brothers as they were leaving was a command that he knew might not be followed. He knew his brothers were a quarrelsome lot. He said to them: "Don't quarrel on the way!" He knew that if his brothers stopped to quarrel and to fight and blame each other for their troubles on their way home, their trip would be unbearable. It would serve no other purpose but to upset them and possibly delay their return to Egypt. Twenty years must have felt like a lifetime to Joseph, but soon he would be able to see his father whom he loved so deeply.

So it was, with some degree of happiness and joy in their hearts, the brothers departed for Canaan, loaded with all of their goods and gifts. This time the brothers made quite a caravan. They were glad to be going home this time because; they had such great news to relate to their father and to their families as well.

But at the same time the brothers must had been a little bit apprehensive as well. Now they would have to tell their father the whole truth about their brother Joseph, and that he was still alive and well. He was not dead as they had lied and said he was before. This terrible lie that they had been packing around in their hearts, and had to live with for twenty years was, about to find them out, as it eventually does to anyone who tells lies. Lies are the work of Satan because he is the father of all lies big or small. There is no such thing as a little white lie and God hates any kind of liar.

There would be no more trips to Egypt for food because, now their families and everything that they possessed would be moving to Egypt, to the land of plenty. All of their families and everything that they possessed would be saved from the famine that was to last another five years. God in His grace and mercy had protected and saved each and every one of His people.

When the small caravan reached home, the brothers began to tell their story to their father Jacob and to their families. Jacob must have had a hard time listening to his sons tell their story because; they all seemed to be talking at once and with great excitement. But soon their excitement and enthusiasm seemed to fade quite abruptly and for no apparent reason.

It was not until after Jacob had asked a few questions, and they had been answered to some degree of satisfaction, that he might have suspected that there was something else on the minds and hearts of his sons. There was something that they had been holding back because; they seemed quite ill at ease. It was also very apparent that, the brothers could not find the right words to express just what they wanted to say to him. But as it was, his sons had been holding back the best news until the very last. However, this good news had a dark side to it as well. It would finally reveal to their father, the awful lie that they had perpetrated some twenty years earlier, about the death of Joseph, the favorite son of Jacob.

But as the minutes went by slowly, they couldn't hold back the horrendous news any longer. Finally, with some hesitation in his voice, Judah spoke up and let out the good news. He said: "Joseph is still alive! In fact, he is the ruler of all Egypt." What a bombshell to drop on an old man of one hundred and thirty years old. Although it was good news to Jacob, he was utterly stunned and you could have knocked him over with a feather. The news was so stunning that He did not and could believe them.

He probably asked them if this was the truth, or just another lie that they had come up with to test his old heart? If the brothers had lied once before, it would be reasonable to assume that they could also lie again. His old heart must have almost stopped beating. It had been over twenty years since he had heard of his beloved son's death, and now his ears are hearing such unbelievable news. His son was alive, and to top it all off, he was a ruler of all Egypt. What tremendous news the Lord had just blessed him with. It was a blessing that he would never be able to forget.

However; he was not fully convinced that it was the whole truth until, they had told him of what Joseph had said, and he seen the carts that Joseph had sent to carry him and his belongs back to Egypt. Only then, did he believe their story. Then Jacob said: "I am convinced! My son Joseph is still alive. I will go and see him before I die." From that time on Jacobs's spirit was revived and he gave praise and thanks to God for His faithfulness. God has blessed Jacob beyond his wildest dreams, and now at last, he had a greater hope for the future to come. Now God is about to reunite Jacob and his beloved son Joseph once again, and never to be separated only in death.

-5-

JACOBS FAMILY MOVES TO EGYPT

After many days of preparation, Jacob, and his sons, along with their families departed for Egypt. The journey to Egypt would be a long slow, process because of the many flocks and herds of animals that they would have to contend with. But to Jacob, it would seem like an eternity because, he was very anxious to see his son Joseph.

Some days had passed the caravan reached the place called Beersheba. It was here that the caravan of Jacob also stopped to rest for a while from their journey to Egypt. This site had been very important to both his grandfather and to his father because; they too had offered sacrifices to God at this particular place. So it was here that, Jacob also offered a sacrifice and to consecrate his family to God before leaving the Promised Land. But in essence it would be a four hundred thirty year sojourn away from the Promised Land of Canaan for Jacob and his family.

When Jacob entered Egypt, his whole family would be reunited once again, under Gods guidance and mercy. His family at that time consisted of seventy people in all, but this number doesn't include the son's wives. The number seventy was regarded by the ancient Israelites as a token of Gods special blessing on them. From the family of Jacob, the nation of Israel would be born.

However; it seems from the scriptures that Jacob may have had some misgivings and doubts about going to Egypt because, he had no way of knowing for sure just what would happen to him and his family while they were in Egypt. But if it were true that his son Joseph was indeed in control of the land of Egypt, then he would have nothing to fear. It is much the same story today for many people who move to different countries to start a new life with their families. They too must feel that their future is uncertain at best, but they must think of the future of their families in the years to come and not just for themselves at that present point in time.

But as it happened in the case of Jacobs's family, he had no doubt placed everything in the hands of the Lord who, was working in their daily lives to bring about His plans for the nation of Israel. God was fulfilling His promise to Abraham to build Israel and His people into a mighty nation. God is now setting the stage for Moses and the great Exodus centuries far into the future.

Now God speaks to Jacob for the seventh time in his long life. One night as Jacob lay on his bed he fell into a deep sleep. While he was sleeping, God spoke to him in a vision. God said to Jacob: "Jacob! Jacob!" Here I am" Jacob replied. Then God said: "I am God, the God of your father; do not be afraid to go down to Egypt, for I will make you into a great nation there. I will go down to Egypt with you, and I will surely bring you back again, and Josephs own hand will close your eyes." To further comfort Jacob, God also promised to go with His people even into the foreign land of Egypt.

This promise is positive proof from God and to anyone else in the world today that, once you have accepted the Lord Jesus Christ as your own personal Savior and Lord, He seals you with the Holy Spirit. From that time on, your name will be written in the Lambs Book of Life and you are His child now and forever throughout all eternity. He will never forsake you or leave you for the rest of your life. The Bible says that He will stick closer to you than a brother.

The last part of Gods promise to Jacob, probably meant a great deal more to him than he wanted to admit because, of the great love that he had for his son Joseph. God promised Jacob, that his beloved son Joseph would be with him at his deathbed. With this God given assurance Jacob, knew that he would be well cared for in Egypt. Now his worries were over, and he could be content and happy, and have the peace of mind that he longed for so much. He knew that without a doubt, God would do just exactly what He said He would do. God has now reaffirmed one aspect of His promise to Abraham.

Also, God has now told Jacob of his death in Egypt, and that He would return him to the Promised Land after his death. Now Jacob could continue his journey to Egypt with peace of mind and with great joy in his heart. With the prospect of seeing his son Joseph for the first time in decades, he pushed on with the renewed strength that God had given him.

Many days have passed now since Jacob and his people had left Canaan, and as the large caravan of people and animals were slowly approaching the boarder of Egypt, Jacob sent his son Judah ahead of him to speak Joseph, so he could get the directions to the Land of Goshen. When the caravan came into the Land of Goshen, Joseph made his chariot ready, and went out to meet Jacob his father.

As soon as Joseph came before Israel he threw his arms around him and wept for a long time. That is how it was, when Joseph, one of the greatest leaders of Egypt, came to meet his family at Goshen where they were to settle. While the two embraced each other, they shed many tears of joy and gave thanks to God for this, the greatest reunion of their lives. After the two of them had dried their tears of joy, Jacob said to Joseph: "Now let me die, since I have seen your face, because you are still alive." This reunion with his son Joseph was one of the crowning events that God gave to Jacob in his long and eventful life.

Although Jacob would have been willing to die and give up his life at that particular time, it was not to happen. God was not finished with Jacob just yet. He had many more blessings to bestow upon him in the years to come. One of the greatest blessings that God had bestowed on Jacob was; the blessing of being able to see his two new grandchildren, and to be able to watch them grow up and to enjoy their company for the many years that were to come. But the greatest blessing of all was the fact that, he now had his whole family together again and he could enjoy the company of his favorite son Joseph once more. God had been very good to him in spite of all of the troubles and heartaches that he had suffered and had to endure in the past years of his life. God would enable Jacob to do this very thing for another seventeen years.

I am quite certain that Jacob must have felt the same way as the people of today do, concerning their children, and their grandchildren. There are but a few words that can really express the love and high esteem that, children are held in the peoples' hearts and lives of today. Your children and your grandchildren are one of Gods richest blessings to the people of all ages.

Now the time has come for Joseph to once again demonstrate the great leadership ability that God had blessed him with throughout his life. He accomplished many of his goals, by maintaining a genuine respectful attitude to those in authority. He also used his great skill in making suggestions to his counselors. Therefore, by having knowledge of the customs of the people, it was easy for him to govern the people.

As Joseph continued to speak to Jacob his father and his entire household: he said; "I will go up and speak to Pharaoh and will say to him: my brothers and those of my father's household, who were living in the land of Canaan, have come to me. The men are shepherds; and they have brought along their flocks and herds and everything they own. When Pharaoh calls you in and he asks you, 'what is your occupation?' 'You should answer: 'your servants have tended livestock from our boyhood on, just as our fathers did. Then you will be allowed to settle in the region of Goshen."

In this indirect way of speaking and telling them what he was going to say to Pharaoh; Joseph was coaching his brothers and his father, as to what they were to say to the great Pharaoh, and how they were to act in his presence. He didn't want his brothers or his father to feel the least bit embarrassed, ashamed, or uncomfortable in the presence of the Pharaoh and his officials. Joseph knew that by custom shepherds were detested by the Egyptian people, and they didn't want to have anything to do with them. They would avoid them like a plague if it were possible.

God used this racial and ethnic prejudice of the Egyptians as a way of preserving the ethnic and spiritual identity of His own people. Jacobs's family had already intermarried with some of the Canaanites, and His people were in danger of losing their identity as Gods people. God always wants the best of everything for His people. So He separated His people from the Egyptians and placed them in the best land in Egypt, in the land of Goshen. God had accomplished all of this through the Pharaoh before Jacobs's family had come to Egypt. As you can see, God used the great Pharaoh, to further benefit and to bless His people. God gave them the best land in Egypt. Nothing is ever too good for Gods people to have and enjoy to the fullest.

The land of Goshen is an area located in the eastern part of the Nile Delta and it is a very fertile land, and it remains so today. It is well watered and is ideally suited for shepherds and their livestock. It was in this region, that another Great Pharaoh, "Rameses the II", would build the great City of "Rameses" But the building of this great city, would not take place until centuries later, when the Egyptian people would use the Hebrew people, as slaves to build it. This area was also known as the "Region of Zoan"

When all of the celebrations were completed and things had settled down to some form of normality. Joseph chose five of his brothers, and presented them before Pharaoh. The Pharaoh did exactly as Joseph had said that he would do. He asked them their occupation. The brothers replied to the Pharaoh in the same manner as Joseph had instructed them to do. But they added a little bit more of an explanation then the one Joseph had mentioned. They said: "Your servants are shepherds, just as our fathers were. We have come to live here for a while, because the famine is so severe in Canaan, and we have no pasture for our flocks. So please, let your servants settle in Goshen."

Pharaoh then said to Joseph: "Your father and your brothers have come to you, and the land of Egypt is before you. Settle your father and your brothers in the best part of the land. Let them live in Goshen. Now the family of Jacob had the full blessing of the Pharaoh and they could settle down to a life of peace and quiet. They would no longer have to fear for their family's safety or for the food that they needed. Josephs plan had worked perfectly, because God Himself had engineered and directed it through His love and grace for Joseph.

By adopting an attitude of humility and humbleness, and stating that they were shepherds from the time that they were young, it earned the brothers an add bonus from the Pharaoh. He said to Joseph: "If you know of any among them with special ability, put them in charge of my own livestock." To be put in the position of head shepherd and overseer of the

Pharaohs livestock, that person would have to assume a great deal of responsibility. But on the other hand, it would carry with it some big advantages and a few other perks as well. That person would have the best of everything that Egypt had to offer. This was another great blessing from God that He had bestowed upon Jacobs family.

Shortly after Joseph had presented his brothers to the Pharaoh, he brought his father Jacob to meet the Pharaoh. This meeting probably would have had more of a party like atmosphere then it had been when Joseph had brought his brothers before Pharaoh. The big difference between the two meetings was because, this time, the Pharaoh was the host. He would no doubt want to make a big impression on the father of his chief overseer as well, so he could prove his good intentions to Joseph. So it had to be a special event with a great deal of fan-fare and dancing. The Pharaoh might have also entertained the thought in his mind of pronouncing a special blessing on Jacob because of his great admiration for Joseph. But instead, the visitor blessed the host in the name of the living God. Literally speaking, Jacob was fulfilling Gods promise to Abraham and his descendants, "to be a blessing to other people."

During the course of the many conversations that went on at the party, Pharaoh recognized the fact that Jacob was very old, and that the years of living in the desert had not been overly kind to him. So he asked Jacob saying: "how old are you?" This was a fitting question to put to a man of Jacobs years. The long years of the patriarchal family were truly exceptional, even for this period of time in history. Jacob responded to the Pharaoh in all honesty and humility. He had experienced sadness as well as evil throughout his lifetime. The years of rivalry with his brother Esau, and the struggles that he had with Laban, had marked the early part of his life with sadness. These kinds of troubles had not made life very pleasurable for him. To add to his misery and discomfort, for long years he had grieved the supposed death of his favorite son Joseph.

He said to the Pharaoh: “The days of the years of my pilgrimage, are one hundred and thirty years. Few and evil have been the days and the years of my life.” He was recognizing the fact that maybe his life was coming to a close. He couldn’t expect to live as long as his father Isaac, who was one hundred eighty years old when he died. Likewise, his grandfather Abraham died when he was one hundred and seventy-five years old. After Jacob had pronounced his blessing on the Pharaoh he left the palace and went home to his family in Goshen.

So now Gods chosen family of seventy people were safe and sound in Egypt. They would be living in the best part of Egypt and under the watchful eye of God, and His chosen caretaker, Joseph. It was Joseph who would see that Jacobs’s family would have all things that they needed, no matter what it was. God would see to their spiritual needs, and Joseph would see to their physical needs. What a combination that was. Jacobs’s family would no longer be threatened by the possibility of starvation. Each family received enough food so they could feed each member of their family and their livestock without the fear of hunger hanging over their heads.

It was near the end of the second year of the famine when, Jacob and his family moved to Egypt. There were five years out of the seven years still remaining, as God had promised. By the end of the second year the famine was very severe in both Canaan and in the land of Egypt. Both countries were made desolate by the famine. Nothing would grow, and the people cried to Joseph for help.

By the time the third year of the famine, was over the people of Egypt and Canaan had used up all of their money to buy their food. Their money had failed them, just like it does too many people in this day and age. It had vanished like the desert wind. Our money of today will do the same thing, if we worship it instead of God. The word money in this context refers to weights of silver and gold, and not coins or paper as we have today. Money hadn't been invented yet, and it would not come into existence for centuries to come. After Joseph had collected all of the money in both Canaan and in Egypt, he took it to Pharaoh in his palace.

After the people's money was all gone, and their food supply was depleted, they came once again to Joseph for food. They said to Joseph "Give us bread, for why we should die in your presence? For the money has failed." The people had nowhere else to turn and they had no idea what to do. How could they continue to buy grain without money? It was a big problem that they were faced with, and it seemed almost imposable for them to solve it.

Then Joseph gave the people the answer that they were searching for. He said to the people: "If your money is gone bring me your livestock. I will sell you food in exchange for your livestock" There was the answer that the people had been searching for. So the people sold all of their livestock to Joseph, and he brought them through the famine for another year. The following year was much the same as the proceeding years were but, this time it was a little different than before. There was no more money, and now, there was no more livestock left for the people to sell for food. It seemed that the two countries would just self-destruct by themselves.

The people cried to Joseph and said: "We cannot hide from our lord the fact, that since our money is gone, and our livestock belongs to you, there is nothing left for our lord, except our bodies and our land. Why should we perish before your eyes and our land as well? Buy us, and our land, in exchange for food, and our land as well as us, will be in bondage to Pharaoh."

This time the people had come up with a solution and they had given Joseph the answer to their dilemma. But God had probably put this same thought in the back of Josephs mind for quite some time. So Joseph did as the people suggested, and he bought up all of the land in Egypt for the Pharaoh in exchange for food. Joseph then reduced all of the people of Egypt to complete servitude, from one end of Egypt to the other.

Now the Pharaoh had control of all of the money, the land, and the livestock, in the whole country of Egypt and Canaan. Because all of the food had belonged to the Egyptian state, the Pharaoh became very wealthy. Along with this wealth, came a great deal of power. It gave Egypt the power to control the destiny of the two countries of Egypt and that of Canaan.

The Pharaohs ownership of the land would eventually lead to the gross abuses of power by the Pharaohs that were to follow the present Pharaoh after his death. As well as being able to hold all of the people in Egypt and Canaan in total bondage, the great Pharaohs could rule with an iron fist, if they so desired.

This very thing would happen to the Hebrew people many years into the future, after the deaths of Joseph and the present Pharaoh. They would become slaves of the Egyptians, and they would be a whole nation under bondage and persecution. However, there was one exception to the rule, and that exception went to the Priests of the land. They were not required to sell their land to sustain their lives because; they received their regular allotment of food and grain from the Pharaoh. Their allotment was enough to sustain their lives. As an added bonus, they were not required to do any manual work to earn their living.

Meanwhile; as the Egyptian people were selling off their land for food, and becoming poorer; Jacob and his family were acquiring huge tracts of land, and they were becoming wealthier as time went on. Their herds and flocks prospered under God care and protection. They didn't have to worry about food because Joseph supplied their every need. It was Gods way of caring for His chosen people.

After Joseph had bought up all of the land in Egypt, he moved all of the people from the outer regions of the country into the cities. This was to be just a temporary move for them because; it would enable him to control any situations that might cause him problems later on. It would also make it a lot easier for him to distribute the grain to the people for food, and for planting, after the famine was over.

You can see here; how God has instilled great wisdom into the mind of Joseph so that he could see far into the future. This is also further positive proof that God was controlling everything that was happening to Joseph and to the country.

After the seven years of famine had passed, the people come to Joseph for seeds to plant the crops. It was then that Joseph imposed a system of taxation on the people. He said to the people: "Indeed I have bought you and your land for Pharaoh. Look, here is seed for you, and you shell sow the land. But when the harvest comes in, give a fifth of it to Pharaoh. The other four-fifths you may keep as seed for the fields and as food for yourselves and your households, and as food for your little ones."

Then Joseph passed it into law shortly after he had decreed it. This type of taxation was the first of its kind, and I believe that it still could be in effect today, but I am not to clear on the subject of Egyptian law. I cannot see the Egyptian government taking that kind of law off of the books. It would be like killing the goose that laid the golden egg, as the saying goes.

The people were so thankful to Joseph that they were willing to remain in bondage to Pharaoh. It didn't matter to them. As far as the people were concerned Joseph had saved their lives and for that they were extremely grateful. As time went on, God made the land to produce all of the crops once more. God sent the rains and the land produced the crops, with great abundance, so much so, that the people continued to express their gratitude to Joseph. But Joseph continued to express his gratitude and thanks to God for being true and steadfast to His word. The Bible does not mention how many people that Joseph may have converted to believe in God, but it does say that his whole household believed in his God. So that would be a substantial amount of people including all of his servants and their families.

-6-

THE BLESSINGS OF JACOBS SONS

As time slipped away, Jacob was becoming very old and tired, and he realized that his death was drawing near. His health and his eyesight had both been failing him for some time. As you may or may not know, blindness was quite a common occurrence to old people who had lived their lives out in the desert. The blazing sun was hard on their eyes, their skin, and their bodies with no exception.

One day as Joseph was attending to his official duties; a messenger came to him and said to him, "your father is ill." So Joseph quickly gathered up his two sons Manasseh and Ephraim and hurried to the tent of his ageing father. When Jacob heard that his son Joseph had arrived, he rallied his strength and sat up on the bed. Then Jacob said to his son Joseph. "God Almighty, spoke to me at Luz, (or Bethel as Jacob had renamed the place) in the land of Canaan, and He said to me: 'I am going to make you fruitful and will increase your numbers. I will make you a community of peoples, and I will give this land as an everlasting possession to your descendants after you."

This is the first time that Joseph had heard his father speak to him about any kind of covenant that God had made with him and with his forefathers. This was all news to him and somewhat of a mystery as well. As he listened intently to what his father was saying, Jacob continued to explain just what he had to do. He said to Joseph: "Now then, your two sons born to you in Egypt before I came to you here will be reckoned as mine." It must have shocked Joseph to some degree when his father made this kind of statement to him, but for now he would just listen and speak later. As Jacob continued to explain further to Joseph he said:"Any children born to you after them will be yours. In the territory that they inherit, they will be reckoned under the names of their brothers. In this particular scripture, Jacob was foretelling of the division of the Promised Land, by Joshua, to the tribes of Israel centuries into the future.

As you can see, Jacob had to adopt Joseph's two sons, Manasseh and Ephraim, so that they could legally come into the family line of Jacob. In this manner, they would be equal to Jacobs's two older sons Reuben and Simeon. Through adoption, they would each receive equal inheritance rights and privileges, and they would be classed as direct descendants of Jacob and not Joseph. Otherwise, they would have been classed as Egyptians, because they were born in Egypt.

Then Jacobs's voice took on a tone of deep sadness and great sorrow that seemed to radiate up into his face, as he told his son Joseph about a very sad day in his life. The aching, and the great pain that had once been in his heart so, long ago still, seemed to linger and be there to a great degree. He told Joseph how his mother, his beloved Rachel, had died on the journey from Paddan in the Land of Canaan. He said: "I buried her beside the road a little distance from Ephrath." (That is the place known today as Bethlehem).

After a short pause in the conversation with his son Joseph, Jacob, noticed the two boys that were with Joseph.

So he asked Joseph who the two lads were that he had with him. Joseph replied and said to his father: "they are the sons that God has given me here." Jacob could have asked this question for a very specific reason. He could have done this because of his blindness and the fact that he couldn't see very well, or he wanted to make sure that these children were truly Joseph's children before he blessed them. Another scenario or thought that he may have been entertaining or recalling in his mind at that time was that, he was remembering how he and his mother had deceived his father Isaac, and how he had stolen his Brother Esau's birthright. At any rate, Jacob had to make sure that he was pronouncing his blessing on the right children. Once a blessing was pronounced on a person, there was no reversing it. It was just like the blessing was carved in stone, never to be removed or replaced.

Then Israel said to Joseph: "Bring them to me so I may bless them." So Joseph put his two boys on his father's knees, and Jacob put his arms around them and embraced them, and kissed them. By this act of embracing, and kissing, it symbolized that the boys, had now become adopted by Jacob, and that they were now his property.

Then Joseph took his sons from his father's knees, and he held them so Jacob could bless them. It was customary, that the oldest son or the firstborn receive the blessing instead of the younger son. Joseph had held Manasseh, his oldest son, in his left arm so that it would be a natural thing for Jacob to be able to place his right hand on Manasseh's head. His youngest son Ephraim was held in Joseph's right arm, so it would be natural for Jacob to lay his left hand on Ephraim's head. But that is not what happened.

Joseph then bowed his head to the ground in front of his father as a sign of respect and reverence to God. Then Jacob crossed his arms and was about to pronounce his blessing on the boys when, Joseph tried to remove Jacobs right hand from Ephraim's head and place it on his oldest sons head.

Joseph was quite upset with his father and he said to his father: "No, my father, this one is the first born; put your right hand on his head." But Jacob said to Joseph, "I know, my son, I know. He too will become a people, and he too will become great. Nevertheless, his younger brother will be greater than he, and his descendants will become a group of nations." This is the second time that God has overturned the expected order of things. The older would serve the younger. It was the same thing that had happened in Jacobs's case. His older brother Esau would serve the younger brother Jacob.

Then Jacob blessed Joseph his son and said; "May the God before whom my father's Abraham, and Isaac, walked. The God who has been my shepherd all my life to this day, the Angel who has delivered me from all harm, may He bless these boys. May they be called by my name and by the names of my father's Abraham and Isaac, and may they increase greatly upon the earth. In your name will Israel pronounce this blessing: 'May God, make you like Ephraim and Manasseh." He had placed Ephraim first over Manasseh, the younger over the oldest.

Now that Jacob had pronounced his blessing upon Joseph and his two children, he could now rest for a little while before he had to continue to carry out the rest of his duty of blessing his other sons. They also had to receive their blessing from their father before he died.

We know for certain, that God has a hand in everything that happens on the Earth and in Heaven. It was God who put everything in Jacobs's heart and mind, as to what he was to do, what he was to say, and who was to receive each blessing. There was no other way, other than by the direct influence of God Himself, that Jacob could have foretold the future so far in advance. Neither, could he have described the events that would take place in the centuries to come.

For example: when Jacob spoke these words and said that: "his younger brother will be greater than he," he spoke nothing but the truth. History proved out centuries later, that Gods chosen people had become a great nation. They were so great a nation that, they would split into two different kingdoms. During the divided monarchy (930-722B.C.) Ephraim's descendants were the most powerful tribe in the north. The name "Ephraim" was often used to refer to the northern kingdom as a whole. This is historical proof that God had put everything in Jacobs's heart at that time as to what was to happen in the future; God is the only one who can predict and fulfill the future, of mankind.

So now Jacob was happy for the time being. The custom that he was required to do before he died was partly completed. But he still had to bless his other sons and explain to them, some of the things that would happen to them and their descendants to come. After he had rested for a while he said to Joseph: "I am about to die, but God will be with you and take you back to the land of your fathers. To you, as one who is over your brothers, I give the ridge of land I took from the Amorites with my sword and my bow."

As you can see, God was directly involved in Jacobs life, and He would continue to be involved in Josephs life as well. Jacob has just foretold what would happen to Joseph and his sons, in the future when he dies, and for him not to worry. He said: "God will take you back to the land of your fathers." As it turned out many years later, that Joseph spoke these very same words "I am about to die." just before he died in the land Egypt.

To further prove to Joseph, that he had received the family birthright, over the rest of his brothers, Jacob gave him one more portion or blessing above his older brothers. It was a ridge of land that Jacob had won in a battle with the Amorites in the land of Canaan. So now, by blessing Joseph's two sons, and putting them on the same level as his own sons, Jacob had adopted Joseph's two sons into his family. Also, by giving him the piece of land in Canaan, Joseph had received the double portion that he was entitled to as part of his birthright. The latter part of his birthright however, would not be fulfilled until the Israelites returned to Canaan to, possess the land that God had given them.

The Bible says that in his last days, Jacob described the future for his descendants. The Bible does not state exactly what day that the blessing of his other sons occurred. But it uses the word days, which could mean most any day. I believe that the blessing of his other sons must have taken place shortly after Jacob had blessed Joseph and his two sons. This blessing is referred to as "The Blessings of Jacob." Its various blessings were intended not only for Jacobs's twelve sons, but they were also intended for the twelve tribes that would descend from them.

When Jacob called his sons altogether for his last time, it was natural for him to address his sons in the order of their birth. The first son to come before Jacob was Reuben. Jacob started to speak warm words of praise to Reuben for his birth, but he ended with words of rebuke. Reuben was the beginning of his strength, or his family. The family would be his strength in the years to come. It was the beginning of Jacobs Excellency, of his dignity, and of his power.

But all was not peaches and cream, in the life of Rueben. He had made some bad choices in his life, and he would pay dearly for at least one of those choices that he had made. The biggest mistake that he had made occurred in his younger days, after the death of his mother Leah. Israel and his family had been moving around in the desert, and had stopped and pitched their tents near Midgal Eder. So Reuben thought, now that his mother was dead, he could claim part of his birthright. It would include claiming Israel's concubine Blihah as his own possession. So he went in and slept with her to solidify his birthright. But his father Jacob heard of it and he was very displeased and angry.

Reuben's act was both arrogant and premature. Because of this he would lose his legal status as the firstborn. He had doomed his cause. As it happened, he was passed over for his younger stepbrother Joseph. Jacob said to him, "You have become as turbulent as the waters. You will no longer excel, (or to be considered as the firstborn) for you went up onto your fathers bed and defiled it." Reuben's descendants were characterized by indecision.

But all was not lost for Reuben. He also had some good points. When the other brothers wanted to kill Joseph, he was the only one of the brothers who did not want to kill him. He was the one who had talked the others into throwing Joseph down an old cistern to die. In this way, he was hoping to rescue Joseph that night, and then take him home to his father. But that was not part of Gods over-all plan for Joseph.

The next two brothers to be blessed were Simeon and Levi. To them Jacob said: "Simeon and Levi are brothers." By this, he meant that the two tribes descending from them would be similar in nature, or they would have the same traits as each other. "Their swords would be weapons of violence." He said that; "They would be full of anger, and cruelty." "Cursed be their anger for it is fierce, and their wrath for it is cruel. I will divide them in Jacob and scatter them in Israel." Jacob had said this because of the fierce and cruel revenge that they had taken against Shechem and his people. (See story in Gen. Ch. 34)

Even though Shechem had raped their sister Dinah, their vengeance was excessive, and an outrage against the sacred rite of circumcision. Their anger was fierce and cruel, and not righteous or zealous for Gods honor. Because of their actions their descendants would be scattered in Israel later in history. Simon's descendants would be dispersed throughout the large tribe of Judah. In (Josh. 19: 1-9) Levis descendants would be scattered in 48 different cities, towns, and pasturelands throughout the land. (Josh.21) Jacob was so appalled at what he saw in their future that, he didn't even want to have his good name to be associated with them. His good name was his honor, and a good name displays a person's integrity.

Now it is Judah's turn to hear what Jacob had to say about him. He probably thought that he was going to receive similar condemnation from his father, but it was just the opposite. He was one of the sons to receive a great deal of praise from Jacob. Judah's, and Jacob's blessings, were the longest of Jacobs's blessings to his sons. Jacobs's praise for Judah was only surpassed by his praise for Joseph. Judah had rose to the leadership of the twelve sons, just as Joseph had passed over Reuben, Simeon, and Levi. They were passed over because they had given up their leadership roles. Judah's self-sacrificing actions to save his younger brother Benjamin from going to prison, when he came before Joseph, were exemplary.

So Jacob said to Judah: "Your brothers will bow down to you. Judah is the lions whelp." (Or cub). The lion is an ancient symbol of royalty. Then he said:" Your hand will be on the neck of your enemies. The Scepter will not depart from Judah. Neither will the rulers staff from between His feet, until He comes to whom it belongs, and the obedience of the nations is His. He will tether His donkey to a vine, His colt to the choicest branch. He will wash His garments in wine His robs in the blood of grapes. His eyes will be darker than wine, His teeth whiter than milk."

Perhaps at this point I should explain some the proceeding scripture, as it is quite hard to understand if you do not have a study Bible handy. It is very important that you the reader understand what the scripture says because it speaks of our Lord and Savior Jesus Christ.

When Jacob said: "Your brothers will bow down to you," he meant Judah's tribe would be preeminent among the twelve tribes of Israel. Also, that he and his descendants would be an ancestor of Jesus Christ. Jesus would come from the line of Judah. It was Jesus, of whom Jacob was speaking about. Jesus was Judah's greatest descendant. As you know, every knee will bow before Him in the Great Judgment to come, and all tongues will confess His name.

The lion cub is a symbol of sovereignty, strength, and courage. Judah is often pictured as a lion in later times. This is specifically mentioned in (Nu.24; 9). Jesus Himself is often referred to as "The Lion of the Tribe of Judah." (Rev. 5:5)

Jacob also said that: "The Scepter shell not depart from Judah." This is very true, because Christ the Son is Eternal as well as the Father and the Holy Spirit.

The Scepter is an ornate staff, or rod, that is a symbol of royal authority. The scepter belongs to Christ, and it is given to Him when He comes to reign on earth as the Lord of all people and nations. The staff between His feet refers to Christ's authority as a lawgiver. Therefore, the tribe of Judah would always have a lawgiver in its ranks. That means that Christ's authority, His power, and His Kingdom, will never end. Also with these words, Jacob predicted that a royal line would rise from Judah's descendants, which it did through Christ Jesus. This is more proof that God speaks words of prophesy through people of His own choosing.

The words "Until Shiloh comes."…. The word Shiloh is an obscure word. But the Bible says that it probably means, "The One "To Whom It Belongs." This means that all authority belongs to the coming Messiah Jesus Christ.

Binding His donkey to the vine, and His donkey's colt to the choice branch. Jacob was referring to the fact that the day is coming, when the descendants of Judah, would someday enjoy a settled and prosperous life.

Then Jacob referred to: "Washing His garments in wine and His robes in the blood of grapes." This part of the scripture, describes the warfare that the Messiah will wage, to establish His reign in the age to come. (Ps.2: 110: Rev.19: 11-21) The wine represents the color of blood.

The color of His eyes and teeth, speak of His vitality and victory. The language that is spoken in this passage, expresses the mystery and the wonder surrounding the "Coming One, The Messiah."

The next in line to receive Jacobs blessing was Issachar, who was the 5th son of Jacob and Leah. But for some reason that is not explained in the Bible, Zebulun, who was the 6th son, was given precedence over his brother Issachar. This time God had chosen the older son over the younger one. Zebulun's blessing, or the allotment of land for his descendants in the coming possession of the Promised Land of Canaan, would be located in the northern coast-lands bordering Phoenicia. Although Zebulun's descendants would be landlocked by the tribes of Asher and Manasseh, they would only be within ten miles of the Mediterranean Sea. They would be able to "feast on the abundance of the sea." Theirs would be a treasure hidden in the sand. This is in reference to maritime wealth. As Jacob had said: "Zebulun will live by the seashore and become a haven for ships." His border will extend toward Sidon.

To Issachar Jacob said: "He is a rawboned donkey lying down between two saddlebags. When he sees how good his resting place is, and how pleasant is his land, he will bend his shoulder to the burden and submit to forced labor." This refers to the fact that his descendants would become an enslaved tribe of people, after a time of plenty. Issachar's allotment of land would be southwest of the Sea of Galilee reaching down to Beth Shan and west to the Jezreel Valley. Mount Tabor marked its northern boundary. There were sixteen towns and their villages that were the inheritance of the tribe of Issachar, clan by clan.

The next in line was Dan, and Jacob said to him: "Dan will provide justice for his people as one of the tribes of

Israel. Dan will be a serpent by the roadside, a viper along the path that bites the horse's heels, so that its rider tumbles backward." The name Dan is related to the word meaning "Judge." When Jacob said that Dan would be a serpent by the roadside, he was referring to a much later time in history. As it happened, a group of Danites would show their treachery, as they slaughtered the people of a city called Laish, and burned it to the ground. The inhabitants of this city were a peaceful and unsuspecting people. They were people who had dealt in commerce with all of the other people around the Mediterranean world. These people had no thoughts of wars, and violence, in their lives. The people had no army or anyone else to defend them, because they were too far from Sidon. They were totally helpless and at the mercy of the Danites. After the Danites captured the city they rebuilt it and renamed it Dan, after their forefather Dan. You can read of this treachery in (Jdg. 18: 27- 28).

Dan became the northernmost settlement of Israel. As Jacob continued he said: "He would be a viper along the path." This part of the statement, according to the Bible, possibly means that some of Dams descendants would abandon their faith in God, and start to fallow the ways of Idol worship. But that doesn't mean that the godly people of the tribe of Dan were condemned along with the ones who fell away from God. The godly could still expect and receive salvation from the Lord.

In the rest of Jacobs's statement that says: "He bites the horses heels." This statement refers to the time in history, when God raised-up Judges to rule the tribes of Israel. It occurred between the time of the death of Joshua, and the time of the monarchy in Israel.

There is one particular event that happened when the Judges ruled, that I would like to mention here in passing. God had raised-up a man by the name of Samson. He was called a Nazirite, and he was born into the tribe of Dan.

At one point in his life, he would single-handedly hold the Philistines at bay and kill hundreds of them with a jawbone of an ass. As it happened, he would kill thousands of them throughout his lifetime. He was a special child of God. That means that he was consecrated to God by a vow. He was never, to drink wine, or allow the hair on his head to be cut. Also, he was never to defile himself by coming into contact with a dead body. His role in God's plan was to deliver the Israelites from the hands of the Philistines. They had oppressed the children of Israel for over forty years. It is a wonderful story and you can read about it in the Bible. The story is found in the book of Judges in chapters (13-16 NIV). Now I must get back to my story.

By this time in his discourse to his sons, Jacob had become very tired. So he paused for a short time and gave thanks to God and he said: "I look for your deliverance O Lord." He was no doubt looking forward to the time of his death, when God would take him home to heaven with Him. But most of all he asking God to grant him the strength to continue on, so he could complete the task of blessing his sons, and foretelling their futures. He was also expressing his deep faith, and that he was relying strictly on God, for the strength that he needed. Jacobs's faith is a wonderful example of faith in God that all believers would do well to heed for their own life.

As he continued to bless his sons, he said to Gad. "Gad will be attacked by a troop, a band of raiders, shall tramp on him but he will attack them at their heels." Gads descendants were to be located east of the Jordan, and they would be open to raids by the Moabites to the south. Although they would endure many hardships, they were assured that the ultimate victory would be theirs.

Asher, who was next in line to receive Jacobs blessing, was blessed in a much different way than Jacobs other sons. Although his words were brief to Asher, Jacobs blessing expressed happiness and hope for his son. This happiness and hope was directly related to Asher's birth because, Leah his mother had expressed so much happiness over the fact, that she now had numerous sons. Jacob said to him: "Asher's food will be rich; he will provide delicacies fit for a King." His descendants would be given land in the rich fertile farmlands of the Mediterranean. This would ensure the prosperity of Asher's descendants.

Naphtali was the next son to be blessed. His blessing was much the same as Asher's. The words that Jacob used were sweet and beautiful words. He said: "Naphtali is a doe set free, that bears beautiful fawns." These words also, were expressing hope and joy in the same manner as Asher's blessing did. But perhaps, they were a reference to the independent spirit that was fostered in the descendants of Naphtali. They would be located in a more isolated area in the hill country, north of the Sea of Galilee. (See Jos.19: 32-38).

Now it came time to bless his favorite son Joseph. He was the "Prince" among his brothers. This was the son whom he loved more than life it's self. Only the promises given to Judah, can rival, the praise Jacob gave to Joseph. As Jacob began to pronounce his blessing on Joseph, he said: "Joseph is a fruitful vine, a fruitful vine near a spring, whose branches climb over a wall." These words were referring to Josephs two sons, and that the younger son Ephraim, would become greater than his older son Manasseh. This was proven out much later in history. The Ephraimites would gain supremacy over the other northern tribes. His descendants were warlike people and were often victorious in battle. (See Jdg.8: 1 - 12:1) (Jos.17: 18).

Then, Jacob used the imagery of archers, to describe the treatment that Joseph had received from his brothers. He said: "With bitterness archers attacked him. They shot at him with hostility. But his bow remained steady, his strong arms stayed limber, because of the hand of the Mighty One of Jacob. Because of the Shepherd the Rock of Israel, because of your father's God who helps you. Because of the Almighty, who blesses you with blessings of the heavens above? Blessings of the deep that lies below: blessings of the breast and the womb." As Jacob continued on and said: "Your father's blessings are greater than the blessing of the ancient mountains, then the bounty of the age-old hills. Let all these rest on the head of Joseph, on the brow of the prince among his brothers." All of these words stress the activity of God in saving and redeeming His people. God was, and still is, the sure defense of Israel.

Throughout the blessing of Joseph by his father Jacob, the words that he spoke expressed his deep love, both for Joseph, and for the God of Heaven and Earth, the one and only true God. Also, throughout Josephs blessing, Jacob used five different names for God.

The first name Jacob used for God: it referred to God as the "Mighty One of Jacob!" It expresses the activity of God in saving and redeeming His people. This could have been a special name that Jacob used to refer to God, because of the experience he had when he wrestled with God earlier in his life. (Ge. 32: 22-30). There are many other places in scripture where God is called Mighty, and it serves as a name for God. By using this special term for God, in his blessing of Joseph, it shows what great affection Jacob had for his son.

1. The second name that Jacob used, he called God the "Great Shepherd!" This name would have great significance for a family of shepherds. God shepherds and cares for His people all of the time, and He is the one and only Good Shepherd, who truly care for His flock. In (Ps. 23) it states this in the first five words, "The Lord is my Shepherd." In (Jn.10: 1-18) Jesus calls Himself the "Good Shepherd." In verses 14-18

Jesus said: "I am the good shepherd; I know my sheep and my sheep know me. Just as the Father knows me, and I know the Father." In (vv17-18) Jesus continues and says:" The reason my Father loves me, is that I lay down my life, only to take it up again. No one takes it from me, but I lay it down of my own accord. I have the authority to lay it down and authority to take it up again. This command I received from my Father." These scriptures alone, tell you who Jesus is and of His Almighty Power. He is the one and only true Son of God. He is the only door to heaven and to eternal life. Even the great Pharaohs of Egypt, who despised shepherds, appeared in statues with a shepherds crook. It represented his benevolent care for his nation.

2. The third name he praised God with was, "The Stone of Israel." On the many occasions that God spoke to him, Jacob (or Israel as he is now known.) erected stone pillars to commemorate the event. (Ge.28-18) the rock typifies the stability and trustworthiness that God had become for him the Stone of Israel.
3. The fourth name Jacob had for God, he referred to God as the "God of your Father." Earlier, Jacob had described the Lord as the God of Abraham and Isaac. But this time he was expressing his great faith and his undying love for his God, who had so richly blessed him throughout his long life. He was proclaiming to his sons that this same God who had blessed and cared for his forefathers was also his God.
4. The last name that Jacob used to refer to God was, the "Almighty." In the Hebrew language it means El Shadai, which means "God of the Mountain." God referred to Himself as God Almighty when He spoke to Moses in the burning bush on the mountain. God is a mountain like God. He is powerful, majestic,

> awe-inspiring, and enduring. Just like a mountain, He provides a shelter from the elements and from all evil. God dwells in His Holy Mountain in Heaven. By using these five names, for God, Jacob was praying manifold blessings on Joseph. Jacobs blessing on Joseph concluded by stating that Joseph was separate from the rest of his brothers. He compared Joseph to a Nazirite. Both Joseph and later Nazirites were separated from others in order to serve Gods holy purposes. Samson was a good example of the Nazirite people. His whole life was dedicated to serving the Lord. The Lord was his refuge and strength until he fell into sin with the Philistine woman Delia who, deceived him and caused him to reveal to her the secret of his great strength.

Finely at last, it came time to bless his youngest son Benjamin. He said: "Benjamin is a ravenous wolf. In the morning he shall devour the prey, and at night he shall divide the spoil." Here, Jacob used the imagery of a wolf. Benjamin's descendants would be characterized by the savagery that they would display in the many battles that were to come in the future.

So now, each one of the sons of Jacob had received their blessings from their father. These twelve sons of Jacob would become the twelve tribes of Israel. Although, some of these blessings are somewhat obscure, others are not. The blessings of Judah and Joseph are clear prophecies from God about their destinies.

As the day of blessing his sons wore on, Jacob had becoming very tired and he could do no more speaking. The blessing of his sons had taken a great toll on him, but he still had one more very important request to make of his sons before he died. That request was to instruct them were he wanted to be buried. He knew that Canaan was the land that

God had promised to his descendants. He certainly didn't want to be buried in the land of Egypt. God had promised Jacob that He would return him to the land of his fathers. So now Jacob challenged his sons for the last time. He said to them: "Bury me with my father's in the cave that is in the field at Machpelah."

It was the same cave where Abraham and Sarah his wife, Isaac and Rebekah his wife, and Leah his other wife were buried. Although Joseph had sworn a solemn oath to Jacob to bury him in Canaan, he wanted to make sure that his other sons understood this as well. He wanted their assurance that his last request would be carried out. Also, there would be no argument from any of the sons as to where he was to be buried. When he had said all these things, he breathed his last breath and died. God took him home to His glory.

When Joseph who was by the bedside of his father, saw that his father was dead, he closed his father's eyes with his hand, as God had said he would, and then kissed his face and wept over him. Joseph was expressing his strong and, genuine love for his father and he didn't care who saw him weep. Then Joseph gave orders to his servants and physicians to embalm his father. The embalming of the body would require forty days, but the Egyptians mourned for him for seventy days. They mourned for an extra thirty days because it was done out of respect for Joseph and his high position. But the seventy days could have been their normal period of mourning for the dead in Egypt at that time.

After the seventy days of mourning were past, Joseph went up to the household of Pharaoh to present his requests to him and to his officials. He said to them: "If I have found favor in your eyes, speak to the Pharaoh for me. Tell him, my father made me swear an oath and said: "I am about to die; bury me in the tomb that I dug for myself in the land of Canaan. Now let me go up and bury my father then I will return." The fact that Joseph could not get into see the

Pharaoh right away, indicates that even Joseph with all of his power and might, didn't necessarily get an immediate audience with the Pharaoh any time that he wanted. When Joseph got in to see the Pharaoh, and the Pharaoh had heard Josephs request, he gave him his blessing and permission to leave the country and go and bury his father in Canaan.

All of Pharaohs officials and all of the dignitaries of his court, as well as the households of Joseph, his brothers, and his father's household, all assembled to go to Canaan to bury Joseph's father. Only their children, their livestock and some servants, were left behind in the land of Goshen. There was also a large number of chariots and horseman sent along with them to protect them on their journey. It was a very large company of people that left Egypt to bury Jacob in his father's tomb in Canaan.

When they reached the threshing floor of Atad, near the Jordan River, they lamented loudly and bitterly. There, Joseph observed another seven-day period of mourning for his father. The threshing floor spoken of is a large circular area made up of either rock or pounded ground. These threshing floors were usually located on an elevated open area that was exposed to the wind. In this way, when the grain was tossed into the air, the chaff and the straw would be blown away by the wind and the grain would be collected on the threshing floor. It was at this same place later on in history that, would become, the entrance to the Promised Land for the Israelites. The Canaanites were so impressed with the party of mourners that they renamed the place "Abel Mizraim, because of the grievous mourning of the Egyptians.

So Jacobs' sons did as he had commanded them, and they buried Jacob in the Land of Canaan, in the cave beside his Father and Grandfather. God had kept His promise to the letter, and He had brought him back to the Promised Land, just as He said he would do. God is always true to His word and He is always trustworthy and unchanging. After Jacob was laid to rest, the whole company of mourners returned to Egypt and carried on with their lives.

As time passed all was not well in the camp of Joseph's brothers. Now that their father was dead and gone, they began to worry about another problem that seemed to be plaguing their minds from time to time. Perhaps: the brothers may have discussed this problem at some length before while; they were not in the presents of Jacob or Joseph. The problem was that, now that their father was gone, they could no longer hide behind him for protection. Joseph would now have the opportunity to seek his own type of revenge on his brothers for what they had done to him. They really feared for their lives. Joseph had the power to enslave them, and their families, or he could have them killed.

As they discussed this problem, they said to one another: "What if Joseph holds a grudge against us, and pays us back for all of the wrongs we did to him?" Their guilt was finely catching up to them. This would have been their typical human way of thinking on their part if what they feared came true. But they should have realized by the way Joseph had been treating them after he had revealed himself to them, and how he had them all move to Egypt that, revenge was not something that he desired or had even thought about.

So, now what were they to do? It seemed to them that they were in a trap, but it was of their own making. So they had to come up with some kind of a plan to protect themselves and their families. At this point in their lives, they were probably quite used to telling a few lies and blaming someone else for their troubles. So they had to come up with a story to fit the problem that they were having. But of course, it would have to contain a lie or two. It would be just like the first time that they had lied to Jacob about Joseph. They had not learned a thing about being honest and truthful.

So they sent messengers to Joseph and told them what to say to him. They said: "This is what you are to say to Joseph.

Your father left these instructions before he died. "I ask you to forgive your brothers, of the sins and the wrongs, they have committed in treating you so badly. Now please forgive the sins of the servants, of the God of your father." When Joseph heard the message that his brothers had sent him, he broke down and wept.

Joseph had accepted the confession of his brothers that was contained in their message to him as a sincere confession of their sins. Joseph may have been saddened by the thought that his brothers had falsely implicated their father in their story of lies, but it was too late the damage was done. Nothing could change that. He may have regretted to some degree that, he had not informed his brothers much earlier that, he had already forgiven them of their sins against him. Because he had not done so, he may have felt that he was partly to blame for his brothers having to come up with more lies to save their hides.

After Joseph had regained his composer, from his weeping, he sent for his brothers to appear before him. He had to set the record straight once and for all, concerning matters involving him and his brothers. There could not be any more deceit, mistrust, or jealousy between him and his brothers. There was nothing that any of the brothers, or Joseph, could do to change anything that had happened to them in the past. The past was the past. They had to move on with their lives and get their relationships back in order. With God's help, they would be able to do just that and live a long and prosperous life together.

When his brothers came before Joseph, as they had been commanded to do, they fell down before him and they said to Joseph: "Behold, we are your servants." This was a final fulfillment of Joseph's earlier dreams. Then Joseph said to his brothers: "Don't be afraid, am I in the place of God? You intended to harm me, but God intended it for good to accomplish what is now being done, the saving of many lives. So then don't be afraid. I will provide for you and your children." These words of reassurance that Joseph spoke must have been sweet music to his brother's ears. The brothers had expected harsh treatment from Joseph, but instead they heard nothing but words of blessing. Now all of their doubts and fears could all be put to rest. They had nothing to fear from Joseph any more. It would be a great and a wonderful thing if, the people of the world today would adopt the same attitude towards their neighbor as Joseph did. He forgives his brothers and he gave all of the glory to God. Can we not as Christians do the same thing?

Joseph didn't take any of the credit for the events of the past, but he gave it all to God. He knew that it was God who had caused all of the events to take place in the past and that he could not control anything that had happened to himself or to his brothers. It was God, who had taken all of the evil things that had been engineered by Satan, and turned them to the good for His people. God had used Joseph's captivity and his rise to power in Egypt, to save and sustain Israel and his sons.

The Egyptian people, and all of the other people that had come to Egypt to buy food in the face of the famine, were truly blessed by God. Also, at the same time, God had demonstrated by these events, that His purpose for the nations of the world is life for all nations. The full purpose of blessing the nations would be accomplished through the descendants of Abraham, just as God had promised Jacob. God is always faithful to His promises, because He is a Holy, Just, and Unchanging God.

After the brothers had departed from Joseph's presence, they hurried back to their families with the great news that, Joseph had forgiven them of their past crimes against him. Now at last, they and their families could all sleep in peace at night, and not have any worries about their future. So now, all was well with Jacobs's family for the first time in decades. God had brought them all together once again and they would all be cared for under the watchful eye of Joseph. They had nothing to fear from God or from anyone else in the land of Egypt.

THE DEATH OF JOSEPH

As time went on, the months faded into years, and the years into decades, and Joseph has now grown old and tired just like his father did before him. He knew he was about to die. He called his brothers to him and made them swear an oath to him, that they would not leave his bones buried in Egypt. He wanted to be buried in the Promised Land of Canaan. The use of the word "Brothers" here refers more, in the broader sense, to the sons of the Israelites, rather than to Joseph's siblings. This is true because Joseph's brothers were older than him, and they could not have possibly out lived him.

After Joseph said to the sons of Israel: "I am about to die," and he had made them swear to take his bones back to the Promised Land; he did the same thing that his father Jacob had done before him. He told them what God had planned for the Israelites in the future. He said: "God will surely come to your aid, and take you up out of this land. To the land that He promised on oath, to Abraham, Isaac and Jacob." But this covenant would not be fulfilled until centuries later, when Moses would lead the Israelites out of Egypt, on the great Exodus. Before Joseph died God permitted him to see his grandson Makir and his children. This was another blessing that God granted Joseph in his old age.

So it was that, the long life of Joseph the favorite son of Jacob came to an end. He lived until he was a hundred and ten years old. Ancient Egyptian records indicate that, one hundred and ten years, was considered to be the ideal life span. To the Egyptians, this would have signified a divine blessing upon Joseph. His life span could be compared to that of his ancestors. Abraham his great grandfather (175 yrs.), Isaac his grandfather (180 yrs.), and Jacob his father (147 yrs.).

When Joseph died he was embalmed and placed in a coffin in Egypt. He was not buried in a grave, but was probably kept in some kind of tomb hewn from a rock or a side of a hill. Hundreds of years later, Moses and the children of Israel, would keep the Israelites' oath, by taking Josephs bones with them into the journey of the wilderness. (Ex.13-19). Then finally, Joshua would bury the bones of Joseph at Shechem, during the conquest of Canaan.

As I was comparing the ages of the patriarchs, another comparison came into my mind. It is the comparison of the life of Jesus Christ our Lord, and the life of Joseph who was a direct ancestor of Jesus Christ. The following are some of the comparisons that I would like to mention at this time.

(1) Joseph was one of twelve brothers——Jesus had twelve disciples.
(2) Joseph had a coat of many colors with purple borders, which repents Royalty. —— Jesus had a coat without any seams. The soldiers gambled for His coat at the foot of His cross.
(3) Joseph was thrown into a pit and was later sold as a slave in Egypt for twenty shekels of silver. — Judas Iscariot one of the disciples, who had lived and traveled with Jesus for three years, sold Jesus out for thirty pieces of silver.

(4) Josephs' brothers rejected him, because he was the favored son of Jacob his father. — Jesus was rejected by the people of His day and was hung on a cross between two thieves like a common criminal.
(5) Joseph was raised to power in Egypt, and he was considered the right hand of the Pharaoh.
(6) Jesus rose from the dead and walked out of the grave, and is alive today in heaven, and He is sitting at the right hand of God the Father in power and great glory.
(7) Joseph through the guidance of God gave food to many people and saved them from starvation. — — Jesus gave His life on the cross and has saved the whole human race from eternal damnation if they believe in Him and God the Father who sent Him.

You must have faith and believe in the Lord Jesus Christ to be saved. Jesus said in (Jn.14: 6) "I am the way the truth and the life. No one comes to the Father except through me." This means exactly what it says, Jesus is the one and only way to heaven. There is no other way that you can even hope to enter heaven. If you believe that, there is any other way to heaven then you have been deceived by Satan.

As I have mentioned before, "Deception," is one of Satan's greatest weapons, and he uses it on all of mankind anytime and anywhere he chooses. The joy and the peace that we as believers (or Christians) will have when we enter eternal life, is beyond our greatest imagination. Our small human minds are incapable of fully comprehending what God has in store for those who believe in Him and His Son Jesus Christ.

These are just a few of the comparisons that I have mentioned, to give you some food for thought. I am sure that there are many more comparisons that a person could make between Jesus our Lord and Joseph. But I feel that the comparisons that I have mentioned above will help you to see the similarity between them. In a small way, God had shown the people of the Old Testament what would happen to His son Jesus Christ in the future.

So ends the wonderful story of Joseph, one of the greatest men of the Bible. Throughout this story I hope you have been able to see Gods awesome power and protection. Also, you can see His deep love for His people, and His divine guidance as well. These blessings God freely gives to all people who love and obey Him and you can't buy them at any price. This includes everyone in the whole human race, good or bad which, He has chosen to call His own, but you must reach out to God in prayer, and in faith, and grab on to what He has to offer.

Please remember that Gods love, and His forgiveness of your sins is free for the taking. It will cost you nothing but your heart, and your love for Him and, it will defiantly save your soul from Hell in the time that is yet to come.

Remember, you only have this one opportunity in life to receive Him while you are alive on this earth because; the second that you draw your last breath here on earth, the next one will be in one of two places, in Heaven with the Lord or in Hell with the Devil in eternal torment. Jesus will never turn you away or leave you. So the question remains to be said!

Will you be one of God's chosen people by accepting Jesus Christ as your own personal savior? It is my fervent prayer that you will accept Him into your heart while you continue your journey throughout the rest of your life. It is Gods will and great desire that everyone worship Him in spirit and in truth. Then, when the day comes, and you stand before Him to be judged, you will hear Him say to you: "Well done good and faithful servant. You have been faithful with a few things; I will put you in charge of many things. Come and share your master's happiness!" (Mt.25: 21).

Part Five

MOSES AND THE EXODUS

-1-

HIS BACKGROUND

The story of Moses and the Exodus of the Israelites out of the land of Egypt is a story that bears repeating to children and adults alike. It is a story that is both awesome and exciting. Throughout this story of Moses, you will be able to see how the God we Christians serve is, a God of Grace, Love, Compassion, and above all He is holy and just. You will see how He chose His people and why He chose them. You will see how He loved and cared for them, how He guided and protected them, and also how He disciplined them as well.

This story starts to takes place in Egypt, and it will end on the east side of the Jordan River before, the Israelites begin the conquest of Canaan. When Jacob, the father of Joseph came to Egypt during the seven-years of famine, he brought with him sixty-six people. But, as you will recall, Jacobs's son Joseph was already in Egypt with his wife and two sons, Ephraim and Manasseh. When you add Jacob and Joseph's family, together you have the grand total of seventy people in all. These seventy people were the corner stone, or the start of God's chosen people the Hebrews, or the Israelites that God would eventually through time, build into a great nation.

As our story begins, centuries have passed since the death of Joseph and his brothers, and all that generation had died and was long forgotten. God, who is always faithful and true to His word, would continue to keep His promise to make Adam and Eve fruitful, and to multiply their descendants. You may recall this promise way back in the Garden of Eden in the story of Creation. This was Gods initial blessing to all of mankind. He has also continued to keep this promise to Abraham, Isaac, and to Jacob. Now God is going to continue to fulfill His promise through the Israelite people.

In (Ex.1: 6) the Bible says that: "The Israelites were fruitful and multiplied greatly, and became exceedingly numerous, so that the land was filled with them." This was indeed another miracle, created by God Himself. God still continued to multiply His people in times of distress and hardship. Also, by Gods great mercy, the Israelites had been left by themselves in Egypt in the land of Goshen for the over four hundred years after Joseph had died.

The scripture say in (Ex.1:8), Then a new King, who did not know about Joseph, came to power in Egypt. He did not know or hear about, all of the great and wonderful things that Joseph had done for Egypt. Also, he was not aware that it was the God of Joseph, who had kept the Egyptians from starvation during the seven years of famine. It was also this same God, who had made their country very wealthy at the same time. But, the Kings lack of knowledge on this subject was probably due mostly to the fact that all most four hundred years had passed since these events had taken place. It may not have been possible for him to know about Joseph and his God because there may not have been any kind of records kept in Egypt of their existence and what had transpired at that particular time.

However, one day the new King said to his officials, "Look," the Israelites have become much too numerous for us. Come, we must deal shrewdly with them or they will become even more numerous and, if war breaks out, will join our enemies, fight against us, and leave the country." So you can see from this passage that the King and his people thought that they had a great deal to be concerned about. But the fear that the Egyptians displayed toward the people of Israel was purely based on nothing but misjudgment and hatred because, of the Israelites prosperity through God.

After the King had spoken to his officials, and his people, about his deep concerns of war with the Israelites, his advisers probably encouraged him to enslave the Israelites. The King that is mentioned here is, probably Ahmose the founder of the 18th dynasty. (1730-1570 B.C.) More than likely, this Pharaoh was one of the Hyksos Kings, who had descended from foreign invaders. Ethnically these Kings were a minority in Egypt.

So the Egyptians forced all of Gods people, the Hebrews, into slavery and put cruel taskmasters over them to afflict them and their burdens. The Egyptians made the children of Israel to serve with rigor and hard bondage. They drove them with the whip and treated them with harshness in every kind of labor. The making of bricks and mortar, and the use of big stones to build the cities was extremely hard and difficult work. Therefore, the lives of the slaves were made very bitter. The Egyptians were trying to break the spirit of the Israelites. But, the more harshly the Egyptians treated them, the more God made them to flourish and to grow. Now the Egyptians thought that they were defiantly becoming the minority, and they were dreading the Israelites even more as time went on.

As the years went slowly by, nearly four centuries have passed now, and the Israelites are still under bondage. By this time, other new Kings had come to power. The Bible says that this new King was probably Thutmose l. This King ruled Egypt from (1539-1514 B.C.) Then the King sent for the two midwives, who were in charge of delivering the Israelite children. Their names were Shiphrah, ("Beautiful One") and Puah ("Splendid One"). Probably these two women ran a group of midwives who would go around and deliver the Israelite children. These midwives were Hebrew, and they knew and loved the Living God.

So the King said to the two midwives that he had summoned before him. "When you help the Hebrew women in childbirth, and observe them on the delivery stool, if it is a boy kill him. "If it is a girl let her live." The "delivery stool" was usually two large stones that were close together, and the women would sit on them when it came time for the delivery of the baby.

But, the midwives did not do as the King had commanded them to do. They did not kill the boys, but they let them live. The midwives chose to obey God rather than man, although this type of disobedience to the King could have cost them their lives. God had given the midwives families of their own, because they had obeyed Him rather than man. Families were usually reserved for men and not for women. When the words "feared God" are used in scripture," it refers to piety, obedience, and the true worship of God from the heart. It does not mean that we should fear God, as we might fear something else in our life that may or may not cause us harm. God does not want us to fear Him, but to love and worship Him both in spirit and in truth.

When the King found out that the midwives were not killing the male Hebrew children, he was very angry, and he sent for them again. He said to them: "Why have you done this thing and saved the male children alive?" So the midwives replied to the King and said: "Because the Hebrew women are not like the Egyptian women; they are vigorous, and give birth before the midwives come to them."

This must have seemed like a logical answer to the King, because he did not order the midwives killed for their disobedience to his commands. So he said to all of the Egyptian people: "Every son who is born you shall cast into the river and every daughter you shall save alive." Because he could not trust the Hebrew midwives to do what he said, he now commanded his people to do. His people were to throw all Hebrew male babies into the Nile River so they would drown. It would be a cruel and certain way for the Hebrew children to die.

It came to pass as time went on, that two special people from the tribe of Levi were married. Their names were Amram and Jochebed, and the woman became pregnant and bore a son. The baby was so beautiful that she could not even think of harming him in any way. This baby was Gods special baby, and God was watching over him. So she hid him for three months, from the Egyptians. But as time went on it was becoming increasingly difficult for her to hide him. So what was she going to do with him? Without a doubt, she had prayed to God many times for an answer to her problem. At this point, I believe that God would relieve her of her stress, by putting in her heart, what He wanted her to do.

Unknown to Jachebed the mother of this special baby, God has now put into motion His plan to deliver the Israelites from bondage but it would take decades before it would really happen. So the mother of Moses fashioned a basket made out of papyrus or bulrushes. The word "Papyrus" is derived from the Egyptian language meaning, "Red Sea" This could possibly be a reflection, of far into the future to the fact that Moses, would have to cross the Red Sea with the Israelites later on in their history.

Then she daubed it with tar and pitch, and laid it in the reeds by the riverbank. Just as the Ark, had saved Noah and his family from a watery death; so now, God would use this miniature Ark, to save His chosen one from a watery grave.

She could only hope with all of her heart that someone would find the boy and adopt him. But for now, she had placed her beautiful little baby boy into Gods capable and loving hands. But if it were possible at that point in time for her to see into the future, her heart would have leaped with great joy and thankfulness to her God.

Then she sent the baby's oldest sister Miriam, to hide in the reeds and to watch over him. She had to know what would happen to him. Miriam at that time would have been in her mid-to-late teens. Aaron, the brother of Moses, had been born three years earlier. Everything in God's plan for life has a time and a place to happen. But we, as humans, sometimes do not want to wait to see what Gods plan is for us. We just trust in our own judgment and get ourselves into all kinds of trouble.

From this point on in the story, you will be able to see God at work in the life of Moses. As it happened, that on the same day as Moses was put in the river, the Pharaohs daughter came down to the river to bathe. She was a Princess, and she had many attendants looking after her welfare as she bathed in the river. She could have been the same Princess who later became Queen Hatshepsut of the 18th dynasty. She lived from (1501-1482 B.C.) and was possibly the woman who adopted Moses. Although the Egyptian people were accustomed to bathing often to keep clean, it was more of a ritual to bathe in the river from time to time because, the Egyptians considered the waters of the Nile to be sacred.

While the Princess was bathing, some of her attendants were walking along the riverbank, and they saw the basket in the reeds and they mentioned it to the princess. So she sent one of her slave girls to get the basket out of the water. When the Princess opened the basket, the baby cried, and God caused her to have great compassion on him.

It is here, that God expressed His great love and care for His Chosen One, Moses. I believe God didn't permit the baby to cry until after the Princess had opened the basket, and he was safe with the person with whom He had chosen to care for Moses and too raise him to manhood. Otherwise, if he would have cried earlier, other prying Egyptian eyes and ears might have heard him and they may have tried to kill him.

As soon as the Princess had unwrapped the infants blanket, she realized that he was a Hebrew baby because, of his blanket and its special markings and pattern. She said to her slave girls: "This is one of the Hebrew babies." When she picked the baby up and put him in her arms her heart must have pounded with great joy! But now, the Princess had created a huge problem for herself. How would she be able to hide the baby from the Pharaoh, and the rest of the Egyptians who also lived in the palace? Also, she had another problem as well. How was she going to feed him? She had no milk in her breasts to feed the baby, and she certainly did not have any way to really caring for the child.

As she was pondering these problems in her heart, the Lord gave her the answers she needed. Miriam the sister of Moses over heard the Princess expressing her concerns to her attendants. So she ran up to the Princess and bowed before her and said to her: "Shall I go and get one of the Hebrew women to nurse the baby for you?" "Yes, go," she answered. Since it was a Hebrew child, who would be better than a Hebrew woman to nurse it?

So Miriam ran home and got her mother, and brought her before the Princess. The Princess said to the baby's mother: "Take this baby and nurse him for me, and I will pay you your wages." Then the Princess would have made her attendants to swear an oath to keep her secret, possibly under the threat of death. So the woman took the baby and nursed him and cared for him until he was weaned at about two or three years of age. Then his mother took him back to the Pharaohs daughter, and Moses became her adopted son. It was at this time that the Princess named him Moses, because she said that, "she drew him out of the water."

In Hebrew the name Moses means: "He who draws out." In this manner also, his name refers to the Living God who is the true "Deliverer." The name would also refer to Moses, who would deliver the Israelites at the Red Sea. The one, who was drawn out of the water, would be the means of drawing the Israelite nation out of the water at the Red Sea. (See Exodus chapters14-15). There are a few interesting thoughts here, that I would like to bring to your attention at this point in the story.

(1) Moses was born a Hebrew, in the clan of Levi.
(2) He was chosen by God Himself to deliver His people from bondage in Egypt.
(3) The Pharaoh tried to kill Moses and all of the male babies when they were born. But God was working through the Hebrew women, and the midwives and He continued to increase their number.
(4) God made sure that the mother of Moses received money from the Pharaohs treasury as wages, so she could raise her own son.
(5) God surrounded Moses with well-educated people, so he could receive the best education that Egypt had to offer.
(6) Throughout his life in the Pharaohs court, he became mighty in words and deeds. (Acts 7:22).
(7) God molded Moses into a leader of people that He would use eighty years into the future.
(8) Throughout his later life, God used Moses as His spokesman and servant to do many wonders and signs.
(9) Moses would have had to learn three different languages. They would have been Egyptian, Acadian, and Hebrew.

At this point in time, the Pharaoh who was in power was ruling Egypt with an iron fist and his word was an absolute law but he too loved Moses much like a father would love any child of his own. Moses was given everything that he needed without question. Although, the Bible does not elaborate on the first forty years that Moses lived in the Pharaohs court, we know from scripture that, God was making him into a great leader of people and a vessel that He could use, another forty years into the future.

As time went on Moses began to grow restless, and he was becoming more and more curious about his nationality and who he really was. It appears from the scriptures at this point that, by now he knew that he was a Hebrew and not an Egyptian. Moses was now forty years old, and life had been good to him up to this point. He lacked nothing in his life. But now a personal crisis was about to confront him for the first time in his life. This crisis would completely change him for the rest of his life. God was about to take Moses from a life of plenty, to a life of meager means. However, God still had to break him down, humble him, and refine his character, to the point where He could use him the way He wanted to.

-2-

MOSES FLEES FROM EGYPT

One day when Moses went out from the palace to see how his fellow Hebrews was doing, his heart became very distressed within him as he watched his adopted people the Egyptians, mistreating his own people. He finely realized for the first time, how cruel the Egyptians were. To make matters even worse, he realized that he had been living a life of disciplined luxury, while his people were being badly abused and beaten to the point of death its self. Although Moses was well loved and had a privileged position in the Pharaoh's court, there was no legal procedure that he could employ to stop the beatings of his people. As Moses watched his people being driven and whipped like animals, his anger and frustration was became too hard for him to control.

One day as he was watching some of his people working and making bricks in the mud pits, one of the taskmasters started to whip one of the workers. It was too much for him too bare. He could not stand by and hear his people's cries of pain in his ears any longer. So being moved by a powerful sense of injustice he looked all around, and there was no one in sight that he could see. So, in a fit of uncontrollable rage, he struck down and killed the Egyptian taskmaster, and buried him in the sand. Now because of his uncontrolled anger he had just committed murder and it would be something that he would regret for the rest of his life. Only God knows for sure how regretful and fearful Moses must have felt because, God is the only one who knows everyone's thoughts before they even think them.

The next day Moses went out again to see his people. This time however, Moses would realize the bitter consequences of his actions from the day before. As he walked about, surveying his people at work, he came upon two of his fellow Hebrews, who were fighting. As he approached the man who had done the wrong, he said to him: "Why are you striking your companion?" Then the man said to Moses: "Who made you prince and judge over us. Do you intend to kill me as you killed the Egyptian?" Then fear struck at the heart of Moses like a piercing knife, and he said to himself: "Surely this thing is known." So now Moses knew that his crime had been found out. To make things even worse for him, he knew that it was a capital crime for anyone to kill an Egyptian. Moses knew the law, and even with his privileged position, he knew that he was as good as dead if the Pharaoh or his officials found out what he had done.

When the Pharaoh heard about what Moses had done, he sought to kill him. Moses has now realized his worst fear. Now, even his own people as well as the Egyptians would have a good reason to reject and kill him. He had no choice but to flee from Pharaoh and the land of Egypt. He knew in his heart that there was absolutely no place where he could go to hide. So it was that, he left Egypt and fled to the land of Midian, with nothing but the clothes on his back.

The land of Midian is located in the region of the Sinai Peninsula and the Arabian Desert. The area also flanks the eastern arm of the Red Sea or the Gulf of Aqaba on either side. The land was dry and desolate. It formed a stark contrast to the home that Moses had once enjoyed in the royal court of the Pharaoh.

Moses wondered in the desert for many days before he reached the land of Midian but it was at this point in time in the life of Moses that, God was refining his character, and driving him on day after day to the place where He wanted him to be. Finally, at the point of total exhaustion, he came to a well of water, and there he collapsed on the ground and fell asleep. He could not go another step farther because he was simply dead on his feet.

The long hot days and the cold nights that, he had spent in the burning desert sun had taken its toll on his body and spirit. The combination of the hot desert sun, and the guilt in his heart of what he had done back in Egypt, would be like a millstone weighing down on his exhausted heart and soul. But now, God has broken Moses down spiritually to where He could start to use him for the exact purpose that He had given him life.

As the day wore on, things began to happen just like they did in the proceeding stories of the Israelite families that made their homes in the desert. You may recall what I had said about the ownership of a well and its water and its use, and how it was very highly prized and sought after in any desert location. It was no different here in this desert than anywhere else in the world. However, you will see that this well of water will play a significant role in the life of Moses.

While he was sleeping by the well, he was awakened by the sound of people's voices and the sound of sheep and goats bleating. Seven unmarried daughters of the Priest of Midian had come to the well to water their fathers flock. Unmarried girls at that time did not enjoy as much protection and freedom as they do today. It was hard work for the girls, but in that ancient world it was typically the women who drew water for the animals and the household. As the girls were filling the water troughs with water for their flock, some other rough and tough shepherds came along with their flock and tried to drive the girls flock away from the watering troughs.

The scriptures reveal that these men had used this very same bullying tactic on these same girls before with great success. But this time things would be a great deal different. This time God had placed a man there to protect them by the name of Moses. Moses; being the man that he was, could not stand idly by and see this great injustice take place, so he came to the girls rescue. He grabbed one of the shepherd's staffs and he proceeded to drive away the other shepherds and their flocks. Then he drew water from the well and helped the girls to water their flock.

Once again Moses has demonstrated his sensitivity to injustice. After the girls flock had been watered, the girls invited Moses to go with them to their home to meet the rest of their family. The father of the girls had a great deal of influence in the surrounding communities of Midian. His name was Reuel or Jethro as he was sometimes called. The Bible says that he was a Priest like "Melchizedek" the Priest-King of Salem. Salem is a shortened form of the name "Jerusalem." In (Ge.14: 18-20) He was a foreigner who had come to worship the true living God. The name Reuel means "friend of God." His other name Jethro means, "His Excellency."

When the seven sisters arrived at home this time, it was earlier than they had ever done before. This surprised their father so much that he questioned them and said: "Why have you returned so early today?" The girls could not hide their excitement as they answered their fathers probing question, and they said: "An Egyptian rescued us from the shepherds. He even drew water for us and watered the flock." The way that Moses appeared, and the way that he was dressed, was enough to confirm the girls suspicions that he was an

Egyptian. He certainly did not look to them like any run of the mill shepherd.

When the girls arrived at the tent of Jethro, Moses did not go directly into the tent, but he remained outside. He did this out of respect for the family, and he wanted to be invited into the tent, as was the custom. While he was alone outside the tent, he no doubt had been thinking of what he should do next, and where he might go from there. After all, he looked like he was an Egyptian, and, as a rule of thumb, shepherds usually didn't want to have anything to do with Egyptians. So he probably thought that he would not be too welcome in their tent under any condition. Little did he know at that time in his life that, it was the Sovereign God of the Universe who was directing his every move and circumstance?

Then Jethro asked his daughters saying: "Where is he? Why did you leave him? Invite him to have something to eat." So when the invitation was extended to Moses, he entered the tent and settled down to enjoy the hospitality that was extended to him by Jethro and his family. However, along with the invitation for Moses to dine and to stay on with his family, Jethro had an ulterior motive. He was hoping to someday, to merry off at least one of his seven daughters to any man who might fit the bill of eligibility. Who knows! Just maybe, he could get lucky with this man Moses.

After a great deal of deliberation and persuasion, Moses agreed to stay and work for Jethro. Now after forty years of high class living in the Pharaohs Palace, God had brought Moses down to a lowly shepherd's tent, and a vessel that He could use to lead His people in the future. Moses would now learn what it would be like to have to earn a living with his bare hands. He had nothing else to offer Jethro but his loyalty and his labor. Being he was a fugitive from Justice, the offer of protection from the mighty Egyptian Pharaoh, a new home, and being accepted into Reuel's household, it was an offer that he could not refuse.

As time went on, Moses fell in love with one of Jethro's daughters and he married her. Her name was Zipporah, which means ("Bird"). Some time had passed after they were married, and she gave birth to a son and Moses named him Gershom, which means (A Stranger), because Moses said that he was a stranger in a foreign land. So now Moses was doubly removed and cast out from his people and from the Egyptian people as well. He was estranged in yet another waiting place. (Ex. 2:22) For all he knew, he would be a stranger and a wonderer for the rest of his days. But for now Moses was becoming very happy and content with his new family. He knew that he could not ask for anything more from life then what he already had. The scriptures say that he dwelt in the land of Midian for forty years.

During this span of forty years Moses, would have had ample time to learn a great deal about the God of the mountain whom his people worshiped, and from his father-in-law Jethro who was the High Priest of Midian. He knew that God existed without any doubt but he had never seen Him. It would have been the only way that Moses could have learned anything about God although, he may have heard some stories from time to time from the slaves that he had contact with before he left Egypt.

It was during this long period of time that King Thutmose 3rd died, (1447B.C) and a new Pharaoh came to power. This Kings death was paramount in the life of Moses. His death would give Moses a new lease on life. It would enable Moses to go back to Egypt, without being under the threat of death. When any King died, the Egyptian authorities dropped all pending charges against people, even in capital cases. So now Moses at last, would be a free man.

During the forty years that Moses was absent from Egypt, the plight of the Israelite people had reached a fever pitch. The Bible says in (Ex. 2: 23-24), "The Israelites groaned in their slavery and cried out, and their cry for help because of their slavery went up to God. God heard their groaning and He remembered His covenant with Abraham, Isaac, and Jacob.

So God looked on the Israelites and He was concerned about them." By this time however, Moses was in his twilight years as we say today, because he was now eighty-years old. Sometimes we call it a ripe old age. But God had no doubt preserved, and maintained his body; in much more of a middle aged mans condition, than what the people enjoy today at eighty years old. From this point on in his life, Moses would be traveling more extensively doing the Lords work, and not sitting around tending sheep.

God had now finished tempering his character, and Moses was now ready to be a vessel that God could use to accomplish His will. Once again Moses was about to experience another drastic change in his life; and God was about to send him where he did not want to go. It would be a change that God had engineered for His purpose, for both the Israelites and for Moses himself long before Moses was even born.

MOSES AND THE BURNING BUSH

One day while Moses was tending a flock of sheep for his father-in-law Jethro, he took the flock to the far side of the desert so he could find better grazing for them. When he arrived at the far side of the desert; it was right where God wanted him to be. God had brought him to a perfect place where he would have a clear view of Mount Horeb, or the mountain of God. The name Horeb means ("Desert or Desolation"), but God would make it a holy place, because of His divine presence there.

As Moses was tending his flock, the Angel of the Lord appeared to him on the side of the mountain in, the form of a burning bush. The expression, the "Angel of the Lord" here, is used interchangeably with the names "The Lord" and "God." God often revealed Himself to people, accompanied by fire and an ominous dark cloud (Ex. 13:21; 19:18; 1ki 18:24, 38).

As he watched the bush, it appeared to be on fire, but it was not burning up, and this intrigued Moses and his curiosity got the better of him. So Moses thought to himself and said: "I will go over and see this strange sight, why the bush doesn't burn up." When God seen that Moses had turned aside to see this great sight, He called to him from the midst of the burning bush and said: "Moses! Moses!" Can you imagine the fear that must have went through the heart of Moses?

After all, this is the first time in his life that Moses has had any real contact with this God of his people. God in His great wisdom and mercy had chosen to use the curiosity of Moses to introduce Himself to His servant. It is possible that, if God had chosen any other way to introduce Himself to Moses, it would have frightened him half to death and Moses may not have ventured anywhere near the mountain because of his fear of the unknown.

When Moses answered the Lord he said: "Here I am" Then God said to Moses: "Do not come any closer. Take off your sandals, for the place where you are standing is Holy Ground. I am the God of your father, the God of Abraham, the God of Isaac, and the God of Jacob." By mentioning the names of the forefathers of Moses, God was assuring Moses, that He was the same God that his ancestors worshiped long ago. Also, that the covenant that He had made with them was still in effect and nothing had changed. As you can see, God doesn't change His mind or His word.

When God told Moses who He was, Moses hid his face in total fear because he was afraid to look at God. But sometime later on when Moses went to meet God on one occasion on Mount Sinai he would ask God to see His glory (Ex. 33:18). Then God said to Moses: "I have indeed seen the misery of my people in Egypt. I have heard them crying out because of their slave drivers, and I am concerned about their suffering. So I have come down to rescue them from the hand of the Egyptians, and to bring them up out of that land into a good and spacious land, a land flowing with milk and honey."

Canaan was the home of the Canaanites, Hittites, Amorites, Perizzites, Hivites, and the Jebusites. So now, God has told Moses about the land that He has promised to His people the Israelites in the future. It would be the land of Canaan, or the Promised Land as it is called in the Bible. God has always been faithful to His word, and always will be no matter what happens in the world even to this very day.

When God used the words "I have come down to rescue them," these words speak of Gods gracious intervention on the earth. (Ps. 40:1). It also prefigures the Incarnation of Jesus Christ. Jesus; Gods only begotten Son, would someday far into the future, come down from Heaven to deliver mankind from Sin Death and the Power of Satan, and to have fellowship with mankind in the form of a man.

He was with us here on the earth for thirty-three years doing His Fathers will. Then Jesus did what He had come to the earth to do. He gave His life, and shed His precious blood on the cross at Calvary, to redeem all of mankind from their sins. When He rose from the grave on that first Easter Sunday, sin, death, and the power of Satan has been totally broken and defeated forever. Through Gods Grace, mankind has now been given the choice of becoming immortals once again. We have once again been declared righteous in Gods eyes through the Blood of the Lord Jesus Christ.

Not only was God showing Moses that He was intimately aware of the troubles of His people, but now He would also act directly on their behalf. The good and large land of Canaan was Gods great pledge to His people. (Ge.12: 7) (15:12-21) (Ex.6:8). In the future he Land of Canaan would, sustain Gods people for the centuries to come. It had large tracks of land ideally suited for agriculture as well as land suited for the support of flocks and herds of all manner of livestock. Under God's blessing, Canaan would truly seem to be a land that flowed with milk and honey.

At this time, Moses was probably wondering why God was telling him all of these things. He certainly did not think that it would involve him to any great degree. He certainly did not consider himself to be involved with God in anyway shape or form. But as he continued to listen to God, the Lord said to him: "So now, go. I am sending you to Pharaoh to bring my people the Israelites out of Egypt." When God said this to Moses, you could have probably knocked him over with a feather. Egypt was the last place on earth that he would ever want to return to because, as far as he was concerned, the Pharaoh still wanted to kill him. For this one reason alone, he had a very valid excuse for not wanting to go back to Egypt.

So with some show of timid hesitation in his voice, Moses said to God: "Who am I that I, should go to Pharaoh and bring the Israelites out of Egypt?" This is the first time of many times to come, that Moses tries to get God to give up on him and not send him back to Egypt. But as God continued to speak with Moses He said to him: "I will be with you, and this will be a sign to you that it is I who sent you. When you have brought the people out of Egypt, you will worship God on this mountain." Now God has just assured Moses that He would be with him when he went back to Egypt, and that He would continue to be with him in all that he was to accomplish there for God.

But good old Moses is still trying to come up with excuses not to go and do what God wants him to do. Moses was only being true to his human nature, like many people do in today's world. He was letting his fear of the unknown control him to the point of sheer rebellion against God.

Then Moses said to the Lord: "suppose I go to the Israelites and say to them: the God of your fathers has sent me to you,' and they ask me, 'What is His name?' Then what shall I tell them?" This seemed like an innocent enough question to Moses, because God had not yet identified Himself to Moses by name. Being that this was the second time that Moses had expressed his reluctance to go to Egypt, he may have thought that God would throw in the towel and give up on him and let him go. But that was not to be the case. God said to Moses: "I AM WHO I AM! This is what you are to say to the Israelites: "I AM" has sent me to you. Say to the Israelites. "The Lord, the God of your fathers, the God of Abraham, the God of Isaac, and the God of Jacob has sent me to you. This is my name forever, the name by which I am to be remembered from generation to generation."

The One who spoke to Moses declared Himself to be the Eternal One, uncaused and independent. Only the Creator of all things can call Himself the "I AM." in the absolute sense. When we speak of God, we say He Is. All other creatures in God's creation are in a position of obligation to Him for their existence. In the Hebrew language the word "Lord" means "Yahweh. In addition to this, God the Great Creator was declaring His absolute existence and His relationship with the people of Israel.

Then God said to Moses: "Go, and assemble the elders of Israel and say to them, 'The Lord, the God of your fathers, the God of Abraham, Isaac, and Jacob appeared to me and said: I have watched over you and have seen what has been done to you in Egypt. I have promised to bring you up out of your misery in Egypt, into the land of the Canaanites, Hittites, Amorites, Perizzites, Hivites and Jebusites, a land flowing with milk and honey."

You may have noticed, God repeats the same words over and over when He wants His instructions followed too the letter, and for the purpose of emphasis. Likewise, it also helps the person who is hearing the message to get it straight in his or her own mind as well. God will not leave anything to chance, or to the hope that it will happen. It is all or nothing with God! You cannot walk the fence with God. Either you love and serve Him, or you don't. It's that simple. The sooner that mankind realizes the truth in these words, and applies this truth to their lives, the better it will be for everyone in the world.

As God continued to talk to Moses, He said to him: "The elders of Israel will listen to you. Then you and the elders are to go to the King of Egypt and say to him, 'The Lord, the God of the Hebrews, has met with us. Let us take a three-day journey into the desert to offer sacrifices to the Lord our God.' But I know that the King of Egypt will not let you go unless a mighty hand compels him. So I will stretch out my hand and strike the Egyptians with all the wonders that I will perform among them. After that he will let you go. I will make the Egyptians favorably disposed towards this people, so that when you leave you will not go empty-handed. Every woman is to ask her neighbor and any woman living in her house, for articles of silver, and gold, and for clothing, which you will put on your sons and daughters, and you will plunder the Egyptians."

This was the same promise that God had made to Abraham centuries before. The Lord said in (Ge. 15-14-16 Ps.105: 37). "And also, the nation whom they serve I will judge; afterward, they shall come out with great possessions." The Lord would be providing His people with great possessions, of clothing, gold, silver, and anything else that the people required for their journey to the Land of Canaan. This was Gods way of ensuring that, His people in turn, would have riches to give back to Him with thanksgiving. Much later in time, the Israelites would be required to give these very same precious goods back to God. These precious goods would be an offering for the Tabernacle that God would require His people to build in the future in the desert on their way to Canaan.

So now God has told Moses in advance, what He was going to do in the future with the Egyptians? When God refers to the wonders that He would perform, He is referring to the ten plagues in (Ex. chs. 7-12) that He would bring upon the Egyptian people. He would do this to punish them for the pain and suffering that they had brought upon the children of Israel. These wonders would be thing only God can do. The words that God spoke were designed to inspire reverence in His worshipers, and fear in the hearts of His enemies.

In the future God would humiliate the Egyptian Pharaoh so much, that his people would turn against him because, of his stubbornness, and the results of the ten plagues. Because of their suffering, the Egyptian people would look with favor on the Israelites, and they would gladly give them whatever they asked for when they were ready to leave Egypt, just to get rid of them and their God.

Even after God had explained all of these things to Moses, and had given him all kinds of assurance, Moses still wasn't convinced in his heart that he wanted to go along with Gods plan for his life. He probably would have given a dozen sheep and a dozen goats, to anyone or to anything else that, would help him to get out of this situation that he now found himself in. How was he to explain to God that, he just wasn't the man for this job? So now Moses, in all his worldly wisdom, dips down in his bag of tricks and comes up with another great "what if," for God to overcome and to think about. This would be his third expression of reluctance, to do what God wanted him to do.

He said to God: "What if they do not believe me or listen to me and say, 'The Lord did not appear to you'?" This was indeed, another very feeble excuse by Moses, so he could bail out on God and not have to go back to Egypt. It seems that we as mankind, even in this day and age all have a great tendency to bail out on God whenever we can if, what He wants us to do will take us out of our comfort zone.

But this time, things would be a bit different and God would shake him up a bit. It would make Moses realize just whom he was dealing with. This time God would show Moses His Almighty Power, and just what He could do anytime He chose to do it.

When Moses had left his flock to investigate the miracle of the burning bush, he had carried with him his shepherd's staff in his hand. So God said to Moses: "What is that in your hand?" "A staff," he replied. Then God said to Moses: "Throw it on the ground." When he threw it on the ground it became a snake. The snake was not just any ordinary run of the mill piousness snake. It was possibly a cobra whose venom is very deadly. This type of snake is quite common in the Middle Eastern countries. Throughout Egyptian history, the Pharaohs wore an emblem made out of pure gold, of a cobra on the front of their headdress. It was warn as a symbol of their sovereignty and power.

When Moses seen that the staff had become a snake, it struck great fear in his heart and he ran from it. God had turned the staff into a snake so that He could demonstrate the reality of His power, and His presence to Moses for his coming mission to Egypt. After God had calmed Moses' and his fears down a little; He said to Moses: "Reach out your hand and take it by the tail, that they may know that the God of their fathers has appeared to you." So when Moses did as God had commanded him, the snake turned into a wooden staff in his hand once again.

As it so happened, Moses still had some lingering doubts about the power of God in his mind. But God knew the thoughts of Moses, and that he was not truly convinced that he was the man for the job. So God decided to demonstrate His Mighty Right Hand one more time to, this mere mortal of a man. It is here at this point in the story, that you can see and understand the great patience of God. So God said to Moses; "Put your hand inside your cloak." So he did as he was told, and when he pulled it out it was as white as snow with "Leprosy." This must have scared Moses half out of his wits. After he looked at his hand for a minute or two, God said to him: "Put your hand back into your cloak." So Moses did as he was instructed and when he pulled it out, his hand had returned to its natural state.

Now at this time, God has given Moses two miraculous, or supernatural, signs of His power. Then God said to Moses: "If they do not believe you or pay attention to the first miraculous sign, they may believe the second. But if they do not believe these two signs, or listen to you, take some water from the Nile and pour it on the dry ground. The water you take from the river will become blood on the ground." This would be the third miracle that God intended do for Moses.

By now you would have thought that Moses might have gotten the message loud and clear from God. But being true to his human nature, Moses was still reluctant to do

Gods bidding. Unfortunately there are a great percentage of people in today's world as well that God, has to really shake up before He gets their attention, and they understand the message that He has for them.

Even when God permits some sickness or disaster, to come into their lives, they still do not want to listen to Him. People still want to go their own way, which is the way of the world and the Devil. But people must remember four very important points. (1) If you follow the ways of the world and keep on living in your sinful ways; (2) if you do not repent of your sins in prayer to God; (3) if you do not believe that the Lord Jesus Christ is the only way to eternal life; (4) you cannot and will not inherit eternal life and live with God throughout all eternity. You will be doomed to spend your eternity in Hell with the Devil in total darkness and torment.

As you can see, God is still showing great patience with Moses. But by now Moses has learned one very important lesson. It is a lesson that he will never forget as long as he lives. He has finely realized the tremendous power that God has at His disposal when He desires to use it. This is true because now, he addresses God as the Lord, and he finally admits to himself and to God, that he is Gods servant, whether he likes it or not. But he is still trying to cling to one small last glimmer of hope that, he can still elude Gods plan and not return to Egypt.

So for the fourth time, Moses expresses his reluctance to the Lord. He came up with another good excuse why; he was not fit to carry out Gods plan for Him. He said to God: "O Lord, I have never been eloquent, neither in the past nor, since you have spoken to your servant. I am slow of speech and tongue." Moses is not complaining, in the sense of a speech impediment. But he was complaining instead, of not being persuasive enough, or quick witted enough, to be able to match wits with the Egyptian King.

This was a valid point for Moses and his last hope to get out of this situation with God. But as far as the Lord was concerned it was a useless point to make. Moses was not as yet; trusting God to do what He said He would do. He still thought that God would give up on him, and let him off the hook. What Moses did not know or understand was that God had raised him up for this very purpose.

The human race is the only ones who will let you off the preverbal hook at times. If God wants to use you in some way for His service, He will prompt you by the Holy Spirit and He will put in your heart what He wants you to do. He will not force you to do anything you don't want to do but, that is because, He has given mankind the free will of choice. But if, you make the right choices, He will guide you throughout your whole life if you will let him. But His will must be done to please Him. You will see that, this is exactly what happened from the following conversation between God and Moses.

Even though God is still showing great patience with Moses at this point, God did not particularly care for his complaining about his slow tongue and slow speech. The Lord said to Moses: "Who gave man his mouth? Who makes him deaf or mute? Who gives him sight or makes him blind? Is it not I, the Lord? Now, go; I will help you speak, and teach you what to say." God has now given Moses the command to go, and to get on with the task that God has given him to do. God has also stressed to Moses the fact that He has fashioned each individual according to His wisdom and not mans wisdom.

You would think that after the miracles that God had just shown Moses to this point and of all the things that God had said to him, it would have convinced him to obey God. But that was not to be the case just yet with Moses. He was still thinking in his own human capacity to do, what he had to do too get out of having to return Egypt.

Now for the fifth time, Moses begs God, not to send him to the Pharaoh. He even used the word "Please," to emphasize the fear that he felt in his heart, in having to carry out Gods command. He said to God: "O Lord, "Please," send someone else to do it." Now the Lord was starting to lose His patience with Moses. The Bible says in (Ex. 4: 14), so the anger of the Lord was kindled against Moses. Now he was about to get a flash of Gods anger. Although the Lord is "slow to anger," He does not withhold His anger or punishment from His disobedient children forever. But God was way ahead of Moses in His thinking. The Lord in His mercy and grace had already solved the problem that Moses had just come up with, when he had complained about his speech. God had already foreseen the problem that He was going to have with Moses, and with this particular complaint about his speech. So now God cuts off the last avenue of escape that seemed open to Moses.

God then said to Moses: "What about your brother Aaron the Levite? I know he can speak well. He is already on his way to meet you, and his heart will be glad when he sees you. You shall speak to him and put words in his mouth. I will help both of you speak and will teach you what to do. He will speak to the people for you, and it will be as if he were your mouth, and as if you were God to him. But take this staff in your hand, so you can perform miraculous signs with it."

This staff was just an ordinary shepherds crook made of wood. But the thing that made it so great was the fact that, it would be the means by which God would demonstrate His great and awesome power to the Pharaoh and his people in Egypt. In and through, the hands of Gods two servants Moses and Aaron, God would work His mighty miracles, and bring Himself great Glory and Honor. In (Ex. 4:27) God had said to Aaron: "Go into the wilderness to meet Moses." So with

Gods guidance Aaron went to meet Moses at the base of the Mount Sinai.

As you can see from scripture that God had already spoken to Aaron, long before His conversation with Moses on the mountain of God. God had already put that part of His plan into motion because it could have taken a few days or even a week, for Aaron to reach his brother Moses on Gods Holy Mountain.

With the conversation between God and Moses now at an end, Moses went back down to the base of the mountain. There like God had said, his brother Aaron met him. When Moses met Aaron, he threw he arms around him and gave him a big bear hug and kissed him on both sides of his face. This was, and still is, a custom of greeting in many of the Middle Eastern Countries of the world today. Their long overdue meeting was probably one of many tears, and two or three bear hugs to be sure. After all, they hadn't seen each other for over forty years. Without a doubt they would have had many things to tell each other because of being apart for such a long period of time. After some time had passed, Moses told Aaron everything that God had requested of him to do. Moses also told him about all of the miraculous signs, that God had commanded him to perform.

Now God has called Moses to be His "Prophet," and the man who will deliver His people from bondage, and to lead them to the Promised Land. A Prophet or a Prophetess's main job was to represent accurately to people, the message of the one who sent him or her. As Moses is now called a Prophet of God, so Aaron was to be a Prophet of Moses. Now God has everything set in place to start His deliverance of the Israelites from Egypt.

The way that God set up His plan was, the way that God wanted it done. God would tell Moses what to say and do, and then Moses would tell Aaron what to say and do. In this manner, everything that was said or done in God's plan would have to come from God first. There would be absolutely no chance of anything going wrong, and God would be in complete control of everything. He was the head of the chain of command. It would be impossible for the Pharaoh to blame Moses and Aaron for anything that would now occur.

After a short rest at the base of the mountain, and some preparation with the flock that Moses had been in charge of, Moses and Aaron departed from the mountain of God and returned to the home of Jethro, his father-in-law. After all of the greetings and excitement was over and the people had settled down for the day, Moses probably told all of the people in the camp once again about, what had happened to him on the mountain without leaving out any of the details. Moses then said to Jethro the words that would hurt his old heart to the core. He said, "Please let me go and return to my own people who are in Egypt, and see whether they are still alive."

Moses had to get permission from Jethro to leave because; he had now become an official part of Jethro's family. This was just a common courtesy that was afforded to families at that time. Once again, Moses was leaving the only real family that he had known in the last forty years. With a great deal of heaviness in his heart Jethro said to Moses: "Go in peace." He didn't know if, he would ever see them again in his lifetime when they left, but he gave Moses and his family his blessing and wished them well.

We as parents, have to do much the same thing to our children when they grow up and want to leave our family. But we will still miss them and love them unconditionally, until we die. But this is all part of Gods great and glorious plan for all of mankind. Now all there was left for Moses to do was to prepare himself and his family to go back to Egypt. But first he would have to wait on the Lord to give him the permission to leave Midian.

-3-

MOSES RETURNS TO EGYPT

So it came to pass that now, another chapter in the life of Moses closes, and God opens another door in his life. But as you will soon see, God will make Moses into one of His greatest Prophets. While Moses and his family were still in Midian in the camp of Jethro, the Lord appeared to Moses and said: "Go back to Egypt, for all the men who wanted to kill you are dead." This was another surprise that God had for Moses, and it could not have come at a better time. Now his fears could all disappear. God also knew that it would give Moses more confidents to go back to Egypt because he would not have the fear of death in his heart.

Now Moses has received the command from the Lord to go to Egypt. So without any hesitation, he loaded up his wife and his two sons' Gershom, and Eliezer, and all of their family possessions on donkeys, and they said their good bye to Jethro and his family, and they departed for Egypt. The Bible doesn't say just how long it took Moses and his family to reach Egypt; or just where they decided to live in Egypt, but this time Moses obeyed God without any argument what so ever, and he had Gods peace in his heart and in his mind.

This is positive proof that the Lord by this time had given Moses, a change of attitude, and he had changed his way of thinking of what he had to do. Now he was developing a good positive relationship with God whom he would now devote his life to. This could have also been due in part, of the result of the great relationship, and the influence of Jethro his father-in-law. It is a well-proven fact that God, will use other people to influence you and get you started in the direction that He wants you to go.

In the last conversation that Moses had with the Lord before he departed for Egypt God had said to him; "When you return to Egypt, see that you perform before Pharaoh all the wonders that I have given you the power to do. But I will harden his heart so that he will not let the people go." There is nine times in the story of the Exodus that the hardening of the Pharaohs heart is ascribed to God. But there are also another nine times that the Pharaoh has said to have harden his own heart against God.

The new Pharaoh that had now come to power was probably, "Amenhotep II" who reigned from, (1447-1421B.C.). He was not simply just a King of Egypt, but he was a symbol of all of those who resisted, and were sworn enemies of God. The Bible also says in (Ex. 9:16), that God had determined Pharaohs negative response to Moses, long before Pharaoh could harden his heart. God had put this particular Pharaoh in power, for the express purpose of demonstrating His power, to the people of Egypt and to His people as well.

Then God said to Moses: "Say to the Pharaoh, thus says the Lord: Israel is my firstborn son, and I told you to "Let my son go, so he may worship me. But you refused to let him go; so I will kill your firstborn son." When God used the words "firstborn son" here, it's used as a figure of speech indicating Israel's special relationship with God, and these words also "Anticipate" what will happen in the tenth plague that will come upon Egypt in the near future.

These words are also used collectively of the Israelites in (Hos. 11:1). But when these words are used later on in scripture in connection with the ten plagues, the words have a completely different meaning, as do the words, "Gods Son." This is because; as time passes all those who believe in Gods son Jesus Christ, and does the will of the Father who sent Him will be called Gods Sons. Some day when all believers die, they will be taken to heaven to live with God throughout all eternity. The scripture in (Jn. 1:12) says: "Yet to all who received Him, to those who believed in His name, He gave the right to become the children of God."

As Moses and his family made their exhausting journey towards Egypt, after some days of travel, they stopped at a lodging place along the way to rest. It was a place where there was plenty of water and some shade trees, and feed for the animals as well. It was one of the few oases that existed in that particular part of the desert.

As you know, for anyone traveling in the desert at that time in history it would be very hot, dry, dusty work. When they seen the lodging place their hearts and spirits must have gotten a real up lifting. They would without a doubt, welcome the opportunity to clean up and to rest up for a little while, before continuing on their journey to Egypt. You must remember that Moses is now eighty years old. He would not be as energetic and as strong as he was when he was in his prime of life. A person's old age has a way of catching up to all of us, if God permits us to live that long.

The Bible does not say just, how long they stayed at the oases, but a very critical experience in the life of Moses happened while he was there. The Bible says in (Ex. 4:24) that the Lord met Moses there and sought to kill him. Evidently, Moses had disobeyed and broken Gods covenant of circumcision, because he hadn't circumcised one of his sons. He possibly had done this so he could please his Midianite wife, who may have been opposed to circumcision of children.

The Midianite males were circumcised just before they were married, and not when they were infants. The neglect of circumcision, by Moses was a crime deserving of death. This was especially true for the future leader of Gods people. It was a sin that God would not put up with because it was disobedience of a direct order by God Himself, so God sought to kill Moses.

When Zipporah the wife of Moses, heard what was about to happen, she took a flint knife and cut off her sons' foreskin and she touched Moses' feet with it. She said: "Surely you are a bridegroom of blood to me." When she said these words to Moses, it was referring to circumcision, and the covenant that God had made with Abraham and his descendants. By committing this act, Zipparah, had actually saved the life of Moses. There is no doubt, that she had sensed the divine displeasure of God and she decided to do the surgery immediately. In those days the people used a flint knife, to do the surgery because it held its edge and it was much sharper then the metal knives that were available at that time. After God seen that the circumcision was done, He left Moses alone and let him live although, He could have struck him dead at any given time.

After some time had passed, Moses and his family left the lodging place, and continued on their journey to Egypt. Moses was unaware at this time that God had spoken to his brother Aaron a second time and had instructed him to go into the desert to meet Moses at the mountain of God. When Moses and his family arrived at the mountain, Aaron was already there to meet them. After their second joyful reunion was over Moses told Aaron everything that the Lord had said to him. He explained to him about all of the miraculous signs that God had commanded him to perform. At the same time, Moses instructed Aaron on how the chain of command had to work that included him. God would speak the message to

Moses, then Moses would repeat it to Aaron, and then Aaron would perform the signs before the people.

When they arrived in Egypt some time later, Moses and Aaron went directly to the Israelites camp and they gathered all of the elders together. After the elders were all assembled, Aaron told them everything that Moses had commanded him to say to them. When the elders heard, that the Lord was concerned about the Israelites and their bitter years of bondage, they bowed down and worshiped the Lord. Their belief was also greatly reinforced because of the signs that Moses and Aaron did in their presences as the Lord had instructed them to do. The elders were fully convinced without any doubt that Moses and Aaron were indeed sent by God as His messengers.

Likewise, the same could have been said for Moses and Aaron. It must have given their faith and confidence quite a boost, when they were able to perform Gods signs with the staff that He told Moses to take with him. Also, being able to do these signs would be absolute proof to them that God was true to His word, and that He was with them as He said He would be.

Now that the first test of their faith had been completed and was behind them, Moses and Aaron would now require a greater leap of faith, and a greater degree of boldness, to complete their second test. They were now on their way to confront the King of Egypt who, was considered by some people to be a real tyrant. This task would take a great deal, more faith and courage on their part, then anything that they had ever encountered in their lives before. This time, they would have to rely strictly on God for everything. God would be their only strength and protection, against this Pharaoh of Egypt, a man that they had never met or had any kind of dealings with before. It would indeed be a monumental test of their faith, and trust in God to do what He had asked them to do.

But the two of them also realized and understood that they must obey God at all cost, no matter what came their way because of His promise to them. He had promised to be with them, to protect them, and to deliver them from the Pharaoh. They were not to doubt God and His power at any time. However the thought may have crossed their minds at one time that, they were going to Egypt strictly on their own faith but, that thought was soon eliminated because God had already performed miracles through them before the Elders of the Israelites. But God had another surprise gift for His two servants waiting for them. It was a gift that they didn't even know about until they arrived at the Palace of the King.

By the time Moses and Aaron had reached the palace, God had instilled in His messengers, a heart of great boldness and courage. Any fears that they may have been possessed with earlier had vanished. This was defiantly something that they did not possess when they left home.

So with this newfound boldness in their hearts, they went directly to the palace and demanded an audience with the Pharaoh. No doubt this tyrant king, wondered who these two people were, and what give them the right to demand an immediate audience with him. It was unheard of for anyone to demand anything of the great Pharaoh. As ruthless and as cruel as this oppressor was, he could have ordered Moses and Aaron killed on the spot, and their bodies thrown to the buzzards without even giving them an audience at all but, God was with them and He was protecting them.

So it was that, Moses and Aaron approached this tyrant King with strong daring words in the name of their God. By using the name of their God, they were able to approach the Pharaoh without any fear in their hearts. Then in the presence of the King, Moses told Aaron what he was to say. He said to the King: "Thus says the Lord God of Israel: 'Let my people go, that they may hold a feast to me in the wilderness.'" When the King replied to Aaron, he not only expressed his arrogance, but his bad attitude, and the hatred that he had against the Hebrews as well. This same arrogant attitude would come back to haunt him as time went on.

He said to Aaron: "Who is the Lord that I should obey His voice and let Israel go?" I do not know the Lord, nor will I let Israel go." So now Moses and Aaron could see that Gods plan was working out just as He had said it would. This would also serve to increase their boldness and faith in God a great deal more also. They would now know for sure, that God would do what He says He would do, and that they would never have anything to fear from this tyrant King any more.

So once more Aaron said to the King: "The God of the Hebrews has met with us. Please let us go three days journey' into the desert and sacrifice to the Lord our God, least He fall upon us with pestilence or with the sword." This was a reasonable request for God to make. It also made the requirement of worship and sacrifice fall squarely on Gods shoulders and not on the shoulders of Moses and Aaron, or on the children of Israel.

Now it appears that the Pharaoh is caught between a rock and a hard place. So now his attitude turns from arrogance, to panic. If he let the Israelites go to worship this God that he did not know, he knew that there would be no reason for them to ever come back to Egypt to die in the mud pits of Egypt. He certainly didn't want to lose his big work force. If he lost his slaves, he would have to rely on Egyptian manpower to complete the two cities of Pithom, and Raamses that they were presently building.

So now the King was backed into a corner and he had to come up with a reason why he could not let his slaves go. He then said to Moses and Aaron: "Why do you take the people from their work? Get back to your work! "Look, the people of the land are numerous now, and you make them rest from their labors." The last thing that the Pharaoh wanted to do for his slaves was, to give them a day off to rest so that they could regain their strength, and maybe rebel against him and his authority. So on the same day that Moses and Aaron came to see the Pharaoh he decided to punish Moses and Aaron for their insolence. He had to show them that he still had power over the Hebrews. As far as he was concerned no god or man for that matter was going to tell him what to do.

It was at that time that, the Pharaoh decided to make life a great deal harder for the Hebrew people. He called in his Egyptian taskmasters, and the Hebrew officers who were in charge of all of the work crews and he said to them: "You shall no longer give the people straw to make bricks as before. Let them go and gather straw for themselves. But require them to make the same amount of bricks. Don't reduce the quota. They are lazy; that is why they are crying out, 'Let us go and sacrifice to our God." Make the men work harder so that they keep working and pay no attention to lies."

Until this point in time, the Egyptians had gathered the straw and brought it to the mud pits to make bricks. But now it was up to the Israelites to go and gather their own straw where they could find it. When they couldn't find enough straw, they had to pull up the stubble and use it to make bricks. This task would now have to be done by the Hebrew officers who were in charge of the work crews as well. This added responsibility, meant that the officers would have to work much harder than they did before. Their easy life was gone. Now, they too, were beaten with the whip, as well as the rest of the slaves. Because of their official position, they thought that they should not be dealt with in such a harsh manner.

As time went on, the officers went and complained more bitterly to the Pharaoh that they had no straw to make bricks and that it was the Egyptians fault that they couldn't possibly meet their daily quota. But it didn't do them any good to complain. The Pharaoh only repeated his same old excuse and scorn and said to them; "Lazy, that's what you are—Lazy! That is why you keep saying: 'Let us go and sacrifice to the Lord.' Now get to work. You will not be given any straw, yet you must produce your full quota of bricks."

When the officers came out from the palace of the Pharaoh, Moses and Aaron were waiting for them. Now they had someone else to blame for their troubles so they turned their anger on Moses and Aaron. They said to Moses and Aaron: "May the Lord look upon you and judge you! You have made us a stench to the Pharaoh and his officials, and have put a sword in their hand to kill us." The people feared that the Pharaoh would deal more harshly with them, because of the words that Moses and Aaron had spoken to him.

This accusation from the officials upset Moses and Aaron a great deal. So Moses complained to the Lord and said: "O Lord, why have you brought trouble upon this people? Is this why you sent me? Ever since I went to Pharaoh to speak in your name, he has brought trouble upon this people, and you have not rescued your people at all." Moses expected the Pharaoh to cave in as soon as he heard the Lords name "Yahweh." But nothing had happened to this point because; God had not acted as yet with His strong right hand. Moses had forgotten one very important thing that the Lord had said to him. It was that He knew that the Pharaoh would harden his heart and not let the people go. When Moses questioned the Lord, he was reflecting on the fact, that he initially was reluctant to be the Lords agent of deliverance.

Unfortunately, there is a great percentage of the human race of today that does not want to do Gods bidding for Him either. They would sooner go their own way and take their chances with life than serve the Lord in any capacity. Also, they would rather serve other gods that are dead, who can't do anything for them, or give them "eternal life. I believe that it must cause a great deal of pain in the heart of God, when mankind rejects Him and His Son Jesus Christ the way that they do. For God has no equal, in heaven and earth. There is no limit on the amount of love that He shares with His Creation and with His children who are believers.

After Moses had settled down a bit and had quit complaining to the Lord, He said to Moses: "Now you will see what I will do to Pharaoh." God said these very empowering words to give Moses some encouragement to continue his work for the Lord. As the Lord continued to speak to Moses, He said: "Because of my mighty hand he will let them go; because of my mighty hand he will drive them out of his country."

This is the second time that God has told Moses what He was going to do. But He didn't give Moses any kind of timetable. As I have mentioned before, God is not in a hurry to do things. He has a time for everything. He has a time for seed, and a time for harvest, a time for reaping, and a time for storing. He has a set time for living, and a set time for dying. Therefore; you must understand; that when you read the Bible, there can be a great deal of time that may have passed between the scriptures, without them saying anything to that effect. Also, you must remember that God knows the end result of everything past, present, and future. Everything is under His control, and there is nothing that He doesn't know or see.

As the Lord continued to talk to Moses, He started to fill Moses in on some of the things that He had done in the past centuries long ago with his ancestors. With the passage of time and with the type of education that Moses had received in the Pharaohs palace, it is quit safe to say, that Moses might not have had much previous knowledge of his ancestors and their commitments to God. In the scriptures (Ex. 6: 2-8), God used the words: "I am the Lord, four different times.

1. To introduce the message to Moses. (v. 2)
2. Based on the (v v.2-5) to confirm Gods promise of redemption of His people. (v.6) this fact would have only been comprehended and understood by the Israelites who were to experience the exodus and their descendants.
3. To underscore Gods intention to adopt Israel as His people. (V.7)
4. To confirm His promise of the Land of Canaan to His people as an inheritance and to conclude the message to Moses. (V.8).

God said to Moses: "I appeared to Abraham, to Isaac, and to Jacob as God Almighty, but by my name the "Lord," I did not make myself known to them." I also established my covenant with them to give them the land of Canaan, where they lived as aliens. Moreover, I have heard the groaning of the Israelites whom the Egyptians are enslaving, and I will remember my covenant. Therefore, say to the Israelites; 'I am the Lord, and I will bring you out from under the yoke of the Egyptians. I will free you from being slaves to them, and I will redeem you with an outstretched arm and with mighty acts of judgment. I will take you as my own people, and I will be your God. Then you will know that I am the Lord your God, who brought you out from under the yoke of the Egyptians. I will bring you to the land that I swore with up lifted hand to give to Abraham, to Isaac, and to Jacob. I will give it to you as a possession, I am the Lord.' "

You can see here from the above paragraph that God has now brought Moses up to date with a brief but great history lesson. Also, at the same time, God was renewing the same covenant with Moses and the Israelites as He had with their ancestor's centuries before. You can also see that God is a covenant God, and that He does nothing for mankind without making a covenant first. God's word in itself is a covenant, and you can say for certain that it is carved in stone because God will not break or change a single word of it.

It is not that, the Israelites had not heard of God's name "The Lord" before but it indicates that they did not fully understand its implications, as the name of the one who would redeem His people. But they had known Him mostly as "God Almighty." They knew a great deal about God, and had experienced His goodness in many ways. But they had never known God in an intimate way, like Moses was to get to know God. God would do many miraculous signs, and wonders through Moses and Aaron, and He would also speak with Moses much more then He had with the other Patriarchs before him.

After God had completed His conversation with Moses, Moses and Aaron went to the Israelite community, and Aaron conveyed to them what the Lord had said. But the Israelites refused to listen to him because of their discouragement and the cruel treatment that they were receiving from their task-masters. Then, Moses and Aaron; returned to their home and waited for further instructions from God.

A short time has passed now, and God has decided to push things along, and shake up the Pharaoh a bit more. So he appeared to Moses and Aaron once again and He said to them: "When Pharaoh says to you, 'perform a miracle,' then say to Aaron, 'take your staff and throw it down before Pharaoh,' and it will become a snake." The staff, that Aaron carried, would figure prominently in several of the ten plagues that were to follow that same year. Now, God has just told both Moses and Aaron together, for the first time, that He is about to perform His first miracle before the great and mighty Pharaoh.

As it was, God had only spoken to Moses alone before, and He hadn't really included Aaron in any of the conversa-tions to any great degree. But from now on Moses would seem like a God to the Pharaoh, and Aaron would seem to be a prophet to Moses. God also instructed Moses specifically to make sure that he told Aaron what to say, and what he had to do. Moses had to follow these last instructions to the letter with no room for error. However, this second time that, Moses and Aaron would appear before the Pharaoh; things would be quite a bit different, because they would be putting Gods Almighty Power on display.

So Gods messengers went before Pharaoh, and they did as God had commanded them to do. When the Pharaoh asked them to perform a miracle, Aaron threw his rod down before Pharaoh, and his officials it turned into a snake. But the Pharaoh was not to be outdone by some God that he didn't know. He called for his wise men, and for his sorcerers. Then he called for his magicians of Egypt, who were able to cast their rods down before Pharaoh, and their rods also turned into snakes.

The power of these persons may have been done by the use of trickery, and slight-of-hand Illusions, or by demonic powers. According to the Bible, two of the magicians who opposed Moses were named Jannes and Jambres. They are mentioned in (2Ti. 3.8) and also in the Dead Sea Scrolls. But these men were no matches for the power of God. But they too would soon see the power of God, right before their very eyes, in the next thing that happened.

As they were watching their snakes on the floor, Moses' snake, swallowed up their snakes. Then Moses reached down and picked up his snake by the tail, and it became a staff once more. When Gods snake devoured the other two snakes, it demonstrated Gods mastery over the Pharaoh and the gods of Egypt. Still, the heart of the Pharaoh grew hard, and he would not listen to them just like the Lord had said it would.

The Pharaoh was not convinced for one minute that, this God of Moses and the Israelites had any special powers. It would take a little more than a year before the Pharaoh would finely realize just how powerful God really was. Now Moses and Aaron have completed their first miracle before the Pharaoh. They have put Gods power on display before the King and his court. But still, they would rebel against God and His messengers. After their encounter with the Pharaoh, Moses and Aaron departed from the palace of the King and went home.

-4-

THE TEN PLAGUES OF EGYPT

The ten plagues that God caused to occur in the land of Egypt, will once again demonstrate to you just how God chooses to use the awesome, and magnificent creative power that, He alone possess. As well, you will see that, there is nothing too hard, too big, or too small that God cannot handle.

The first nine plagues of Egypt can be divided into three groups of three plagues each. The first, the fourth, and the seventh plagues were introduced by Moses and Aaron, in the mornings as the Pharaoh went to the Nile to worship the god Hopi. When the other plagues occurred, there was no warning to the Pharaoh and his people. The first nine plagues may have been a series of miraculous intensifications of natural events, taking place in less than a year. If this were the case, the first plagues would have resulted from the Nile flooding in late summer and early fall. Large quantities of red sediment could have been washed down from Ethiopia, causing the water to become as red as blood.

For God to turn all of the water in the land of Egypt, into real blood, it would not have been too practical to serve His purpose. But, it would not have been impossible for Him to do so, if that is what He intended to do. Whenever the plagues did occur, they came at Gods bidding and timing because, there is no other power in the whole universe that could accomplish such miracles.

At this time, there are two things that I wish to convey to all people who read the Bible. I have discovered that throughout the use of reading and studying the Bible that; when you use the scriptures as a daily food to feed your hungry soul and spirit and for your own enjoyment as well, you will gain unbelievable wisdom and knowledge from God through the guidance of the Holy Spirit. He will give you insights into what He wants you to know and do.

The second thing that you must remember is that, in many of the scriptures in the Bible, a great deal of time may have elapsed between each of the scriptures or sections. Sometimes, it could be days, months, years, or even centuries from one scripture to another. Also, you must remember that God doesn't measure time the way we do, and He cannot be restricted by time or space because He is eternal and we are not. One of His days is like a thousand of our years to Him. I am certain that you will see and realize these two important points in the scriptures and in the great stories that you can read in the Bible. As you become more familiar with them, you will understand just what I mean.

The First Plague: "The Waters Turned To Blood." (Ex. 7:14-24)

Some time has passed since Moses and Aaron had appeared the second time to the Pharaoh in his palace, and God had turned the staff of Moses into a snake. Once again the Lord spoke to Moses and said: "The Pharaohs heart is hard, and he refuses to let the people go. Go to the Pharaoh in the morning, as he goes out to the water. Wait on the bank of the Nile to meet him, and take in your hand the staff that was changed to a snake. Then say to him, 'The Lord, the God of the Hebrews, has sent me to say to you: Let my people go, so that they may worship me in the desert, but until now you have not listened. This is what the Lord says: By this you will know that I am the Lord: With the staff that is in my hand I will strike the water of the Nile, and it will be changed into blood. The fish in the Nile will die, and the river will stink; the Egyptians will not be able to drink its water.'" 'Tell Aaron: Take your staff and stretch out your hand over the waters of Egypt. Over the streams, canals, over the ponds and all the reservoirs, even in the wooden buckets and stone jars, and they will all turn to blood.'"

Early the next morning, Moses and Aaron met the Pharaoh by the river and they did exactly what the Lord had commanded them to do. Aaron struck the waters with his staff and the waters in the Nile turned to blood. The blood was everywhere in Egypt. However, the Egyptian magicians were able to do the same act with their secret arts. There is no doubt that their power came strictly from the Devil. So the Pharaoh hardened his heart, and he went back into his palace and he wouldn't even listen to Moses and Aaron, just as the Lord had said he would do.

He was totally oblivious to the suffering of his people and what was happening to the whole country. When he turned and went back into his palace, he displayed his utter contempt for the revelation of Gods power over the Nile to all of the people and his officials who were there in his presence at the time. To be able to get good clean water to drink now while the Nile River water was unusable, the people of Egypt had to dig along the side of the riverbank to get water. After the water was filtered through the sandy soil along the riverbank, the polluted water would become safe for drinking. As you can see, God had given Moses and Aaron very specific instructions as to what they were to say and do. He left nothing to chance. For example:

(1) God told Moses what to expect from Pharaoh, that his heart would be hardened, and he would not listen to him or let the people go.
(2) God told Moses to meet the Pharaoh by the riverbank in the morning when he went down to the river to worship.
(3) God also told him to take his staff with him.
(4) God forcefully identified Himself to the Pharaoh and his court when He said: "The Lord, the God of the Hebrews," has sent me to say to you: 'Let my people go.'" God also made the Pharaoh to understand very clearly, that the Hebrew people were His chosen people.
(5) God told the Pharaoh that until now He had not listened, and because he had not listened, God was about to punish him and his people. By turning the water into blood, all of the fish would die, and the river would stink throughout the land. Then the Pharaoh would know for certain that He was the Lord.
(6) The staff of God in Aaron's hand would do all of these miracles.
(7) The Second Plague: "The Plague of Frogs" (Ex 8: 1-15).

Seven days have passed now, since the Lord had struck the waters in the Nile and all over Egypt, and made it the color of blood. This is one of the rare times that we are given any kind of a time frame that the plagues, happened at a specific time. It is also an indication that; the plagues did not follow one right after the other in rapid succession.

The Lord said to Moses: "Go to Pharaoh and say to him, this is what the Lord says: 'Let my people go, so they may worship me. If you refuse to let them go I will plague your whole country with frogs. The Nile will teem with frogs.

They will come up into your palace and your bedroom, and onto your bed, into the houses of your officials, and on your people, and into your ovens and kneading troughs. Tell Aaron, to "stretch out your hand with your staff, over the streams canals, and ponds, and make frogs come up and cover the land of Egypt."

Aaron did as the Lord commanded him, and frogs (or toads) came up immediately out of the waters of Egypt and covered the land. But the Pharaohs magicians were able to do the same thing by using their demonic powers. But all they did was to compound the problem of the frogs. It is possible that the frogs abandoned the river because, of the high concentration of bacteria-laden algae, that had by now proved fatal to most of the fish, thus polluting the river.

This kind of scenario could well of happened naturally, if and when the natural events that occur each year along the river were allowed to happen without interruption. But this time however, things would happen by Gods command, and at His timing. The miraculous nature of this plague lay in the timing and the magnitude of the invasion. God did not create new frogs from nothing. But He caused the frogs to come up in unnaturally large numbers, and at exactly the right time, and then to die at exactly the right time.

The frog was considered to be a sign of life renewal and happiness to the Egyptian people. They also worshiped the goddess Heqt, who was suppose to assist women in child-birth. Even though the Pharaoh and his people worshiped the frog; now they would became nothing but terrible pests, and the smell was hard for the people to bear.

They were in the people's beds, houses, ovens, kneading troughs, and anything else that they could get into. It was probably enough to drive the people out of their minds. After a few days had passed, the Pharaoh could not put up with the complaining of the people and the smell of the dead and dying frogs any longer. This time however, he didn't consult with any of his local magicians, because he knew that they could do nothing to get rid of the frogs. So he didn't waste any time on them. He sent a messenger and summoned Moses and Aaron to come and get rid of the frogs. In his mind he had concluded that, he had come to the point of desperation. He was smart enough this time to realize that now he had to bypass his magicians and go right to the source of his trouble, which would be Moses and Aaron. They would have to intercede between him and their God to get rid of the frogs.

When Gods messengers arrived in the presents of the Pharaoh, the Pharaoh said to Moses: "Pray to the Lord, to take the frogs away from me and my people, and I will let your people go to offer sacrifices to the Lord." The Pharaoh knew in his heart, that what he said to Moses was just a big lie. He had no intention in the world of letting the Hebrew go. After all, he had lied before, and he had gotten away with it, so why not try again. He probably thought that two lies were better than one and besides, why should he change now?

"Unfortunately" There is a huge number of the world population, in today's world, that does this exact same thing. They lie because the truth is not in them. There is no such thing as a little white lie. They are all big lies. As a result, the lies that they tell will cause nothing but more lies and trouble for themselves as they continue their journey through life. They sometimes, have to tell a second and maybe a third lies to cover up the first one. Sooner or later, at some point in their life, they will be branded as a liar, and no one will have anything to do with them because no one can believe a word that they say.

When you lie, you are following Satan, who is the father of all lies, and you are headed on the path to destruction, and to hell it's self. The Lord hates a liar, and He say so in (Proverbs 6:17.) The Lord says, "He hates haughty eyes, and a lying tongue." Also in (Proverbs 12:22), God says, "the Lord detests lying lips, but He delights in men who are truthful." This is God's word pure and simple and it will not change. The spoken truth will always prove that you have integrity, but a spoken lie will bring you down to death and destruction. If you always tell the truth no matter what the consequences may bring, you cannot be proven wrong. But if you tell lies you can be proven wrong, and be classed as a liar, and then suffer a great deal of disgrace in the eyes of people.

As soon as the Pharaoh had spoken to Moses and Aaron, about removing the frogs from the land and its people's homes, Moses said to the Pharaoh: "Accept the honor of saying when I shall intercede for you, your servants, and your people, to destroy the frogs from you and the land. They will remain in the river only." Then the Pharaoh said to Moses: "Tomorrow!" Moses then replied to the Pharaoh and said: "It will be as you say, so that you may know there is <u>"no one like the Lord our God."</u> The frogs will leave you and your people, and remain only in the Nile." These words are expressed again, and again, in the prophetic books of the Bible.

In the request for intercession, the Pharaoh had hurled at least two hidden challenge at Moses. The Pharaoh probably wanted to see if Moses had the power to intercede for him with this God of his or not. Also, it was a clever trap set for Moses, so he would be at fault, and not the Pharaoh, if things didn't work out the way the Pharaoh wanted them to. He was making Moses the scapegoat for his problems.

However, there was one thing that the Pharaoh had not counted on. That was; that the God of Moses, was the "God of All Creation," and the "God of the Living," and not a God of the dead. He was not like the dead gods that the Egyptians worshiped. Their Gods were made out of sticks, and stones, and metal objects. But Moses, through Gods grace and guidance, turned the tables on the Pharaoh. Moses invited the Pharaoh, to set the time for Egypt's deliverance from the frogs. This way, the Pharaoh would not be able to say, that it was just a coincidence that the frogs began to abate at a certain time. He was caught in his own trap, just like many people are today, when they live by lying, stealing, cheating and any form of deception. These are all the trademarks of the Devil. After Moses had finished speaking to the Pharaoh, they departed for home.

Moses then cried out to the Lord, when he got home, to get rid of the frogs for Pharaoh and his people as he had requested. The Hebrew verb "cry", here places emphasis on the need at hand, and suggests Gods willingness, to stoop down or to reach down from heaven to answer that need. This same sort of prayer provoked the Lord to rescue His people.

The Lord listened to Moses, and He did what he asked Him to do, and all of the frogs died in the houses, in the courtyards, in the palace, and throughout the whole land of Egypt the next day. There were so many dead frogs, that they had to be piled in heaps and the land reeked from the smell of them. The only place that the frogs remained alive was in the river, as Moses had declared them to be. By this act alone, Moses would appear more like a God to the Pharaoh, and Aaron as his prophet. Gods plan was working perfectly because it was His will, and not mans will.

After a few days had passed, and Pharaoh seen that there was relief from the frogs in the land, he returned to his old stubborn self and he refused to let Gods people go. As you can see, the Pharaohs behavior exhibits a certain pattern. It is an all too familiar pattern that is exhibited by millions of people all around the world. The pattern has never changed, because the people have never changed in their thinking. People pray to God and ask for His help in times of trouble and stress. But when the good times return oftentimes, they forget to even thank God for His blessings, and His help. They just go their own way without giving God a second thought. After God has blessed people with good health, and all of the amenities that this life has to offer today, the people still think that they have done it all without Gods help. They will not give God credit for anything in their lives. It is a sad situation, but true nonetheless.

<u>The Third Plague:</u> <u>"The Plague of Gnats "</u>

The Plague of Gnats was the third Plague to come upon the Egyptian people within a short time. But this time the people and the Pharaoh did not have any warning from God, like they had with the two previous plagues. Sometimes, God will discipline people without warning. He does this because He wants to get their attention. Once He has their full attention, He will help them to work through, whatever it is that He wants them to know. This shows you that He has a deep and abiding love for all who honor and serve Him.

Once again God speaks to Moses, and He tells him exactly what the two of them are to do, and what they are to say to the Pharaoh. God said to Moses: "Tell Aaron, stretch out your staff and strike the dust of the ground, and the dust will become gnats throughout the land of Egypt," As soon as Aaron did this, men and animals throughout all of the land of Egypt became infected with the insects. The gnats were so thick and so bad that, it just about drove the people and the animals out of their minds with terrible itching and scratching. There was no peace of mind for man or beast.

Not to be out done by Moses this time, the Pharaohs magicians tried to produce gnats too. But they could not, no matter how hard they tried. To save face and to protect their own lives, one of them came up with an astounding statement that might have caused the Pharaoh to start thinking that this God of Moses was really a God to be reckoned with. The magician said to Pharaoh: "This is the finger of God." It is possible that they too were starting to believe in the God of Moses. But still the heart of the Pharaoh was hardened and he would not listen to anyone. The gnats would have had a natural breading ground, in the flooded fields of Egypt in late autumn. So, from this we can possibly judge at what time of year that this plague could have taken place.

When the magicians used the words "The finger of God," it was an act that would be repeated by the Lord Jesus Christ, later on in the history of the world when He, would walk the earth. In the scripture in (Lk. 11:20) Jesus said: "But if I drive out demons by the finger of God, then the kingdom of God has come to you indeed." The Kingdom of God has come to all of mankind through the Lord Jesus Christ, but the world would not accept Him as the God and Creator of all things.

<u>The Fourth Plague:</u> <u>"The Plague of Flies."</u>

By this time as the fourth plague comes along, the Pharaoh must have started to get the message from God that, He was the God Almighty and that He, was in control of the Plagues that were occurring and not anyone else. Some time has passed now and God sends another plague to increase the misery of the Egyptian people and the Pharaoh. As each of the plagues manifested themselves, they became more and more intense each time, and the people suffered much more each time as well.

The Lord said to Moses: "Get up early in the morning and confront Pharaoh as he goes to the water and say to him, 'this is what the Lord says: Let my people go, so that they may worship me. If you do not let my people go, I will send swarms of flies on you and your officials, on your people and into your houses. The houses of the Egyptians will be full of flies, even the ground where they are. 'But on that day I will deal differently with the land of Goshen, where my People live. No swarms of flies will be there, so that you will know that I, the Lord am in this land. I will make a distinction between my people and your people. This miraculous sign will occur tomorrow.'"

The following passages are quite clear; in (Ex. 8:22, 9:4, 10:23, 11:7) they say that God protected the Hebrew people from any effects of the plagues. God says that, He would make a distinct difference that would be noticed by the Egyptian people between them and His people when the plague of flies occurred. It was a clear and precise statement by God to proclaim to the Pharaoh, His "Almighty Power." It also, demonstrated to the Pharaoh, that because He was God, He could preserve His own people, while He was judging Egypt.

So Moses did as the Lord commanded him to do. Early the next morning, Moses delivered Gods message, and God did as Moses said. Then swarms of flies filled all of the houses of the Pharaoh, and his people. But not one fly came near the land of Goshen, and Gods people. It was by this means that God would make Himself known among all of the people in Egypt. In some ways, this exclusion is the most remarkable aspect of the plagues, especially in the last plague. There was no relief from the flies, no matter what the people tried to do to get rid of them. The flies would multiply rapidly as the receding Nile left breeding places in its wake. These full-grown flies would infect people and their animals alike. Their incessant horrible biting, would be just about unbearable and beyond human endurance.

I can well imagine just how the people of Egypt must have felt, when all of these problems and troubles were happening to no one but them. It was bad enough at first that, they had to dig in the sand on the riverbank, to get their drinking water, when Aaron and Moses turned the waters to blood. This plague had not been too hard for them to handle. But then along came the second plague, the plague of the frogs. This was totally a different situation. The problem of not getting enough sleep, and having to put up with the smell of the frogs, plus the constant croaking noise that they would make, it would be enough to drive a person mad.

Now, to make matters even worse, and to cause the people even more discomfort, the Lord sent the third plague, the plague of Gnats. This plague would have a terrible effect on the people's body. The flies would make you itchy, and cause you to scratch yourself until you bled. A persons discomfort would be unbelievable, and horrifying, to say the least. The big difference between this third plague, and first two plagues was that, this plague came without warning. It also demonstrated to the Pharaoh that, God could do whatever He wants because; God has no boundaries like His earthly creations do.

Now the fourth plague has come along, and the people had to put up with multitudes of biting flies. The flies were making the Egyptian people's lives so unbearably painful, that some of the people went to the Pharaoh to complain. The misery, and hardship, that they had to endure, was more than any human being should have to put up with. It was possible at this time that, the Egyptian people began to find out that it was the Pharaohs fault all along that; they were suffering all of these terrible plagues.

There is no doubt that as Moses and Aaron departed for home that day, they were leaving behind them a very angry Pharaoh who was wondering what to do next. All that he could do for now was to put up with the swarms of flies, and the Gnats that might have been left from the third plague. But, he could always hope, that the dead gods that he worshiped, would be able to bail him out. But as we know, his gods were totally lifeless, useless, and hopeless, and they could do absolutely nothing to help him and his people in their misery.

The Bible does not say just how long it was before the Pharaoh caved in, to his own discomfort, and the constant complaining of his people. But I would suspect that it was not more than a few days or a week at the most. Finely, he was compelled to send for Moses and Aaron once again. It would probably not sit too well with him and his officials that he would have to knuckle under to Gods messengers again. But then, what choice did he have? He undoubtedly knew that Moses, who was starting to seem like a God to him, was the only one who could help him with the plague of flies.

When Gods messengers arrived back at the palace, the Pharaoh was waiting for them with open arms. He knew that he had to put on a happy face for Moses, because he wanted something from him. He probably had a grin from ear to ear as they say. But behind the smile that he put on, there was nothing but pure anger, and hatred for the Israelites, their God, and his prophets.

The Pharaoh said to Moses: "Go sacrifice to your God <u>here in the land</u>." This was another clever trap that he had set for Moses. If Moses had agreed to the exact words that the Pharaoh had said, Moses and his people would not have been able to take a three-day journey into the desert to worship the Lord. The Pharaoh was playing a game of words with Moses. Just like the Devil had done with Eve centuries before in the Garden of Eden. He said that the people would only be able to sacrifice to their God "here in this land." That would mean that the Israelites would not be permitted to leave Egyptian soil. He knew that he stood to lose control of the Hebrew people, and his huge work force. This was one of the Pharaohs greatest fears.

However, the one thing that he had forgotten about was the fact that he was dealing with God and not Moses. So God put into the heart of Moses, the answer that he needed to have, so that he wouldn't fall into the Pharaohs trap. He said to the Pharaoh: "It is not right. The sacrifices that we offer to the Lord our God would be detestable to the Egyptians. If we offer sacrifices that are detestable in their eyes, will they not stone us? We must take a three-day journey into the desert to offer sacrifices to the Lord our God, as He commands us."

To counter the demand that Moses made, the Pharaoh said: "I will let you go, but you must not go very far. Now pray for me." This was a request that would undoubtedly hurt his pride right down to the core. It would leave a bitter taste in his mouth because; he was now humbling himself before Moses, Aaron, and their God, plus all of his officials. It was not an image that the Pharaoh wanted to portray before his people but, God had put him in a position, where he had no choice but to accept the terms that Moses had put forth to him.

Then Moses replied to the Pharaoh and said: "As soon as I leave you I will pray to the Lord, and tomorrow the flies will leave the Pharaoh and his officials and his people. Only be sure that Pharaoh does not act deceitfully again by not letting the people go." This was a stern warning from Moses to the Pharaoh. Soon after Moses had left the Palace, he prayed to the Lord, and God did what Moses asked Him to do. The next day all of the swarms of flies left the land of Egypt, and peace was restored to the people and its land.

It appears that the Pharaoh was not a man to let any stone go unturned. He had to see if this God of Moses had done what He said He would do. He had to know the truth of the matter without leaving any lingering doubts in his mind. He had to know for certain, whether the Hebrew people had been protected from the swarms of flies or not, or, was it just a lie trumped up by this God of Moses? Was this God of the Hebrews as powerful as he said He was or not? As soon as Moses had departed, he sent a messenger whom he trusted above anyone else, to investigate the Land of Goshen. When the messenger returned with the news that the Land of Goshen had indeed remained free of all flies, it would have been like a sword being driven through the angry and bitter heart of the Pharaoh.

After some time had passed, and the Pharaoh and his people were getting back to some degree of a normal way of life, the Pharaoh did what he did the best. He reverted back to his same old way of thinking. He probably thought that he had beaten Moses and his God once again. So his stubbornness returned with more determination than it had before, and he refused to let Gods people go.

<u>The Fifth Plague: "The Plague on Livestock."</u>

The fifth plague that the Lord sent upon Egypt and its people would be more devastating than any of the preceding plagues. This time the plague would affect the livestock of the Egyptians. It would destroy much of the economy of Egypt, as well as its military preparedness, that was so very important to the safety of the country. This time however, God made four specific distinctions in the way that He did things.

(1) This plague did not affect any of the Hebrew livestock.
(2) The Egyptian people, who had come to believe in the Lord through Moses and the Israelites, had their livestock spared when they brought them in from the field and put them in shelters.
(3) God Himself set the time that the plague would take place.
(4) God used His "Mighty Hand" to produce the plague, and not the rod of Moses.

By producing the fifth plague the way He did, God was demonstrating once again to the Pharaoh that He was in total control of everything that had been happening to him and his people. It was by His Mighty Right Hand that He was protecting His people. Also, even though He could not be seen, He was God and the ruler of heaven and the earth, and the creator of all living things. These were three points that God was trying to hammer home to the Pharaoh. But still he would not listen or heed Gods warnings.

A short time after the fourth plague had happened and God had taken the swarms of flies away, God spoke again to Moses. He said to Moses: "Go to Pharaoh and say to him: 'this is what the Lord, the God of the Hebrews says:' Let my people go, so that they may worship me. If you refuse to let them go and continue to hold them back, the hand of the Lord will bring a terrible plague on your livestock in the field. But the Lord will make a distinction between the livestock of Israel and that of Egypt, so that no animal belonging to the Israelites will die. 'Tomorrow the Lord will do this in the land.'"

"However, this time in this plague, God expressed His great mercy to some of the Egyptian people that feared Him. When God had said, that the plague would not occur until "Tomorrow;" God was giving these people enough time to bring their livestock in from the fields to shelter, so that they would be able to save them from the plague that was to come.

So now, the Lord has set the conditions as well as a time limit, for the fifth plague to occur. It was to follow within twenty-four hours of Moses speaking the message to the Pharaoh. There would be nothing that the Pharaoh or any of his magicians could do about it. They were doomed to suffer another plague, because of the stubbornness of the Pharaoh, and it would cost the Egyptian people dearly. They wouldn't have any hope of restitution from the Pharaoh, because God was controlling the situation. This plague would cripple the economy of Egypt to a great extent, and cause untold misery for the country and its people.

It is possible that the Lord may have used the flies of the fourth plague, to spread the anthrax bacteria into the Egyptians animals. The flies would now infect all of the animals that had been left out in the fields. As you know, the Egyptians worshiped a number of idols at that time. They worshiped many animals and animal-headed deities, including the bull-gods Apis and Mnevis, the cow-god Hathor, and the ram-god Khnum. But these gods were man-made and totally useless to anyone. So once again the Egyptian religion is rebuked, ridiculed, and under attack by God.

The next day, God did what He said He would do. As soon as the plague struck, all of the Egyptian livestock that was left out in the fields died, but all of the Egyptian livestock that had been put in shelters was not affected by the plague. Also, not one head of livestock that belonged to the Israelites died. When the Pharaoh sent men to investigate the land of Goshen, as he had done before, they found that not one, of the Israelites livestock had died. This was further proof to the Pharaoh that the God of Israel was in control, and not the gods that he worshiped. Yet his heart was unyielding and he would not let Gods people go.

The sixth Plague: "The plague of Boils."

The sixth plague would be much more severe than the proceeding ones because, this plague would affect the bodies of the Egyptian people themselves, and some of their remaining animals. The scriptures do not say how much time had passed, between the fifth and the sixth plagues. But I would suspect that they occurred quit close together. This was the second plague to come from God without any warning to the Pharaoh and his people.

God said to Moses and Aaron, "Take handfuls of soot from a furnace, and toss it into the air in the presence of Pharaoh. It will become fine dust over the whole land of Egypt, and festering boils will break out on men and animals throughout the land." Then Moses and Aaron went into the presence of the Pharaoh and tossed the soot into the air, as the Lord had instructed them to, and immediately festering boils broke out on men and animals throughout the land. These festering boils were probably a variety of skin anthrax that had struck the animals a few days before. But the boils that appeared on the people were black burning abscess that develops into a pustule, causing great pain and suffering on all of the people of Egypt.

However, the magicians who were in the presence of Moses and the Pharaoh that day did not fare so well either. The Bible says in (Ex.9: -11) that, the magicians were unable to stand before Moses, because of the boils on their knees and the legs. It is possible that now, the Pharaoh, who had more than likely been affected with boils as well, was about to give into Gods demands. At the very least, he must have been giving Gods demands some very serious thought about letting the people go. But God in His great wisdom, and mercy, was not through punishing the Pharaoh and his people just yet. There would be a great deal more misery and sorrow to come. As in the plagues before, the Bible says that the God hardened his heart, and he would not let the people go.

<u>The Seventh Plague:</u> <u>"The Plague of Hail."</u>

After some time had passed and God had permitted the Pharaoh and his people to suffer the sixth plague for a while, He decided that another plague was in order. This time however, God was about to provide another startling revelation to the Pharaoh. God had all ready proven to the Pharaoh how mighty and powerful He was through the first six plagues. But now God would show him that He also controlled the weather and all of the other elements as well.

So God said to Moses: "Get up early in the morning, confront Pharaoh and say to him; 'this is what the Lord, the

God of the Hebrews says: Let my people go, so that they may worship me, or this time I will send the full force of my plagues against you and against your officials and your people. So that you may know, that there is no one like me in all the earth. For by now, I could have stretched out my hand and struck you and your people with a plague that would have wiped you off the earth. But I have raised you up for this very purpose, that I might show you my power, and that my name might be proclaimed in all the earth. You still set yourself against my people and will not let them go. Therefore, at this time tomorrow, I will send the worst hailstorm that has ever fallen on Egypt, from the day it was founded until now. Give an order now, to bring your livestock and everything you have in the field to a place of shelter. The hail will fall on every man and animal, that has not been brought in and is still out in the field, and they will die."

So now the die is cast for the seventh plague. God has declared, what will happen in the land of Egypt when the seventh plague arrives. Early the next morning Moses and Aaron went to the Pharaoh and reported to him, word for word, just exactly what the Lord had instructed him to say. It is very likely by this time that the Pharaoh also had a strong nagging suspicion that, this God, whoever He was, would continue to do just exactly what He said He would do. The hail would come at the exact time that the Lord had declared it to happen. Then Moses and Aaron left the Pharaohs palace and went home. This time just like before, they were leaving the Pharaoh perplexed, angry, and full of hate against God, and His messengers, and the Hebrew people. As it happened in the fifth plague, it also happens here in the seventh plague. God does things quite a bit different then He did before. For example:

- God told the Pharaoh to obey Him or else he would face the full wrath of Gods plagues on him, and his people.
- God informed the Pharaoh that there was not another God like Him in all the earth.
- God has told the Pharaoh in no uncertain terms that, He could have wiped him and his people right off of the face of the earth in a twinkling of an eye, if that was His desire to do so.
- God told the Pharaoh that He was the one who had raised him to power, so that He could show His power through the Pharaoh, and His name could be declared in all the earth.
- God explained to the Pharaoh that, it was his stubbornness, and his unwillingness to obey God that was causing Him to bring the plagues on him and his people. This is why he would not let Gods people go.
- God told him what He the Sovereign God, was about to do to the land of Egypt and its people.
- God in His great mercy, warned the Egyptian people who feared the Lord and His power, to bring their livestock and servants in from the field, to protect them from the hailstorm that was to come. Anything left in the fields would certainly die. But anything that was brought into shelter would be spared.
- God gave the time that the storm was to begin. He said "Tomorrow about this same time." God was probably referring to the time that Moses delivered the message to the Pharaoh.
- God told him that the hail would destroy all of the herbs, and crops in the field.
- This time God used the rod of Moses to perform the miracle.

- God told the Pharaoh through Moses, that he and his officials would still harden their hearts and not let His people go.

The next day, God, who is always true to His word, said to Moses: "Stretch out your hand toward heaven that there may be hail in all the land of Egypt, on man, on beast, and on every herb of the field throughout the land of Egypt. When Moses stretched out his hand while holding his staff in it, God sent the hail, along with the lighting, and the fire, as He said He would. The word "fire here," probably refers to the lighting strikes that would occur along with the hail.

While God was judging Egypt with these plagues, it was not a sign that He was not also being merciful to the people at the same time. Those Egyptian officials, and some of the people, who seriously regarded the word of the Lord, listened to the message that Moses had delivered. They brought their livestock and their servants in from the fields, and they were all saved from the hailstorm and its destructive force. But those who did not fear the Lord and His word, and left their livestock and their servants in the fields, they were all killed. God had delivered His judgment as He had declared.

The hail was so severe that, it even broke down the trees, and stripped them of their leaves and branches. It made the country appear like a war zone. The only crops that were saved from the hail were the wheat and the spelt. Spelt is a member of the grass family allied to wheat. Although it is inferior to wheat, it grows well in poorer and drier soil. Some of this special grain has been found in the ancient pyramids of the Pharaohs in the last century.

These crops had not germinated as yet because of the time of year that the hailstorm occurred. The hailstorm probably occurred in January or February when the flax and the barley crops were in bloom. This would put the hailstorm in its proper chronological order. In the first six plagues God could have used a sequence of events that stemmed directly from the flooding of the Nile River. However, in the next three plagues, God would use the forces of nature, to implement His plan that He intended to carry out against the Pharaoh and the people of Egypt.

However, in the land of Goshen where the children of Israel lived, not one hailstone fell. This was truly a miracle that God had done, but only a few people may have realized it at the time. It took a miracle to start the hailstorm, and another miracle to stop it. In this manner God was demonstrating His awesome power over the elements as well as everything else on the earth. This should have been enough positive proof to the Pharaoh, that this God of Moses and the Hebrews, was a God to be feared and respected.

In the world today, God continues to protect His people and their property, if they ask Him to. But you must ask Him, without doubting Him. You must also believe that He will do as you ask if it is in His will to do so. We hear from time to time in the world today, of terrible hailstorms, and of hail as big as baseballs. So it is not too hard to believe that these storms can happen and leave their devastating affects behind. They can be killers of people and animals, as well as crops in the field. The wording of this text also says that no hailstorm has ever been as bad as this one, in the history of the world.

The Bible does not say how long the storm lasted. But it must have lasted for quite some time because; it scared the life out of the Pharaoh. He was probably shaking in his boots with a heart filled with fear. Sometime during this terrible storm, the Pharaoh summoned Moses and Aaron. Here was another miracle that God produced, and no one but possibly Moses and Aaron even gave it a second thought. The fact that Moses and Aaron, would have had to come some distance to get to the Pharaohs palace, they walked through this wicked hailstorm, and they were not injured by any hail or fire. Not one hailstone toughed them.

The Pharaoh said to them: "This time I have sinned. The Lord is right, and my people and I are in the wrong. Pray to the Lord, for we have had enough thunder and hail. I will let you go; you don't have to stay any longer." Then Moses replied, "When I have gone out of the city, I will spread out my hands in prayer to the Lord. The thunder will stop and there will be no more hail, so that you may know that the earth is the Lords. But I know that you and your officials still do not fear the Lord God."

Then Moses left the city, and he did as he said he would do. He lifted his open hands toward heaven in a gesture of prayer to the Lord, and God stopped the terrible hailstorm, the lighting, and the thunder. After God had stopped the terrible storm, things happened just as the Lord had said through Moses. The Pharaoh remained his stubborn old self and he and his officials hardened their hearts, and they would not let the Israelites go.

There are two facts that had happened as this plague ended, that I would like to bring to your attention at this time. Fact No.1: This is the first time that the Pharaoh has acknowledged his sinfulness, and he perceives its devastating results. It also showed that, He was starting to yield under the pressure because of the destruction of his country, and the cries and the suffering of his people. For such an arrogant man to even say that, "I have sinned," it was in its self, a stunning admission of his guilt. Fact No.2: He finally has admitted that the Lord is righteous. This would be a hard lump for him to swallow and to admit to in the presence of his officials and his people. In a true sense, he would be admitting that the gods that he and his people served and worshiped were totally powerless and useless to him.

<u>The Eighth Plague:</u> <u>"The Plague of Locusts.</u>

As time passed, it was getting late and into the summer months, and it was through the natural process of the seasons that, the Lord sent another judgment or plague, on the Pharaoh and his people. It was the time of year when the short horned grasshoppers would normally appear and raise havoc with the crops in the fields. So now God uses the natural occurrence of these destructive critters, as His eighth plague. But this time the swarms of grasshoppers, or locusts as they are called in the Bible, would be so intense that they would further devastate the land and its people. It would also create unbelievable anger and frustration in the hearts and minds of the people and the Pharaoh.

God knew that the Pharaoh and his officials were starting to buckle under the pressure of the seven proceeding plagues, so this time He hardened the Pharaohs and his official's hearts once again. God, in His judgment of Egypt and the Pharaoh, was not ready to let them off of the proverbial hook just yet. The Lord still had more punishment in store for the Pharaoh and his beleaguered people. There would be no rest for them until God had completely fulfilled His plans and His purpose.

This same fact still holds true for the people of today's world as well. God in His Grace and Mercy has a specific plan for each and every one of His children. "There is only one way that Gods plans can change for us." That is if; we as His children, make the wrong choices in our lives, and reject God and His Son Jesus Christ. God has provided the one and only true way to eternal life, and that is through Jesus Christ our Lord. When Jesus spoke in scripture in (Jn. 14:6). He said these words. "I am the way the truth and the life. No one comes to the Father except through me." He meant exactly what he said. He is mankind's only hope of salvation. "He is The Bright and Morning Star, the King of all Creation and the Light of the World."

When God had decided it was time to present the Pharaoh with a much greater problem then He had ever faced before, He spoke to Moses and said: "Go to Pharaoh, for I have hardened his heart and the hearts of his officials, so that I may perform these miraculous signs of mine among them. That you may tell your children and your grandchildren, how I dealt harshly with the Egyptians, and how I performed my signs among them, and that you may know that I am the Lord." As you can see by the scripture that, this time, it was God who had hardened the hearts of the Pharaoh and his officials, to further His plan to punish Egypt and its King.

So Moses and Aaron went to the Pharaoh as God had instructed them and Aaron repeated to him what the Lord had said: "This is what the Lord the God of the Hebrews says: 'How long will you refuse to humble yourself before me? Let my people go, so that they may worship me. If you refuse to let them go, I will bring locusts into your country tomorrow. They will cover the face of the ground so that it cannot be seen. They will devour what little you have left after the hail, including every tree that is growing in your fields. They will fill your houses, and those of your officials and all the Egyptians; something neither your fathers nor your forefathers have ever seen from the day they settled in this land till now.' "

God left no room for doubt with this last statement that; the coming plague of locusts would be a horrifying demonstration of His Almighty Power. Once again, the Pharaoh and his people were in for more punishment from the Lord because of the Pharaoh and his arrogance and stubbornness. Then with a great deal of anger still raging inside of the Pharaohs heart, Moses and Aaron turned and left him, pondering over his coming fate with the locusts. It would be safe to say that the Pharaoh probably didn't sleep much that night because, of the terrible news that Moses had just delivered to him.

There are several very interesting points that I would like to mention here that, you may or may not have thought about. They are quite interesting to say the least.

(1) This plague is the eighth time that God has punished the Pharaoh for his arrogant and stubborn ways. He was no different at that time than many people in the world today. They will remain very stubborn, and carry on in their own prideful and sinful ways rather than, seek out the Lord Jesus Christ and is saved from eternal death and destruction. But these people have made their choice, and nothing will change their minds. These kinds of people are only concerned about material things, and the pleasures that this world has to offer. They are not concerned about eternal life or anything in the spiritual realm.

(2) There was a warning, preceding this plague from God in the message that Moses delivered to the Pharaoh. God had hardened the heart of the Pharaoh this time for a specific reason. He wanted to perform these miraculous signs among the Egyptians and the Israelites. This was done so the Israelite people would be able to tell their children and their grandchildren, how the Lord had dealt so harshly with the Egyptians. There is no doubt in my mind that, this story has been, repeated time and time again to many Egyptian and Israelite children, and to many other children of other nations as well, down through the years.

(3) The memories of Gods redemptive acts are, to be kept alive by reciting them over and over to our descendants throughout the ages. By doing this simple act, we keep God active and alive in our hearts and minds as well, as in our children's hearts and minds. This eighth plague would be more devastating to the land

and its people than anything that had happened in the past. Not even the trees would survive what was to come.

(4) God stressed in this message, that He was the Lord.

(5) In the beginning of this plague, the Lord changed the direction of the wind, from the West to the East. Through this demonstration of changing of the wind direction, Gods Almighty Power was displayed before the people of Egypt and their stubborn King. They would know for certain that even the elements were compelled to obey Gods Sovereign Will.

When Pharaohs officials heard the message, they finely decided to act and they got on the Pharaohs case once again because, they were the ones who had to listen to the complaints of the people. They knew that the country was in ruins and something had to be done. It was high time that the Pharaoh realized just what his stubbornness was costing the country and its people. Ironically, the officials echoed the same phrase that Moses had used when he had delivered the message to the Pharaoh.

They said to the Pharaoh: "How long will this man be a snare to us? Let the people go, so that they may worship the Lord their God. Do you not yet realize that Egypt is ruined?" This statement is further proof that human rebellion and disobedience to God always leaves death and destruction in their wake. Also, this admission by Pharaohs counselors fulfilled Gods prediction that the Egyptians would soon acknowledge Gods supremacy over the Pharaoh and the gods of Egypt.

After much haggling and arguing with his officials for some time, the Pharaoh finely gave in to them, and he sent for Moses and Aaron again. I would suspect, by this time that he had developed a greater and a deeper hatred for Gods messengers but he dared not show it. It would be a sign of great weakness on his part.

When Moses and Aaron arrived back at the palace, the Pharaoh met them with a preposterous question that was right off the wall. It was a question that carried a condition with it. Also, it clearly implied that he was not serious about letting Gods people go. He said to Moses: "Who are the ones that are going?" You could have probably knocked Moses over with a feather, because Moses had been demanding the release of the entire Hebrew population from day one, and not just the men. Typically, it was only the men who participated fully in the worship service to God at that time.

However, being true to form, the Pharaoh had a hidden agenda that he was not about to disclose to Gods messengers. For example: He was not releasing the women and children, or any of their possessions. They were to stay behind as hostages. This would be done, to make sure that the men would return and not just disappear. After all, the men were his main work force. He had to keep the Hebrew people under his control. He must have thought and felt that, a bird in the hand was worth much more than two in the bush.

So Moses replied to the Pharaoh and said: "We will go with our young and our old; with our sons and daughters, with our flocks and our herds we will go, for we must hold a feast to the Lord." Once again, Moses had repeated the same demand as he had done before. There could be no misunderstanding of Gods directive to the Pharaoh.

Then with cold irony in his voice the Pharaoh said to Moses: "The Lord had better be with you when I let you and your little ones go." This was a clear and precise threat given by the Pharaoh. He wanted to show Moses and his God, that he had clearly seen through their plot and that he was not fooled by it. As he continued to speak, he said: "Clearly you are bent on evil. No" he said. Have only the men go; and worship the Lord, since that's what you have been asking for." Again, he refused to comply with Gods demands. His stubborn, hateful, and cruel human will, still persisted. So this time with a great show of anger and frustration, so that he could impress his officials and save his face before them, he drove Moses and Aaron out of the palace.

It was shortly after Moses and Aaron had left the palace, and because of the Pharaohs obstinate behavior that God said to Moses. "Stretch out your hand over Egypt so that the locusts will swarm over the land and devour everything growing in the fields, everything left by the hail." So Moses stretched out his staff over Egypt, and the Lord made an east wind to blow across the land all that day and all that night. By morning the wind had brought the locusts. They invaded Egypt in uncountable numbers but the locusts did not affect Gods people in the land of Goshen.

Never before had there been such a plague of locusts, nor will there ever be again. They covered the face of the whole earth. This is a hyperbolic way of expressing that this was an unprecedented disaster in all the land of Egypt. This would also demonstrate and prove to the Pharaoh, that God was in total control of this plague also. So the Pharaoh did what he could, and he called for his magicians. As usual but they were totally powerless against the locusts.

When the Pharaoh finely saw the devastating effect that the locusts had on the land, and the problems that they were causing, he must have went half out of his mind with anger. But seeing the magnitude of the situation, he wasted no time in sending for Moses and Aaron again. I do believe that he was starting to see the light at the end of the tunnel, so to speak. So at long last the King was going to have to finally acknowledge the God of Moses, for whom He was, "The God of all Creation." He was not a god of wood, stone, or metal. The proof of this statement is contained in the words that he said when he came face to face with Moses and Aaron, after they arrived back at the palace.

The King said to Moses: "I have sinned against the Lord your God and against you. Now forgive my sin once more, and pray to the Lord your God to take this deadly plague away from me." Now he has just admitted two very important facts to Moses and Aaron. They are: (a) That it was God who had to stop the plague of locusts, because He was the only one who had the power to do so, and (b) it was up to Moses to intercede for him through prayer to his God and no one else.

We as Christians, have a God given privilege to be able to intercede in prayer before God for other people in our prayers today as well. God always hears our prayers, and He always answers them, in due course and in His own time. It must have given Moses and Aaron a great deal of satisfaction and joy, to see the Lord working for them and His people. God was winning the battle with the Pharaoh, and He would be the ultimate winner in any case.

So Moses did as the Pharaoh had requested him to do after they had left the palace. He prayed to the Lord, and the Lord caused a strong west wind to blow and it blew all of the locusts into the Red Sea. Not one locust remained in the entire land of Egypt. Once again the Pharaoh has seen Gods power over the forces of nature, as God had shown him in the plagues of the frogs, and the hail. It appears now from the scriptures in (Ex.10: 16-20) that the Pharaoh is about to give in to Gods demands, and let His people go. But God was not through punishing him and the people of Egypt, just yet. In (Ex. 10: 20) the scripture says: "But the Lord hardened Pharaohs heart, and he would not let the Israelites go."

The Ninth Plague: "Darkness"

As time passed, God set the stage for yet another plague because; He was still playing His game with the Pharaoh and his people. But this plague, like all of the other plagues, will only affect the people of Egypt, and not the Israelites. Also, like the third, and the sixth plagues, God did not announce the ninth plague in advance. Shortly after God had taken the plague of locusts away from Egypt, He said to Moses: "Stretch out your hand toward heaven, that there may be darkness over the land of Egypt, darkness which may even be felt."

So with his staff that he held in his hand, he stretched it out toward heaven and there was a thick darkness that appeared over the whole land of Egypt, and it would last for three days. The darkness that is described in this passage is the kind of darkness that you could only experience deep down in a cave somewhere in the earth. It was so dark, that you couldn't see your hand right in front of your face. The darkness was like a thick black blanket of evil, that had came over the land. There was absolutely no light in the whole land of Egypt except, were the Israelites lived. The Pharaoh and all of his people could not leave their homes, because they were unable to see what they were doing or where they were going. The thick darkness was now holding the people in total captivity. It filled their hearts with such great fear, that they did not rise up from their beds for three days.

This calamity of darkness, would have affected the Egyptians in other ways as well. It would cause them to lose their faith in one of the many gods that they worshiped and prayed to. The sun god Ra or Re was one of their most revered gods. The people could do absolutely nothing to help themselves in this situation. Even a normal solar eclipse would have had an impact on the people and their fears. But now on top of all of this, God added a thick enshrouding blanket of darkness that would last for three days. The people must have been terrified with unprecedented fear that was beyond their wildest imaginations.

This was a deliberate frontal attack by the Lord, on the people of Egypt and an insult to their gods. Also, it was a slap in the face to the Pharaoh and his counselors who, were considered by the people to be like gods. They were supposed to be able to control nature. But they were just as helpless as anyone else. It should have proven to the people at this point that they had believed in fairy tales all their life. However there is no doubt that, there were many of the Egyptian people by this time, starting to believe in the God of Moses. But they probably feared for their lives and dared not say so publicly.

The generations of today are no different. They have heard of God and His Son Jesus Christ, but still they will not acknowledge Him, for fear of being ridiculed and mocked by other people. But this generation must also realize that, Jesus Christ is the only one who can save them from certain spiritual death which is the second death that, they will suffer when they come before the Judgment Seat of Christ. If, they reject Him, they will be doomed to Hell for All Eternity. The Bible says in (Ac.4: 12): "Salvation is found in no one else, for there is no other name under heaven given to men by which we must be saved." This scripture is speaking specifically of the Lord Jesus Christ and no one else.

After the three days of darkness had passed and God had taken the darkness away, the Pharaoh sent for Moses again and he said to him: "Go serve the Lord; even your woman and children may go with you; only leave your flocks and herds behind." Moses then said to Pharaoh: "You must allow us to have sacrifices and burnt offerings to present to the Lord our God. Our livestock too must go with us; not a hoof is to be left behind. We have to use some of them in worshiping the Lord our God. Until we get there we will not know what we are to use, to worship the Lord." The Pharaoh was still trying desperately to hang onto some of the Israelite's possessions. Deep in his heart, he knew that the Israelites would not come back if they were ever allowed to go free.

So once more the Lord hardened the wicked heart of the Pharaoh for His own purpose and the Pharaoh would not let the Israelites go. This time however things were a great deal different than any other time that Moses had appeared before the Pharaoh. This time both Moses and the Pharaoh were screaming at each other face to face.

For this reason, it makes the following statement that was made by the Pharaoh somewhat ironic. He said: "Get out of my sight! Make sure that you do not appear before me again" The day you see my face you will die." Now the Pharaoh has closed the door, on any chance of ever granting Moses another audience with him in the future. Moses then said to Pharaoh: "Just as you say, I will never appear before you again." This time it would be the final meeting between Moses and the Pharaoh.

The Tenth Plague: "The Plague on the First Born."

Before Moses had gone to see the Pharaoh, for the last time during the plague of darkness, God had instructed Moses what he had to do, and what God Himself was going to do. The Lord had said to Moses: "I will bring one more plague on Pharaoh and on Egypt. After that, he will let you go from here. When he does, he will drive you out completely. Tell the people that men and women alike are to ask their neighbors for articles of silver and gold."

Many of these articles of silver and gold would be used by the Israelites in the future as, a gift that would be given back to God for the express purpose of, building of Gods temple in the desert. This temple would be a large tent that was specially designed inside and out by God Himself. It would be Gods dwelling place as the Israelites made their journey to the Promised Land of Canaan. God would literally be right in the presence of His chosen people. The Israelites and the High Priest were to worship and make sacrifices to the Lord at this temple.

I would suspect that maybe a question might have come into your mind at this time, as to what God was doing. But as you know, God does what His will dictates and what fits His purpose. You might be asking yourself this kind of question! How would a people, who had been slaves to the Egyptians for four hundred years, ever be able to ask, or demand anything, from their captors? The answer to this question is quite simple to answer.

God Our Father, who is a God of love, mercy, and grace, would not expect His people to leave the land of Egypt empty handed and with nothing, to show for, after four hundred years of oppression. So, while all of the trouble with the plagues was happening to the Egyptian people, God was working behind the scenes to further help His people. He was preparing the hearts of Pharaohs officials, and the Egyptian people for the day when His people would leave Egypt for good. The Bible says in (Ex.11: 3) that the Lord had made the Egyptians favorably disposed toward His people. Moses himself was highly regarded in Egypt by Pharaohs officials as well.

You can see by this scripture that it was in God's plan from the beginning that His people not leave Egypt before His people had relieved Egypt of some of its wealth. This was another demonstration of God expressing His great love for His people. God does the same for the people of today's world as well. He will always love you, and care for you, no matter what happens to you. All you have to do is have faith in Him, love and trust Him, and He will do the rest.

The tenth plague would be the final plague that God would bring upon the Pharaoh and his people. This Plague however, would be the worst plague that had ever occurred in the land of Egypt, as far as pain and suffering was concerned. It would involve each and every Egyptian family including the Pharaoh himself. The cry of agony and pain would be unbelievably great throughout the land of Egypt. The only exception that God would make would be for His people the Israelites.

God would show the Pharaoh and his people once and for all, that He was the Lord, the God of all Creation. They would know without a doubt that He held life and death in His hands, and that He could do what He pleases when He pleases. This time as well, He would make a much greater distinction between the Egyptians and the Israelites as further proof of His great and magnificent power.

After Moses had said to the Pharaoh: "Just as you say! I will never appear before you again," he continued to speak to the Pharaoh with great anger, and power in his voice. He said: 'this is what the Lord says: "about midnight I will go throughout Egypt. Every firstborn son in Egypt will die, from the firstborn son of Pharaoh who sits on the throne, to the firstborn son of the slave girl, who is at her hand mill and all the firstborn of the cattle as well. There will be loud wailing throughout Egypt, worse than there has ever been, or ever will be again. But among the Israelites not a dog will bark at any man or animal. Then you will know that the Lord makes a distinction between Egypt and Israel."

There would be no way now that the Pharaoh could not fully understand Gods sovereignty and power. It would also show the Egyptian people as well as the Pharaoh, that the gods that they honored, and worshiped, were totally lifeless and useless. They would be absolutely powerless against God and His Mighty Right Hand. But God hardened the heart of Pharaoh one last time, and he would not let the Israelites go. God did this so He could multiply His wonders in Egypt, which would include the tenth and final plague.

After Moses had paused for a moment to catch his breath and control his anger, he continued to speak to Pharaoh, saying: "All these officials of yours will come to me, bowing down before me and saying: "Go, you and all the people who follow you!' After that I will leave." Then Moses, still hot with anger, left the presence of the Pharaoh and his officials and went home. As soon as he arrived back home he proceeded to tell the leaders of the Israelites, what they were expected to do as they had been commanded by God.

THE DEATH OF THE FIRSTBORN

The tenth plague would cause a major turnaround in the lives of God's chosen people, the Israelites. Several different events would happen to the people from that time on, and these events would affect them as a people and as a nation for centuries to come. For example:

The people would have to put their trust in Moses and Aaron to lead them on this journey through the desert because they were the mediators between God and His people.

They had no way of knowing where they were going, or in what direction they were to travel.

They didn't know how they would be clothed or fed after their supplies ran out.

a. Who would supply one of the most important necessities of life that is so necessary to sustain human life in the desert? <u>"WATER."</u>
b. Who would protect them from any enemies that might come against them on their journey through the desert?
c. Who would make decisions for them when troubles arose among the people?
d. Above all else, the people had to trust a God whom they had never seen.
e. Although they had seen His almighty power demonstrated to them during the plagues, could they still trust God to care for them completely for all of their daily needs?
f. Each family would have to make animal sacrifices to God, and observe certain special holidays. This was an area in which the people would know little or nothing about because God had not as yet instructed them or Moses in these matters.

g. The people would now be required to obey and to keep Gods commandments throughout their lives, and to worship God with their hearts, as well as with their animal sacrifices.

These are only a few of the questions that may have been put to Moses and Aaron by the people as they prepared to start their journey to Canaan. However, there were many more proceedings that did have a profound effect on the Israelites throughout their history as a people but they are too numerous to mention at this particular time.

Now the time has come and God is ready to deal His last devastating blow to the Egyptian people and to the Pharaoh their evil leader. This final plague would be different from the other nine plagues in one respect. Although God was the power behind all of the other nine plagues, and the possibility that He may have used the natural flow of nature and the elements to produce the plagues, He had not been personally involved in the first nine plagues like He would be in the tenth and final plague that was to come.

As you may have noticed, that when Moses relayed Gods message to the Pharaoh in (Ex.11: 4), God Himself had said "About midnight I will go out in the midst of Egypt and all of the firstborn in the land of Egypt shall die." This part of the scripture specifically declares that God Himself would be personally involved in the killing of Egypt's firstborn. Not even the faults gods of Egypt would do the Egyptian people any good. Now God would show the people and their evil King that He was and still is, in complete control of everything in this great universe of ours. His will and His power have no equal.

This last message to the Pharaoh from Moses must, have struck a devastating kind of fear in the hearts and minds of the Pharaoh and his officials. It is also possible that he may have wanted to in some small way give in to the demands of

Moses, so God had to harden the heart of the Pharaoh once more and he refused to let the Israelites go. The Pharaoh was still being true to his old stubborn self to the bitter end, but now that same stubbornness would cost him dearly. It would cost him the life of his firstborn son.

Now the Pharaoh had became more upset and angry at this point, than he had ever been before at Moses and Aaron because, of the devastating message that Moses had just delivered to him. Perhaps; his thinking could have been; "It is not possible that this God, whoever He was, had the power over life and death?" This kind of thinking would have been a big mistake on his part, and it would now become his down fall. He may have also thought that this God of Moses and the Israelites would not do what He said He was going to do. After midnight he would know the full truth about this God of Moses and His power.

As you know, God is always true to His word, for He cannot tell a lie because; "He is holy and Righteous" and it's impossible for Him to lie. Satan is the father of all lies and all sin. God is the father of all truth, love, mercy and grace. He is the only one who has the free gift of eternal life but, you must seek Him out in prayer and He will answer you.

Just as God had said He would do, He went throughout the land of Egypt that very same night at midnight, and He killed every firstborn son or daughter of the Egyptians, as well as the firstborn of all of the livestock. Not one Egyptian family escaped as God had declared it. But the Israelites and their families, as well as their livestock were untouched by the Angle of Death, because God had made His distinction between His people and the Egyptians. The crying, the pain, and the agony of the people losing their firstborn, was an unbearable sound throughout the entire land of Egypt. The sights and sounds, of what was happening that night, served only to intensify the great tragedy that was taking place. God had kept His word to the letter.

To lose their firstborn son was without a doubt, one of the most devastating blows that the Lord could have brought upon the fathers of the Egyptian families. This was the ultimate disaster because; all of the plans, the hopes, and the dreams of the fathers were centered on their firstborn sons. The killing of the firstborn also represented judgment on the entire community, right down to the lowly slave girl, which was the lowliest of all occupations. It would also serve as a judgment on all of the faults gods of the Egyptians.

Likewise, the killing of the first-born son was also a preview of what God was going to do centuries later far into the future. God would sacrifice His only begotten Son Jesus Christ on the cross at Calvary to redeem the world from sin. God fulfilled this scripture to the letter in (Jn.3: 16). It says; "God so loved the world that He gave His only begotten Son, that whosoever believes in Him should not parish but have everlasting life." This is Gods seal that He puts on His word that is written in His Holy Bible.

THE FIRST PASSOVER IS INSTITUTED (NIV.) (EX. 12:1-28)

In the last message that Moses had just delivered to the Pharaoh, God had said that He would make a "distinction" between the Egyptians and the Israelites to further prove that He was the Lord. This time however, God made the distinction more pronounced than at any other time when He had declared it. This time, the distinction would become known as the Passover. The Passover was to be a celebration that would be celebrated each year by the Israelites throughout their history. God instituted the celebration or feast, to accentuate the deliverance of the Israelites out of the land of Egypt. It would also prove to the Pharaoh and his people beyond a shadow of a doubt that God, can, and will, always protect His people, no matter what the circumstances are.

Before Moses had delivered his message to Pharaoh, God had instructed Moses and Aaron on just what they were to tell the leaders of the Israelites, and what they the people were required to do, and how they were to do it. The people were to follow Gods instructions to the letter. God had said to Moses: "This month (March-April) is to be for you the first month; the first month of your year." It was here at this time that God inaugurated the first religious Hebrew, or Jewish calendar. Normally in the Middle East, the New Year festivals usually coincided with the new season of life in nature. This would be in April or May.

The designation of this month as Israel's religious New Year, would always remind Israel that her life as the people of God, was grounded in Gods redemptive act of the great exodus from Egypt. This would also serve as a counter in time for the Israelites. It is similar to the way the Christian Calendar is use today, as a marker in time. The Christians of today use the Birth of Christ as a marker in time. Israel's agricultural calendar began in the fall, in mid-September to mid-October. The calendar used by Judaism was developed at a later date in time. Judaism today uses only the calendar that begins in the fall in (September-October).

As God continued to speak to Moses He said: "Tell the whole community of Israel that on the tenth day of this month each man is to take a lamb for his family, one for each household. The animals you choose must be year-old males without defect. You may take them from the sheep or the goats. Take care of them until the fourteenth day of the month, when all the people of the community of Israel must slaughter them at twilight."

The reason that the people had to keep the lamb, or goat, for four days after they had selected it was because, they had to inspect it to make sure that it was perfect in all respects, without spot or blemish. After they had killed it, they were to take some of the blood and put it on the sides and tops of the doorframes of the houses where they lived. That same night, they were to eat the meat roasted over the fire, along with bitter herbs, and bread made without yeast. The eating of Unleavened Bread made without yeast, and the eating of bitter herbs, was another feast that was directly tied in with the Passover.

The bitter herbs would serve as a reminder for the Israelites and their descendants, of the bitterness of their centuries of captivity and bondage. As the Lord continued to speak He said: "Do not eat the meat raw or cooked in water, but roast it over the fire—head, legs and inner parts. Do not leave any of it till morning. If some is left till morning, you must burn it. This is how you are to eat it, with your cloak tucked into your belt, your sandals on your feet and your staff in your hand. Eat it in hast; it is the Lords Passover. On that same night I will pass through Egypt and strike down every firstborn, both men and animals. I will bring judgment on all the gods of Egypt. I am the Lord." The blood will be a sign for you on the houses where you are; and when I see the blood, I will pass over you. No destructive plague will touch you when I strike Egypt.

This is a day that you are to commemorate for the generations to come you shall celebrate it as a festival to the Lord, a lasting ordinance. For seven days you are to eat bread made without yeast. On the first day you are to remove the yeast from your houses, for whoever eats anything with yeast in it from the first day through the seventh must be cut off from Israel. On the first day hold a sacred assembly, and another one on the seventh day. Do not work at all on these days except to prepare food for everyone to eat. That is all you may do. Celebrate the feast of Unleavened Bread, because it was on this very day that I brought your divisions out of Egypt."

The same time God had instituted the Passover, He also gave Moses some rules and regulations, or laws that the Israelites would be required to follow. These laws or covenant that God had made were first mentioned to Abraham in (Gen.17: 9-14). Now the Lord reaffirms them to Moses and Aaron in (Ex.12: 1-13; Ex.12: 43-49).

The Lord said to Moses and Aaron; "These are the regulations for the Passover. No foreigner is to eat of it. Any slave you have bought may eat of it after you have circumcised him. But a temporary resident and a hired worker may not eat of it. It must be eaten inside one house; take none of the meat outside of the house. Do not break any of the bones. The whole community of Israel must celebrate it. An alien living among you, who wants to celebrate the Lords Passover, must have all of the males in his household circumcised. Then he may take part like one born in the land. No uncircumcised male may eat of it. The same law applies to the native-born and to the alien living among you."

The Passover also represented what God had planned for, far into the future. It represented and pointed to the coming "Deliverer and Savior of all people, "Jesus Christ."

The New Testament in the Bible specifically identifies Jesus Christ as the type of the Passover Lamb. The word "type" is defined as a divinely ordained correspondence between a person, an event, or institution and its antitype or fulfillment. Most biblical types were fulfilled in the person and work of Jesus.

It was right at the beginning of the ministry of Jesus that, John the Baptist prophetically announced that Jesus was the "Lamb of God who takes away the sins of the world." (Jn.1: 29). The great Apostle Paul wrote in (1Cor. 5:7) that Christ our Passover Lamb has been sacrificed for us. He has taken our place on the cross. Likewise, Peter identified Jesus as the "Lamb without blemish and without spot." (1:Pet.1: 19). All of these scripture references allude to the fact that Jesus Christ is our Passover Lamb. The following are some comparisons that I would like to use to further substantiate the fact that, the Passover Lamb represented none other than Jesus Christ our Lord, who was to come centuries into the future. For example:

a. The Passover Lamb had to be without spot or blemish. — Jesus was sinless and perfect in His humanity.
b. The animal had to be Male. —Jesus was Male.
c. The lamb had to be young. — Jesus was still a young man when He died on the cross. He was only 33 years old.
d. The lamb had to be examined four days before it was to be sacrificed. — Jesus lived a meticulously examined life, because whatever He did, it was always done in public.
e. The animal had to be slain in public. — Jesus was hung necked on the cross for the entire world to see. He was not spared any indignity even at His death.

f. None of its bones were to be broken. — Despite the brutality of His death, none of Jesus' bones were broken.
g. The animal's blood on the doorposts of the Israelites houses was a sign to God, that He should pass over and not destroy that family's firstborn. — The blood of Jesus is the sign of His death. When God looks down from heaven today, He looks through the "Blood of Christ" and He sees our sins no more. The blood of Christ has taken away all of our sins. But we as sinners must ask, and want His forgiveness. He offers His complete forgiveness free for the taking. — Through Jesus' death, and resurrection, we as believers, are also saved from the coming judgment. (Rom. 5:9; Eph. 2:13; Col. 1; 14; Heb. 9:22; 10:19; 1Pet. 1:2; 1Jn. 1:7; Rev.1: 5; 7:14). In all respects, Jesus fulfilled the divinely ordained prophetic picture that God had presented to the Israelites at the first Passover. He is indeed, our "Passover Lamb. He is humanity's only hope of Redemption and Eternal Life."

Like Gods people the Israelites, who in that time period had to celebrate the Passover each year on an exact date, so it is celebrated in a like manner by the people of the Christian faith today but, with some exceptions? Many churches today celebrate the Lords Supper on a regular base once a month. Christ instituted the Last Supper at the same time of year as the first Passover Supper was celebrated. But from that time on and for the centuries to come, this celebration now represents the body and the blood of Christ. The bread represents His body, and the wine represents the blood of Christ that was shed on the cross for the remission of all of mankind's sins. This is another example of how Christ is our Passover Lamb.

Just like the Israelites who, at that time were placed under the blood of the sacrificial lamb for their own protection from the "Angel of Death," so it is with the Christians of today who believe in the Lord Jesus Christ. They are placed under the blood of Jesus Christ our crucified Lord. God in His great wisdom, and mercy, knew that Christ would be the end of all animal sacrifices to Him. So Christ, on the same night that He was betrayed by Judas, instituted the Lords Supper. It was the last meal that Jesus ate with His disciples before He was crucified on the cross.

Now the people were going to be sent into the hot desolate Sinai Desert, lead by Moses and Aaron to the land of Canaan. It was called, the Promised Land by God Himself who said, "It was a land flowing with milk and honey."

So it was that now, God was bringing to a climax, the final days of slavery for the people that He would call His own. His people whom, He had built into a small nation were about to depart from Egypt, never again to return to that bitter land of bondage. From the time that Jacob had first entered Egypt in 1876 B. C.; to the time when God delivered His people out of Egypt, God had kept His people in Egypt for four hundred and thirty years to the day.

It was sometime after midnight in the early morning hours, after God had gone throughout the land of Egypt and killed the entire firstborn of the Egyptians and their animals; that the Pharaoh sent for Moses and Aaron. He was no longer stubborn and rebellious. He was stricken to the core with utter grief and pain because, he too had lost his own firstborn son. It must have dealt a terrible blow to his already deflated ego.

You may recall the bitter words that he had said to Moses the last time that they had met. He said that he would not permit Moses to see his face again. Now in the middle of the night, he was forced to back down on his word and grant Moses and Aaron one more audience with him. This was further humiliation for him to swallow and to choke on. It must have made him utterly sick to his stomach. To make matters even worse now, he had to bow down to Moses and Aaron once again, and grant them Gods demands in front of all of the officials of his court, and to the people of his country.

When Moses and Aaron arrived at the Kings palace, he said to them, “Up! Leave my people, you and the Israelites. Go, and worship the Lord as you have requested. Take your flocks and herds, as you have said, and go, and bless me.” Now at long last, the Pharaoh is a broken man, and he finely has to admit to all concerned that the Lord has totally defeated him. It would indeed be a bitter pill for him to swallow.

Moses and the people were now permitted to leave Egypt with all of their possessions. Not even one animal was to be left behind. Now at last, they could go and worship their God out in the desert. It would have seemed like a great blessing to the Pharaoh and his people, if the Israelites would just up and leave the country but, by the same token, the Pharaoh would be losing his great work force. At this point the Pharaoh, his officials, and all of the people of Egypt must have feared for their lives as well because, they may have thought that God would kill them too at any time. The fear of the Lord must have been great and very heavy in their hearts after, they had seen what He had the power to do.

The people of Egypt had suffered enough. At this point, they would do anything to get rid of the Israelites so they could have some peace of mind. By getting rid of the Israelites, they may have thought that, they would be getting rid of their God as well. The people certainly didn’t want a god around that might kill them at any given moment.

After Moses and Aaron had left the Pharaoh for the last time, they hurriedly assembled the people with all of their possessions and prepared them so that they could leave the next day.

Now God has put another part of the plan that He had for His people into motion He was about to lead them to the Promised Land. It was the land that He had promised to the Israelites' forefathers Abraham, Isaac, and Jacob. God, who never forgets a promise, was about to start fulfilling the covenant that He had made with these three people centuries in the past.

As I stated before, God had been working behind the scenes and had made the Egyptian people favorably disposed, toward the Israelites and even to Moses himself. Moses, as well as many of the Israelite people was well liked by a great number of the Egyptian people. But now, because the Egyptian people had lost their firstborn, they were all to glad to get rid of the Israelites before more tragedy came upon them.

Before the people were able to start their long journey to the Promised Land, Moses delivered another message from God to His people. To all of the people he said: "Ask the Egyptians for articles of silver and gold, and for clothing."

This done, the Egyptians gave them whatever the Israelites asked for without any argument what so ever. The generosity that was displayed by the Egyptians was the work of the Lord who had planned it from the beginning. When God was speaking to Moses in (Ex. 3:21-22), the Lord said to him: "I will make the Egyptians favorably disposed toward this people. So that when you leave you will not go empty-handed. Every woman is to ask her neighbor, and any woman living in her house, for articles of silver, and gold, and for clothing, which you will put on your sons and daughters. You will plunder the Egyptians."

So you can see by these two passages of scripture that, the Lord deeply loves and cares for His children no matter when or where they are. The next day, when they would finely depart from Egypt, it would be a new beginning for all of Gods people. They would continue to celebrate this day of deliverance for the rest of their lives, as well as many other events that God would ordain for His chosen people much later in their lives.

CONSECRATION OF THE FIRSTBORN

The scriptures say in (Ex. 13:11) that God would now require the children of Israel to consecrate all of their firstborn males, both human and animal, to Him when they were born because He claimed them for His own. However, God made an exception when a donkey was born. Every firstborn of a donkey was to be redeemed by sacrificing a lamb in its place. God made this exception because, of the important role that the donkey played in the transportation of people and commercial goods. If by chance, it was not to be redeemed because of some defect or some other reason, then the people were to break its neck.

The redemption of the people's firstborn children was to be done by the family sacrificing a lamb in the place of their son. God would not permit His people to sacrifice their sons, or to make any other kind of human sacrifice to Him. The only other requirement that God insisted on was, for the parents to present their firstborn males in a ceremony to the Lord in front of a priest. Humans were to be consecrated to the Lord by their life, not by their death. In this manner, all of the firstborn males of the Israelites were to belong to God. Also for this reason, His people were dramatically reminded of the extent to which the Lord had gone to free them from slavery. He had spared their firstborn sons, even as He slew the firstborn of Egypt, human and animal. The lamb was killed to buy the firstborns freedom. Later on in history, the Lord would claim the Levites for Himself in exchange for the firstborn sons of the people. (Num.3: 40-51). Jesus, who was the firstborn son of Mary and Joseph, was presented to the Lord in accordance with this law, eight days after His birth. You can read about it in (Lk. 2:22-23 NIV.).

-5-

THE EXODUS BEGINS

The great Exodus of Gods people from Egypt began the very next day as God said it would. But God Himself kept a vigil all that night so that nothing would happen to any of the Israelites. Because God had kept this vigil that night, now the Israelites would also be required to keep that night each year as a vigil to honor God for the generations to come.

While the Egyptians were busy burying their dead first-born children, Gods people were preparing for the journey to the Promised Land. Their journey would begin from the city of Rameses in the land of Goshen. It was one of the cities that the Israelites had been forced to build for the Egyptians. It was also there, that thousands of them throughout the centuries had paid the ultimate price. The price was blood, sweat, tears, and in the end many times they paid with their lives. There was no mercy shown to them from their Egyptian taskmasters. The Bible says that the exodus began from the city of Rameses in the year, 1446 B.C.

Because of the command of the Lord, the people had to leave Egypt in such hast that they didn't even take time to bake their bread for the journey. The people left Egypt with the dough that they had made before the yeast had been added to their bread. The people carried it on their shoulders and in their kneading troughs and wrapped in their clothing. They did not put the yeast in the bread because they had to eat unleavened bread for the next seven days as instructed by God through Moses. From that time on as the years passed by, the Israelites would celebrate the "Feast of Unleavened Bread."

When the people were all gathered together the Bible says that there were 603,550 fighting men, not counting women and children under the age of twenty years old. At the age of 20 years old, a male was considered old enough to be put in the army to fight, so this is why this number appears so low, at the time of the departure from Egypt.

In today's world in Israel, both male and female who are eighteen years of age, are conscripted into the military, and they must serve their country for a period of two years or more depending on the situation. When you include all of the women and children, and other ethnic groups that tagged along with the Israelites, there would probably be more like three million people. To the Egyptian people who observed this great exodus of humanity, they must have thought that half of the population of the country was leaving Egypt. So it was that the Israelites marched out of Egypt in full view of the Egyptians with Moses and Aaron in the lead.

The mixed multitude of people that went with the Israelites included some Egyptians and some other ethnic groups who, for reasons of their own, went along with the Israelites. This was probably due to the fact that they may have wanted to get out from under Egyptian rule because; the Pharaoh was such a wicked and cruel ruler. It is also possible, that many of them may have come to know and fear the Lord, through Moses and the Israelites. Whatever the case may be; they decided to tag along with the Israelites.

They too, were glad to be leaving Egypt, the land of many heartaches and sorrows.

However, because of this mixed multitude of people, everything would not go all that smooth for the Israelites on their journey to the Promised Land. This mixed multitude of people would soon cause many problems for Moses and the Israelites. There would be many times throughout the journey that Moses would have to deal with them on separate bases. Along with all of their herds and flocks, and all of their possessions packed on camel, and donkeys, or in wagons, they marched off into the desert trusting in Moses and Aaron to show them the way.

When the Israelites departed from Egypt, they took with them the bones of Joseph that had been preserved in a tomb centuries before. They took his bones because he had made the sons of Israel swear an oath to him at his deathbed. He had said to them: "God will surely come to your aid, and then you must carry my bones up with you from this place." For many of Gods people, it would seem to them like they were leaving a land of many sorrows and extreme hardships but, they were no doubt thankful to God for their first taste of freedom.

They did not make their first camp until they came to Succoth. It was about a three-day journey from the city of Rameses. Succoth was probably more of an area location rather than a city location, although it could have been both. The Bible says it was probably the modern Tell el-Maskhutah in the Wadi Tumeilat west of the Bitter Lakes. The Bible identifies forty significantly different campsites in the book of Numbers, between Rameses and the plains of Moab. But most of the sites were desert encampments not cities, with lasting archaeological records that could be positively identified as specific locations. After leaving Succoth they camped at Etham on the edge of the desert or the wilderness of the Red Sea.

It would have been a much shorter route, for the Israelites to reach Canaan, by going in a more northerly direction along the coastal plains. But God chose to lead them in a more southerly direction. The northern route that went through the plains later on would become known as the Land of the Philistines. Although, at that time there were some Philistine people living in that particular region, their main invasion and settlement of this land did not occur until the middle of the 12th century B.C.

However, the Egyptians had already heavily fortified this coastal route for their own defensive purposes. This northern route could have caused a great deal of war, or harassment and related problems for the Israelites on their journey to Canaan if they had taken that route. As you can see, God did not want His people to be involved in any wars with other nations at that particular point in their journey. He knew that the Israelites were not organized enough to do battle with any army, although God would have protected them in any case.

It is quite possible that the Israelites would only be armed with nothing more than a few spears, bow and arrows, or slings, or whatever they were able to get from the Egyptians when they left Egypt. They certainly would not have had much for horses, and they certainly would not have had any chariots. This was because they had left Egypt in such a hurry. They would not have had time to make any swords, or any other kind of war like weapons for their defense.

However, this would not be the case when Gods people would eventually cross the Jordan River decades later. They would be well prepared for battle by that time. But for now and in their immediate future, God would fight their battles for them.

The scriptures say in (Ex.13: 17) that when the Egyptians let the people go; God had said to Himself; "If they face war, they might change their minds and return to Egypt." By this scripture, God clearly shows you that He knows peoples thoughts even before they think them. The people could have very easily wanted to change their minds and returned to Egypt, after they had completed their worship and sacrifices to God, at Succoth or Etham. But God had foreseen this problem and He took them away from that problem before it happened. God still protects His people in this same manner in today's world as well. Sometimes He may take you out of a potential problem before you get into it, but you may not realize that He has done this until sometime later in life.

For this reason and for the fact that Egypt had heavily fortified that particular part of their border, God chose to lead His people by a desert road that ran in a southeasterly direction, towards the wilderness of the Red Sea. This route would eventually lead them to Mount Sinai where God had made other plans for His people.

As you know, God has His reasons for doing what He does. Although we may not quite understand things at the time they happen, we must trust Him and His judgment and go on with our daily lives. Many times in our lives God will lead us through peaks and valleys of trouble, so that we can glorify Him and His Son Jesus Christ in some way. But when we eventually reach the mountaintop of our troubles, He delivers us from them in His own time and pleasure. God will always lead you out of your troubles if you ask Him to do so, but you must ask Him in faith and trust him to deliver you. Without faith you can do nothing. God is our ever-present help in all of our needs without question.

God went before His people to lead and protect them. He guided them by day in a pillar of cloud, and by a pillar of fire by night to give them light so that they could travel both day and night if God wanted them to. It was also a dramatic visible symbol of God's presence for all of the Israelites to see. By these and other wonderful signs He made Himself unforgettable in the sight and in the minds of His people.

God is a spirit and the Bible confirms this statement in (Jn.4: 24). It says, God is Spirit, and His worshipers must worship in spirit and in truth. It was a mark of His gracious character that He made His presence seen and felt among His people. If the people had focused on the fact that His presence was right before their eyes, they would not have needed to fear anything that would have come their way. God stayed with His people in some sort of visible manner throughout the whole journey to the Promised Land.

THE CROSSING OF THE RED SEA

The crossing of the Red Sea (or Sea of Reeds) is indeed a dramatic part of the exodus from Egypt, and in the history of the Israelites. There were however, many other events of lesser significance that occurred in the Israelites journey to the Promised Land. They also need to be mentioned at some point in the Israelites journey. In each of these events God manifests His great and magnificent power, to the Israelites and to any other nation of people who might get involved with the Israelites. You can be sure that the plight of the Israelites would spread to other countries very quickly without much of a problem. But to the Egyptians who were now pursuing the Israelites, it would be a final devastating blow to the Pharaoh and his people. The Egyptian people would learn firsthand, that God was the one true God and that He held all power over nature and everything in the universe.

Now once again, God speaks to Moses. He said to him: "Tell the Israelites to turn back and encamp near Pi Hahiroth between Migdol and the sea, directly opposite Baal Zephon. Pharaoh will think, 'The Israelites are wondering around the land in confusion hemmed in by the desert.' I will harden Pharaohs heart, and he will pursue them. But I will gain glory for myself through Pharaoh and his army, and the Egyptians will know that I am the Lord." Although the people might not have completely understood Gods reasoning, the Israelites broke camp and turned back northward, as God had commanded. Because God had created this deception, it is clear that the Pharaoh must have had someone watching the Israelites every move. They would then report back to him their location and what they were doing. This would have been a smart thing for him to do because he didn't trust Moses and the Israelites to return to Egypt.

After three days had passed and the people had not return to Egypt, it was then that the Pharaoh realized one of his greatest fears. The people were not coming back on their own accord and now he has lost his big work force. At this point his anger at being deceived by God and Moses was completely out of control. He had lost all sense of reasoning, and the Devil had taken complete control of him. He was thinking exactly what God wanted him to think. The people were lost, and they would be easy prey for him because of their confused state. But unknown to the Pharaoh, it was God who was not quite finished with punishing him and his people for the enslavement of the Israelites. God had another great and horrific disaster planned for them and now He was about to put it into effect. As more time passed, it could have been possibly a week or more, before the Pharaoh said to his officials: "What have we done? We have let the Israelites go and have lost their services!" It appears at this point that the Pharaoh was trying to put some of the blame on his officials and not just himself.

As the Lord continued to harden the Pharaohs heart, his uncontrollable anger and hatred welled up inside of him more and more with each passing day. He realized now that the Lord had humiliated and beaten him in front of his own people. This humility was more than he could take, so at one particular moment in time, he thought that there was only one solution to the whole matter. He would have his revenge on the Israelites and their God. He would totally, wipe the Israelites from the face of the earth. He would have his sweet revenge at all cost.

So he threw all caution to the wind. It made no difference to him now in his angry condition, and in his present state of mind how much he and his people had suffered; at the hand of this God just a short time ago. As far as he was concerned, it was payback time for being deceived. Perhaps, the thought of having lost his firstborn son also blinded his thinking, but it is not known for certain just what his exact thoughts may have been. Only God the Father in Heaven and the Pharaoh would ever know what transpired at that exact point in time when, he finely decided to go after the Israelites and wipe them from the face of the earth.

Unfortunately, people in the world today are no better off than the Pharaoh was at that time. Many people today carry grudges and bitter hatred around in their hearts for years against a person who may have wronged them at some point in time. They let the wrong that was committed against them steal their joy, their happiness, and their peace of mind from them. They do not grant their neighbor forgiveness for the wrong that was committed against them, and move on. They only seek their full-blown revenge, and do not care about the consequences just, like the Pharaoh in our story. People must realize that they should let God settle the score for them and move on with their life. The one who commits the wrong will pay for their wrong deeds some time, somewhere down the road in their life.

It is Gods command that we forgive each other seventy-times seven, which means all of the time, not just once in awhile. The scripture in (Deut. 32:35) God says that "Vengeance is mine, and recompense; their foot shall slip in due time; for the day of their calamity is at hand, and the things to come hasten upon them.' If you do not forgive your neighbor his wrongs or (sin) against you, neither can the Lord forgive your trespasses against Him. Jesus said this in (Mt. 6:14) not me. Only God, who is "Righteous and Just," can judge and make right all the wrongs committed against each other. There will be a time for Gods vindication.

Now the time has come, and now God will cause the Pharaoh to make one of the biggest mistakes of his life. With his anger still burning hot within him, the Pharaoh gave orders to his officers who were in charge of 600 of his best chariots, and all of his horsemen, and his foot soldiers, to get ready to go after the Israelites.

So it came to pass after a day of preparation and readiness' with the Pharaoh at the head of his army, in his special chariot he started out in pursuit of the Israelites. It must have been a very impressive sight to see indeed with, such a huge army marching off into the desert. All of the people in the Pharaohs army probably had only one thought in mind and that was, to seek the Pharaohs revenge for him, and to turn the desert sand into a killing field. But little did they know that, they were marching of to the last battle of their life.

After a few days of travel, it was late in the afternoon near twilight that the Pharaoh and his army caught up with the Israelites who were now camped near the shore of the Red Sea. This must have thrilled the Pharaoh beyond his wildest dreams. He had the Israelites trapped between his army and the sea. He must have been overjoyed at what he saw because; the Israelites appeared to have no place to retreat. Unless everyone and everything could swim the sea, the Israelites were totally hopeless and helpless. It seemed like it would be a swift and bloody victory for him and his army. This would have certainly been the case if God had not been the one who had set the trap, and was using the people as bait to trap him and his army. The people would not have stood much of a chance against the Pharaohs army and his chariots if, things would have went the way that the Pharaoh thought it would go.

As the Pharaoh and his army closed the distance between them and the Israelites, it would have been impossible for the Pharaoh not to see the pillar of fire, and the pillar of cloud that was the visible sign of God's presence. But at a great distance he may have thought that some kind of sand storm was brewing up. Sand storms are quite common in the desert. But as he drew closer to the multitude of people, he would have seen the pillar of cloud and the pillar of fire that was there. There is no doubt that in his mind he must have wondered about the phenomenon his eyes were witnessing but he probably didn't care. It was something totally different and unknown to him and his army.

When the Israelites who were bringing up the rear of the people, looked up and saw that the Egyptian army was pursuing them, they became extremely terrified. They cried out to Moses in anger and with great fear. It is not a sin to show fear in the face of danger, but it is a sin not to trust God when you are faced with that fear. Some people said to Moses: "Was it because there were no graves in Egypt that you brought us to the desert to die? What have you done to us by bringing us out of Egypt? Didn't we say to you in Egypt, 'Leave us alone; let us serve the Egyptians'? It would have been better for us to serve the Egyptians then to die in the desert.'"

This was only the beginning of the much bitter complaining, that Moses and Aaron would experience from the people throughout the journey to the Promised Land. It is ironic, just how soon people forget Gods goodness and start to complain about their circumstances. The complaining by the people, expressed their total lack of faith in God to care for them and their daily needs. But Moses on the other hand, showed his great faith in God by saying what he did. Moses did not use harsh words to rebuke the complaints of the Israelites. Instead, he sought to encourage them and to give them hope with a promise that they would see the salvation of the Lord.

He did the only thing that his faith would allow him to do. He gave all of the glory to God. He knew that God would be the only one who would be able to deliver the people from their present situation. Being that the Israelites could see that they were trapped between the sea and Pharaohs army, with no place to go, it would have created a great deal of stress and pressure on them. However, Gods plan was working perfectly.

In (Ex.14: 13) Moses said to the people: “Do not be afraid! Stand still and see the salvation of the Lord, which He will accomplish for you today. For the Egyptians whom you see today, you shall see again no more forever. The Lord will fight for you; you need only to be still.” This was a necessary reminder from God through Moses to the people. Although Israel may have been able to fight to some small degree, and would have marched out boldly, no one but God Himself would win this particular battle. The salvation that Moses spoke of was to come from the Lord Himself, and He was pleased in His heart to provide it.

Then God spoke to Moses again in (Ex. 14:15-18) and said: “Why do you cry out to me? Tell the children of Israel to go forward.” They were to go forward and not go back and not give up. ‘But lift up your rod, and stretch out your hand over the sea and divide it. The children of Israel shall go on dry ground through the midst of the sea. I indeed will harden the hearts of the Egyptians, and they shall follow them. So I will gain honor over Pharaoh and over all his army, his chariots, and his horseman. Then the Egyptians shall know that I am the Lord, when I have gained honor for myself over Pharaoh, his chariots and his horsemen.” There was Gods great plan in a nutshell.

When God had finished speaking to Moses, the cloud that had been leading the Israelites, moved, and went behind them and joined up with the pillar of fire. They both came between the Israelites and the Egyptians to fully protect the Israelites. The cloud that had been before the Israelites became darkness on the one side that faced the Egyptian camp. But it provided light for the Israelites on the other side so that they could go forward through the sea.

In this way, the two camps could not come together. So God’s children would be totally protected from the Egyptians throughout the night. The darkness of the cloud on the Egyptian side also prevented the Egyptians from seeing the

Israelites when they were crossing the sea. God had made the pillar of cloud and the pillar of fire two different realities for everyone to see. It was a curse to the Egyptians, but a blessing to the entrapped Israelites. All that night in the darkness God caused mass confusion in the Egyptians camp.

As soon as the pillars had moved behind the Israelites, Moses stretched out his rod over the sea, and the Lord caused a strong east wind to blow all that night. It blew so hard that the sea was divided and it formed a pathway of dry ground so the Israelites could cross over the sea. Try to picture this in your mind if you will; and see an exceedingly strong wind with a narrow point of focus, driving a wedge into the water and forming two high walls of water on both sides and drying up the ground as well. In your imagination, you can probably form a pretty good picture of how the wind could divide the waters. But it was Gods Almighty Power that held the walls of waters up. The people crossed over the sea all that night and when morning came they were safely on the other side of the sea. Because of the magnitude of this miracle, it would indeed be a miracle that a person could not easily forget no matter who they are.

In today's industrial world we use compressed air or pinpoints of air or water to do cutting of hard materials for us. In this case however, God used an east wind to accomplish and to show the Power of His Mighty right hand. This is one more time that God used the forces of nature that He has created to come at His beck and call. He did not have to wait for a windy day to produce the results that He wanted. The Lord waited until the time was just right. God is never in a hurry to accomplish His will.

It came to pass in the morning watch while it was still dark, that God looked down from the cloud and the pillar of fire on the army of Egyptians. He then troubled the army a great deal more. He took off their chariot wheels. This would make them impossible to drive. Now the chariots had become more of a liability than a threat to the Israelites. Some of the Egyptians said: "Let us flee from the face of Israel, for the Lord fights for them against the Egyptians." It is quite possible that from the above scripture that some members of Pharaohs army may have come to know God and to fear Him as well.

It took the Israelites all night to cross to the other side of the sea but God left the pathway open for the Egyptians to see. Then God hardened the hearts of the Pharaoh and his whole army again so that they became very impatient and angry. He then removed the cloud and the pillar of fire that had been protecting the Israelites. Now with Gods protection seemingly gone, the whole Egyptian army saw their chance to continue their pursuit of the Israelites. They wasted no time as they went after the Israelites, and followed them into the midst of the seabed.

As soon as the Pharaohs army reached the middle of the seabed and without any hope of escape, God said to Moses: "Stretch out your hand over the sea that the waters may come back upon the Egyptians, on their chariots, and on their horsemen." So while the Egyptians were in the middle of the seabed, God caused the chariots and their horses, and all of the horsemen, and most of the army to become bogged down and they were all drowned.

It was near daybreak when Moses stretched out his hand over the sea; and the walls of water collapsed and the sea returned to its normal depth. God also threw the foot soldiers, which had been fleeing toward the sea but were still on dry ground, into the sea. Not one member of the entire Egyptian army that had pursued the Israelites survived. The one thing that the Pharaoh had not counted on was the fact that God was the sole protector of the Israelites. God had totally defeated him and his army. God's victory was complete.

At the beginning of their journey, when the Israelites were leaving Egypt, they did not have very much faith in the leadership of Moses, or God, for that matter. But now that they had seen how God had delivered them from the hand of the Egyptians. It was entirely a different matter at this point. So now they praised God for His deliverance from the Egyptians, and they had truly become a nation under Gods protection. From this point on in their relationship with God, the people had a good reason to place their faith in God and the leadership of Moses. But that faith would be short lived, as you will soon see. But for the present, the people no longer complained to Moses about going back to Egypt. However, that didn't necessarily mean that they would stop their complaining completely.

After God had delivered the Israelites from the Egyptians at the Red Sea, the multitude continued on their journey to the Promised Land. To celebrate the Lords great victory at the Red Sea, Moses and the Israelites composed a song and sung it to the Lord. It was sung as part of the first worship services to God, after He had delivered them from the Egyptians. You can read this Hymn or psalm in (Ex.15: 1-21) (NIV). Miriam, who was the younger sister of Moses, led the women in their singing and dancing while they played their tambourines. Singing and expressive dances played an important part in the culture of the people at that time. Certain movements in the dances would often depict some part in the people's history.

Although there is no record of any prophetess ever serving as a priest in ancient Israel, women did serve as prophetess. Miriam was called a prophetess, because she often spoke from God. But, neither she nor her brother Aaron ever enjoyed the intimacy that Moses did with God. Moses and God often spoke directly to each other but only in a verbal manner, and not by sight. The only person, who has ever seen God the Father, is God the Son, who is none other than Jesus Christ Himself.

Pause here for a moment; and let your imagination take you back into that great Biblical time when this fantastic event occurred. Everything that occurred at the Red Sea you must agree that, it had to be one of the most spectacular sites and happenings that have ever occurred in the history of mankind. It must have held the people spell bound and staring for most of the night and the next day as well. Just think of the magnitude of the event itself! For all of these millions of people, to be able to stand on the seashore, and witness the act of God parting the waters of the sea with His mighty wind, it would have been breathtaking to say the least. For the people to see the high walls of water that were towering over their heads, and standing straight up above them, it would have been an awe inspiring sight as well.

Also, the people were able to see that God had made the ground dry, so they could cross the seabed with no problems. It must have truly amazed the people beyond their wildest dreams. Then to make the scene all the more astounding and dramatic; the people could see Moses when he stretch out his staff over the sea and cause the waters to close back over Pharaohs army, his horses and chariots. To see all the dead, animals and people washed up on the seashore, Gods people must have shouted with great joy. It had to be a miracle that a person would never forget, and they would talk about it for years to come.

This is a true biblical story it is not fiction. It has been told down through the ages, and it will never grow old. You should tell it to your children, your grandchildren, strangers, or anyone who would be willing to listen to you. It will be an opportunity for you to make yourself into a storyteller for God. God will bless you without a doubt, for telling people of His great and magnificent power, for the love and protection that He displayed to His people, and for the way that He led them to the Promised Land.

After the miracle at the Red Sea, Moses led the people into the wilderness of Shur. This desert was located east of Egypt in the northwestern part of the Sinai Peninsula. In another scripture in (Nu. 33:8) it calls this desert the desert of Etham, which is an Egyptian word. In the Hebrew language, the desert is called Shur.

After the people had departed from the Red Sea area and they had been traveling in the desert for some time, their water supply was depleted and they could find no water to drink. When they came to a place that was called Marah, they found the water that they so badly needed. When the people tried to drink the water however, it was to bitter and they could not drink it. So they started to grumble and complain to their favorite target, Moses. He would be the one who would face the brunt of the people's anger, each time that they found themselves in any kind of trouble. He would become their favorite whipping boy.

But God had warned the people, against grumbling and complaining to Him once before. In (Ex. 16:8) He warned the Israelites, and then in (Co.10: 10), Paul also warns people who live in the world today, not to follow their example. In reality then, when you are grumbling and complaining against the situation that you have gotten yourself into, you are doing so against God, and not the situation it's self. It could be that, God may be testing you to see what you will do in that particular situation or circumstance. By putting you through some tests in your life, God is molding your character and making your faith in Him much stronger, and then you will turn to Him for help in every need because this is what He desires from you.

When the people complained to Moses, Moses took their complaint to the Lord. He knew that God was his only source for wisdom and strength. God was the only one who could help him and he depended on God for everything. Now it was time for God to display His awesome power to His people once again, and another miracle was in order. So the Lord showed Moses a piece of wood and told him to throw it into the water. When he threw it into the water, the water became sweet and great for drinking and the people's problem was solved. Now the people were happy to say the least. Now the people could stop their complaining and drink all the water they wanted. They had water for themselves as well as for all of their livestock. Once again God has come to the peoples rescue with another miracle. But soon, they would find something else to belly ache about. But that is the way people are, even in the world today. When things don't go as people think they should, they belly ache and complain to anyone who will listen to them. We ourselves are often like the Israelites in many ways; we turn from praising God to complaining far too easily when we are in a tuff situation.

In many cases, we will blame God for our problems and not ourselves. I somehow believe that, in the case of the Israelites that, it was some of the other ethnic groups of people that had tagged along with the Israelites, who may have been doing a great deal of the complaining. I suspect this would be the problem because; these other ethnic groups might not have had the faith that the Israelite people had. God would be only a convenient source of help for them and for their material needs. The lack of water in this area would prove to be a constant test of Israel's faith in God. God could have changed the water to sweet water by using any method that He chose. But He chose to use a piece of wood because it made the miracle of the cleansing of the water easier to understand for the people. It is a proven fact, that when people see some miracle done before their eyes, they are more likely to believe it and that it came from God. Each time God would produce a miracle for the people, He would be glorified before them. It is because of our human weakness that, God is and can be glorified.

It was at that same time while the people were all still gathered there, God made a decree or an ordinance with them. He did this to test them once more. Through Moses; He said to them "If you listen carefully to the voice of the Lord your God and do what is right in His eyes; if you pay attention to His commands and keep all His decrees, I will not bring on you any of the diseases I brought on the Egyptians, for I am the Lord who heals you." These words testify to the mercy and power of God. God's promise of His healing power for His people still holds true today. He will heal you no matter what diseases may come your way "if you believe and trust Him and it is in His will to do so." All healing comes from the Lord but you must believe in Him, and have faith in Him to do what you ask Him to do.

By making the water sweet and good to drink, God was protecting His people's health and giving them a sense of comfort as well. It was also a good reminder for them that, God would provide everything that they needed no matter what it was. After the people had taken on all of the water that they needed for themselves and for their livestock; they rested for some time and then they continued on to a place called Elim. At this particular place there were twelve wells of water (or springs) and seventy palm trees. It was here that they made their camp. No doubt the Lord let the Israelites rest at Elim for a few days or maybe a week or so, before He continued to lead them farther on their journey to Canaan.

Elim was located seventy miles south of Ain Hawarah in the well-watered valley of Gharandel, near the traditional southerly site of Mount Sinai. The word Elim means "Place of Trees." The wells of water, and the shade of the palm trees, would bring a welcome relief from the blazing sun and the barrenness of the wasteland that the Israelites were in. Any relief from the hot burning sun in the desert would be a true blessing from God. Many times the Bible compares wells and springs to salvation, and palm trees to blessings.

For example; in the very first psalm in the Bible it says; "Blessed is the man who does not walk in the counsel of the wicked, or stand in the way of sinners, or sit in the seat of mockers. But his delight is in the law of the Lord, and on His law he mediates day and night. He is like a tree planted by streams of living water, which yields its fruit in season and whose leaf does not wither. Whatever he does prospers."

MANNA FROM HEAVEN

When it became time for the people to pull up camp and to move on, God led the Israelites into the wasteland of Sin. This word Sin, or the name of this particular desert, has absolutely no connection with the word that is used in the English language, for human sins. The word was more than likely derived from the word Sinai. Its location was in the southwestern Sinai, probably in the region that is known today as Debbet er-Ramleh. The Israelites arrived there on the fifteenth day of the second month. It had taken them exactly one month after leaving Egypt, to reach this point in their journey. So now you can see how slowly the people had to travel because, of their livestock and carts and the many other things that they had to contend with every day.

When they arrived there, they were no doubt, dusty, tired, out of sorts and out of food and water. So the people did what they did the best; and that was to complain to Moses. So Moses took the peoples problem to the Lord and the Lord told him what He would do for His people. He said, "I will rain down bread from heaven for you. The people are to go out and gather enough for that day. In this way I will test them and see whether they will follow my instructions. On the sixth day they are to prepare what they bring in, and that is to be twice as much as they gathered on the other days. I have heard the complaints of the children of Israel. Tell them at twilight you will eat meat, and in the morning you will be filled with bread. Then you will know that I am the Lord your God."

It's totally amazing just how fickle the people were and how soon they would forget God and His mercy. Stop and think for a minute about how ironic it is? After all the many miracles that God had done for them in just the short span of one month's time; they still complained and grumbled. To top it all off, they could see that Gods presence was with them in the form of a cloud and a pillar of fire all of the time? It's enough to make a person wonder if the people could ever be satisfied with anything God would do for them.

It seems odd to me as I relate this story to you that, they could not understand that God, who was so merciful, so good, and so powerful, would He not have the power also to supply food for them as well if, that was what was needed? It would be a small thing for God to do. Could they not realize that God would certainly not have gone to the trouble to deliver the Israelites from the hands of the Egyptians, and then let them starve to death somewhere in the desert? God would not deliver a person from their bad situations then throw them back into the fire. The Lord doesn't operate that way. Only Satan would do something like that because he is the father of all lies and the truth is not in him.

Now the people would experience Gods power and presence in a renewed way, and it would be further evidence of God's mercy and grace. From now on God will feed the Israelites bread from heaven in the morning and give them meat to eat in the evening. God is still doing the same for all of the people that are in the world today who are believers but, it in a much different way. Instead of sending us bread from heaven, He sent us His son Jesus Christ to feed our souls with living water and give all believers in Christ eternal life. We as Christians today are experiencing a renewed evidence of God's presence and power through Jesus Christ as you can see by the following scriptures.

The scriptures in (Jn. 6:32) Jesus called Himself the "true bread from heaven." In (Jn. (6:33) Jesus referred to Himself as the "bread of God." In (Jn.6: 35-48) Jesus said, "He was the bread of life." In (Jn.6: 51) Jesus said that He was the "living bread that came down from heaven." When Jesus was speaking, He was speaking in a spiritual sense and not in the physical sense.

So Moses and Aaron went before the people and said to them: "In the evening you will know that it was the Lord who brought you out of Egypt. In the morning you will see the glory of the Lord, because He has heard you're grumbling against Him. Who are we that you should grumble against us? You will know that it was the Lord when he gives you meat to eat in the evening, and all the bread you want in the morning. He has heard you're grumbling against Him. You are not grumbling against us, but against the Lord." Moses and Aaron could not see why the people blamed them for all of their problems. After all, they were only human like everyone else, and they had no special powers or control over anything that had been happening to the people. They were powerless, like the rest of the people.

The Lords response was a response of both love and concern for His people. Instead of being angry with the people, who He had a perfect right to be from a human standpoint, He chose to make them a promise that only He could keep. He promised to supply all of their food for them. It was a promise that He would keep for forty years, as long as the Israelites were on their desert journey to the Promised Land. But the Israelites reception of this wonderful blessing from God was already tarnished, because of their bad attitude. What should have been a happy and joyful discovery, when God delivered their first morning bread; it turned into a bittersweet one for the people instead.

Then Moses said to Aaron "Say to the entire Israelite community. 'Come before the Lord, for He has heard your grumbling.'" While Aaron was still speaking, the people looked toward the desert and the glory of the Lord appeared in a cloud before them. This was more positive visual proof for the people that God was with them day and night.

That same evening, quail came and covered the camp. The Lord had timed the quail's arrival in camp, with their natural migration pattern, which only He could do. They also came in great numbers. There would be a sufficient supply of meat for everyone in the evenings. In the morning there was a layer of dew around the camp. When the dew was gone, thin flakes like frost on the ground appeared on the desert floor. When the Israelites saw it, they marveled at it and said to each other; "What is it?" They didn't have the faintest idea of what it could be.

Then Moses said to them; "It is the bread that the Lord has given you to eat, and you are to take as much as you need." An Omar for each person you have in your tent." The Manna resembled a thin wafer and it tasted like honey. It was both tasty and nutritious. It could also be made into the bread that the people needed for their daily use. An Omer was a Hebrew measurement that is equivalent to about two quarts, or one tenth of an ephah, which would equal about one tenth of a bushel of grain.

When the Lord promised the Israelites bread each morning He put a certain quota or amount, of Manna that the people were allowed to gather each morning. They were only to gather enough for each person that was living in their tent. No more, no less. It was to be gathered in the morning on a daily bases, and not stored up for the next day. The only exception to the rule was that, on the sixth day, they were to gather twice as much. This was to be done, so that they would have enough to prepare for the next day, which would be the seventh day of the week. The people were not to work at all on the seventh day. It was to be a day of rest for them, as well as a day that was committed to the Lord in worship and praise. The people were to keep the "Sabbath Day Holy."

This is the second time that God has initiated or instructed His people to rest on the Sabbath day. The first time was back in the time of Abraham. God made these rules because He wanted to test the people to see if they would listen to His instructions or not and obey Him. He would supply the bread or Manna fresh each morning, and the meat in the evening at twilight.

However, there was no doubt that the people were not too happy about having to live under more rules and regulations from the Lord. Rules are sometimes a hard pill to swallow for many people and to some people; rules are only made to be broken. Such was the case with the Israelites at that time, and it's still true for the generations of today.

The people are no better now than before. Our generations today do exactly the same thing as the people did in the time of Moses. They break Gods and man rules and regulations, every day, and think nothing of it. As long as they can get ahead of everything, or everyone they are happy, and they think that they are Number1 no matter what it cost them. The price that they have to pay means nothing to them. They think that they have won the race over everyone, but that is not the way that God wants us to live or feel and be His people. He wants us to help our fellowman (or neighbor) with love and kindness in our hearts. When we do this small thing, we will have joy in our heart, and peace in our mind knowing that we have done what the Lord has commanded us to do.

When Moses told the people that they were not to keep any of the manna until morning, his message seemed to fall on some deaf ears. These were the kind of people who thought that the message was only meant for everyone else but them. They possibly thought that they could get away with keeping some manna overnight regardless of what God thought. This of course, was breaking Gods command but God had a big surprise waiting for those who did not obey His command.

When the people woke up in the morning they woke up to a terrible smell in their tents because the manna was full of worms or maggots and it stunk very badly. So the saving of the manna did those people absolutely no good. All it did was to get them in trouble with God and Moses. The people who disobeyed Gods command and saved the manna, showed their lack of faith in God and His ability to provide their daily bread.

There are several interesting points here that the Lord may have been making to the people while at the same time providing them with food. For example:

(a) God was testing the faith of His people. Would they listen to Him or not.
(b) They were not to doubt His word no matter what came their way.
(c) They were to put their complete trust in the Lord for their daily bread and protection.
(d) After the people had gathered all the manna that they needed, what was left on the ground disappeared. God didn't leave it around so the people could get the manna whenever they wanted.
(e) The extra manna that the people gathered on the sixth day, which was twice as much as any other day of the week, it never went bad. On the Sabbath day when the people needed it for food, it was just as fresh as if it had been just gathered up. All other days of the week it turned bad.
(f) It proved to the people that the manna was not a natural occurring substance on the desert floor. It truly was a gift from God each day.
(g) Last but not least, it was a built in reminder of how important the Sabbath Day was to become for the people of Israel. It was to be a day of rest for the people, as well as a day of worship and praise to the Lord. God created the Sabbath Day as a day of rest because; on the seventh day of creation He rested, after He had finished creating the world and everything in the whole universe.

Sometime later, Moses had more instructions for the people and he said to them; "This is the thing that the Lord has commanded: 'take an Omer of manna and keep it for the generations to come, so they can see the bread that I gave you to eat in the desert, when I brought you out of Egypt.'" Then Moses told Aaron to take a jar and put an Omer of manna in it. Then place it before the Lord to be kept for Generations to come. As the Lord commanded Moses, so Moses commanded Aaron. This chain of command would remain in effect and in this order until Moses was dead. As soon as the Israelites had celebrated their first Passover in Canaan decades later the Lord stopped giving the Israelites the manna from heaven.

Then Aaron put the manna in front of the Testimony that it might be kept. The word testimony in this passage is a synonym for the Ark of the Covenant that the Israelites would build at a later date. The jar, in which the manna was placed, was made of pure gold. It had to be made of pure gold because it would later be placed in the tabernacle in the gold covered Ark of the Covenant in the Most Holy Place. Anything that was to be placed before the Lord in the Most Holy Place was to be made of pure Gold.

There is one other interesting aspect to the manna that the Lord had provided that I would like to bring to your attention at this time. That is; the manna that was put before the Lord in the gold jar lasted for centuries and it never went bad. It is still in the Ark to this day as far as anyone knows. This was one more miracle that God had done for His people, as a memorial to His great works.

It would also serve as a reminder for His people, and for the coming generations, that God provided bread for them from heaven. The Bible says that the manna was placed in the Ark of the Covenant, along with the staff of Moses, and the two stone tablets that God wrote the Ten Commandments on. These treasures including the Ark of the Covenant have been missing for centuries, and no one but God knows exactly where they are located for sure.

WATER FROM THE ROCK OF HOREB

When God decided to move the Israelite camp once more, the Bible says that they moved from place to place. This would probably mean that the people did not remain in those particular places very long or, that nothing specifically happened too them while they were there.

As the people moved on at the command of the Lord, they came to a place called Rephidim in the southwestern part of the Sinai Peninsula. When they arrived there they had the same problem, as before, there was no water for them to drink or to water their flocks. The lack of water in the desert would cause an ongoing problem for them, and it would also create a great deal of stress on the people at the same time. The lack of water would also continue to test the people's faith in the Lord as to the supplying of their daily needs for water.

Because of the great number of people and their flocks, it would have taken a huge amount of water to fill their needs. So, true to the people's nature, the lack of water would once again cause the people to complain and grumble against the Lord and Moses.

They said to Moses; "Why did you bring us up out of Egypt to make us and our children and livestock die of thirst?" Once again, they were blaming Moses for the lack of water. They should have been asking him to take their problem to the Lord. If they would have done this and had not complained, the Lord would have been greatly pleased with the people. However that was not to be. The people were so angry and upset that they were almost ready to stone Moses to death.

Moses said to the people; "Why do you contend with me? Why do you temp the Lord?" He said this because he felt that the people were grumbling against the Lord as well as himself. In essence, they were complaining against the

Lord and His mercy. This type of attitude was an added cause of frustration for Moses. Then Moses cried out to the Lord and said; "What shall I do with this people?" His frustration with the people was so great that, this time he literally cried out before the Lord in anguish. This example of Moses literally crying out before the Lord is exactly what the people of today should do when they are in any kind of trouble. Without any doubt what so ever, God will hear you and He will come to your rescue in some way that pleases Him.

The Lord then said to Moses, "Walk ahead of the people. Take with you some of the elders of Israel, and take in your hand the staff with which you struck the Nile. Go to the Rock of Horeb, and I shall stand there on the rock before you, and when you strike it, water will come out that the people may drink."

Through the active participation of the elders of Israel in this particular miracle that God was about to perform for his people; it shows that not all of the people were complaining to Moses or showing him a great deal of disrespect.

When the enveloping presence of the Lord appeared on the rock before Moses and the people, it must have been an awesome sight to see. It was living proof to them that the continuing presence of the Lord was with them, and that it was the Lord who was actually supplying the water and doing His work through Moses His chosen leader.

Paul may have had this event in mind when he wrote in the scriptures in (1 C o. 10; 4) "and they drank the same spiritual drink, for they drank from the spiritual rock that accompanied them, and that rock was Christ." Here, he was speaking about the Israelites.

The striking of the rock, pictured the coming death of Jesus who is our Rock of Salvation. The water that came from the rock could satisfy their present physical need for water. But one day far into the future when Christ would come to earth, He would supply the living spiritual water that is needed to satisfy our every spiritual need.

The Bible implies, that the water continued to flow from the rock as long as it was needed. When the rest of the people seen the miracle that the Lord had done, they too were in awe of God and His Almighty Power. So Moses did as the Lord had commanded him to do in the presence of the elders of Israel, and God brought forth water for His people from the Rock of Horeb. Moses then named the place Massah which means "testing," and Meribah, which means "rebellion."

THE ISRAELITES FIRST BATTLE

While the Israelites were camped at Rephidim, they came under attack by the Amalekites. The Amalekites were the descendants of Esau. He was the son of Isaac and Rebekah and the grandson of Abraham. The Amalekites were a tribal people that lived in the southwestern part of the Sinai desert.

The attack on the Israelites was unprovoked, and the Israelites as well the Lord considered this attack particularly heinous. This was the first time that the Israelites had experienced any kind of war like activity on their journey to the Promised Land. But God was on their side so there was no great cause for alarm as far as God was concerned.

The Lord who could never be caught off guard, had been working behind the scenes, and He had been grooming one particular man for the leadership of His people in the time of war. This man was called Hoshea the son of Nun, but Moses later renamed him Joshua. It was quite common in Biblical times to change a person's name from one name to another. The name "Hoshea" means "salvation" while "Joshua" means "the Lord saves." The Greek form of the name Joshua is the same as that of the name Jesus.

Joshua was from the tribe of Ephraim, which would become one of the most powerful of the twelve tribes of Israel. His military prowess uniquely suited him to be the conqueror of Canaan forty years later. His faith in God and his loyalty to Moses suited him well to be an aide to Moses, as well as his successor. Likewise, by the changing of Hoshea's name to Joshua, it was a statement anticipating the later prominence of Joshua and his military leadership, plus all of the other duties that would befall him in his lifetime. Just as God had trained Moses for his leadership, He was about to start training Joshua in the same manner. Joshua would now become Gods "Field General."

The attack on the Israelites was more than likely just a type of hit and run attack rather than a sustained attack. As soon as Moses realized that they were under attack by the Amalekites, he sent for Joshua and said to him. "Choose some of our men and go out to fight the Amalekites. Tomorrow I will stand on top of the hill with the staff of God in my hands."

This statement by Moses was clearly a statement of trust and obedience to God. Although this particular scripture does not say so, the implication is quite clear. God told Moses where he had to go and what he had to do the next day. Because of his love for God, Moses would not have done anything of his own volition where God was directly involved. When Moses told Joshua to take some men to fight the Amalekites, he didn't give him a specific number of men that he was to take with him.

Because God was going to be directly involved in this battle, it was for certain that its eventual outcome would be a complete victory for the Israelites. So Joshua gathered his army the next day and they went to war against Amalek and his army. Moses, Aaron, and a man named Hur, who was also a close aide to Moses, went to the top of the hill like he said he would do.

As long as Moses held up his hands with the staff of God in it, which was a visible sign that Israel's victory was in God's hands alone, the Israelites would be winning the battle. But as soon as his arms grew tired and his staff was lowered, the Amalekites would start to win the battle over the Israelites. At the time that this battle took place, Moses, was well up in years and he would become tired quite easily. So it is fair to assume that he could not hold the staff up for any great length of time. Even a young person's arm would soon become tired and they too would have to let the staff down.

When Aaron and Hur seen that Moses was having trouble holding the staff up, they found a large rock for him to sit on. Then they positioned themselves one on each side of Moses, and helped him to hold up his arms so that his hands were steady until sunset. It was only in this way that Israel would prevail and win the battle because; it was truly only in Gods power that the battle would be won. When the sun had set that day, God had totally defeated Amalek and his army by the sword, through Joshua His new Field General.

After the battle was all over and peace had been restored to the Israelite camp, the Lord spoke again to Moses and said; "Write this on a scroll as something to be remembered, and make sure that Joshua hears it, because I will completely blot out the memory of Amalek from under heaven." Then Moses proceeded to build his customary alter to the Lord and he called it, "The Lord is my Banner," for hands were lifted up to the throne of the Lord. The Lord will be at war against the Amalekites from generation to generation."

King David would fulfill this prophecy by the Lord in (2 Sa.1-1) after he became King of Israel, some seven hundred years later." Although the Lord had taken centuries to fulfill His promise, to the Amalekites He had in no way changed His mind. God never changes His mind once He decrees what He will and will not do. As you know, with God time doesn't exist because He is eternal. Time and age, are two of the conditions that God has placed on mankind and all of His other creations.

-6-

ARRIVAL AT MOUNT SINAI

The Bible docs not say just how long the Israelites remained camped at Rephidim, but I would suspect that it wasn't much longer than a week or two. After they departed from Rephidim, the community of people arrived at Mount Sinai in the southeastern part of the Sinai Peninsula. It was there that the Israelites made their camp in a close proximity to the mountain.

They arrived there exactly on the fourteenth day of the third month, which was two months to the day after they had departed from Egypt. No doubt, Moses was quite surprised and elated at Gods perfect timing. Gods perfect timing, would have served to increase his faith in the fact, that God is always true to His word, and that He will always keep His promises no matter what happens.

Moses would also realize that, God was now, fulfilling the promise that He had made to him earlier, when He first spoke to him on the mountain. God had told Moses, that the Israelites would come back there to worship Him on this mountain, after He had brought the Israelites out of Egypt. It is here at Mount Sinai or the "Mountain of God" as it is sometimes referred too; that many things would happen to shape the history of the Israelites. For example:

(a) God would give the people more rules and laws to live by.
(b) They would be given more customs that they would have to keep throughout their lifetime.
(c) They would be given the Ten Commandments that God expected them and for all of mankind to follow later on.
(d) When the Israelites arrived at Mount Sinai it was a momentous event for both Moses and Aaron. As you may recall that;

(a) It was on this same Mountain that Moses had his first encounter with God, at the burning bush. At that particular time God also told Moses of his mission in life.
(b) It was at the base of this Mountain where Moses and his brother Aaron first met, after forty years of separation.
(c) Also, it was at this same Mountain that Moses first told Aaron that he would be his spokes man in the presence of the Pharaoh.
(d) It would also be the first time that Moses would see his wife Zipporah and his two sons' since he had sent them back to her father Jethro, when He returned to Egypt to confront the Pharaoh.

So you can see that, when Moses came to the mountain for the second time, his mind must have been flooded with the memories of his first visit there. It was shortly after the people had arrived at Mount Sinai that God, who is always merciful and full of grace; had an extra special blessing for his servant Moses.

Jethro the Priest of Midian, who was his father-in-law, had sent a messenger to Moses and he said; "I your father-in-law Jethro, am coming to you with your wife and her two sons." Moses must have been overjoyed when he received this message because he had not seen his family for over a year. Jethro had heard through the grape vine of everything that God had done for Moses and for His people Israel, and how He the Lord, had brought Israel out of bondage in Egypt. It is quite possible that Jethro wanted to see and to hear for himself, directly from Moses, just exactly how true the rumors were. He didn't want to leave any stone unturned as to the truth of the news that he had been hearing about his son-in-law Moses.

When Jethro arrived at the mountain, Moses went out to meet him and he bowed down before him and kissed him, as was the custom at that time. You may recall that I had stated before that the act of bowing low and kissing a person on each cheek was not an act of worship but it was a sign of respect. It was also a reminder of the obligations that may have existed between the two people.

After their formal greeting was over, Moses took Jethro into his tent and told him everything that God had done to the Pharaoh and the Egyptians. He also told him of how the Lord, had done mighty works on behalf of His people Israel, and how He the Lord, had led His people from Egypt, to the "Mountain of God" to worship Him. As Moses related the many stories to Jethro, it must have filled his heart with a great deal of joy, as well as giving him a tremendous peace of mind. It would also serve to erase any doubts that he might have had about what God could do at His own bidding and pleasure.

After Moses finished telling his stories to Jethro, he praised the Lord and said: "Blessed be the Lord who has delivered you out of the hand of the Egyptians, and out of the hand of Pharaoh. Now I know that the Lord is greater than all the gods, for He did this to those who treated Israel arrogantly." By his confession of the above words, they may imply that he had once regarded the Lord as one among many gods, or perhaps as the principal god among them. But now he declares his full faith in God as the "Supreme Deity." He no longer has any doubt as to which god is the true God of all Creation.

The next day Moses went before the people as he had done many times before to oversee, any disputes that may have come up. He was compelled to listen to all of their winning and complaining because of his high position as their leader. Moses had taken it upon himself to be the judge and jury for the people in all of their disagreements no matter how small or how big they were. He had become the one person in whom everyone could confide in and be satisfied with his decisions and judgments. He had also become the peoples "Mediator" between themselves and God.

In this respect, Moses was in the likeness of Christ. Christ, who is our Lord and Savior, is our Mediator between God the Father and all believers of the Christian Faith. He intercedes for us in heaven before the Father on our behalf. Now: through Christ, we have direct access to the Father. We can come directly into the Fathers presence with our requests and desires through prayer.

When Jethro seen how hard it was on Moses, to be the mediator between the people and their arguments with each other, and how he was so worn out at the end of the day, he said to Moses. "What is this thing that you are doing for the people? Why do you alone sit as judge, while all of these people stand around you from morning till evening?" Moses replied to Jethro and said: "Because the people come to me and seek Gods will and I inform them of Gods decrees and laws." Then Jethro said to Moses: "What you are doing is not good. You and these people who come to you will only wear yourselves out. The work is too heavy for you. You cannot handle it alone. Now listen to me and I will give you some advice and may God be with you."

The lively interchange of words between Moses and his father-in-law Jethro showed the very human side of Moses. Although he had a very special relationship with God, he was driven by the human desire to do everything perfectly himself. In this way the people would not be able to find any fault with him and his decisions.

At that particular moment in time, Moses was not unlike many people of the world today. It is bad news to them if they make a mistake and people find out about it. They just seem to worry themselves sick over some silly little mistake that they've made, and they let it bothers them for days or weeks, or even months.

This is not Gods way for you to live your life. God doesn't want you wallowing in your own self-pity and having a bad case of low esteem. You are Gods prized possession because, He has created you in His own image, and He wants nothing but the best for you and all of mankind. That is why His son Jesus Christ had to die on the cross and shed His precious blood for you and for me. Through His blood we have been redeemed and our sins are forgiven. Now, all believers in Christ can inherit eternal life. But you must have faith and believe in Him and in His Father who sent Him.

Now Jethro was about to give Moses more good advice. This kind of good advice would be carried on throughout Israel's history. He said to Moses: "You must be the people's representative before God and bring their disputes to Him. Teach them the decrees and laws and show them the way they are to live, and the duties that they are to perform. But select capable men from the people that will make your load lighter because they will share it with you. If you do this and God so commands, you will be able to endure the strain and all these people will go home satisfied."

This was good sound advice that Moses had just received from Jethro. It was Gods way of helping Moses with a huge problem that had come his way, and that he didn't quite know how to solve it. So God solved it for him through Jethro. Many times in the lives of people, God will use other people or an event, to get too the people that He has a message for. The men that Moses was to choose had to possess certain qualities. They could not be just any person that came to his mind. For example: They had to be men who feared God. The term for fear in the Bible means to hold God in awe, which is the central idea of piety.

(a) They were to show, piety, reverence, godly humility, and ready obedience.
(c) They had to be trustworthy or truthful men, who hated dishonest gain, and they had to be able men, having strength, efficiency, and wealth.
(d) They had to be haters of covetousness, so they could not be bribed.
(e) They were to be ranked with the rulers who were over them. In other words, each man was to be held accountable to someone else who had a greater degree of authority in the chain of command such as, God Moses, and then Aaron. Our military is run in the same kind of manner.

After Moses had chosen these men, he was to appoint them as officials or judges, over a certain number of people all of the time. Some of them were to have thousands, hundreds, fifties, or tens of people, under their jurisdiction. These Judges would solve the lesser important cases, but the most difficult cases were to be brought before Moses himself. Then He would take the most serious problems to the Lord. God would be the ultimate judge in all-unsolvable cases.

Because of the great relationship that existed between Moses and his father-in-law Jethro, Moses, was not ashamed to take the good advice that had been offered to him. But it is also possible, that he may have realized that the advice had come from God through Jethro. So Moses took the advice of Jethro and he set up a system of judges over the people of Israel. They would now judge and run the affairs of the people in the new nation that God was creating.

Also, it is my opinion that God has now put into motion, a system that most of the governments of the world have adopted throughout the history of mankind. The only difference today is that we have changed the names of the people who hold these different positions. We call them government ministers with a portfolio. They have different duties to perform for each position that they hold.

After Moses had completed the task of choosing all of the judges that he required, the Bible says that Moses let his father-in-law Jethro depart, and he returned to his own country. So it is safe to assume, that Jethro stayed in the company of Moses long enough to help him to set up this new form of government. Although he was now the head of this new government, Moses was still accountable to God.

When Jethro returned to his own country, he was no doubt a different person in many respects. Because of his position as the Priest of Midian he probably would have had a great deal of influence on his people at home. When he related his stories to the people, he probably did so with feelings of great joy and happiness. This was possible because he had now developed a newfound faith in the one true God. As far as he was concerned, the stories that he had heard from Moses, and the things that he had witnessed while he was visiting Moses, it was all of the proof that he needed to confirm his faith in the God of heaven and earth. Through his latest experience, he was now in a position to expand the knowledge of the true God to the people of his country.

Jethro the Priest of Midian had now become Jethro Minister of the Lord.

It was some time after the departure of Jethro that, God made His presence known to Moses on the mountain once again. It was the first time that Moses went up on the mountain to talk to God since his return from Egypt. After he had reached a certain place on the mountain he stopped, and God called to him and said: "This is what you are to say to the house of Jacob and what you are to tell the people of Israel. You yourselves have seen what I did to Egypt, and how I carried you on eagle's wings and brought you to myself. Now if you obey me fully and keep my covenant then, out of all nations you will be my treasured possession. Although the whole earth is mine, you will be for me a kingdom of priests and a holy nation. These are the words you are to speak to the Israelites."

When God had finished speaking, Moses went back down the mountain to the people. When he had called all of the elders of the Israelites together, he told them word for word what the Lord had spoken to him. When all of the people had heard the words that Moses had relayed to the elders, they all said together in one accord: "We will do everything the Lord has said." Then Moses returned to the mountain and he gave the peoples answer to the Lord.

The covenant that the Lord had just spoken of to Moses about was, an expanded version of the same covenant that, the Lord had made with Abraham and his descendants six hundred years earlier. Now the Lord was making this same expanded covenant with the Israelites and Moses at Mount Sinai.

This Mosaic Covenant; was the first covenant that God has made with the entire nation of Israel. The word Covenant would be used many times later in the history of the Israelites. This was because they would be required to make treaties or agreements, with other nations in the future conquest of Canaan, Gods Promised Land.

To be a participant or a part of the divine blessing that went with the covenant, the people had two very important conditions that they were required to meet. The first condition was that they had to be obedient to the Lord and keep His commandments and laws. The second one was to have faith in God, and that He would do everything that He said He would do, and that He would supply all of their daily needs both bodily and spiritually. God came to the Israelites as the Great King. It was a treaty that was made between the Superior Sovereign King of heaven and earth, and His inferior servants the Israelites.

The first thing that God did was to remind the Israelites of who He was and how He had acted in their behalf. He was their Savior. He was the one who had whisked them away from their Egyptian oppressors "as of on eagles wings. The scripture in (Ex. 19:4) God promised to make the Israelites His special treasure. They would be a kingdom of priests and a holy nation, because God Himself is Holy They would be a separate and a distinct nation that would be separate from all other nations because, of the special relationship that they would have with God.

Through this special relationship with God, Israel would become the means, by which all other nations of the earth would learn of the living God through the Bible. Also it would be through the nation of Israel that God would keep His promise to Abraham, and bless all of the other nations of the world. These words are the absolute truth to this very day. If all of the other nations of the world would treat Israel the way that they should be treated, then they too would receive Gods richest blessing and prosper abundantly. But that is not the case in the world today. There are only a few nations throughout the world today that will stand and fight for Israel's rights and freedom. The Bible says that Israel is the "Apple of God's Eye" and that He is the keeper of His people, and that He neither slumbers nor sleeps. All other nations of the world would do well to heed Gods warning for they will not go unpunished in the end when Christ returns to the earth.

As Gods people, they were to live a certain way. It had to be Gods way and not their way. God's way would make them at peace with their Creator. But if they chose to live their way, which would be the way of the flesh and the Devil, they would be doomed. It is because of this covenant that God has made with them that; the Israelite nation of today is in a very enviable position. They are still Gods chosen people and God specially blesses them because of His grace and this covenant. All the nations of the world are still being blessed today because of this covenant with Israel.

When the Lord used the beautiful poetic expression "on eagle's wings I bore you," this description best fits one of Gods greatest and most magnificent creations, "The female Golden Eagle." God was also expressing His great and abiding love for His people. It was His loving way of describing His people's swift deliverance from Egypt and Israel's salvation from slavery. In like manner, it can also describe our salvation from sin through Jesus Christ.

Now the Lord is about to create another miracle right before His people. He is going to show His people His deep love and compassion for them. It will also at this particular time, reinforce the leadership roll of Moses to the people. The Lord knew of the many problems that Moses was having in making the people listen to him. They did not fully understand that he was only doing what God had commanded him to do.

This kind understanding was badly needed for some of them, but not necessarily for all of the people. Also, it would make the people fully realize that Moses was Gods called and ordained servant and leader. He was not just to be their whipping boy whenever they chose to use him as such. The people had to fully realize that he was also a man to be honored, respected, and held in very high esteem.

While Moses was still on the mountain talking to God, the Lord said to Moses: "I am going to come to you in a dense cloud, so that the people will hear me speaking with you, and will always put their trust in you and believe you forever. Go to the people and consecrate them today and tomorrow. Have them wash their cloths and be ready by the third day. On that day the Lord will come down on Mount Sinai in the sight of all the people. Put limits around the mountain and tell them, be careful that you do not go up to the mountain or touch the base of it. Whoever touches the mountain shall surely be put to death. He shall surely be stoned or shot with arrows; not a hand is to be laid on him. Whether man or animal he shall not be permitted to live. Only when the ram's horn sounds long blasts they shall come near the mountain." Once the Lord had finished speaking to Moses, he departed from the presence of the Lord and went back down the mountain to report Gods message to the Elders and the people.

As he delivered Gods message to the people, Moses also told them how they were to consecrate themselves in preparation for the meeting with the Living God within three days. He said to the people: "Wash your clothes, and do not have sexual intercourse with your wife for those three days." Even the priests, who were to approach the Lord, had to consecrate themselves as well or the Lord will break out against them. This statement by the Lord raised a question in the mind of Moses and he had said to the Lord, "The people cannot come up to Mount Sinai because you yourself warned us. 'Put limits around the mountain and set it apart as holy.'" It was a very appropriate question as far as Moses was concerned from a human standpoint, but he was not committed to the point of getting into an argument with God his Creator.

There are several reasons why God set the rules that He did for the people whenever He would visit the mountain. For example:

a. God would only reveal so much of His splendor to the people who would be totally unprepared for a full revelation of His Glory. Therefore, He had to hide Himself in a thick dark cloud.
b. The people had to wash their cloths and their bodies, so that they would be clean and presentable before the Lord. This washing would take care of their outward appearance, but not their hearts and minds which would be their inner self. The people were to abstain from sexual intercourse as well for three days, before they went to the meeting with God. Intercourse in its self is not sinful, but it is one of the desires of the flesh that would have made the people ritually unclean before God. They had to consecrate themselves before the Lord. This meant that the people were to, go through purifying rites so that they would be ceremonially prepared for the meeting with the Lord. The purifying ceremony would include the killing and the sacrificing of some animals, and some of their blood would then be sprinkled on Gods alter by the priests. This service washed away the people's sins, and purified their inner self before God.
c. God had to put a limit or boundaries around the mountain because, when He descended on the mountain, the whole mountain would become holy and not just part of it. If any animal or human touched even the base of the mountain, then the mountain would have become defiled and unclean. God would not, and could not, tolerate this because; He is a perfect and a Holy God.

d. The Lord also knew that if He didn't set limits around the mountain, the people might try to cross the boundaries and storm the mountain to get a look at Him. So God threatened the people and their animals with certain death. The threat of certain death would demonstrate to the people the seriousness of this particular command, and also because of the event that was about to take place within three days time.

The people were to stay in their camp and wait, until they heard the sound of a along loud blast from a trumpet (or rams horn). This would be the peoples signal from God, to move closer to the mountain in an orderly manner, so that they could hear God speak to Moses, but they were only to come up to the boundaries that Moses had set for them.

You may recall, that in (Ex. 3:5) God commanded Moses to remove his sandals from his feet when, he spoke to God the first time on this mountain, at the burning bush. It was because he was standing on holy ground and because of the Lords presence was there on the mountain. This situation would be the same as it was the first time when God spoke to Moses on the mountain.

Then it came to pass on the third day in the morning, there was thundering and lighting with a thick cloud over the mountain. As a very loud trumpet blast sounded, the people in the camp shook with great fear. The sound was so loud that the people shrunk back in fear, and they were afraid to move forward. The tremendous sound of the trumpet and the sight of the thunder and lightning demonstrated to the people, the awesome power of the Lord. They had never experienced such a loud sound in their lives. There was thick black smoke billowing up from the mountain like the smoke from a huge furnace, and the whole mountain trembled violently like an earthquake. As the people looked on in fear at, this tremendous spectacle the sound of the trumpet grew louder and louder. The whole mountain was covered in smoke because the Lord had descended on it in fire.

When the sound of the trumpet had subsided, Moses led the people out of the camp to the boundaries at the foot of the mountain. With a great deal of fear still in their hearts, they all waited for God to speak. After God had descended on the mountain, He called Moses up to the top of the mountain. God did this because He wanted to be close to Moses when He spoke to him. In this manner it would leave no doubt in the minds of the people just who was doing the speaking. When Moses spoke, the voice of God answered him so that the people heard every word that the Lord was speaking to Him. Now the people would know without a doubt that, God had been instructing Moses all this time in everything that he had been telling the people.

It would have been a very impressive sight indeed for the people to witness, when God descended on the mountain. The people would learn firsthand that; it was the living God and He alone that had surrounded Him in a thick cloud and it was He who had sent forth thunder and lightning that illuminated the whole mountain, and it was He who filled the heavens with His wonders.

However, there was one other amazing fact that also occurred at that same time. It was the fact that, it was a heavenly visitor who had blew the trumpet for the Lord, rather than someone from the camp of the Israelites. The hearts of the people must have been completely overwhelmed with fear. No doubt, that the people still had a very vivid memories of how God who was now so close to them on the mountain, had destroyed the whole Egyptian army with the swoop of His mighty right hand. The people must have realized that God could do the same thing to them if it was in His will to do so.

As you may well know, God is a God of love and patience and He was not out to harm or to kill any of His people. So to be on the safe side He further instructed Moses and said: "Go down and warn the people so they do not force their way through to see the Lord, and many of them perish. The Lord knew that with such a huge number of people that, the people in the rear may try to push forward to see better, and in this way cause many people in the front to come in contact with the base of the mountain, and for this reason be killed.

Although Moses didn't fully understand Gods reasoning at the time, God knew what the people were thinking and what was about to happen. It is very clear that God knew that some of the people were becoming daring and unruly. The scriptures imply that some of the priests and some of the other people may have been willing to take a chance with their lives. They were probably thinking of coming up the mountain to see this God, who had saved them from the Egyptians, and who was so Almighty and Powerful.

So God repeated His command once more with some urgency in His voice, and He said to Moses: "Away! Get down and then come up, and bring Aaron up with you. But do not let the priests and the people break through to come up to the Lord, or He will break out against them."

But much to his surprise when he had returned down the mountain, Moses could see the fear in the eyes of the people. The display of Gods Almighty Power scared them half out of their wits, and they had stayed at a safe distance from the mountain. The people were so afraid of God that they said to Moses: "Speak to us yourself and we will listen. But do not have God speak to us or we will die."

Now the people at last had made a formal and a verbal request to Moses to be their mediator between God and themselves. It was a role that Moses had already been fulfilling from the very beginning, but the people didn't want to accept his leadership. God had now accomplished exactly what He had set out to do. Subsequently Prophets and Priests would fill the role of a mediator for the people much later on in history as, the Israelites continued on through the pages of time.

Moses realized the moment that he saw how the people had reacted to God that, he must calm their fears quickly. So without any hesitation, he explained to them that God was not there to cause them harm in anyway. He was only there to test them, and to make a binding covenant or a contract with them, and to reassure the people that He was with them on their journey. Also with Gods presence on the mountain, He could show His love, His protection, and also show that He would provide for their every need. The people should have realized what Gods intentions were because, God had just told them that they were His chosen people and that they would be a treasure to Him, and a nation of priests.

If the people truly feared (or loved) the Lord, they would not deliberately sin against Him and break His commandments and laws. That was what the covenant and His appearance on the mountain was all about. God wanted to have a close relationship with His people and be the God that the people would honor, praise, and worship because He is the Creator of the World, the Universe, and everything in it.

As Moses continued to converse with the people he said: "The Lord heard you when you spoke to me, and the Lord said: 'I have heard what this people said to you. Everything they said was good. Oh! That their hearts would be inclined to fear me and keep all my commands always; so that it may go well with them and their children forever. Go tell them to return to their tents. But you stay here with me so, that I may give you all the commands, decrees, and laws that you are to teach them to follow, in the land I am giving them to possess. So be careful, to do what the Lord your God has commanded you. Do not turn aside to the right or to the left. Walk in all the way that the Lord your God has commanded you, so that you may live and prosper and prolong your days, in the land that you will possess."

In (Dt.6: 4-7), Moses continued his speech to the people and said: "Here, O Israel: The Lord our God, the Lord is one. Love the Lord your God with all your heart and with all your soul and with all your strength. These commandments that I give you today are to be upon your hearts. Impress them on your children. Talk about them when you sit at home and when you walk along the road, when you lie down and when you get up."

Throughout this discourse that Moses had just repeated to the people; God has said many things that still pertain to all people today. Some of them, you may or may not be aware of at this point in time. For example:

a. People who love and obey God are not to fear the Lord in any sense of the word that stresses the fear of retaliation or death to people by God. However, He could certainly kill you in a single heartbeat if it is His will to do so. The Bible says that we are to fear, love, and trust, obey, and reverence Him in all respects. We can all receive His great mercy, His love, and His magnificent healing power, that He will so freely and amply give to all people if they ask for it. Every day of our lives, God gives us our daily bread, and meets our every need without a word of thanks from many of the people that He loves so much.
b. We can approach God and come right into His spiritual presence in prayer, if that is our desire. We do not have to fear any reprisals from Him. We can take all of our cares and problems to Him without any reservations what so ever.
c. Through Gods grace, and because of the work of our Lord and Savior Jesus Christ and the shedding of His blood on the cross, His death and resurrection from the grave, we as His people have been sanctified and made Holy before God. God has washed all of our

sins away and He will remember them no more. It is only because of Jesus that we are no longer required to make animal sacrifices to God, or to do anything else for our redemption from sin. Jesus is the only person who has completed our salvation for us and no one else.

d. The Israelites had Moses as a mediator, between them and God. We have the Lord Jesus Christ who sits on the right hand of God as our one and only mediator between our Father and us, in heaven.

After Moses had finished delivering his message from God to the people, he returned to the top of the mountain to receive further instructions from the Lord. The people probably stood watching in awe as, Moses disappeared into the thick dark cloud that surrounded the Lord. Then the people returned to their tents and went about their daily routines with joy in their hearts, instead of fearing God as they had a short time earlier in the day. However, there is no doubt that, there were a great many of the people who were wondering about what had happened to their leader, and their one and only mediator between themselves and God, after He had disappeared into the thick dark cloud.

-7-

THE TEN COMMANDMENTS

When Moses had returned to the mountain to receive further instructions from the Lord, he no doubt approached the Lord without any fear in his heart. He probably felt very comfortable talking with the Lord at this point in time. This would have been quite possible because, of the many times that he had appeared before the Lord, and the Lord had not harmed him in any way. I believe that it must have given Moses a real sense of peace in his tired mind, and a great deal of joy in his old heart to be able to come into the presence of the Lord and not be afraid of Him.

In speaking from my own experience as a father, it is one of the many wonderful blessings that God has given my family and I to, be able to come right into His presence in prayer and tell Him of all that we desire of Him. Jesus won this privilege for all believers when He gave His life on the cross for you and for me. Just like Moses; we too are able to speak with Him directly and tell Him all of our troubles without any fear in our hearts what so ever. We are to come "Boldly" before the Throne of Grace, and present our prayers to Him without any fear. The Bible states this very clearly in (Eph.2: 18) which says: "For through Him we both have access to the Father by one Spirit." Also in (Eph.4: 12) it says: "In Him and through faith in Him we may approach God with freedom and confidence." These scriptures are speaking of Jesus Christ Himself. He is not a God of fear, but a God of peace and love.

As God spoke to Moses, He gave Moses all kinds of instructions as to how the people were to live, the customs that they were to keep, and the way they were to worship, sacrifice, and honor Him throughout their entire lives. One; of the most important sets of laws, that God ever gave mankind was, The Ten Commandments. God has intended these commandments, not just for the use of the Israelite of the past, but they also apply to the people in today's world as well.

Although most of the Governments that exist in the world today; have declared Gods Ten Commandments unconstitutional and not of value, or that they are no longer politically correct, they are by no means less important to obey, than they were at the time when they were given by God to Moses. They are still Gods perfect guidelines to follow if; you want to keep your life in line with God, and His commandments, and His laws. These laws are still in effect and will not change until you die, or before the Lord Jesus returns when the Rapture occurs in the time to come.

The Lord Jesus Himself issued the following warnings to the Pharisees, and the scribes, who were the teachers of the law, when Jesus walked here on the earth. Jesus said in (Lk. 11:52), "Woe to you experts of the law, because you have taken away the keys of knowledge. You yourselves have not entered, and you have hindered those who were entering." Likewise, in (Mt.23: 13), the Lord quoted the same warning. He said: "Woe to you teachers of the law and Pharisees, you hypocrites! You shut the kingdom of heaven in men's faces. You yourselves do not enter, nor will you let those enter who are trying to."

This is a very stern warning from Christ our Lord to the Governments, to the Lawyers, and to the Judges who hold power over the people in all the nations of the world today. They will not go unpunished when they stand before the Lord to be judged. Jesus will not enjoy giving them their sentence to eternal death but it was their choice. Jesus will have no other choice either, but to do what He has already put into motion long ago. I believe; Satan will enjoy hearing God pass down their death sentence to them because he was able to deceive them from the beginning.

Jesus also spoke one of the greatest sayings that has ever been spoken and no doubt, has been expressed by millions people all over the world today. He said it in just six short words, "You will reap what you sow!" If you sow good seed, you will reap good thing, but if you sow evil, you will reap evil. It's just that simple. Then He said in another scripture, "and the house fell with a great crash." Here the Lord was speaking of people, "spiritually." But He used the builder of a house to demonstrate what He was talking about, and the point that He was trying to get across to the people. If you reject the Lord Jesus in your lifetime while you are here on earth, then when you die, you will have no chance of life in eternity with the Lord. You will spend your eternity in hell with the Devil. Then great will be the fall of your spiritual house.

The meaning of these passages of scripture are quite clear and not that difficult to understand. Jesus charged the instructors of the law at that time, with doing the exact opposite of what they claimed they were called to be. He called them hypocrites. Rather than bringing people nearer to God, they did the exact opposite. They were turning people away from God. They had even gone so far as to completely remove the possibility of themselves ever entering into that knowledge which was the knowledge of God, and His word and His laws. But because of the way that they were living, and what they were doing to the people, through the oppression of their laws, (not Gods laws), they were keeping themselves and others in total ignorance to the way of salvation. They had truly shut the kingdom of heaven in the people's faces."

The key to wisdom and knowledge is the studying of God's word, and doing His will in our lives. Although we can never hope to be perfect like Jesus because, He was sinless and the only man to walk the earth who was perfect, we should try and follow His examples whenever we can; even if this means putting other people's needs far above our own needs at times.

The following commandments of God are known as the Laws of Moses. However, Moses was only Gods Prophet or the mouthpiece for Gods words. This Law is really the Law of God. When God started this particular conversation with Moses, the first thing that He did was to identify Himself by His name, as the great I AM. In that way, the people would know for certain that, it was God who was giving them the instructions, and that they were not coming from Moses His servant.

When God spoke to Moses this time as well, He proceeded to give Moses the following Ten Commands. God said: "I AM the Lord your God, who brought you out of the land of Egypt, out of the house of bondage." then He said:

(1) "You shall have no other gods before me."

This commandment is one of the greatest commandments that God has written for all people to obey, and for His own glory. God put it before all of the other commands for good reason. The Israelites were not to be like the other nations or people that were in the world at that time. There were many nations who worshiped gods of carved wood and stone, or of animals and birds, and the elements as well. They worshiped anything that they thought would help them to have a better life, or what their Kings and other rulers decreed for them to worship. But as you have seen, God has proven to the Pharaoh and the people of Egypt and the whole world in general that, He is the only power behind all things in the whole Universe. God is not to be viewed by Israel, or anyone else, as one God among many, or the best of the gods. <u>He is, the only Living God.</u> He alone is to be the only God worshiped, obeyed, adored, and honored by the Israelites at that time and by all of the people of the world today. The Israelites were forbidden to create, any kind of idol or image, or any other substitute from the very beginning of their existence. They were not permitted to make anything that would distract them from the exclusive worship of the living God. Because God has no specific visible form, any idol that would be intended to resemble Him in anyway would be a sinful misrepresentation of Him. However, it was not Gods intention to prohibit the fashioning of fine art and jewelry throughout the world. You can have statues of different things around you to, beautify your surrounding if you desire. But you must not worship them, or serve them in any way as gods. You must not let them take the place of God the Father your Creator.

(2) <u>"You shall not misuse the name of the Lord your God."</u>

This means that you should not take the name of the Lord your God in vain (Profanity). It means that people should not curse, swear, or employ the use of satanic arts, or deceive people by the use of God's name. The scripture in (Mt. 5:33-37), Jesus said: "But I tell you. Do not swear at all: by heaven for it is Gods throne; or by the earth for it is His footstool; by Jerusalem, for it is the city of the great King, (meaning Jesus). Simply let your' Yes be yes' and your 'No,' No,' anything beyond this comes from the evil one." We are only permitted to use Gods name when we are to take an oath in a court of law, oath of office, or your wedding vows.

We are to reverence Gods name at all times. When we take an oath in God's name, we are actually asking God to be a witness that what we say is the truth and not a lie. If we lie or break our promise, we are calling on God to punish us.

(3) "Remember the Sabbath Day by keeping it Holy."

The Sabbath day is to be a day of rest, relaxation and worship to God for all of mankind. God made the Sabbath holy because, He rested on the seventh day when He created the universe, the world, and everything in it. Also, the Sabbath became a sign of the covenant between God and the Israelites at Mount Sinai. We are not to despise preaching and His word, but hold it sacred and gladly hear and learn it. But mankind in this modern day and age has made a mockery out of it. There is no rest for many people on the Sabbath because of the almighty dollar. There are a great percentage of people in our society that have no choice but to work, if they want to keep their jobs. Our society of today has put Gods word and His laws on the back shelf somewhere out of sight and out of mind. They do not want to be reminded of how wicked and vile this generation is.

(4) "Honor your Father and your Mother."

The fourth commandment is the first commandment with a promise. If the children obey and honor this commandment, God has promised to give them a long life on the earth. The first word of this commandment (Honor) was and still is very important to all of the generations of the world to adhere to today. But that is not the case in many of the countries around the world. The parents of the younger generation in many countries are not cared for like they should be. They are cursed; hated, and despised by their children, instead of being loved and cherished. The word honor has several meanings, some of which are very important to many people. For example: We are to hold our parents in high esteem. This requires respect, praise, love, and obedience, from the younger generation of people. We are not to despise, curse, or speak evil of them. But the parents also, have a God given command, to provide for their children's daily needs, and to return their children's love at all times no matter what the cost.

(5) <u>"You shall not murder." (Kill)</u>

This commandment means exactly what it says. We are not to hurt nor harm our neighbor in his body in any way, but help and support him in every physical need. The word "Murder" refers to a premeditated and deliberate act of killing another human being. The Bible says that this does not include capital punishment, or the killing of another person in times of war. The first murder in the history of the world was committed when Cain killed his brother Able. (Gen.4:8).

(6) <u>"You shall not commit adultery"</u>

The sixth commandment refers to husbands and their wives. It is a great sin against God and against the other marriage partner, if either partner commits a sexual act of adultery. The act of marriage is a sacred trust, and a symbol of faithfulness that God has ordained between a man and a woman. Jesus said in (Mt. 5: 28) "I tell you that anyone who looks at a woman lustfully, has already committed adultery with her in his heart." Any other act, or any kind of marriage that is permitted by mankind is, an abomination in the eyes of the Lord. They will not go unpunished.

(7) <u>"You shall not steal."</u>

In this commandment God forbids a person from all forms of stealing no matter what it is. From the taking of a small piece of candy, to the robbing of a city bank, it's all the same. There is no difference because, you took something that you did not earn, or pay for. If you borrow something and do not return it, that is stealing. If you gain possession of something by dishonest means, that is stealing. The Bible says in (Lev. 19:35). Do not use dishonest standards when measuring length, weight or quantity. Also in (Ps.37: 21) it says, that the wicked borrow and do not repay, but the righteous give generously.

(8) "You shall not bear false witness against your neighbor."

God forbids people to lie to their neighbor or about their neighbor in a court of law, or otherwise. If you lie about anything, you are bearing false witness. When people brand you as a liar, you will never live it down, and the truth is not in you. God hates a liar, and liars will have no place in heaven but God has already made a reservation for them in Hell if they do not repent. Only through the changing of their ways, the repentance of their sins to the Lord, and their acceptance of Jesus Christ as their Savior will a liar have any hope of escaping Hell.

(9) "You shall not covet your neighbor's house."

In the ninth commandment, God gave it to man so he could live in contentment on the earth. The word "Covet" means that you have a sinful desire for anyone, or anything that belongs to your neighbor. It does not matter whither, you desire your neighbors goods in your mind, or if you actually get them openly by trickery. It's all the same thing and God calls it coveting. Godliness with contentment is great gain (1Tim. 6:6). Also in (Heb. 13:5) God said: "Keep your lives free from the love of money and be content with what you have, because He has said, 'Never will I leave you; never will I forsake you.' "

(10) "You shall not covet your neighbor's wife, or his manservant, or his <u>maidservant, his ox or donkey, or anything that belongs to your neighbor.</u>

In this commandment, God has forbidden people to force away from their neighbor, his wife, his workers, or his animals. But we are to urge them to stay and do their duty. We should be content with the helpers God has given us and not try to entice anything away from our neighbor at anytime.

You may have noticed that, the ninth and the tenth commandments say about the same thing. In Gods sight, evil desires and coveting, is indeed sin and deserves condemnation. But the scripture in (Ps.37: 4) says: "Delight yourself in the Lord and He will give you the desires of your heart." Whatever you want, God has it. So ask Him for whatever concerns you, He will not turn you away. The first four commandments deal with our relationship to God. The other six deal with our relationship to people.

As you can see, God has put a great deal of emphasis on our relationship with other people. We are to care, love, honor, trust, and help, other people who are in need whenever we can. The golden rule says; that we are to do unto to others, as we would have them do unto to you. If you do this, you are sowing good seed into good ground, and you will reap a rich harvest of blessings from God and your fellow man. Good seed can only produce good fruit, and bad seed can only produce bad fruit. Jesus summed up these commandments into two other commandments in (Mt.22: 37-40). He said: "'Love the Lord your God with all your heart with all your soul with your entire mind. And the second is like it: 'Love your neighbor as yourself.' All the Law and the Prophets hang on these two"

The Ten Commandments were not the only laws that God gave to Moses at that time while he was on the mountain.

God gave him other laws that he had to explain to the people. He told them what they had to do in respect to their Altars, Servants, Personal Injuries, Protection of Property, Social Responsibilities, Laws of Justice and Mercy, and Sabbath Laws. As well, there were three Annual Festivals that the people were to keep. They were the Feast of Un-leavened Bread, the Feast of the Harvest, and the Feast of Ingathering. It was at these three Festivals that all of the men would have to appear before the Lord as a family unit, if they had one.

While God was having this long meeting with Moses on the mountain, He gave Moses a solemn promise accompanied with a very stern warning. He promised to send His Angel ahead of Moses and His people to lead, and to protect them on their journey to the Promised Land. But there was a severe condition that was attached to that promise. God said: "Pay attention to him and listen to what he says. Do not rebel against him; he will not forgive your rebellion since My Name is in Him. If you listen carefully to what he says, and do all that I say, I will be an enemy to your enemies and will oppose those who oppose you. My angel will go ahead of you and bring you into the land of the Amorites, Hittites, Perizzites, Canaanites, Hivites, and the Jebusites, and I will wipe them out."

This promise that God made to the Israelites long ago is, still in effect for all people of today as well. God didn't make this promise, or any of the other promises that are in the Bible just, for the Israelites at that time. He made them for all people who believe in Him and His Son, Jesus Christ. They will always be in effect, until the end of time, as we know it. However, all believers today are under Gods grace, His love, His care, and His protection because of what Jesus accomplished on the Cross-at Calvary. There is no Principality or Power in heaven or on the earth that will ever be able to pluck a single believer out of hands Gods. Also, there is not one of Gods promises that will ever be broken by Him now, or in the future to come.

The conditions that God put on this covenant with His people were quite understandable and reasonable. He said: "Do not bow down before their gods, worship them, or follow their practices. You must demolish them and break their sacred stones to pieces. Do not make a covenant with them or with their gods. Do not let them live in your land, or they will cause you to sin against me, because the worship of their gods will certainly be a snare to you."

This was a stern warning from God, and He told His people in advance what would happen to them. God; is the only God that His people are to honor and worship, and nothing else. Likewise, this is what God still requires from all people today. All people who are of the Christian faith will Love, Honor, Praise, and Obey Gods will because this is His command. God will not share His Glory, His honor, or His worship, with anything or any Idol. The Lord said in (Is.42:8), "I am the Lord; that is my name! I will not give my glory to another or my praise to idols."

After God had declared these conditions in the covenant, He came right back with more promises for the Israelites, if they would worship the Lord their God. He promised to:

(a) Bless their food and water.
(b) Take away sickness from among them.
(c) The women would not miscarry or be barren.
(d) God would give them a full span of life.
(e) God would send His terror into the hearts of the people ahead of the Israelites, and their enemies would turn their backs and run from them.
(f) God promised to establish the borders for His people, where they were to settle and occupy the land that He was giving them.

(g) God promised to hand over to the Israelites, the people who lived in the land.
(h) God promised to send Hornets ahead of the Israelites to drive out their enemies.
(i) God also promised to protect the land for His people by, not driving their enemies out of the land to far in advance. This was so that, wild animals would not become too numerous and then become a problem for the Israelites. Also, the land would become desolate because of its lack of use, and its productivity would be lost when they took over the land.

As you can see God has left no stone unturned as far as caring for His people. After God had verbally given these promises to Moses, God sent Moses back down the mountain to the people. Moses then explained the conditions and the promises that God had made pertaining to His covenant with the people. Then Moses wrote down on scrolls, all of the instructions that the Lord had given him.

A scroll was a long strip of leather or papyrus, on which people could write whatever they wanted to preserve in writing for future generations. The scrolls were then treated with some kind of preservative, then rolled and sealed in containers to protect them. As the centuries rolled on, scroll writing would eventually give way to the book form of keeping records and manuscripts. The book form is still widely used today but it too, is slowly starting to give way to other forms of storage for the preservation of all kinds of information.

Early the next morning after Moses had returned from the mountain, he rose up and built an altar at the foot of the mountain. He then set up twelve stone pillars, which would represent the twelve tribes of Israel that were to come into being in the future. Then he read what he had written on the scrolls to the people and they agreed in unison to abide by the terms of the covenant that God had set before them. The people all said; "We will do everything the Lord has said; we will obey." It was not until the people had agreed verbally to obey Gods laws, that they would become a part of Gods covenant. This was the second time that the people had made a solemn oath of obedience to the Lord.

Moses then sent some young Israelite men out to the herds of cattle, and they killed and offered burnt offerings of young bulls as a fellowship offering to the Lord. After they had killed the animals, Moses collected the blood in bowls. One half of the blood he sprinkled on the altar that he had built for the Lord. This symbolized God's forgiveness and His acceptance of the offering. The other half he sprinkled on the seventy Elders who were of authority. They would represent the sealing of the covenant with all of the people. It bound all of the people to an oath of obedience to the Lord. The people who were sprinkled with the blood were the seventy people that Moses and Jethro had chosen earlier to oversee the many problems of the people. It is just the same in today's world as well. Priests or ministers can represent many people in a church or in a community today. So now these seventy leaders of the Israelites represented the millions of people that were involved in this covenant with God.

Just as the Israelite houses had been under the blood at the time of the first Passover in Egypt, now the peoples themselves were brought under "the blood covenant of the Lord." This also resembles our own relationship to God, which is made possible by the blood of the Lamb of God, who is Jesus Christ. The scripture in (1Pet.1: 2) clearly states that all believers in Christ are sprinkled with His blood, and are therefore a part of His redemption. The sanctifying work of the Holy Spirit keeps a person in obedience to God's word, and leads us to a saving faith and the cleansing from all sin.

In this scripture, you can see the work of all three persons of the Trinity, the Father, the Son, and the Holy Spirit.

After Moses had completed the cleansing ceremony of the people, God called Moses up to the top of the mountain once again. But this time he didn't go by himself. This time he took Aaron and his two sons Nadir and Abhor who were to become Priests for the Israelites. He also, took with him, the seventy Elders. But they were only permitted to accompany him part of the way up the mountain. They were not permitted to approach God or to come into His presents.

It was only because of God's grace that any of these seventy-three people were allowed to come near to God, and to see what they were permitted see. Everything had to be done on Gods terms. They were to worship at a distance as God had instructed Moses. Only Moses was permitted to come into the presence of God and to speak to Him. The word worship here means that the people were to literally bow down with their faces to the earth.

Because of Gods great and magnificent glory, the people were only permitted to see the ground that He stood on, His feet, and His hand. The mention of His feet and His hand indicates that they saw a manifestation of God in human form. The lack of details reminds us that any attempt to describe the glory of God is always inadequate and futile. The scripture only describes what was under His feet. It says in (Ex.24: 9-10) that, "under his feet was something like a pavement made of sapphire stone, clear as the sky itself."

Although the seventy-three people were in a close proximity to God and Moses, God did not raise His hand against these leaders of the Israelites. They would now become the corner stone's of the Israelite society that God had been establishing for them. Also, God had called them up on the mountain so that He could reveal Himself to them in the manner that He did. By revealing Himself to the elders, God was proving to them that He truly was God and that He truly existed. He was now sealing His covenant with them and His people. Then they all sat down and they ate and drank together.

The eating of a meal and the drinking of wine was in accordance with the customs that many nations practiced at that time. The parties, who were involved in the covenant or contract, would celebrate by having a meal and drink wine together to seal the covenant and make it binding to both parties. The meal would probably consist of bread and wine, and the meat from the peace offerings. This festive covenant meal was indeed something to be remembered by the Israelites and Moses. It was a grand celebration in the presence of the living God, which would make this celebration all the more memorable for the people who were involved.

This meal was also a prophetic glimpse of, the supper that the Lord Jesus and His disciples had on the night that He was betrayed before His crucifixion. It was at that time that Jesus transformed the ancient symbols of the blood of animals and their sacrifices to God to, the bread and wine that are used in churches today. The bread and wine are symbols of "His Body and His Blood." The celebration of the Lords Supper is a celebration of the new blood covenant sealed by Christ's death on the cross.

The scriptures in (1Co. 11: 25-26) say: In the same way, after supper He took the cup, saying, "This cup is the new covenant in my blood; do this, whenever you drink it, in remembrance of me." Whenever Christian believers in Christ partake of this precious sacrament, they receive forgiveness of their sins and are greatly blessed by God. They bring honor to Christ each time that they partake of it.

Up until this time, Moses, had been at the same place on the mountain as the other seventy-three people. But now God calls Moses to come up higher on the mountain and to stay there. Before Moses left the people, he instructed them to stay there and to wait for him and Joshua to return. But it appears that they got tired of waiting and they returned to their camp.

So Moses took Joshua who by this time had become his very close aide, farther up the mountain with him. But Joshua was not permitted to come to close to the Lord, so he stayed at a safe distance and waited for Moses to return. It would be safe to assume that, Joshua stayed within hearing distance so that he could hear the conversation between God and Moses. After sometime had passed Joshua and Moses returned to the camp and Moses relayed the Lords instructions to the Elders and to the people.

However, this time the glory of the Lord remained on the mountain for six days in the form of a cloud, but to the Israelites, the glory of the Lord looked like a consuming fire. On the seventh day, which would have been the Sabbath, God called again to Moses out of the cloud, and Moses went back up the mountain and walked into the cloud to meet the Lord. All the people could do was to watch in awe at the splendor of Gods Glory that was right before their eyes.

At this point you may recall, that I had said earlier that, God used certain numbers in the Bible to demonstrate certain events in His plan for mankind and the world. For example He used the number forty in:

(a) The time of Noah and the flood, it rained for forty days and forty nights.
(b) Moses was on Mount Sinai for forty days and forty nights receiving instructions from God.
(c) Jesus spent forty days and forty nights in the desert being tempted by the Devil.
(d) The Israelites wondered in the desert for forty years because of their disobedience to God.
(e) The twelve spies that Moses sent out to spy out the land of Canaan had taken forty days to complete their journey.

These are but a few of the examples where God is consistent, in using numbers in His plans for the world. The Lord is always perfect and consistent in everything that He does. There are no half measures with Our Lord.

-8-

THE WORSHIP OF THE GOLDEN CALF

The story of the Israelites worship of the Golden Calf reveals both the unfaithfulness of the Israelites, and Gods everlasting love and mercy. Even though they had broken their promise to obey Him in such a short time, God forgives their sin and He begins again with them.

This part of our story begins on a very human level and it exposes the dark and the fickle side of mankind. Moses had been gone for a long time, and the people were lost without Him to confide in. They were like sheep without a shepherd. The people were the redeemed of Israel, but in their discouragement they wondered back to other gods. They had run out of patience waiting for Moses to return. The Bible says that Moses stayed on the mountain this time for period of forty days and forty nights.

The reason Moses stayed on the mountain this time was because, God wanted to give him the Ten Commandments that He had written on two stone tablets. He also gave Moses instructions on how the people were to build The Ark of the Covenant, and the Tabernacle that was to be used for the peoples worship to God. The Tabernacle would be a place where God could dwell among His people. He also instructed Moses on the details for all of their furnishings. God wanted a specific place so that the people could worship and bring their offerings to Him.

It is safe to assume, that the majority of the people who were defying God and committing this great sin of idol worship, were not all Israelites. They were more than likely the people who had tagged along with the Israelites to escape the cruel Egyptian ruler. There is no doubt however that, some of the Israelites may have been coaxed into the charade leading to their down fall as well.

It was no different at that time, and then it is today. Some people today, think life is a big party and they will do anything to be a part of it. They throw caution to the wind and do not think of the consequences that will surely follow their shortsighted decisions. They have no faith in what they cannot see or touch. Reality is only the here and now, and they forget about the consequences that they may have to put up with later on in the life to come. As you know, God knows and sees everything that we think, say, and do. You cannot hide anything from the Lord; you are an open book to Him.

After the Lord had finished instructing Moses on His laws and commandments, He alerted Moses to the fact of the Israelites sin. He said to Moses: "Go down, because your people whom you brought up out of Egypt have become corrupt. They have been quick to turn away from what I have commanded them. They have made themselves an idol in the shape of a calf. They have bowed down and sacrificed to it and have said: 'These are your gods, O Israel who brought you up out of Egypt.' "The Lord was totally disgusted with His people.

From the scriptures in (Ex. 32: 9-15) you can see how deeply the sin of the Israelites, caused great pain in the heart of God, and it made the Lord angry. He said to Moses: "I have seen these people, and they are a stiff-necked people."

This means that the people were stubborn as an ox and they were not willing to be under Gods control and to follow Gods laws and commands.

As the Lord continued to speak to Moses He said: "Now leave me alone, so that my anger may burn against them and that I may destroy them. Then I will make you into a great nation." In this statement Gods words turned very ominous. He threatened to destroy the entire nation of Israel, and wipe them from the face of the earth and then start anew with Moses. It would have been an instant replay, of the time when God had destroyed all of mankind with the flood in the time of Noah.

So Moses pleaded with the Lord and said: "O Lord." "Why should your anger burn hot against your people who you brought out of the land of Egypt with great power, and with a mighty hand? Why should the Egyptians say: 'it was with evil intent that He brought them out to kill them on this mountain, and to wipe them from the face of the earth? '" "Turn from your fierce anger and relent, and do not bring this disaster on your people. Remember your servants, Abraham, Isaac, and Jacob by whom you swore by your own self: 'I will make your descendants as numerous as the stars in the sky. I will give your descendants all this land I promised them. It will be their inheritance forever."

If God had done what He said that He would do, it would have destroyed the line of Abraham and his descendants and He would have broken His covenant with Abraham. It appears that when God used the words "your people" He had completely disowned the Israelites. He wanted nothing to do with a nation of people who would not obey Him.

We as people in general, are much the same in our feelings with our fellowman, many times throughout our lives. If someone doesn't like us, we go out of our way to avoid him or her and want nothing to do with him or her. But God says we should try to reconcile our differences with each other if we can, and get on with life. It is far better to go through each day of your life with a joyful heart than, with a heart that is bitter with resentment and anger. Anger will eventually destroy you and you will have nothing but a miserable life. That is not in God's plan for you as a child of God.

Then the Lord relented, and He would not bring His threatened disaster on His people. It was because Moses loved the people so much, he knew that he had to intercede for them before the living God. He actually argued with God about His purposed plan. In his intercessory prayer, Moses used three principal arguments to try and cool down the anger of the Lord.

The first principal he used was that of reminding the Lord that it was only He and He alone who had delivered the Israelites out of Egypt. He also reminded God that the Israelites were His people and not that of Moses. So how could He abandon His people now, even if they had committed such a great sin?

In his second argument, Moses expressed his great zeal and love for the Lord as well as his love for the Israelites. He said that the Egyptians would hear of the judgment that God had passed on His people, and then they would believe that they had triumphed over the God of the Israelites. It would certainly prove to the Egyptians that the God of the Israelites was a cruel and an unforgiving God. They would class Him as no different than any other god that they worshiped, so how could He destroy them now?

The third argument that he used, he asked God to remember the covenant that He had made with His servants Abraham, Isaac, and Jacob centuries before. So how could He destroy His own people and wipe out the entire descendant line of His chosen people. To Moses' way of thinking, he had put up a good argument with the Lord, and that it was he who had changed the Lords mind. But that was not case, as you will see.

When we look a little deeper into what the Lord did, when He relented, we can see that He had a specific purpose in mind in doing what He did. God had set up the whole conversation to test His servant Moses. God had no intention of destroying His people. He wanted to test the faith of Moses to see how strong it was. God was doing the same thing in this situation with Moses that He had done with Abraham when, God told him to sacrifice his son Isaac. The prayer of Moses is a wonderful example of the interaction of faithful intercessory prayer and the purpose of the Lord. God drew Moses into the whole process by causing him to pray for the right outcome of the situation, and not so much for Gods intended disaster. Oftentimes, the Lord will use our prayers combined with His own determination to make His will come to pass in our lives. When all is said and done, it is always Gods will that will be done no matter what.

When the scriptures said that the Lord relented; once more God was displaying to Moses that He was a God of love and great mercy, and not a God that was without compassion. Although, He was a God of mercy and compassion, He would most certainly discipline the Israelites so that they could learn from their mistakes. However, this mistake of disobedience by the people would cost three thousand of them their lives.

Then Moses turned away from the Lord, and went down the mountain. He took with him, the two stone tablets of Testimony that had been written by the "finger of God" on both sides, in his arms. He would then present them before the people as God had commanded him.

Moses had been gone so long, that some of the clan leaders might have thought that Moses must have died on the mountain. As far as they knew, God could have killed Moses like He did the Egyptians. Plus it was a known fact that, Moses had last been seen, walking into the cloud on the mountain and he had just disappeared from sight. It would have been enough to start some people to thinking that something had gone terribly wrong.

So some of the clan leaders went and confronted Aaron. They said to him: "Come make us Gods who will go before us. As for this fellow Moses who brought us up out of Egypt, we do not know what has happened to him." Perhaps it was the work of satanic forces, working in the hearts and minds of these people along with plain stupidity that made them do what they did. But I believe that Satan had an awful lot to do with their bad actions and their bad behavior.

The words "this Moses," are words that were spoken in scathing satanic, and demeaning tones. It is a well-known fact that even in today's world; we too have to deal with satanic forces. But as you will see, these people will pay for their rebellion against God and His commands. God is a God of love and mercy, but He will only put up with a persons' rebellion so long. Then He will give them an attitude adjustment that, He feels will get them back on track to where He wants them to be.

It is shocking and hard to believe the role that Aaron, the faithful brother of Moses, played in the downfall of these unfaithful people. You would have thought that, after all that he had been through and the things that he had witnessed while being in the company of Moses, that he would have kept his faith in God. But Aaron too fell by the way side and sinned against God. What he consented to do would truly display his human nature? People demonstrate this same kind of human nature even today. Nothing has changed as far as mankind is concerned. Only the people and their names have changed.

Although the Bible does not say so; the people who came to him may have threaten Aaron's life and the life of his family, if he didn't go along with their request. But this is not fact. It is also possible that, some of the unbelievers or Pagans who were in the midst of the Israelites took advantage of the situation to spread some of their evil lies about their gods to the people. Satan, who is the father of all doubt and lies, would not miss an opportunity like this; to use these kinds of people to disrupt Gods plan for His people.

Then Aaron said to the leaders of the rebellion, "Take off the gold earrings that your wives, your sons, and your daughters are wearing, and bring them to me." As you may recall that, when the Israelites left Egypt, God put it into the hearts of the Egyptian people to give the Israelites anything that they wanted. A great deal of the gold and silver that had been taken from the Egyptians by the Israelites was taken in the form of jewelry. As well, the people had taken bronze, silver, precious stones, clothes, and material for making many things.

After Aaron had melted down the gold into a liquid form, he fashioned a statue of a Golden Calf with some hand tools he had. He probably could have chosen any kind of idol that he wanted to for the people to worship, but he chose the calf. He probably did this because of the Egyptians and the gods that they worshiped and served. The molded calf was an ominous symbol of worship, which means that, it had a menacing and alarming character, foreshadowing evil or disaster. It was not necessarily a statue of beauty. The bull and the cow were both worshiped in Egypt, but the bull god that was called Apis, was a familiar embodiment of Baal that was seen and worshiped in Canaan.

As soon as Aaron had finished making the statue, he gave it to the people and said to them; "This is your god, O Israel that brought you out of the land of Egypt." When he had finished speaking, Aaron built an altar before it and made a proclamation before the people, and said: "Tomorrow is a feast to the Lord." With this statement, it shows that Aaron had not completely given himself over to the people and their evil. He was trying in some small way to control the mob of rebellious people that had gone astray. He knew that these people were committing a great sin against God. They had made a graven image; and they were going to use the Lords name in false worship to it.

God had repeatedly made it very clear that, it was He and only He who had brought the Israelites out of Egypt. After all, these people had witnessed and were a part of the great event that God had accomplished in the Exodus. It must have broken the Lords heart to see His people committing this sinful act, in such a short period of time.

The next day the people who had gone the way of the wicked rose up early. They ate and drank and made sacrifices to their idol, and committed all kinds of immoral and perverse acts against the Lord. They were completely consumed by their own lusts and desires. They had thrown all caution to the wind and they could care less about the consequences of their action.

It is clear in the scriptures that Joshua did not take part in the worship of the idol. He had probably returned near the base of the mountain several times while Moses was away to see if he could see Moses. It is possible however, that when the time was right, God could have given Joshua some indication or direction in his heart as to when Moses was returning down the mountain.

As soon as Joshua seen Moses at the base of the mountain, he ran to meet him. When he reached him, he reported to Moses that, from his vantage point near the mountain that he had heard what he thought was the sound of war in the camp. But Moses knew exactly what it was because the Lord had told him what was happening in the Israelite camp. Moses replied to Joshua and said: "It is not the sound of victory or of defeat, but it is music that you hear coming from the Israelite camp below. The people are dancing and singing, around the statue of a Golden Calf."

When Moses approached the camp and he saw what was happening, and how the wicked people were committing all kinds of sinful and immoral acts against the Lord, his fierce anger boiled up inside of him and He lost total control of his temper. He threw the two stone tablets that God had written on with His finger, down on the ground in front of the people and their alter, breaking them into pieces. He did this as a testimony against the Israelites, that they had broken the covenant of the Lord.

Then Moses melted down the statue and ground it into powder. He then spread it on some water and made some of the people drink it. After Moses had completed destroying the statue, he went to his brother Aaron to find out just what had happened. Aaron knew that he was in trouble with Moses and that he had to come up with some sort of story to bail himself out of trouble. So Aaron in his desperation told Moses a couple of lies.

The first lie he told was that, it was the people who had caused him to commit this great sin because they were evil. It was kind of a lame duck excuse because; people can only make you commit a sin or a crime only if you let them. It is you and you alone who must give into it unless of course, you are threatened with death.

The second lie that he committed was more preposterous than the first one. He said to Moses: "The people told me to make them gods that would go before them. Then I asked for any gold jewelry that the people were wearing and to take it off. Then they gave it to me and I threw the gold into the fire and out came this calf." He would not place any of the blame on himself. As far as he was concerned, he was completely innocent of all wrongdoing. It is hard to believe that he would expect Moses to believe such a laughable story. But that was his story and he was sticking to it.

Unfortunately this is the same kind of scenario that many people use in today's world as well. They will tell a lie to try and get them out of a bad situation. But just like Aaron, they have to tell a second lie to cover up for the first one. This makes the first lie even worse. But Satan enjoys this kind of life style because; he knows that he has already beaten you, and that he has accomplished what he set out to do. The Devil; likes nothing better than to pull you away from God, and the great love that He has for you. But give thanks to God and His Grace that we have, forgiveness of our sins through Jesus Christ our Lord.

Despite the return of Moses, a huge number of the people remained unrestrained and continued on in their perverted sexual ways. It seemed nothing could stop them from doing whatever they wanted to do, not even Moses himself. The people were running around wildly and committing their perverted sexual acts without any sense of shame. The Devil had complete control over them.

Moses knew that if, this kind of worship and disobedience were allowed to go unchecked and allowed to continue, it would spread throughout the rest of the camp like a consuming fire. This kind of pagan or Devil worship was the exact kind of worship that God intended to blot out in the land of Canaan. God had already warned His people to refrain from such worship, and such kinds of sexual acts. It had to be stopped at any cost. Moses knew that this was a problem that only the Lord could handle.

So Moses consulted the Lord over this grievous problem that he was faced with. After he had spoken to the Lord he went to the entrance of the camp and he called out to the people and said to them: "Whoever is on the Lords side, come to me." Then all of the Levites who were not a part of the worship of the Golden Calf, rallied around their leader Moses. Then Moses said to them: "This is what the Lord the God of Israel says; 'each man strap a sword to his side. Go back and forth through the camp from one end to the other, each killing his brother and friend and neighbor.' "

It must have been a very hard task for the Levites to do because; some of their brothers and sisters had been involved in the worship of the Golden Calf as well. They were to kill everyone and anyone, regardless of who they were that, had anything to do with disobeying the Lord, and worshiping the Idol. Not one person was to be spared from the sword.

When the Levites started to kill these people, they ran wildly throughout the camp to try and hid, but it was to no avail. Not one person escaped the judgment of the Lord. All of those wicked people had received a swift and severe judgment at the hand of the Lord. They paid with their lives for what they had done. That day, about three thousand people died. It was far better that, these few wicked people had to die, rather than for the whole Israelite camp to come under the judgment of the Lord.

Moses knew how hard it was for the Levites to do what the Lord had decreed. So when it was all over, he called the Levites together again and he said to them: "You have been set apart to the Lord today, for you were against your own sons and brothers and He has blessed you this day. As a reward for their zeal for the Lord, the Levites were set apart to be the caretakers of the tabernacle and aids to the priests that was yet to come.

The next day, Moses went before the people and said to them: "You have committed a great sin. But now I will go up to the Lord; perhaps I can make atonement for your sin." It is clear from this scripture that Moses knew that he had to try to be a mediator between God and the Israelites. Perhaps he also felt that he stood a good chance of saving his people because, he thought that he had been able to change Gods mind once before. It was this kind of thinking that would have driven him to speak with God as soon as possible. The stain of the terrible sin that the people had committed had to be removed as far as he was concerned.

So Moses left the camp once more and made his way up the mountain to confront God with a plea for mercy for the Israelites. As Moses came into the presence of the Lord this time, he came right to the point. As he spoke to the Lord he said: "Oh what a great sin these people have committed! They have made themselves a god of gold. But now, please forgive their sin. But if not, blot me out of the book you have written."

As you can see, Moses was demonstrating to God his great love for the people, and he was willing to put his life on the line to prove it. What else could a mere mortal man offer his God who is his creator? This was the most touching moment in Moses' leadership of the Israelites.

The Lord replied to Moses and said: "Whoever has sinned against me, I will blot out of my book. Now go, lead the people to the place I spoke of and my angel will go before you. However, when the time comes for me to punish, I will punish them for their sin."

You can see from Gods promise that, He was still willing to lead the people with His angel but, at the same time He also issued a solemn threat of punishment for disobedience. It is not clear however by the scripture here if, God is referring to the punishment that the people had already received or, if a plague would occur at some later date on the journey to Canaan. It is possible that it refers to both case because, certain plagues would befall the Israelites in the wilderness because they continued to disobey the Lord at times.

Although Moses was willing to make this great sacrifice for the people, God could not accept his offer. The reason God could not accept the offer from Moses is because; each person is responsible for his or her own sins. But this was indeed, a very sincere and selfless gesture on the part of Moses. It also resembles the self-sacrificing life of Jesus Christ, which, God has accepted as the atonement for the sins of every generation of humanity. Jesus is the only one who is able to forgive or accept another person's sins upon Himself. There is no other name given under heaven and earth whereby, man can be saved except by the name of Jesus.

After Moses had returned this time from talking to God on the mountain, and trying to intercede for the people, he moved his tent outside some distance from the Israelite camp. Mosses called it the Tabernacle of meeting. Whenever the people sought the Lord, and required Gods Devine Wisdom through Moses they would come to his tent. This tent would be a forerunner of the true tabernacle that the Israelites would build later on for the Lord.

The people could still watch Moses at the door of his tent whenever, he came out of his tent. Every time Moses came out of the tent, all of the people rose and stood at the entrances to their tents but, they dared not go anywhere near Moses and his tent because, Moses had warned them to keep their distance. When Moses went into the tent the pillar of cloud would come down and stay at the entrance, while the Lord spoke with Moses. At that precise time, the people would bow down before the Lord and worship Him at the entrance of their own tents to show reverence toward God.

The Lord spoke face to face with Moses just like a friend would speak to a friend. But Moses was not permitted to see Gods face. He did not cringe or shy away from God in fear anymore because, by now he had a close and wonderful working relationship with the Lord. All of mankind today can have this same kind of relationship with the Lord if they try, and if they desire it in their hearts. All we have to do is to come to the Lord in prayer, and He will hear us. He will not forsake or fail us in anyway, because He is our Creator.

Because of Gods instructions; whenever Moses left his tent and returned to the mountain or the camp, his young aide Joshua the son of Nun would remain at the tent to guard it against any intruders. It is here that we get another brief glimpse of this bold young man of God, who would become a successor to Moses. By just guarding the tent, God was training Joshua to perform some of the duties that he would be required to do later on in life.

One day while God was speaking with Moses on the mountain, He said to him "Leave this place you and the people you brought out of Egypt. Go up to the land I promised on an oath to Abraham, Isaac, and Jacob. Go up to the land flowing with Milk and Honey, but I will not go with you because, you are a stiff-necked people and I might destroy you on the way."

You may have noticed here that, God appears to have disowned the Israelites once more. God calls them the people "you brought out of Egypt," and not His people. He also uses the word "you" instead of the word "I." This shows the utter contempt that God had for the Israelites and their stubbornness. Because of their willingness to disobey God and His commands, God was almost ready to eliminate the Israelites altogether and start over with Moses. He could have done this very thing; if it had suited His purpose to do so.

But now God gives Moses the one thing that He had been pressing Him for all along. The Lord in His great mercy has now assured Moses that He will continue His covenant with the wayward people of Israel, and that He will without a doubt fulfill His promise concerning the Land of Canaan.

But there was also some bad news that accompanied Gods promise. It was that, He would not go with them and be in their midst as before. It was a message that the people did not want to hear or believe. So the people mourned loudly with great pain in their hearts to God because of it. The command to move on without the presence of the Lord was a bitter pill for the people to swallow. So now, what were the people to do to try and appease the Lords anger? Once more God displays too His people, just how much He loves them, and He gives them an opportunity to redeem themselves.

Recall if you will; that the people had been worshiping the Lord by bowing down at the entrance of their tents whenever He appeared at the tent of Moses. This was to display reverence to the Lord, and it was their way of repenting in some small way, for the way they had sinned against God.

For the Lord had said to Moses; "Say to the children of Israel, 'you are a stiff-necked people. I could come up into your midst in one moment and consume you. Now therefore, take off your ornaments, that I may know what to do to you.'"

Then immediately, and without any hesitation or grumbling, the people removed all of their ornaments from their bodies in total compliance to Gods command. The immediate removal of their ornaments would be proof to God that, the people had genuinely repented of their sin, and that they truly wanted to have a good working relationship with God. It was this kind of wonderful relationship that Moses enjoyed with the Lord that kept him in the good grace of the Lord and steadfast in his faith. For this reason alone, Moses felt comfortable talking with the Lord like a friend would talk to a friend, and he could now reason with the Lord on the many different issues that would develop throughout the years to come.

But for now, it was this terrible issue that God was threatening to withdraw His presence from Moses and the Israelites. The questions that could have flashed through their minds would be very troublesome to say the least. For Example: What would the people do if God left them on their own in this hot dry desert? They could most certainly starve to death, or worse yet, they would be overcome by their enemies and be slaughtered or, taken as slaves again. The people were now faced with these real possibilities. It was a dilemma that they did not want to face, if God did not go with them. The Hebrew words "My Presence" literally means "My Face" So when the word "Presence" is used here and in the following scriptures it refers to the "Face of God."

When God told Moses that he was to take his people (not Gods people because God had appeared to have disown them.) and depart for Canaan, it troubled Moses a great deal. He knew that it would be impossible for him to do anything on his own without God to help him. As Moses was speaking to God on the mountain in (Ex.33: 12-17) he said to Him "You have been telling me, Lead these people but you have not let me know whom you will send with me. You have said, 'I know you by name and you have found favor with me. If you are pleased with me teach me your ways, so I may know you and to continue to find favor with you. Remember that this nation is your people."

So now that Moses has expressed his great concerns to the Lord, he was hopeful that God would have a change of heart and continue to be with Him and the Israelites. But just having Gods angel to guide them, it was not enough to satisfy Moses. He objects that, a mere angel is no substitute for Gods own presence. The only condition that would be acceptable for further advancement to Canaan would be Gods own presence among His people. Only the "Lords Presence," would demonstrate to the surrounding nations that, Israel's deliverance was really the work of the one and only true and merciful God. So Moses would settle for nothing less than Gods own presents. When God used the words "I know you by name," He was telling Moses that He had chosen him for His special purpose. God was also expressing His own personal and intimate love and care for Moses as well.

As the Lord continued to speak to Moses He said; "My Presence will go with you and I will give you rest." Moses then replied and said to the Lord: "If your Presence does not go with us, do not send us up from here. How will anyone know that you are pleased with me and with your people unless you go with us? What else will distinguish me and your people from all the other people on the face of the earth?"

Moses had now presented God with a very good argument. So God said to Moses; "I will do the very thing you have asked, because I am pleased with you and I know you by name." God also knows each and every one of us on the whole face of the earth by our own name, and He will do whatever you ask Him to do if, you believe and trust in Him to do it. But you must also remember that, whatever you ask Him for, it must be in His will to grant you your requests. But, He will do it on His own terms and not necessarily when you or I want it to happen.

Amazingly as it may seem at this point, Moses had one more request or favor to ask of God while he still had His full attention. Now Moses tells God that he desires to receive an even greater sense of God's Presence. He said to God: "Now show me your glory." This had never been granted to any mortal man before. This was a request that the Sovereign God of the Universe did not have to grant Moses, but God responded positively to his appeal. In (Ex.33: 19-20) the Lord said to Moses: "I will cause my goodness to pass in front of you, and I will proclaim my name "The Lord," in your presence. I will have mercy on which I will have mercy, and I will have compassion on which I will have compassion. But you cannot see my face, for no one may see me and live."

So now God tenderly grants this audacious request of His servant Moses. But it had to be done in Gods way, and not necessarily the way Moses would have liked it to be done. It is in the following verses in (Ex. 33:21-23) God speaks of Himself more in human terms rather than in His spiritual terms. God said to Moses: "There is a place near me where you may stand on a rock. When my glory passes by, I will put you in a cleft in the rock, and cover you with my hand until I have passed by. Then I will remove my hand and you will see my back; but my face must not be seen."

From the proceeding scripture you can see that God can, and will do, whatever He desires to do. His Sovereignty is paramount when it comes to dealing with people. The human language is simply too limited, to fully express the mysteries and the divine attributes of our Living God. Jesus said in (Jn. 4:24) "God is a spirit, and His worshipers must worship in spirit and in truth." The place of worship is irrelevant, because you cannot contain God in any type of building or any kind structure. You must truly worship God in your own heart, and in your spirit, and in your whole being. True worship, must be in keeping with Gods nature, which is spirit. In Johns Gospel, the word truth is associated with Jesus Christ. This is a fact that has great importance for the proper understanding of Christian worship.

All three persons of the Trinity are linked with the word truth. Jesus explained this very clearly in (Jn. 14:6-7). He said: "I am the way the truth and the life. No one comes to the Father except through me. If you really knew me, you would know my Father as well. From now on you do know Him and have seen Him." Also, in (Jn.1: 18) the scripture states, "No one has ever seen God but God the One and only, who is at the Fathers side, has made Him known." This scripture also declares the true deity of Christ our Savior.

Now God gives Moses more instructions in (Ex. 34:1-10) He said; "Chisel out two stone tablets like the first ones, and I will write on them the words that were on the first tablets, which you broke. Be ready in the morning, and then come up on Mount Sinai. Present yourself to me there on top of the mountain. No one is to come with you or be seen anywhere on the mountain; not even the flocks and herds may graze in front of the mountain."

By making Moses chisel out the second set of stone tablets, God was in a small way punishing Moses, for his display of anger when he threw down the first set of stone tablets and broke them. But it also is a great demonstration of God's mercy towards Moses, because God Himself would write the commands again with His finger like He did the first ones, instead of requiring Moses to do the work himself.

Although God at one point had appeared to disown the Israelites because of their sin, once again He displays His great love and concern for them. He issues the same stern warning that He had issued before. No man or animals were to come near the mountain because the whole mountain was sacred ground.It was meant mainly to protect the careless or the curious people who might try to trespass on holy ground. Also, by issuing this same warning the second time to the people, God was showing the people that He was willing to begin all over again with them, and that He was still willing to establish a new covenant with them. God is also very willing to do the same for us each and every day that we wake up in the morning. He gives us a brand new start each day to enjoy His companionship and love.

So Moses did as the Lord had commanded him. Early the following morning Moses ascended the mountain with the two tablets in his arms to present them to God. When he had reached the point on the mountain where God had told him to be, God came down in the form of a cloud and stood there with him. Then God did just exactly for Moses what He had promised. He passed in front of Moses proclaiming His name saying: "The Lord, the Lord, the compassionate and gracious God, slow to anger, abounding in love, and faithfulness, maintaining love to thousands, and forgiving wickedness, rebellion and sin. Yet He does not leave the guilty unpunished. He punishes the children and their children for the sin of their fathers to the third and fourth generations."

Then God showed Moses His glory and Moses bowed before the Lord in an act of total worship. But Moses said once again to the Lord: "O Lord, if I have found favor in your eyes, then let the Lord go with us. Although this is a stiff-necked people, forgive our wickedness and our sin, and take us as your inheritance." God then said to Moses: "I am making a covenant with you (meaning Moses). Before all your people I will do wonders never before done in any nation in the entire world. The people you live among will see how awesome is the work that I, the Lord, will do for you."

When Moses returned this time from the mountain however, his appearance had changed dramatically, and his face glowed or shone like a bright light. His face was so bright that the people could not look at his face and they turned away from him in fear. But Moses was totally unaware that his face glowed until some of the people told him about it. Then Moses covered his face with a cloth so that he could talk to the people without blinding them.

The Bible does not say just how long the face of Moses' glowed but it was positive proof to the Israelites that he had indeed seen part of Gods glory. It was not possible for God to show Moses all of His glory because, Moses was a mortal man and he could not have lived after if God had done so. Moses had been in the Presence of the Lord for forty days and forty nights. That is why his face shone so brightly. Throughout those forty days and nights, the Lord had totally sustained Moses and his body. This was indeed, another miracle from God that He had performed without any one realizing that He had done so.

In this new covenant God gave Moses some new rules, and repeated some old laws and regulations that the people were to obey as well. For example:

a. The people were to work only six days, and they were not allowed to even light a fire in their dwellings on the Sabbath Day. This was a law that could not be broken. Whoever did not obey this law was to be put to death.

b. The people were to take some of the plunder that they had taken from the Egyptians in the form of gold, silver, bronze, blue, purple and scarlet yarn, and fine linen, goat hair, ram skins dyed red, and hides of sea cows, acacia wood, olive oil for the light spices for the anointing oil and for the fragrant incense, onyx stones and other gems to be mounted on the ephod and breast piece. All of these things were to be a free will offering to the Lord for the building of His Tabernacle.
c. Every person who, God had given the talent and the skills and the willingness to get the job done, were to perform the many different tasks that were required of them to bring about, the building of a Tabernacle or the Tent of Meeting, and the Ark of the Covenant for God. They were, to come and make everything the Lord had commanded without any reservations what so ever.
d. There were also three feasts that they were to observe throughout the year, and throughout their history.
e. God would drive out the enemies of the Israelites before them. In this way, God would show His people and all of the other nations, His awesome power, and He would also gain great Glory from His works.
f. The Israelites were not to make any treaties with the people of Canaan, because they would become a snare or a trap to the Israelites.
g. The Israelites were to break down their enemy's altars, smash their sacred stones, and cut down their Asherah poles.
h. God's people were not to worship any of the gods or idols that the people worshiped who lived in the land.

If the Sons of the Israelites went and took some of the peoples daughters that lived in the land for their wives, their wives could lead them away from God. This is very true even in the world today as well. When, a Christian marries a non-Christian they too can and possibly will fall away from God and go the way of the world, and their souls could be a lost to Satan forever.

Now God has not only continued to keep His original covenant that He had committed Himself to with Abraham, Isaac, and Jacob, but now He has renewed it, and He has declared another covenant with Moses and the Israelites. Plus now at this time, He has added another duty for Moses to perform. He was to have the added responsibility of writing down everything that the Lord had commanded him to do. God said to him; "Write down these words, for in accordance with these words I have made a covenant with you and Israel." As you can see this time, God includes Israel once again as His people. God is slow to anger and very quick to forgive. So Moses did as the Lord commanded him, and he wrote down everything on scrolls that would later serve as records for the whole world to see.

Here again, God shows us His great and magnificent power. There is no way that Moses who was only human, could have had the mental capacity to remember all of the small details of Gods commands and laws, and then write them down word for word. The Holy Spirit would have had to bring back to his memory many of the rules and regulations that He had mentioned to Moses.

God in His infinite wisdom knew that, some form of records must be kept for all of mankind to see and to read, in the centuries that were yet to come. So He instilled in the hearts of all of mankind the ability, the knowledge, the will, and the desire, to keep records of the past events of history. If God had not established some form of record keeping of His laws and commands to Moses and the people who were to follow him; then where would we be in this day and age? Just pause here for a moment, and think about it! If God had left mankind on its own, and the Prophets and the Apostles had not been inspired by the Holy Sprite to write down the Old Testament, and the Gospels that are the New Testament; the people of today would not have had any knowledge of the work of Jesus Christ the Son of God, and His redemptive work on the cross.

Likewise, we would have never known of the eternal plans that God has for all of mankind. God in His infinite wisdom and mercy has now just created another miracle for us to wonder and marvel about. God's wisdom is so far above anyone or anything else that, all we as humans can do is to marvel and wonder about it and try to understand it. Every word that is written in the Bible is the inerrant word of the living God our Creator.

After he had received Gods instructions, he went back down the mountain to explain them to the people. His instructions included the building and the furnishing of a tent that God would use for a Tabernacle and the Ark of the Covenant. As our story continues, some time has passed now, since Moses has returned from the mountain and his last meeting with the Lord. Now he has called a special meeting of all the people so that he could instruct them in the building of Gods special place of worship.

He called all of the people before him in whom God had placed His specific skills and talents to do all of the work. After enough gold, silver, perishes stones, gems, and all of the other materials that were required had been collected from the people; Gods craftsmen set about the building of His Temple. It would have taken quite some time to complete, because everything had to be made and designed by hand. But God has plenty of time and so did the Israelite. It must have made the old heart of Moses very happy and full of joy to see, the people working together in harmony instead of fighting and quarreling among themselves.

As soon as the people had completed all of the tasks that God had required of them, Moses then inspected their work to see that it had been done exactly to Gods specifications. Then Moses blessed all of the people who had taken part in the work for the Lord, and he also blessed all of the people for their faithfulness in which the Israelites had donated their gifts, time, and talents, in the building of the Tabernacle and its furnishings. The Tabernacle would now be a dwelling place where God would come to whenever He spoke to Moses, and where the priests and the people could offer sacrifices and worship their God. But Gods visible appearance would still remain the same as before, in the form of a dark cloud for all of the people to see.

The Lord then said to Moses: "Set up the Tabernacle, the tent of Meeting on the first day of the first month. Place the Ark of the Testimony in it and shield it with the curtain." As you can see, the Ark was a very important part of the Tabernacle therefore; it occupied a very special place in the Tabernacle. It was placed in the most Holy Place in the Tabernacle because God would dwell there while He led His people to the Promised Land. The Ark would also play a very important role in the history of the Israelites later on in their history.

When the cloud covered the Tent of the Meeting and the glory of the Lord filled the Tabernacle, not even Moses was permitted to enter the tent because of the Lords presence there. From now on, there would be only five people allowed inside of the Tabernacle. Aaron and His four sons, Nadab who was Aaron's firstborn son, Abihu, Eleazar, and Ithamar, whom God had appointed as Priests when they were on the mountain with God and Moses. They would be the only people permitted to enter the Tabernacle; and that would be only at certain times. Aaron, who was the High Priest was, the only one who would be permitted to enter the Most Holy Place. Anyone else who even came near the sanctuary would be put to death.

I would like to mention at this time, that two of Aaron's sons Nadab and Abihu would be struck dead before the Lord sometime later on when, they made an offering with unauthorized or a profane fire before the Lord. They had no sons to take their place so; that only left Eleazar and Ithamar to serve as priests during the lifetime of their father Aaron. The two sons of Aaron who had sinned against God must have been a huge disappointment to their father because; God had given them such a high position that, carried with it a great deal of honor and prestige. This tragedy in the life of Aaron happened while the Israelites were still at Mount Sinai.

Throughout the rest of the journey, the Israelites would move camp whenever the cloud lifted from above the Tabernacle. But if the cloud did not lift, they would not move. The cloud was over the Tabernacle by day, and there was fire in the cloud by night. God continued to guard His people to keep them from all harm as He said He would. By this kind of action alone, the people should have realized that God was always true to His word.

After the covenant with Moses and the people was completed and fully established by God at Mount Sinai, Israel has now became the earthly representation of Gods kingdom. God as their Lord and King; would now establish His administration over all aspects of Israel's life and not just part of it. God would not settle to be second best to any other god, or idol, or to anything else. The Lord is the same today as He was then. He never changes. He must be first in your life, and then you are His disciples indeed.

Over a full year has passed now since the institution of the Passover and the Israelites departure from Egypt. It was time for the Israelites to celebrate the Passover for the second time in their short history. The Lord then spoke to Moses in the first month of the second year, after the Israelites had left Egypt and He said; "Have the Israelites celebrate the Passover at the appointed time. Celebrate it at the appointed time, at twilight on the fourteenth day of this month, in accordance with all its rules and regulations." So this time the Israelites obeyed the Lord without any grumbling or complaining, and they celebrated the Passover at twilight. Twilight, according to Jewish tradition was the end of the day, and the beginning of the next day.

However, some of the people who were ceremonially unclean because they had to deal with a dead body, or for some other reason had not been able to attend the ceremony on that particular day were very upset. So they complained to Moses and Aaron. What were they to do? Then Moses did the only thing that he could do. He took the problem to the Lord and asked Him what to do. God had not given Moses the authority to deal with such a matter as this.

The Lord replied to Moses and said: "Tell the Israelites; when any of you or your descendants is unclean because of a dead body, or is away on a journey, they may still celebrate the Lords Passover. They are to celebrate it on the fourteenth day of the second month at twilight." Although God had said that He had disowned the Israelites a short time before, He still shows His great love and concern for the people. He gives the people who may have had a problem attending the regular Passover day with the other people, an extra month to prepare them for the celebration. But they must celebrate the Passover. The Lord made no exceptions. If a man was ceremonially clean and not on a journey, and he did not attend the Passover celebration then, he was to be cut off from his people because he did not present the Lords offering at the appointed time.

It was a little over a month later after the second Passover had been celebrated that, God once again spoke to Moses and said; "Make two trumpets of hammered silver, and use them for calling the community together and for having the camps set out." From this scripture, we learn that God has now split the main camp into twelve different groups or camps. Each camp would have its own leader and standard that would go before it as they marched out on their journey.

These trumpets were not to be just the run of the mill curved ram horns that were used many times before by some of the Israelite tribes. These were to be a special kind of trumpet long and slender and flared out like a bell at one end. They were played similar to the way you would play a bugle.

As the Lord continued to speak He said; "When both trumpets are sounded, the whole community is to assemble before you at the entrance of the Tent of Meeting. If only one trumpet is sounded, only the clan leaders are to assemble before you. To gather the assembly, blow the trumpets but not with the same signal. The sons of Aaron the priest are to blow the trumpets. When you go into battle in your own land against an enemy who is oppressing you, sound a blast on the trumpets. Then you will be remembered by the Lord your God and rescued from your enemies. Also; in the day of rejoicing in your appointed feasts, the New Moon festivals, at the beginning of your months, over your burnt offerings and the sacrifices of your peace offerings, and the trumpets will be a memorial for you before your God. I am the Lord your God."

As you can see God is not leaving anything to the Israelites to do on their own. He has planned every step and every move that His people were to take, right down to the smallest detail. God did not want the Israelites to have to worry about a single detail of their journey to His promised land. If God had not given the Israelites such detailed instructions, they probably would not have been very organized in the way that they marched out from camp, each time that they had to move.

The people were to march out in a specific order with each clan leader leading his people under their own banner or standard. They were not to move in just any old way or direction that their hearts desired. As you know, God does everything in a perfect order. So now, His people must also do everything in the same orderly manner.

The tribe of Judah would lead all of the other eleven tribes. The tribe of Judah received special consideration from God because; Judah was the tribe from which Jesus our Lord would be born into. Therefore, God placed the tribe of Judah in the lead column of His people. God had also instructed Moses on how and where, each of the clans and tribes were to be located around the Tabernacle when they stopped and camped for any period of time.

God had also instructed Moses to have each clan and tribal leader, to give Moses the number of people in their respective tribes. Out of each clan and tribe, the leaders were to choose all of the males who were twenty years old and older who were able to fight. They were to be drafted into the Lords army for His purpose. The Lord only needed an army so that He could display His mighty works through it, and not to win His battles for Him. The army would give the people a great deal of moral support and a greater sense of security, as they continued their journey. The total number of fighting men that were mustard for Gods army was numbered at 603,550.This would indeed be a formidable army of men that could ward of any sort of an enemy attack that Gods people may encounter on their journey to the Promised Land if it was needed.

-9-

THE JOURNEY CONTINUES

So it camc to pass after spending eleven months in the region of Mount Sinai that, God gave the people the order to move. On the twentieth day of the second month of the second year, the cloud lifted from above the Tabernacle, and the Israelites set out from the desert of Sinai with the Lord leading His people. When the people marched out from Mount Sinai, they marched out in orderly columns as the Lord had commanded, with each tribal leader and their standard in the lead. As you can see this is one time for a change that, the people obeyed the Lord without grumbling and complaining.

It appears that even the people who were considered rabble among the Israelites had quieted their tongues to some degree. Many times they would use every kind of discomfort that happened to come along, as an excuse to agitate and cause rebellion against God and His appointed leader Moses. But, God had warned Moses that these people would be a thorn in the side of the Israelites throughout their whole journey to the Promised Land.

Whenever the Ark set out, Moses would offer a prayer to the Lord and say; "Rise up, O Lord! Let your enemies be scattered, and let those who hate you flee before you." In like manner, when the Ark rested, he prayed: "Return, O Lord, to the many thousands of Israel." As the people traveled by day, the cloud of the Lord stayed above them. But by night the cloud took on the appearance of fire, to give light to the Israelites and to direct their path.

They traveled from place to place until the cloud came to rest in the desert of Paran. After the people had finished setting up their camp, some of the rabble or troublemakers, and no doubt some of the Israelites as well, started to complain bitterly to Moses. They complained about many things, but mainly about the constant diet of manna that God provided fresh each morning. The lack of water, and the lack of meat or vegetables to eat like they had in Egypt was, a big sore point with many of the people.

Now that the multitude of people had to contend with a new type of distress and discomfort, they romanticized about their past life in Egypt, and minimized its discomforts. The people said to Moses: "If only we had meat to eat! We remember the fish we ate in Egypt at no cost. As well, the cucumbers, leeks, melons, onions, and garlic. But now we have lost our appetite; we never see anything but this manna!"

The people's complaint about the manna was a direct complaint against God and His mercy. It was also a blatant form of disobedience to God and His great goodness. The people had once again failed Gods test of faith, even after the many great miracles that He had done right before their eyes. The people had reverted back to the same lack of faith as they had one year earlier, after being delivered at the Red Sea from the Pharaoh and his army.

The Lord heard their complaining, and His anger was once again kindled against His people. So the Lord sent a fire around the outside of the whole camp and it caused the people to be very much afraid of the Lord. Now, to make matters worse, they also had too fear Gods anger as well but, that didn't matter to some of them. So, in true mob fashion they went directly to their favorite whipping boy, Moses! Then Moses prayed to the Lord and the fire died down.

As Moses prayed and talked to the Lord, he said to the Lord: "Why have you brought this trouble on your servant? What have I done to displease you that you put the burden of all these people on me? Where can I get meat for all these people? I cannot carry all these people by myself; the burden is too heavy for me. If this is how you are going to treat me, put me to death right now?"

It appears as if Moses had come to the end of his rope. He was so tired of listening to the complaints of the people that he was willing to give up his life if that's what it took. He felt like he could no longer continue as the leader of such an ungrateful and disobedient people. It was a prayer of great distress filled with urgency, irony, and passion. He was having himself a real pity party.

Undoubtedly, this is how many people in today's world respond to God when, they get themselves into some kind of trouble or some kind of sickness comes their way. If they cannot see their way out of the problem that they themselves have created or, that someone else may have created for them they will complain bitterly against God or someone else. In many cases they may say to themselves; "Why is this or that, happening to me? What have I done to deserve this or that problem?" But God doesn't cause anything to happen to us, but He does permit things to happen to us. He does this so that, He can see how well we will react to the problems that we face, and whether or not we will take our problems to Him and let Him solve them for us. But, you must ask Him to help you bare up under any problems that may come your way.

Whenever you are depressed, and you seem to be walking through a valley of sorrows that you find yourself in, God will always hear your prayers and deliver you from all of your troubles. God clearly stated this in (Ps. 34: 6-7) when He said; "This poor man called, and the Lord heard him; and He saved him out of all his troubles." In verse 7 it says; the angel of the Lord encamps around those who fear Him, and He delivers them.

God; is a God of love and grace, and not a God of evil. He is always in complete control of the world and everything in it. This includes all of mankind, from Adam to the very last person that will be born on this earth. He would not give up His control of the world to anything, or to anyone because; He loves His creation so much. Jesus proved this in the scriptures in the Bible in (Jn. 3:16 -17) when He said; "For God so loved the world that He gave His one and only Son, that whoever believes in Him shall not perish but have eternal life. For God did not send His Son into the world to condemn the world, but to save the world through Him."

The Lord also states in the Bible in (2Co.1: 3-4) that He is the Father of compassion, and the God of all comfort, who comforts us in all of our troubles, so that we can comfort those in any trouble with the comfort we ourselves have received from God. These are the words of the one and only God of all truth. God cannot tell a lie because He is a Holy God.

Now the time has come and God will show Moses, just how simple it will be for Him to solve the problems that Moses was having with the Israelites. So God replies to Moses and said: "Bring me seventy of Israel's elders! Have them come to the Tent of the Meeting that they may stand there with you. I will come down and speak with you there. I will take the Spirit that is on you and put the Spirit on them. They will help you carry the burden of the people so that you will not have to carry it alone.

Tell the people "Consecrate yourselves in preparation for tomorrow, when you will eat meat". The Lord heard you when you wailed. Now the Lord will give you meat and you will eat it. You will not eat it for just one or two day, but for a whole month, until it comes out your nostrils and you loathe it, because you have rejected the Lord who is among you." 'Then Moses did as the Lord commanded him, and he summoned the elders to appear before him at the Tent of Meeting. However, only sixty-eight elders came to the tent but two of them remained in their camp.

As you can see, God will now relieve Moses of some of his many duties and pass them on to the seventy Israelite leaders. Now it will be the seventy chosen leaders, who will bear the brunt of the many problems and complaints that concerns the Israelite people. God has now solved some of the problems that Moses had complained to Him about. This was also Gods way of establishing the first real form of Government for His people.

The next day when God took the Spirit from Moses and put the Spirit on the elders, they all prophesied before the people. This also included the two who were nowhere near the Tent of the meeting but had remained in the Israelite camp. When the word prophesied is used in this section of scripture, it means that the elders gave out with an elated expression to an intense religious experience. But they did not do so again at any other given time.

It appears that the temporary gift of prophecy was given to the elders by God to establish their creditability as Spirit Empowered leaders. Because two of the elders were not present at the tent, it also shows that the Holy Spirit is never restricted to any one place at any one time. Now at last it would seem that Moses will have some rest and peace of mind in his old age.

As Moses continued to complain to God he said to Him: "Here I am among six hundred thousand men on foot, and you say, 'I will give them meat to eat for a whole month!' Would they have enough if flocks and the herds were slaughtered for them? Would they have enough if all of the fish in the sea were caught for them?"

It's quite ironic here that in this part of the conversation, Moses was only thinking in human terms because; he too had seen and had been a part of so many miracles that God had performed right before his own eyes in the past. But it also appears from the scripture that it was because of his great depression, and his present state of mind that he, could not think too clearly. He may have forgotten for a second or two that he was talking to the Great Sovereign Creator of the Universe. With God all things are possible, but with mankind a great many things are impossible for them to do.

God's awesome power is manifested and He is glorified in mankind's weakness. To illustrate the above statement: I will refer you to the two times in scripture in the New Testament when, Jesus fed a multitude of people on two separate occasions in the wilderness. It is truly a story within a story, but it also coincides with God feeding and caring for the Israelites. Although this little story will take us away from our present story, I feel that I must relate it to you the reader of this book. I know there will be a great many people who do not have a Bible so they can read this story for themselves, so I feel that I must relate it to them for their enjoyment. You can read this story in the Bible if you have one at your disposal. You can locate it in four different places in the NIV. Bible in Jn. 6:1-13, Mt. 14:13-21, Mk. 6: 32-44, Lk. 9:10-17.

This little story takes place centuries into the future when Jesus walked here on earth. Jesus had been teaching and healing people in a remote area by the Sea of Galilee. Jesus and His disciples had probably been resting and relaxing in a boat on the Sea of Galilee. When they came to the shore of the lake, the people came from the surrounding towns and villages to hear Him speak. By this time in Jesus' ministry, His fame as a great teacher and healer had spread like wildfire throughout the country. The people brought with them the sick, the lame, the blind, the deaf, and anyone who had any kind of sickness or disease to be healed.

Although, many of the people may or may not have ever seen or heard Jesus speak before, they all wanted to be healed by Jesus or, they came just to hear what He had to say. As it was true in the time of Jesus, so it is still true in today's world as well. When a great storyteller is present among people, he is greatly revered and he is held in very high esteem.

Time had passed quickly that day, and when Jesus had finished teaching and healing all of the sick people that were there. Jesus looked on the multitude of people with love and compassion. He knew that the people were hungry and that many of them had not eaten all day. When His disciples came to Him and said to Him: "Send the people away so that they can go to the villages and buy themselves some food." Jesus replied to them and said, "They do not need to go away. You give them something to eat! "This of course, would have been impossible for the disciples to do. But with God, all things are possible.

Then the disciples said to Jesus: "We have here only five loaves of bread and two fish." Then Jesus said to them: "Bring them here to me!" On this occasion in (Mt.14: 13-21) Jesus fed more than five thousand men besides women and children. The word Men here, in the scripture appears to be mentioned as a separate entity. This is probably because Mathew was writing to the Jews at the time, and the Jews did not permit women and children to eat with the men in public. So they would have been in a place by themselves. Then Jesus commanded the people to sit down on the grass.

As Jesus prayed and gave thanks, He looked up to heaven, and He blessed and broke the bread, and then gave it to His disciples. They in turn distributed it to the multitude of people. After everyone had eaten their fill and was satisfied, the disciples went about and collected twelve more basketfuls of broken pieces that were left over. The baskets that the scripture refers to here could well have been the lunch baskets that the twelve apostles would carry their lunch in when they were going about the country with Jesus. This is possibly why the twelve baskets were mentioned. After the multitude of people had been fed and cared for, Jesus and His disciples departed and went into the region of Tyre and Sidon.

While He was there in that region, Jesus performed a different kind of miracle. As it happened, a Canaanite woman came to Him and his disciples and requested His help to free her daughter, who was suffering from a terrible case of demon-possession. Someone must have told her at some point in time that; this Jesus who was traveling around the country healing all manner of diseases could help her with her daughter's problem, so she sought Him out. But His disciples tried to send her away because she was crying out to Him. After she had explained her problem to Jesus, He said to her, "Woman you have great faith!" Your request is granted, and her daughter was healed from that very hour. As you can see even Satan and his demons are powerless against God.

The second feeding of a multitude of people occurred when Jesus and His disciples again returned to the shores of Galilee. He remained in this region for another three days teaching and healing the great multitude of people who had gathered to hear Him and to receive His healing touch. The people were totally amazed when they saw the mute speaking, the deaf made to hear, the crippled made well, the blind seeing, and the lame walking, and they praised the God of Israel.

Then Jesus said to His disciples: "I have compassion for these peoples; they have already been with me three days and have nothing to eat. I do not want to send them away hungry, or they may collapse on the way." As you can see, Jesus was concerned about the people's physical needs as well as their spiritual needs. Then His disciples asked Him a typical question that only a human being could ask when, they are blinded to the truth of who Jesus is. "Where could we get enough bread in this remote place to feed such a crowd?"

As you will notice from the scripture, that Jesus didn't have to ask His disciples if they had any food kicking around that they themselves could spare. Jesus, who is God in the flesh, already knew what He was going to do. He already knew just what was at hand because; He is an omniscient (possess all-knowledge) as well as being an omnipotent God, (possesses absolute power). Now Jesus, who is the possessor of all things visible and invisible, would demonstrate His awesome power as well as His great love for the people by feeding them. By the following words that He spoke you can tell that He knows all things before they happen. Then Jesus asked His disciples: "How many loaves do you have?" He did not say, "Do you have any bread?" He worded His question this way because He already knew what He had to do.

One of the disciples replied to Jesus and said: "Seven, and a few small fish." So Jesus commanded the people to sit down on the ground. Then He took the seven loaves and the fish, and after He had prayed and given thanks, He broke them and gave them to His disciples. They in turn distributed the pieces to the people. After all of the people had eaten and were satisfied, the disciples went about and collected seven basketfuls of broken pieces that were left over. On this occasion, four thousand men besides women and children were fed and cared for by Jesus. Then Jesus sent the crowed away and He departed by boat, and went to the vicinity of Magadan or Magdala as it was also called, where Mary Magdalene lived.

In these two examples alone: God has shown us His tremendous power, His love, and His compassion, to provide for His people who are the jewels in His crown of Creation.

God did for His people what man was powerless to do, as He has done throughout the entire history of the world. So ends this little story within a story. I hope that you have been able to see the similarity or the comparison that I spoke of between the two different situations because, they happened centuries apart. Now let us get back to our main story of Moses and his problems with the Israelites.

Now please recall that, Moses and God were having a conversation at the door of the Tabernacle, with the elders listing in on the conversation. The people had been complaining about not having meat to eat. As the Lord continued to speak with Moses He said: "Is the Lords arm too short? You will now see whether or not what I say will come true for you." Once again, God is about to demonstrate His great and awesome power that He, alone possess over all of His Creation. The Israelites would now fully realize once again that the Lords arm is never too short to do His bidding. God has no limit on His authority, His abilities, or His power.

After God had concluded His conversation with Moses and the elders, they all returned to their respective camps. Moses then relayed the entire message word for word that the Lord had spoken to him to the people. They were to wait for another miracle from the Lord the following day.

It came to pass on the very next day just as God had said it would, that He caused a wind to blow, and it drove quail in from the sea. The wind brought them down all around the camp to about three feet above the ground, and as far as a day's walk in any direction. Being the birds were so close to the ground, they could be easily caught by the people. All that day and night, and all the next day, the people who had craved meat ran franticly about the camp catching and killing the quail.

Those who had complained so bitterly about Gods gracious provision of manna, more than likely went out and gathered more quail then some of the other people. Their greed and the lust for meat had taken complete control of their thinking. It is a proven fact that greed in most people will, at some point in their lives, make them do many things that they would not normally do. Greed is a very powerful tool that the Devil uses to deceive people and pull them away from God. If a person's faith is not strong and well grounded in the Lord, they will certainly get themselves into trouble at some time in their life. Greedy people are unable to resist the Devil when he puts the temptation right in front of them. No one is totally immune from being caught in Satan's trap at some time in his or her lifetime.

The people still did not trust God to continually supply their food for them as He had done with the manna in the past. The complainers had described God's gift of manna as something that had dried up their being. Now God was going to give them so much meat that it would make the people physically ill. This would make them realize what a great gift the manna really was. The people had never gotten sick or died from eating it. In essence, when the people rejected Gods provision of manna, they were really rejecting God who was the Provider.

No one gathered less than ten homers of the birds for food. Then the people spread them out all around the camp. After preparing the meat to eat, the complainers sat down to enjoy what would become their last meal here on earth. The Bible says in (Nu.11: 33), that while the meat was still between their teeth, even before it could be consumed in their stomachs, the Lords anger burned against them, and He struck them with a severe plague and it killed all of those who had craved other food. This was one instance when, God chose to display His great displeasure and wrath against the Israelites and their sin against Him without hesitation.

So it was that the camp now became a death camp; and it would be marked with the graves of those who had rebelled against Gods food of mercy, that was called manna or Gods bread from heaven. God had provided the people with manna from heaven for over a year, and now those who had rejected it would be dead and buried. God had totally cut them off from His people. The principle issue in this case was not the meat at all; but it was the failure of the people to demonstrate proper gratitude to the Lord, who was present in their midst and who was their constant source of goodness.

Shortly after the people had buried all of their dead at Kibroth Hattaavah, (which means "Graves of Craving") the people moved there camp from there and stopped again to rest at a place called Hazeroth. This was a place where God allowed the people another short respite from their journey and its judgments.

As time passed and the people had settled into their daily routines, discontent and jealousy began to show its ugly head involving Miriam and Aaron, against their brother Moses. They were jealous to the core, but it was without just cause. Moses could not understand why his brother and sister would speak against him as they did, because Moses had done nothing to displease them as far as he knew. The bitter and arrogant attitude that was displayed by his two siblings, whom he dearly loved, must have devastated Moses to the point of total frustration.

Miriam, who was considered to be a prophetess, enjoyed having a very high status in the community. There is no doubt that her position in the community would command a large following of people. But she was not totally satisfied, and she sought to have a more prestigious position. On the other hand Aaron her brother was, ministering before God as the high priest for the people. His position was also one of the privileged positions to have in the community.

These two people had everything going for them, but still they wanted to have more. They had become greedy for the sake of power. Satan had caused jealousy and envy to enter their hearts, and it would in turn cause God to intervene directly on the behalf of His humble servant Moses. The Bible mentions that Moses was one of the most humble men to walk the earth at that time.

When all was said and done, it appeared that they were criticizing him for no other reason than the fact that he had married a Cushite woman. But this was only a pretext to the real trouble, and not the main reason for attacking Moses. The real underlying reason of course was because of the special relationship that Moses enjoyed with the Lord. Although they too enjoyed high positions in the community, they were not called personally by the Lord, or permitted to come into His presence as Moses was.

From the scriptures it appears that Miriam was the instigator of the attack against Moses, because she was the person that the Lord dealt most severely with. The scripture says in (Nu.12: 2), "Has the Lord spoken only through Moses? Has He not spoken through us also?" As soon as Miriam had spoken these words, God heard them and He was very angry with both Miriam and Aaron. They were publicly disgracing Moses as well as disgracing God at the same time. God acted very quickly and He commanded the three of them to come before Him at the Tent of the Meeting. God was not going to let anyone speak against Him and His chosen faithful leader and get away with it.

All three came out to the Tent of the Meeting immediately without hesitation. Then the Lord came down in a pillar of cloud and He stood in the door of the Tabernacle, and He called to Aaron and Miriam, and they both stepped forward to meet Him.

As the Lord spoke to them He said;"Listen to my words; when a prophet of the Lord is among you I reveal myself to him in visions. I speak to him in dreams. But this is not true of my servant Moses; he is faithful in my entire house. With him I speak face to face clearly and not in riddles; he sees the form of the Lord. Why then were you not afraid to speak against my servant Moses?" Then the anger of the Lord burned against them and He departed from them. When the cloud lifted from above the tent, there stood Miriam, white as snow. God had made her leprous as a punishment for her sin of jealousy.

When Aaron turned toward Miriam and he seen what the Lord had done to her, he cried to Moses and said; "Oh, my Lord! Please do not lay this sin on us, in which we have done foolishly and in which we have sinned. Please do not let her be as one dead, whose flesh is half eaten away when he comes out of his mother's womb!" The sincere repentance of Aaron before Moses is touching indeed. He was honestly begging Moses to intercede before God, for him and for his sister Miriam. This act of repentance also demonstrated to Moses that, their jealousy over his relationship with Lord was unfounded and not called for.

So Moses cried to the Lord and said; "O God please heal her!" Then the Lord listened to Moses, but Gods words were a stern warning against such things as public humiliation. He said to Moses; "If her father had spit in her face, would she not have been in disgrace for seven days? Confine her outside the camp for seven days, after that she can be brought back." We are not told what would have provoked a father to spit in the face of his daughter, but it would have to be something that was very disgraceful and uncalled for. The incident that had occurred was not considered by God to be a trivial matter, but you can see that Gods grace was abundant.

Now Miriam, who was the principal offender against her brother Moses, has become an outcast from the community of Israel. Because she now suffers from this terrible skin disease, she is no longer permitted to live in the camp. Under Gods law, she had to be expelled from the community and live outside of the camp for seven days. It was a period of public rebuke and shame. Seven days was the standard time for uncleanness. It would be the same thing as coming into contact with a dead body.

The scriptures say that the Israelites did not move camp until Miriam had completed her seven-day cleansing period as was required by Gods Law. So it appears that this incident with Moses occurred just before the Israelites were to move their camp and continue their journey to the Promised Land. The wording of the scriptures also indicates the high regard that Moses and the people had for Miriam although; she had committed this sin against God and Moses.

The people were willing to delay their journey to accommodate Miriam. Just as Gods grace was abundant for her, the peoples delayed journey was also their expression of their love for her. When the seven days were completed the Israelites moved and continued their journey until they encamped in the Desert of Paran at a place called Kadesh Barnea. The name Kadesh is associated with the Hebrew word that means "Holy."

-10-

THE DOWNFALL OF GODS PEOPLE

Kadesh Barnea was an oasis in the Negev, fifty miles southwest of Beersheba. This area figured prominently in the story of the wilderness wandering of the Israelites in (Nu.13: -14). It was here in this part of their journey that things really went wrong for the Israelites and their relationship with God. To coin an old phrase, "the bottom really fell out of everything." God almost wiped the whole nation of Israel out of existence.

However, if the story had turned out differently, this name Kadesh Barnea would have been associated with great positive memories for the Israelites instead of a death sentence. It would have been here that, the people would have prepared and sanctified themselves for their future campaign of the conquest of Canaan.

This desert was the people's destination since they had set out from Mount Sinai, or Mount Horeb, as it is sometimes referred to. The Desert of Paran or the Wilderness of Paran was located southeast of the land of Canaan, and it was the southernmost region of the Promised Land. It would be an ideal staging place for a northward sweep of the spies, and later for the armies of Israel in the conquest of Canaan. As you can see God had a specific plan in mind when He positioned the Israelites camp where He did.

Some time after the people had set up camp and had settled themselves into some sort of daily routine, the Lord spoke to Moses and said; "Send out some men to spy out the land of Canaan which I am giving to the children of Israel. From each tribe of their fathers, you shall send a man, everyone a leader among them."

These men were not just ordinary men picked at random from the tribes. They had to possess certain special skills and qualities, of which God had specified the first one as being a good leader. For example: To be a good leader you must have a great deal of "Integrity." You have to be honest and trust worthy, truthful, fearless, totally committed to your cause, and above all you must be persistent. The second thing that they had to be was young, strong and intelligent. Without most of these qualities it is impossible to be a good leader. These men that were chosen by Moses were not only regarded as leaders in their tribal units, but also as men who were physically and spiritually capable of great exploits. So you might say that these leaders were to be the cream of the crop so to speak.

In (Nu.13-2) the Lord had instructed Moses to send out the spies, but in (Dt.1: 21-23) the scriptures seem to say that the people also had made a similar suggestion to Moses. I would suspect that the people were putting in their suggestion to Moses well after he had told them what the Lord had said. Then God instructed Moses to proceed with the plan.

After Moses had chosen a leader from each of the twelve ancestral tribes he then gave them very specific instructions as to what they were to do, the way that they were to go, and what they were to look for. He said to them, "Go northward up through the Negev and on into the hill country. See what the land is like, whether the people are strong, weak, few, or many. What are the towns like? Are they unwalled or are they fortified? Is the land good or bad? How is the soil? Is it fertile? Are there trees on it or not? Bring back some of the fruit of the land!"

The commands that Moses had given to the spies were broad but very definite. They were not to very one way or the other. They were to spy out the land, determine what they could about the people and their cities, and observe the produce and forests, and bring back some of the fruit of the land. At that time of the year when the spies went out, it was the season for the first crop of grapes to be picked. The whole mission was cut and dried, with no stone unturned.

If Moses had been speaking in a military sense at that time, it would have been like a reconnaissance mission. The militaries that have excited throughout the history of the world have, usually carried out this type of mission long before the main body of soldiers was to attack the enemy. It was also the plan of the world's greatest general who is none other than God Himself.

However, before the spies left on their journey, Moses changed the name of Hoshea to Joshua. This was quite a common practice in that era. By doing this simple act in public before the people, it openly declared the high esteem that Moses held for Joshua, the son of Nun. It was also an act of ritual adoption. God often changed the names of some of the people that He had a special relationship with.

For example, God changed the name of Abram to Abraham and his wife's name from Sarai to Sarah. So now at this time, Moses has changed the name of Hoshea to Joshua. The name Hoshea means "Salvation" and the name Joshua means, "The Lord saves." Joshua and Jesus are two forms of the same name. Moses probably did this because He had been prompted to by the Lord to do so or; it was because Joshua would eventually become his spiritual heir and he would be the one who would lead Gods people into the Promised Land

and not Moses or; because Moses may have put Joshua in charge of the twelve spies who were being sent out to check out the Land of Canaan.

The Bible only records a few details of the spies' journey when they went to spy out the land of Canaan. However, emphasis is given to the city of Hebron and to the Valley of Eshcol. The spies did as Moses had instructed them and they went as far north as the region of Syria.

The city of Hebron was a large city, and the first city that the twelve spies came to. Being that it was such a large city with many inhabitants, it would have naturally been heavily fortified. The size of the city and its fortifications totally amazed the twelve spies. It was here that the spies first encountered the countries inhabitants. They were the descendants of Anak and they were called the Anakites. The Anakites were men of great stature. They were very tall and strong and their physical size struck great fear into the hearts of the spies. At the time of the spies visit; there were three notable Anak descendants living in Hebron. They were Sheshai, Ahiman, and Talmai. Much later on in the years to come, Caleb would drive them from this city.

Four centuries before this time, Hebron was the city where the Israelites ancestors had lived. It was here that God promised Abraham that He would give this land to his descendants. In Abraham's time, Hebron had not been a great city. At that time, it had only possessed small dwellings and it was just a trading place for shepherds and herdsmen. It was here at Hebron; that Sarah, Abraham, Isaac, and Jacob were all buried in the field that Abraham had purchase from Ephron the Hittite for four hundred shekels of silver.

When the spies reached the valley of Eshcol, on their return journey, they cut down a large cluster of grapes to take back with them. They did this so that they could show the people what the fruit of the land looked like. But at the same time they were obeying the instructions that Moses had given them. The cluster of grapes was so large, that it took two people to carry it on a pole between them, because of its size and weight. They also brought back some pomegranates and figs.

The journey that had started in the southernmost extremity of the Desert of Zin, and had taken the twelve spies to the northernmost point Rehob near Syria, covered a distance of about five hundred miles, if you round off the numbers (250 miles each way). The complete journey would have taken them forty days. This means that, they would have to have traveled at least twelve and half miles or, 20.12 Km. per day to be able to return in forty days which would not have been imposable to do.

It was here, at this point in the story, where everything started to go wrong for the spies and the rest of the Israelites. As the spies made their report to Moses and Aaron, and to the whole assembly of people, their story took on the form of great exaggerations coupled with a few lies, as many stories often do at times. Whenever a person exaggerates the facts to make their story sound good, or more pleasing to the ear, they are not telling the whole truth, and their story becomes a lie.

Even in today's world, people do the exact same thing. But God will not let this kind of thing go unpunished or uncorrected for too long. People may get away with a lie or an exaggeration for a little while but, when they are found out, they will be branded as liars and they will not be trusted by other people to tell the truth any more. People will simply not believe anything that they say regardless, if it is the truth or not. God will punish them in the end when they stand before Him on Judgment Day. Liars will have their day in hell because they cannot and will not enter Gods Kingdom unless they get on their knees and repent of their sins before God. This is Gods solemn promise.

The first part of the spies' story was true to the letter, but from then on their fears and their true human nature took over. Their story became nothing but a pack of lies and total exaggerations from start to finish. The powerful people, who lived there in the land, offset the goodness of the land in their fearful eyes. The Promised Land was a good land, a gracious gift from God. But by speaking bad things about it, the faithless spies were speaking evil of the Lord. The following is the way their story went as it is written in the scriptures in (Nu. 13: 27-33 NIV.)

The spies said; to Moses and the people; "We went into the land to which you sent us, and it does flow with milk and honey. Here is its fruit. But the people who live there are powerful and the cities are fortified and very large. We even saw descendants of Anak there. The Amalekites live in the Negev; the Hittites, Jebusites, and Amorites live in the hill country; and the Canaanites live near the sea and along the Jordon River.

Then Caleb and Joshua, who were Gods faithful servants and prompted by their faith in God, gave Moses a good report on the land. They alone were the only two of the twelve spies to tell the truth about the land. Their faith was steadfast and strong in the Lord. They had not forgotten the miracles that God had done for the people as the others had done. They knew that God and His great power would protect them and they shouted out against the mob of people and said; "We should go up and take possession of the land, for we can certainly do it." They knew without a doubt that God would be true to His word and be with His people and bring them into the land that He had promised them. But the other ten men who had gone up with them would have no part of what they said. They shouted all the more and said; "We can't attack those people; they are stronger than we are."

Then they continued to spread more lies about the land to the people and said; "the land we explored devours those living in it. All the people we saw there are of great size, we saw the Nephilim there. We seemed like grasshoppers in our own eyes, and we looked the same to them." The Nephilim were people of great size and of great strength. They were like giants. In the Hebrew language the word Nephilim means "Fallen Ones." This is referring to some of the one third of the Angels that had followed Satan and they had rebelled against God and were cast out of Heaven to the Earth.

As you can see, the story of the ten spies is full of lies and fabrications. It seems that no matter what Caleb and Joshua said or did, the whole assembly of people complained all the more. By now the anger of the people had gotten out of control, and they had worked themselves into frenzy. A good portion of the angry crowd cried and complained all night long.

They said to Moses and Aaron: "If only we had died in Egypt! Or in this desert! Why is the Lord bringing us to this land only to let us fall by the sword? Our wives and children will be taken as plunder. Wouldn't it be better for us to go back to Egypt? We should choose a leader and go back to Egypt." These angry words were very slanderous to God and His Goodness. But the people's tears were not just caused because of the lies that the ten spies had told them. It was also because many of the people felt that they had lost the dream that God had promised them, of the Promised Land that was yet to come. But by their actions and behavior at this point, they still had not put their trust in the Lord who, was constantly in their presence like they should have done.

Many of the angry people, who by now were out of control, were relying on their own volition instead of the strength of the Lord. They too had been sucked in to the violence by the shouts and screams of the ten unfaithful ring-leaders. As you know, it only takes the shouts and screams of one or two discontented people in a crowd, to turn them into a mob of violence. This kind of behavior is still quite a common occurrence in many countries in the world today.

As you know, "fear and doubt" are two of the main tools that the Devil uses to entice people to go against God and His desire for you. God has nothing but blessings and love for you. If Satan can get you to go against God in any way shape or form, he has done what he has set out to do. However, his ultimate goal is to eventually destroy you completely, and all of the relationships that you may have with other people throughout your whole lifetime. You can rest assured that, he will never give up trying to do you in, no matter what comes your way.

Many times, Caleb and Joshua stood up and rebuked the lies and the testimony of the other ten spies. They shouted back to the people and said, "The land that we passed through and explored is exceedingly good. If the Lord is pleased with us, He will lead us into that land. A land flowing with milk and honey, and He will give it to us. Only do not rebel against the Lord, and do not be afraid of the people of the land, because we will swallow them up. Their protection is gone, but the Lord is with us."

Now the real truth was shouted out again, and reported to the people by Gods two faithful spies Caleb and Joshua but that did not matter to the mob. When Caleb said; "the Lord is with us," he was proclaiming before God and all of the people his great faith in God. He was trusting in God to do just what He said He was going to do. He knew that there were no walls, no fortifications of any size, and certainly no other gods, that could withstand the onslaught of Israel's army when the Lord is with them.

Caleb fully realized this truth and felt this very strong conviction as he argued with the people. But the angry mob would not even stop to consider the truth in Caleb's words. Instead they threatened to stone Gods four servants, to death and find another leader. There was nothing further that God's servants could do to appease the angry mob. So with shear frustration in their hearts, Gods four servants lay face down on the ground in front of the mob, and shed bitter tears in total disbelief. Their tears were also shed because the people had once again committed another great sin against their God and His mercy.

There is a sharp contrast between the people's tears and the tears of Gods faithful servants. God's servants had done their very best in leading the people as far as they did, with little or no thanks from the people. But now it was too late! The people had made the foolish mistake of believing the lies of the unfaithful spies who had only their best interests at heart and not that of the people.

Unfortunately, there are many people in the world today that will believe a lie quicker than they will the truth. They too, will tell a lie or two so that they can prove the point that they are trying to make. The ten faithless spies were doing the same thing here, but they were also displaying their cowardice and fears of going to war, and a complete mistrust in God. Their controversial description of the land, its people, and the size of the cities were nothing but scandalous lies. But, they had accomplished the goal that they had set out to do and that was, to sway the people to their way of thinking.

Also, by speaking against Moses and Aaron as they did, and causing them to fear for their lives, was a sin that God would not permit to go unpunished. It too would be the same as speaking against God who had appointed them as the leaders of His people. They had forgotten all of the miracles that the Lord had done for them and how He had protected them. They despised His mercies, and spurned His might. Through their ingratitude to the Lord, it showed that they preferred death instead of obedience to the Lord. Now there was no going back and escaping Gods coming judgment.

Soon, these people would experience God's wrath in a way that they least expected.

Unfortunately, this will be the fate of many unbelievers in the world today as well. They too are rejecting the Lord Jesus Christ and God the Father who sent Him. They are headed for eternal death and destruction. These are not mans words of warning, but they are Gods words from the Bible. As I have said before, that His words that are written in the Bible are carved in stone. They can never be changed or erased by mankind.

No sooner had Gods four servants cried out to Him in their frustration and sorrow that, the Lord in His glory appeared at the door of the Tabernacle. God did not waste a second in coming to the aid of His servants. He protected them, and He would not even cause a hair on their heads to be harmed or ruffled by the people. His sudden appearance before the whole community of people would have been a brilliant and magnificent occurrence before the tent of the meeting. Not one eye in the whole camp of the Israelites could have missed what was happening at that precise moment in time.

Then the Lord said to Moses; "How long will these people treat me with contempt?" How long will they refuse to believe in me, in spite of all the miraculous signs I have performed among them? I will strike them down with a plague and destroy them, but I will make you into a nation greater and stronger than them." You can see by the response of the Lord to Moses that, the Lords wrath was justified. After everything that He had done for the people, they still didn't want to put their trust in Him, His promises, or His power. The leaders of Israel in Jesus' day when He walked among the people were no better off than the Israelites. They and the people at that time also rejected Gods miraculous signs and they refused to believe in Him as the Messiah.

In like manner, it is the same thing that happens in our world today. There are millions upon millions of people who do not believe in God and in His Son Jesus Christ. Their unbelief in God, and the committing of terrible sins that come from their hearts, has continued on down through the ages. This stumbling block of unbelief comes straight from the Devil. He has blinded the unbeliever's eyes to Gods truth, and many people will remain stubborn until the bitter end. They will spend their eternity in hell with the Devil, which will be their final and just reward. You must remember that, "Eternity" is forever; there is no end to it.

God's preliminary judgment was to utterly reject the entire Israelite nation because of a few people and their disobedience. The people as a whole had rejected Him as their God, their provider, and their protector. So they were ripe for Gods judgment.

But just like one apple can spoil a whole barrel of apples, so can a few people spoil a whole nation of people. This fact has been proven time and time again throughout the course of history. This is the second time that God has threatened to totally destroy the Israelites for their disobedience and arrogance and to start over again with Moses. You May recall the first time was when the people had sinned against God by worshiping the Golden calf. The most reprehensible charge against Gods grace was concerning their children. For the people to even think, that God, after delivering them from the Egyptians would, bring them into the desert and just let them die, it too was a thought straight from the Devil.

It would have been very easy for Moses to step aside and let God do as He said He would do. But, several times in the Bible, Moses is referred to as being like Christ. The fact that he was always interceding between the Israelites and God, and the fact that he spoke face to face with God in His presence, is proof of the above statement. So Moses did the only thing that he could do because he was only a human being. He interceded and spoke up on behalf of the people and begged God to forgive their sin and rebellion.

We as Christians can do the same thing. We can pray and intercede for all kinds of people and their situations, and on their behalf before God, any time and in any place. God has no restrictions on prayer because He delights in the prayers of His people. In this small way, we bring Him the honor and the glory that He so richly deserves.

You may recall that, back in the story of Abraham in (Ge. Ch.22), Abraham was divinely tested by God. It was there that God asked him to sacrifice his only son Isaac as a burnt offering on Mount Moriah. Now Moses is facing the same kind of divine testing from God as Abraham did in his time. Now let us see how Moses who is God's chosen vessel, chooses to handle what God has purposed to do to the whole Israelite community for the second time.

As I said before, it would have been a simple thing for Moses to stand aside, and let God sweep the desert clean of all of these rebellious people. After all was said and done, what could a mere mortal man like Moses do against the God of all Creation? I would say in a human way of thinking; "Absolutely Nothing." He could have just gone along with the flow of things that were to happen and say, "What will be will be." But this was not so with Moses! He did what we as Christians all should do; and that is to, come boldly to the Throne of Grace and laid our petitions before the Lord. Christ our Lord has won this privilege for us on the cross, and He still intercedes for anyone who is in need of Gods goodness and grace. If we do this, God will reward us openly here in this lifetime, or when we get to heaven. But we as Christians will in no way loose our reward from God.

The Bible records the intersession of Moses on behalf of the people in (Nu. 14: 13-19). Moses dearly loved these rebellious people in spite of their sin against God and himself. He openly showed his love before the people and God in the way he presented his prayer before God.

He said to the Lord; "The Egyptians will hear about it! By your power you brought these people up from among them. They will tell the inhabitants of this land about it. They have already heard that you, O Lord, are with these people. That you, O Lord, have been seen face-to-face, that your cloud stays over them. That you go before them in a pillar of cloud by day, and a pillar of fire by night. If you put these people to death all at one time, the nations who have heard this report about you will say, 'The Lord was not able to bring these people into the land He promised them on oath; so He slaughtered them in the desert. Now may the Lords strength be displayed, just as you have declared? The Lord is slow to anger, abounding in love, and forgiving sin and rebellion. Yet He does not leave the guilty unpunished. He punishes the children for the sin of the fathers to the third and fourth generation. In accordance with your great love, forgive the sin of these people, just as you have pardoned them from the time they left Egypt until now.'"

If you look closely at the intercessory prayer of Moses, you will see that Moses had appealed in three different ways to the Lord. His first appeal was to protect Gods "Reputation." When he said, "the Egyptians will hear about it." He had a deep desire to protect Gods reputation and he didn't want anything or anyone to taint Gods name. The second appeal he made was to "Gods power." When he used the words,"the Lord was not able to bring these people into the land He promised them on oath." He feared that other countries and their people would pour nothing but slanderous contempt on Gods awesome power. The third appeal that he used was to appeal to God's "Nature." It is Gods nature to display His strength in showing patience with His people, being slow to anger, abounding in love, and forgiving sin and rebellion.

Because of his great love for the Israelites, Moses has done the only thing that was humanly possible for him to do. Now he has put the ball back into the hands of the Lord so to speak. It was now up to the Lord to forgive the Israelites once again, and not totally destroy them as He had planned. Moses has now, in his own mind, presented God with another opportunity to display His great love for His people. He knew that God was a loving, gracious, and forgiving God who; could forgive the peoples sin as He had done so many times before, if He was asked to do so. He also knew that, God would receive the glory and honor that He so richly deserved, if He did as Moses requested. However, unknown to Moses at that time, once again God was challenging Moses to a colossal test of his own faith. But it was a divine test that, God had orchestrated to test him and his faith. It was not a test of the will of Moses against the will of God.

God will operate much in the same manner with people in today's world as well to test their faith in Him and His power. He wants to see if people will be obedient to Him and do what He wants them to do. He has only their best interest at heart and He wants to bestow His richest blessings on them. When you deliberately refuse to obey Him and you know that what you have done is wrong, you are refusing the blessings that He has for you. Instead, you are heaping scorn and rebellion upon His mercy and goodness.

As soon as Moses had finished His prayer of intercession, God said to him; "I have forgiven them as you asked." God's forgiveness was instant for the people because, of the intercessory prayer of Moses, but His punishment was, and would be, entirely another matter. Now God is going to pass His death sentence on the Israelite people because of their rebellion against Him. His punishment would be complete, but it would take the next forty years to do so.

As God continued to speak to Moses He said: "How long will this wicked community grumble against me?"I have heard the complaints of these grumbling Israelites. So tell them, 'as surely as I live, declares the Lord, I will do to you the very things I heard you say: In the desert your bodies will fall. Every one of you twenty years old or more, who was counted in the census, and who have grumbled against me, and treated me with contempt. Not one of you will enter the land I swore with up lifted hand to make your home, except Caleb son of Jephunneh and Joshua son of Nun. But because my servant Caleb has a different spirit, and follows me wholeheartedly, I will bring him into the land he went to, and his descendants will inherit it. As you can see, God in His great mercy has immediately rewarded His two faithful servants Caleb and Joshua.

When the people had said that, "they would rather die in this desert," God used these same words to convict and sentence them to death. They were condemned by the words out of their own mouths. You may recall that, the exact same thing happened to the Pharaoh in Egypt. God used the Pharaohs own words that he had spoken, and He killed the entire first born of Egypt, just before the Exodus began.

As God continued to speak and to pass His death sentence on the people He said: "As for your children that you said that would be taken as plunder, I will bring them in to enjoy the land you have rejected. But you! Your bodies will fall in this desert. Your children will be shepherds here for forty years, suffering for your unfaithfulness, until the last of your bodies lies in the desert. "Forty years!" One year for each of the forty days that you explored the land. You will suffer for your sins and know what it is like to have me against you. I the Lord have spoken!"

This was the people's final down fall with God and His leaders. There would be no official pardon this time from God. It was the final insult that God would tolerate from these ungrateful Israelites. He would not put up with their arrogance and rebellion any more.

After the Lord had finished speaking to Moses, the Lord struck the ten unfaithful spies with a plague, right there before all of the people. They died immediately, with their lies still hot on their tongues. For them, their punishment from God was swift, without mercy or warning. The ten spies paid the ultimate price for their lies. They paid with their lives. So it shall be, for all liars and unbelievers on the Day of Judgment. For those people who do not repent of their sins and do not change their ways, it will be a day of unspeakable horror and regret, for God will not hold them guiltless.

So now God has declared to Moses, the punishment that now faces the Israelites for their disobedience. Although God is a merciful loving God, and He is slow to anger, He also has His limits. He will not put up with anyone's sin and rebellion forever. You must repent of your sins, and ask Him for His forgiveness and then change your ways. He is always willing and able to forgive your sins, no matter what they are, because God knows what's in your heart, and you can't hide anything from Him.

It is quite ironic to say the least that; after all of the miracles and wonders that the Lord had performed before the Israelites to this point in their short journey, that they still would not obey Him or keep His commandments. Now, anyone who is twenty years old or more, has been condemned to die in the desert. The only adults that would survive after the next forty years would be Caleb and Joshua. Not even Moses; Gods trusted servant would be permitted to enter Gods Promised Land.

The people were now condemned to a, life of wondering, throughout the desert regions without any purpose what so ever. They were doomed to wonder around in the desert for a period of forty years, until all of the older generation was dead, buried, and forgotten. This would be their just reward for their disobedience to God. Their children too, just as God had said, would have to pay for the sins of their parents because; they too had to wonder with their parents as part of the family unit.

After Moses had repeated word for word to the whole community of people, what God had said, they mourned bitterly. Now the people would fully realized that they had made a terrible mistake, but it was far too late. God has condemned them to an appalling death in the desert. Only their children, who were not yet twenty years old, would be permitted to enter Canaan, for the Lord had spoken and the people's fate was now sealed. Now the people would reap what they had sown. So it will be for all of mankind throughout all the ages. Whatever seed you sow you will reap. This is Gods promise to all of mankind.

Although God had delivered His swift and sure judgment on the ten unfaithful spies, even in His great wrath, He remembered to be merciful to His two faithful servants Caleb and Joshua. God will never forsake or depart from those who love and obey Him.

It would be fair to assume at this point, that the whole community of people probably wept and mourned about their fate all night long until early in the morning. Their grief over losing their long held dream of a homeland, with great prosperity and the blessings and the protection from the Lord was now gone forever. Only their children would reap Gods great reward, and the land flowing with milk and honey. The older generation of people were now doomed to extinction.

Early the next morning after a sleepless night, many of the men of the Israelites went to Moses and said; "We have sinned! We will go up to the place the Lord promised us." By admitting to Moses that they had sinned, and also agreeing to go into the land of Canaan to fight the Canaanites and the Amalekites, the people probably thought that Moses would intercede for them as he had done before and God would change His mind and reverse His decree. But as you might say, it was a pure case of too little too late. It would make no difference to the Lord at this point what the people said or did; God would not reverse His decision.

Then Moses said to them; "it is too late! Now you are disobeying the Lords orders to return to the wilderness. Don't go ahead with your plan or your enemies will crush you, for the Lord is not with you. You have deserted the Lord, and now He will desert you." But being pig headed and stubborn as they were, some of the men went anyway to fight a war that they could not possibly win. They were totally defeated by the Amalekites and the Canaanites who, lived in the hill country in that part of the land.

Although God had now judged and sentenced the older generation of the Israelites to a death in the desert, He did not abandon them completely. God would now fulfill and keep His promise to bring the Israelites into the land of Canaan, but He would do it only through the younger generation of Israelites.

So it came to pass that; God compelled the Israelites to wonder aimlessly in the desert for forty years until all of the older generation was dead and buried. Their primary source of food was the manna that God had so graciously provided for them each morning. There were many other occasions throughout the forty years of the wonderings of the Israelites, that the authority of Moses and Aaron was challenged to the limit. It seemed like it was a never-ending battle for Moses and his brother Aaron to have to prove their integrity to the community of people. Even after the many times that God had defended Moses and Aaron in front of the people, the people still remained unjustly angry and jealous toward them. But through all of their troubles and woes, the two remained faithful and true to the people that they served and to the Lord they're God.

In the fortieth year of their wondering in the dessert, the younger generation of Israelites again returned to the place where God had sentenced their parents to death in the dessert. They had finely returned to Kadesh Barnea for the second time. Now it was the younger generations turn to prepare to enter Gods Promised Land that, He had promised their ancestors Abraham, Isaac, and Jacob.

It was in the first month after the end of their sojourn of forty years in the desert that Miriam, who was a prophetess and the older sister of Moses and Aaron, died and was buried there. Then the whole community of people mourned her death for thirty days. It was a sad beginning for Israel's last year of wondering in the desert.

The old saying "like father like son" now comes true for the younger generation of Israelites. They too like their parents began to grumble and complain against God and His leaders. It was in a sense; history repeating it's self all over again only now, it was forty years later. This time, just like the first time, there was no water anywhere insight. This was the cause of the first crisis that had confronted the Israelites on their journey out of Egypt. Now just like before, it provoked the same kind of ingratitude and anger from these rebellious people.

So Moses and Aaron went to the door of the Tabernacle and fell on their faces and the glory of the Lord appeared to them. The Lord spoke to them and said: "Take the staff, you and your brother Aaron, gather the assembly together and <u>speak to the rock before their eyes</u> and it will pour out its water. You will bring water out of the rock for the community so they and their livestock can drink."

Then Moses did as the Lord had commanded him, and He took his staff and went before the people with his brother Aaron. But this time however, that's as far as Moses went with his obedience to the Lord. Now he makes one of the biggest mistakes of his life. It was a mistake that would haunt him until his death. This time when Moses and Aaron stood before the people and the rock, Moses did the one thing that he should have never done. He lost his temper with the people. As people say today, "he lost his cool." All of the anger, the bitterness, and the frustration that had built up in him over the past forty years came to the surfaces and he let the people have it all.

With uncontrollable anger in his voice, Moses said to the people; "Listen, you rebels, must we bring you water out of this rock?" Then Moses lifted his hand and struck the rock twice with his rod, and water gushed out and the community of people and all of their livestock could drink. The words that Moses spoke must have come as a big shock to the people but not to the Lord. These words were the words of one who had crossed the line. They were the words of man who had run out of patience, one whose patience had been tried to the breaking point.

In his fit of rage, Moses did not speak to the rock as God had commanded him to do. Instead, he raised his rod and struck the rock twice. When he disobeyed God, Moses violated all that he had stood for over the last forty years. God was not displaying anger when He told Moses what to do. But Moses fell into a deliberate unrighteous anger. Because of his anger now on this one occasion, Moses too has lost his own stake in the Promised Land. What a huge blow and loss it must have been for Moses and, it was all because of one moment of disobedience. Forty years earlier when he was first instructed by the Lord to get water from a rock, he followed the Lords instructions to the letter. This second time however, he did not, and Gods judgment came in the form of unexpected severity given the nature of Moses' offense. He had dishonored God in front of His people, and he had not followed Gods instructions to the letter.

God said to Moses and Aaron; "Because you did not trust in me enough to honor me as holy in the sight of the Israelites, you will not bring this community into the land I give them. It was indeed a very stern rebuke from the Lord. This angry action that was displayed by Moses showed a lack of respect and awe for Gods holiness Therefore, God has now charged Moses with the double sin of not totally believing in

God, and not hallowing Him before the Israelites. The word Hallow here means, "To treat as holy."

This one time that, Moses had permitted his anger to get the best of him, it would now also have far reaching consequences for his brother Aaron as well. Because Moses had displayed his deep anger against the people, no doubt Aaron became caught up in his angry rage as well. Also, Aaron was a part of Gods leadership team and a full partner with Moses, in what he did. Now, he too, was sentenced to the same fate that the older generation of Israelites had been sentenced to. He along with Moses would die in the desert. Neither one of them would be permitted to enter the land of Promise.

This would have indeed been, a very devastating blow to both Moses and his brother Aaron, because they had both enjoyed such a close relationship with the living God their Creator. But for Moses, it must have been a terrible crushing, and heart-rending experience. His ego must have taken a real nosedive. This would be because, God had told him point blank of the sin that he was guilty of. There is no doubt that his old heart would have been filled with a great deal of pain and remorse. He knew that he had committed a great sin against the God he loved and that it had damaged his special relationship with Him. It was the last thing in the world that he ever wanted to do but it had happened, and He could not change the past. What is past is past, and no one can change it.

Some time has passed now since Moses had received his bad news from God about not being able to enter the Promised Land. Now it is time for the Israelites to move their camp once again from Kadesh Barnea, and continue on their journey to Canaan. Moses had been rebuffed by the Lord, forty years earlier and told not to enter or make war with the people of the land of the Edom, Moab, and Ammon. God made this decree because these people were blood relatives of the Israelites. The Edomites were the descendants of

Esau the brother of Jacob. Their territory was located south and southeast of the Dead Sea. The Moabites and the people of Ammon were the descendants of Lot, who was the brother of Abraham. So Moses knew that he could not go north to enter Canaan. This posed a real problem for Moses and the Israelites. It would have been much shorter for the Israelites to pass through the land of Edom on their way to Canaan then to go around Edom.

So Moses sent some messengers to the King of Edom and asked for his permission to cross his land on their way to Canaan. But the King refused to grant the Hebrews permission to cross their land. Even through peaceful negotiations, or offering payment for services rendered, he could not gain access to the land and the route that he wanted to take. The King was so adamant about not letting the Israelites cross his territory that he massed his huge army on his border as a show of force. They would not even permit the Israelites to set one foot over the borderline. It was Gods way of leading Moses and His people in the direction that He wanted them to go. God was now directing and completing another part of His great plan that would be fulfilled through His people.

So it came to pass that, Moses went south to Elath, then north and east, bypassing Edom and Moab. This route would eventually bring the Israelites to a position north of the Arnon River, and on the east side of the Jordon River. But things would not go well for the Israelites as they worked their way south from Kadesh Barnea. When King Arad of the Canaanites who dwelt in the south heard that Israel was coming on the road to Atharim he came and attacked Israel and took some of them prisoners. It was an unprovoked attack on Israel. They had done nothing wrong. So then Israel went before the Lord and made a vow to Him and said, "If you will deliver these people into our hands, we will totally destroy their cities."

So the Lord listened to Israel's plea and He gave the Canaanites completely over to the Israelites. This was their first military victory over the Canaanites. But there would be more battles to come. The Israelites would have to fight against the Canaanites many more times in the future, but this time at lest the victory was theirs for sure because, the Lord was with them. The victory was bittersweet one for the Israelites because, just a generation before they had been defeated by the Amalekites, and the Canaanites. This victory would be the beginning of Israel's triumphant march that would eventually bring them into the Promised Land. It was like nothing that they had ever experienced before. Truly, it was a new day for them.

As they traveled on this circuitous route, the problems for this younger generation of Israelites would become more than they could bear. They could do no better, than their dead parents had done. They too would rebel against their God, and put Him to the test, just like their parents did.

One of the many tests that they would have to face was of course, the unrelenting sun, and the unbearable heat of the dry desert. Looking after and caring for their ever growing flocks, their herds of livestock, and trying to keep them separated as well as going in one direction, this in its self, would be a monumental task. It could well be a task that, if it were not kept fully under control, it would lead to a great deal of conflict and irritation, for the shepherds and the herdsman alike.

As the people continued on their tiring trek through the desert, they came to a mountain called Mount Hor. The Bible does not mention too much about this mountain except that it was possibly Jabel Madurah, and it is on the direct route from Kadesh Barnea to wilderness of Moab. The mountain was located about fifteen miles northeast of Kadesh Barnea, on the northwest border of Edom. It would be a mountain of sad memories and great sorrow, for the whole congregation of Israel because of what took place there.

Shortly after the Israelites had stopped there, and had settled in for a well-deserved rest from their travels; they received the sad news from God that Aaron who was their first High Priest, would die there on that mountain. What a shocking bit of news it must have been for the people to hear. After all of the many years of service that he had given the people, it must have seemed to them that he and Moses alike would never die. But that was all in God's plan for His servant Aaron. What God has ordained and decreed for all of mankind cannot be changed or altered in any way shape or form.

God said to Moses and Aaron: "Aaron will be gathered to his people. He will not enter the land that I give to the Israelites, because you both rebelled against my command at the waters of Meribah. Get Aaron and his son Eleazar and take them up Mount Hor. Remove Aaron's garments and put them on his Son Eleazar, for Aaron will be gathered to his people; he will die there."

So Moses did as God had commanded him. He took his brother Aaron, and Aaron's youngest son Eleazar up the mountain. There in plain sight of the whole community of people, he removed Aaron's priestly robs for the last time and put them on his son Eleazar, and then he said his good-bys to his brother and Aaron died there on the mountain.

The reason Moses removed Aaron's priestly robs in front of the whole community of people before he died, and put them on Aaron's son Eleazar was because, he wanted to make sure the people fully understood who their next High Priest would be. It was also to show the people that, it was God who had done the choosing of the High Priest for the people and not Moses. Without a doubt, it must have been a very difficult task for Moses to do from a human stand point. After all, he and his brother had probably become very close to each other, after all of those years of working together serving the Living God.

But on the other hand! From a Christian's standpoint, let us look at the far greater and more beautiful side of our bodily death here on earth. It is only this worn out old body that dies and it is buried and then it turns to dust. It is not your soul and your spirit. They go to heaven if you believe in God the Father, and in His Son Jesus Christ who has paid your sin debt in full on the cross. But if you reject the Lord Jesus Christ your soul and your spirit will most certainly go to Hell.

Jesus is your only ticket to Gods Kingdom and eternal life. There is no other way to get there. The scripture state this fact very clearly in (Jn.14: 6). It says; "I am the way, the truth and the life. No one comes to the Father except through me." Once again, you can repeat the same old phrase that has been echoed many times before down through the age and say that, these words are carved in stone. These words remove all doubt as to "who Jesus really is," and there is no mistaking their full meaning and intent. It is also very possible that Moses could have been somewhat relieved and quite happy for his brother Aaron because, he knew without a shadow of doubt that God the Father was taking Aaron home to spend eternity with Him from that time on. His earthly work had come to an end and he was heaven bound. Also, Moses already knew that God would soon be taking him home to heaven as well. His earthly work would be completed and he would once again see and be with his brother Aaron and his ancestors.

So it was; that Aaron was gathered to his people. When you say these words, they give you a feeling of calmness and peacefulness because, Gods truth is in them, and because God used these words, and not man. In essence, what God is saying through these words is that, there is a life after our death here on earth? Aaron like everyone else, who had gone on before him, now has joined his ancestors or deceased relatives in death. Aaron died when he was110 years old. Then the whole community of people mourned for Aaron for thirty days, as was the custom for a person who was held in very high esteem.

After the thirty days of mourning had passed, the people moved from Mount Hor by the way of the Red Sea, to go around the land of Edom. Because Moses was so determined not to engage the Edomites in battle, the detour that he was taking was causing a great deal of discomfort and misery for the people. They were becoming very impatient and discouraged with Moses once again. They blamed God and Moses for all of their misfortunes. They grumbled about most everything that came to their minds including, having to leave Egypt and dying in the desert.

As they continued complaining they said; "There is no food, and no water, and our soul loathes this worthless bread." By speaking against Gods manna from heaven, the people blasphemed God. This was much more serious than one might think. Rejecting the manna from heaven was equivalent to spurning Gods grace.

The people had become so ungrateful and negative toward God, and Moses, that once more Gods anger was kindled against His people. This time, Gods discipline came upon the people swiftly and without warning. He displayed His wrath in the form of fiery serpents. The snakes had such poisonous venom in their bites that it caused raging fevers in the people and it ended in an agonizing death. To make matters worse, there was no such thing as an antidote for the poison that the snakes injected into a person when they were bitten. Not like there is today. At that time, if you were bitten, you were as good as dead. I would suspect that the snakes could well have been the deadly Cobra Snakes or vipers. These snakes are quite common in those countries, and throughout the desert regions of the Middle East.

It didn't take very long before the people realized that it was God who was punishing them for their sin. So they ran to Moses for help. The pain from the venomous bites was so excruciating that it actually drove the people to repentance. They begged, and cried, to Moses to intervene on their behalf, to take the snakes away. So once again Moses interceded in prayer to the Lord, as he had done so many times before for the people. Then the Lord instructed Moses to make an image of a serpent and put it on a pole. Anyone who was bitten could look at it and live. So Moses did as the Lord commanded him, and he made an image of a snake and raised it up on a pole. No one died after that, because they could look at the image of the snake and live.

There is a similar story in the New Testament that comes to mind when you look at this story of the serpent up on a pole. It was such a contemptible symbol on a pole that it would ordinarily cause people to turn away from it and to be totally repulsed by it. However in this case the Israelite had to look at it so that they could live. The story that I am referring to occurred in the dialogue that Jesus had with Nicodemus in (Jn.3: 14-15). Jesus pointed to this stunning image as He spoke to Nicodemus. Jesus was speaking of Himself here.

The scripture says; "Just as Moses lifted up the snake in the desert, so the Son of Man must be lifted up, that everyone who believes in Him may have eternal life." As you can see Jesus used this image to show, or to explain, how He would die. Jesus did this because He is the Savior of the world, and His prime purpose in coming to the earth was to redeem mankind from their sins. Jesus, like the snake of Moses in the wilderness, would be lifted up at His own execution and be nailed to a cross. There He would be hung between two thieves, between Heaven and the Earth, for the entire world to see, to revile and ridicule Him. It was the worst and the most painful way that a person could die, and it still holds true today. But, just like the Israelites who had to look at the serpent to be able to live at that point in time; so we to can use our imaginations today and see Christ on the cross and look to Him for our deliverance from sin.

As time passed and the Israelites continued on their long journey in the wilderness, they made several stops to rest up and to replenish their ever-dwindling water supply. At one particular place where they stopped and rested, it was called Beer. The word Beer in this instance means "well and it does not refer to the beer that we drink in the world today. Once again, the Lord displayed His grace and mercy to His people in their time of need.

It was at this location that He spoke to Moses and said; "Gather the people together and I will give them water." But this time however, God chose to give them water in a far different way than He did before. This time they were to dig a well to find an adequate water supply. By having to dig a well to get their water supply, God was giving the people a taste of how they would get their water in the land that they would soon occupy. Soon, they would get their water from the wells that the other people had dug in the Promised Land.

When the people finely arrived at the Arnon Wadi or Oasis; they were no doubt filled with great joy, and relief. It must have seemed to them like they had died and gone to heaven. The Oasis with its shade and water supply would have been such a welcome relief from their desert travels that; they no doubt gave thanks to the Lord without question. The people knew that they were very close to Canaan, the land of Gods promise. It was probably at this point in time that, the people must have realized that their long journey through the desert was coming to an end. Soon the people would cease their wondering ways and they would have a land that they could call their own.

The Oasis served as the border marker between the Desert of Moab and the region of the Amorites. From where the

Israelites were camped now, the Arnon River flows west into the midpoint of the Dead Sea. The region of the Amorites was located in what was called the Trans-Jordan area. It was located between the Arnon River and the Jabbok River that flows into the Jordan some twenty-four miles north of the Dead Sea. It was from this vantage point on the east side of the Jordan River, and directly across from the well-known city of Jericho that, the Israelites created a perfect staging area for the future conquest of Canaan.

When God promised the Israelites a land flowing with milk and honey, He didn't promise them that they could just walk into the land and take it over. The people would have to take possession of the land by force. It was by this force, that God would be able to display His great and magnificent power. His awesome power and glory would be displayed to His people, once again and to the people of the surrounding nations as well. Just like God had delivered His people from the mighty hand of the Pharaoh in Egypt; so now, He would change thing around a bit, and begin to deliver the people of the surrounding nations into the hands of the Israelites.

It was shortly after the Israelites had settled into their daily routine of living, and they were enjoying their new surroundings at the Oasis that; Moses sent messengers to King Sihon, the King of the Amorites, who lived in the city of Heshbon. The only thing that he requested was permission to cross the territory of the Amorites. Moses did nothing different than what he had done before with the King of Edom. Although he had failed miserably the first time, he probably thought that he would give his diplomatic skills another shot with this King, and see what would happen.

Moses even tried to further sharpen his diplomatic skills once again by elaborating on were, and how, the Israelites would cross the land of the Amorites. In the message that he sent to the King he said; "let us pass through your country. We will not turn aside into any field or vineyard, or drink water from any well. We will travel along the Kings highway until we have passed through your territory."

The King's highway was a major north-south road or trade route within the Trans-Jordan area. It extended from Arabia to Damascus. The route that Moses had chosen, could not have possibly posed any hardship or distress on the King or his people because, it was a major trade route. But try as he may, Moses failed once again. By failing as he did for the second time, Moses must have thought that as a human; his way and his plan, was not the way of the Sovereign God of Heaven and Earth. But God would use the Kings refusal to further His plans for the war against the Amorites.

When King Sihon refused to give Moses and the Israelites permission to cross his territory, it would prove to be his first fatal mistake. Too make matters even worse; the King had mustered his entire army and he had come out into the desert to make war against the Israelites. He possibly thought at the time that, a big show of force would scare the Israelites into running away. This was his second and most serious mistake. When he reached Jahaz, he fought against the Israelites and he was totally annihilated. He never stood a chance because, he was not only fighting against the Israelites, but he was also fighting against the Sovereign God of the Universe.

You may recall that, the Amorites and the Canaanites were some of the people to whom God had commissioned Israel to uproot and totally destroy because of their wicked way of life. In the coming years, the whole country of Canaan would feel the wrath of the Living God upon them and their cities.

This was the first of Israel's wars on the east side of the Jordan River. As Israel continued its war campaign against the Amorites, God gave every Amorite city into their hands, and they proceeded to occupy each city as the war progressed. It was all part of Gods plan from the beginning that the Israelites, would live in the cities of their vanquished foes.

The mighty acts of God through the Israelites filled the surrounding nations with fear and dread. This fear of God and the Israelites, would serve to soften up the nations for the future times of conquests that were to come. Also, the dispersal of the foreknowledge to the other nations, about God and His Almighty Power and miracles, would bring honor and glory Him without question.

Although God had delivered the Amorites into the hands of the Israelites, He had put some restrictions on what, and whom they were to kill, and on what they were allowed to take as the spoils of war. Exceptions would only be permitted with the permission of the Lord. In the case of the Amorites and their cities, the Israelites killed everything except the livestock. They also kept what was left in the houses as the spoils of war. They killed all of the men, women, and children including babies. No human remained alive. This was one time that the Israelites had followed Gods directive to the letter.

Immediately after the Israelites had completely defeated King Sihon of the Amorites and his army, they returned to regroup in the restaging area on the east side of the Jordon. Now they could focus their full attention on the Amorite people further north toward Bashan. Bashan was an Amorite city that was located in the region northeast of the Sea of Galilee.

When OG the King of Bashan heard that the Israelites had just defeated King Sihon of the Amorites, he marched out to do battle with the Israelites at Edrei. However, before the battle took place the Lord had spoken to Moses and said to him, "Do not be afraid of him, for I have handed him over to you, with his whole army and his land. Do to him what you did to Sihon King of the Amorites." The total annihilation of the Amorites was specifically designed by God to protect His people from following the Amorites ways of living, and then falling into their evil practices that were so much a part of their everyday lives.

So now God has sealed the fate of this Amorite King, his entire army, and all of the people in his city as well. When the Israelites proceeded to go up against him, they put King OG, his sons, and his entire army, and all of his people to the sword. The Israelites totally wiped them from the face of the earth. Then the Israelites proceeded to take possession of their land and everything in it.

These early victories were part of the holy war of God, and they were celebrated by Israel as part of their worship traditions. Through these victories, God has righteously and faithfully fulfilled His ancient covenant or promise to Abraham that He had made to him back in (Gen.15: 7-21). Although it took centuries for God to fulfill His promise, nonetheless, He fulfilled it to the letter. The people of Israel had now taken total control of all the land on the east side of the Jordan River, and north of the Arnon River.

Now the Israelites were poised and ready to strike at a moment's notice if, God had required them to do so. Because of their last two great victories at war, Gods people would have now accumulated a great deal of plunder from their defeated foes. The plunder would include such things as, livestock, horse's wagons, swords, bows and arrows and many other things that people would normally use for fighting their wars at that point in time. They would be more equipped now militarily just because of, the weapons that they would accumulate from the other dead armies.

The next city that they would invade would be none other than the ancient old city of Jericho. But for now at least, Gods people and their army would rest up and wait for further instructions from the Lord because, they could do nothing without Him to protect them.

Since the last great battle that the Israelites had with King OG of Bashan; some time has passed now, and Moses was setting in the shade of his tent in the staging area. Then God spoke to him once again. This time the Lord spoke to Moses so that He could reinforce His plan and His instructions to the people about the upcoming conquest of Canaan. The Lord told Moses that the Israelites were to completely exterminate the Canaanites, and take full possession of their land.

Centuries earlier at the time of Gods covenant with Abraham, God had spoken to the Canaanites and warned them that, a time would come when He would punish the sinfulness of the Canaanites. As far as God was concerned, it was because of their continual wicked acts, and their idol worships that, were the deciding factors in why they were condemned by Him. The, Canaanites had no right to continue to, live in the land of Canaan with His people. It was Gods land flowing with milk and honey and it had to be cleansed to His liking.

Now God, who is the one and only true owner of all the land on the entire face of the earth, puts His plan into motion. He is about to start transferring the land of Canaan and all of its goodness from the Canaanites to His people Israel. There would be no questions asked, no negations, and certainly no haggling with the Canaanites over the land. The question was settled and done with when the Lord spoke these few words, "for I have given you the land to possess." You will notice here that, God said that He had given the Israelites the land to possess, and not to own. Therefore, these words came from God as a divine legal transfer of the land of Canaan to the Israelites and no one else. The deal was sealed by Gods own spoken word.

But God had some extra words of caution for the Israelites at the same time. If the Israelites did not drive out the inhabitants of the land, and if the idolatrous Canaanites were allowed to live among His people, they would be a constant source of trouble for the Israelites. They would be like an irritant in the eye, or like a thorn in the side of Gods people. To say the least, they would become much like some of the people who had left Egypt with the Israelites and had caused them problems since day one of their journey so far.

Also, the Israelites would become just like the Canaanites in their way of living. It is sad but true, this very thing did happen to the Israelites during and after they had taken over the Promised Land from the Canaanites. This would in time, necessitate the expulsion of Israel from the land that, God had given them, and the land that they had fought and died to keep.

Some time has passed now, since Gods people had taken full possession of all of the land on the east side of the Jordan River. It was then that Moses began to see some division in the ranks of the tribes of Israel. Three of the tribal leaders from the tribes of Reuben, Gad, and from one half of the tribe of Manasseh, went to Moses with a request. The scripture here doesn't say why the tribe of Manasseh was divided in half, but one half had joined up with the tribe of Reuben. Their request was that, they wanted to take possession of all the land that had just been conquered east of the Jordan River.

Their request was a reasonable one because, they had seen that the land was very good land. By this time, their flocks and their herds of livestock had become so large that they needed a great deal of land to support them. Also, all of the people that made up the two and half tribes were all in agreement that, it would be a great place to settle down and make a home for their people. The land provided everything that they needed.

However, this request up set Moses to the degree that it made him very angry. He thought that they were trying to get out of their God given responsibility of helping the other nine and half tribes in their conquest of Canaan. But this was not the case at all. They were not trying to get out of the upcoming battles of Canaan. They were loyal to the core. All they wanted to do was to build some provisions for their wives and families while they were gone off to war with the rest of Israel's army.

They said "We will not return to our wives until every tribe has received its inheritance." With this solemn promise to do their duty, Moses finally agreed to their request and the land was then divided between the two and-half tribes. After the division of the land, the people renamed many of the towns and cities that they occupied. By renaming the towns and cities, it was a clear demonstration to the people that God had kept His promise and He had led His people to the Promised Land.

So it was; that the journey from the land of bondage in Egypt, to Gods Promised Land in Canaan has finally come to an end for the Israelites. It was indeed a journey of hardship and tears for the people. But the hardships and especially the tears, would have been much easier for the people to endure if, they hadn't rebelled against God their Creator so many times. A journey that should have taken no more than eleven days, by the people, had taken no less than forty years to complete. That was the price that Gods people had to pay for their disobedience to Him.

As time went on, Moses continued to intercede for the people before God many more times. He also gave them many more instructions on, the rules and regulations that they were commanded to keep before the Lord as; they took possession of the land of Canaan. All of these instructions that he received from the Lord are written down in Gods book the Bible, for everyone to read. This was to become one of his finial acts just before he died.

THE DEATH OF MOSES

The time for Moses to be gathered to his people was now fast approaching, and God would be taking His friend and faithful servant home with Him to Heaven. As you may recall, God had told him that he would not be able to enter the Promised Land because; he had not treated God as Holy before the people, when he brought the water from the rock at Meribah Kadesh in the Desert of Zin. Now his time has come to die and to give his final address to his beloved people. Even after all of the hardships and troubles that, the people had caused him, he still forgave them, and he loved them to the end of his life. So it is, with millions of parents in today's world. They will forgive and love their children with the last breath that God gives them.

Shortly after Moses had instructed Joshua about what, they were to do with the Canaanites; he went out and spoke before the whole assembly of people for the last time. He said to them; "I am now one hundred-twenty years old. I am no longer able to lead you. The Lord has said to me, you shell not cross over the Jordan. The Lord your God Himself will cross over ahead you. He will destroy these nations before you and you will take possession of their land. Joshua also will cross over ahead of you as the Lord said. And the Lord will do to them what He did to Sihon an OG the Kings of the Amorites, whom He destroyed along with their land. The Lord will deliver them to you, and you must do to them, all that I have commanded you. Be strong and courageous. Do not be afraid or terrified of them, for the Lord your God goes with you. He will never leave you or forsake you." These same words that were spoken by Moses are the same words that God has spoken to all of mankind down through the centuries of time. From the prophets to the apostles, God has always been true to His word because His word cannot and will not change.

As soon as Moses had finished speaking to the people, he laid his hands on Joshua his faithful servant, and he pronounced his blessing on him. Then Moses instructed him to be strong, courageous, and above all else to, trust in God and keep His commands. Because Moses had laid his hands on Joshua and blessed him, God filled him with the spirit of wisdom so that the people would listen to Joshua, and follow him as they had done with Moses.

When Moses said that he was not able to lead the people any more, he was not referring to himself as being physical disabled in anyway. In (Dt.34: 7) the scriptures say that, "Moses was a hundred and twenty years old when he died, yet his eyes were not weak and his strength was not gone."

It is quiet easy to see from this story that, God had bestowed many, many, blessings upon His beloved servant Moses. In the last conversation that God had with Moses on earth, He said to him; "Go to Mount Nebo; and from the plains of Moab across from Jericho, climb the mountain, and I will show you the whole land that I promised on oath to Abraham, Isaac, and Jacob, when 'I said I will give it to your descendants.' I have let you see it with your eyes, but you will not cross over into it." This last blessing from the Lord was without a doubt, a very special treat for Moses. Although he was not permitted to enter the Promised Land, God in His mercy granted Moses the good eyes to see it. Then Moses died there on the mountain, and God buried him in Moab in the valley opposite Beth Peor, but to this day no one knows where his grave is. The whole assembly of people grieved for Moses for thirty days, until the time of weeping and mourning was over.

The Bible says that; since then, no Prophet has risen in Israel like Moses, whom the Lord knew face to face, who did all those miraculous signs and wonders the Lord sent him to do. No one has ever shown the mighty power, or performed the awesome deeds that Moses did in the sight of Israel. It was not until our Lord Jesus Christ, the Son of God came upon this earth that, there was a man superior to Moses. Moses was a man in the full sense of the word. But Christ is our Lord and King who, came to all of mankind in human form to redeem the world that; had been lost because of Satan and the sin that he has caused long before the beginning of time began.

The scriptures state this very clearly in (Heb. 3:1-6). The scriptures are speaking about Jesus. It says; "therefore, holy brothers, who share in the heavenly calling, fix your thoughts on Jesus, the apostle and high priest whom we confess. He was faithful to the one who appointed Him, just as Moses was faithful in all Gods house. Jesus has been found worthy of greater honor than Moses, just as the builder of a house has greater honor than the house itself. Someone builds every house, but God is the builder of everything. Moses was faithful as a servant in all Gods house, testifying to what would be said in the future. But Christ is faithful as a Son over Gods house and we are His houses, if we hold on to our courage and the hope of which we boast. "Jesus is truly The Light of the World." He is the "King of Kings and the Lord of Lords."

No one can come to the Father except through Jesus Christ (Jn.14: 6). the big question still remains the same; where will you spend your eternity?" Will it be in heaven with the Lord, or will you spend your eternity with the Devil in Hell in unbelievable pain and suffering, and in total darkness cut off completely from the God who loves you.

As I have clearly stated in the Preface of this book, which I feel must be repeating one last time. It is your free choice to make. God has granted every human being that has ever lived, or will ever live on this earth the freedom of choice. It is my fervent prayer and desired hope that, you will accept the Lord Jesus Christ as your own personal Lord and Savior. Then someday God willing, you and I will meet in

Heaven around Gods Great Throne. Then we can all worship Him together face to face in perfect peace and harmony throughout our time in eternity. It is my heartfelt prayer that the God of Heaven and Earth, grant you the reader of this book, the Peace of Mind, and the Joy in your Heart that, you have so long been searching for. He will grant you many rich and wonderful blessings throughout your life that is still to come if, you Love and obey Him? "Jesus is the Light of the World." God Bless.

BOOK REFERENCES

ABOUT THE AUTHOR

After graduating from College, I served as a Sunday school Superintendant and teacher for many years at our local church. God has taught me throughout the years that through the study of His word, there is something new and exciting every time that I pick up my Bible. The insights that God has given me into His word are simply awesome and inspiring, as it can be with you the reader of this book.

Everything that I have ever written or taught has to be Gods absolute truth. So it is, with this book "The Light of the World." It carries with it to you the reader, Gods Truth in His Holy Word, my name, my character and my integrity which are all very important to me as it will be with you.

Printed in the United States
137816LV00001B/6/P

9 781606 476710